UNPROFITABLE IVORY: THE COMPLETE

TALES OF KINGI BWANA, VOLUME 2

UNPROFITABLE IVORY:
THE COMPLETE TALES OF
KINGI BWANA
VOLUME 2

GORDON
MacCREAGH

ALTUS PRESS • 2014

EDITED AND DESIGNED BY

Matthew Moring

PUBLISHING HISTORY

"Quill Gold" originally appeared in the February 1, 1931 issue of *Adventure* magazine. Copyright 1931 by The Ridgway Company. Copyright renewed 1959 and assigned to Adventure Pulp LLC. All Rights Reserved.

"Unprofitable Ivory" originally appeared in the June 15, 1931 issue of *Adventure* magazine. Copyright 1931 by The Ridgway Company. Copyright renewed 1959 and assigned to Adventure Pulp LLC. All Rights Reserved.

"The Witch Casting" originally appeared in the November 1, 1931 issue of *Adventure* magazine. Copyright 1931 by The Ridgway Company. Copyright renewed 1959 and assigned to Adventure Pulp LLC. All Rights Reserved.

"Stangers of the Amulet" originally appeared in the April 15 & May 1, 1933 issues of *Adventure* magazine. Copyright 1933 by The Ridgway Company. Copyright renewed 1961 and assigned to Adventure Pulp LLC. All Rights Reserved.

"The Ivory Killers" originally appeared in the June, 1933 issue of *Adventure* magazine. Copyright 1933 by The Ridgway Company. Copyright renewed 1961 and assigned to Adventure Pulp LLC. All Rights Reserved.

THANKS TO

Doug Ellis, Joel Frieman, Everard P. Digges LaTouche, Rob Preston and Gerd Pircher.

TABLE OF CONTENTS

Quill Gold 1

Unprofitable Ivory 38

The Witch Casting 95

Strangers of the Amulet 163

The Ivory Killers 255

QUILL GOLD

THE MAN in the tree stirred into silent activity. His vigil was coming to an end. Far up the *donga* cautious steps were approaching. The man's brows twitched down over his eyes in an overhanging ridge and the rudimentary muscles of his ears strained forward as actively as a monkey's in critical listening. It was black African night and his vision, keen as it was, availed him nothing.

The man's listening was nervously tense; he must make no mistake about those steps. A leopard strolling carelessly to his lie-up after his hunting might dislodge loose pebbles just like that. So might a hamadryas baboon, for that matter; or even a bush bok—and he had known both those latter beasts upon occasion to have mysterious night errands. He didn't want to fire at any such inadvertent decoy and so give warning to the whole neighborhood.

The strained ears relaxed, the brows retreated and the man nodded. There was no mistake now. Those cautious steps were man—and booted: white man. Surely, therefore, *the* man. No other would walk so cat-like down the rock and pebble strewn bed of a *donga* by night. The watcher's eyelids screwed in a silent grin.

He took advantage of a flurry of wind down the ravine to shift his position in the low crotch of his tree and to wrap his legs more securely round the limb while he hitched his gun to

the fore—a shotgun; he was taking no chances with a rifle in the tricky dark.

From the *donga's* steep lip above him a thin drizzle of sand pattered sharply through the sparse leaves of the man's tree. Startled, he peered upward and showed angrily clenched teeth.

The tree was a half naked limbed euphorbia that had long ago found lodgment in a crevice close to the steep *donga* wall, had grown to its height and now sent its sprawling roots out in a vain hunt for sufficient nourishment among the washed out rocks and sand, and struggled to maintain clumps of undersized leaves on its gaunt arms.

Against the dense net of stars the man could distinguish the dark grotesques of the leaf masses and the thick roadways of the twisted branches. Up at these he snarled in silent rage. Above all things he did not want to be disturbed just at that vital moment.

What the devil and all might have loosened that sandfall?

He could see nothing other than the fantastic tree shapes. His quick twitching ears could hear nothing more. In angry anxiety he peered and reasoned through a swift elimination of causes.

Elimination was really quite easy; at all events of all the larger and possibly dangerous causes. Lions would not be stalking along a *donga* edge. A prowling leopard would have caused a landslide. A porcupine was a clumsy beast, too. A jackal would have made more noise. It must have been one of the lesser cats—a genet probably, walking, as they love to, along the sheer edge of nothing. Or the wind alone might well have dislodged the little sand shower; the wind was swishing quite briskly down the ravine now. Anyway, if it had been some beast he would have heard it again.

The man grunted and settled to concentrate on the important business in hand. He must be sure and let no bungle spoil the thing. Down this *donga* his man—*the* man—must come. For twenty miles it cut a dry road—like a vast trench, twenty feet across and forty deep—through the plain till it tumbled in a huge succession of straggling leaps down the escarpment to Lake Rudolf. There was no other road because innumerable smaller *dongas*, scoured out by the monsoon rain, emptied into this main artery and cut up the plain into a crazy checkerboard.

And past that tree the man must come; past that patch of white sand where his bulk would show up in the starlight a sure mark—an almost sure mark—for a shotgun.

That was why the man in the tree had chosen just that tree. Because its very sparseness of foliage gave a clear view and because a tree offered a good deal more security than a rock ambush in case of any mischance. There would be a safe opportunity for a second shot to remedy any mischance; and that was a matter of vital importance.

For that other man who stepped so cautiously down the dry *donga* was the very devil. Cunning as a leopard and as uncannily fast, so the stories ran. The natives had the most incredible tales to relate about his prowess. Of course those were just native yarns, the man in the tree knew; but there was a sufficiency of other evidence about the fellow to make this night ambush business a matter of quite some nervous strain. A mistake, a bungle, might mean… The watcher drew in his breath sharply to think just what it might mean.

THE THICK, empty branches above him creaked in the night wind. Distorted limbs they were, twisted in the throes of malnutrition; swollen with huge warty growths like the limbs of similarly undernourished natives who suffered from elephantiasis. They creaked and groaned as in pain, as if in slow, heaving efforts to rid themselves of their parasitic encumbrances.

They seemed to succeed. A great wart that lay along one of the dim branches silhouetted against the *donga* rim shook loose and dropped swiftly to a lower limb, where it clung lumpily, as though loath to leave its parent host.

In its quick transition against the skyline it might have been anything; huge fragment of moss and orchid root, or leopard, or more likely ape. Only, had it been moss it would hardly have landed so fortuitously on the next limb.

But the watcher was not watching the skyline. He was straining his eyes up the dark *donga* bottom to catch those footsteps.

The footsteps came softly nearer; picking their way with an instinctive habit of noiselessness. They dragged interminably; hesitant, feeling out, cautious. Damn it, why couldn't the fellow hurry up and get the thing over with?

The tree man's tension grew. He rubbed his thumb over the bead of his shotgun to renew its luminosity. It didn't satisfy him. With a jerky movement he snatched a tiny vial of radium paint from his shirt pocket and daubed a hasty spot on the bead. That didn't satisfy him either; but, curse it, it would have to do; he couldn't go fooling over the niceties now.

The footsteps were on the very edge of that patch of white sand now. In another second the bulk of the man ought to loom dark against the pale floor. With infinite caution the watcher pushed his gun barrel to the fore—that other man was said to have a diabolical hearing. The clumsy luminous patch on the bead glowed a broad smudge—no sort of a sight. Still, at that range, a shotgun and a charge of buckshot ought to settle the business without any mishap. Just one more second, now.

It was an interminable second. A nerve racking passage of long drawn out time. At the very edge of the patch of sand the footsteps hesitated. The man was there, somewhere in the black shadow; but no farther would he come.

A foliage mass above the tree watcher's head swished more violently than was permissible to the wind. The watcher squinted a quick glance upward; but looked as quickly away again. His every faculty was focused now on the edge of that patch of sand. He dared not be distracted. His hands holding that devastating shotgun at point trembled with pent excitement. Those damnable footsteps! Instead of coming on they seemed to be climbing to skirt that pale target patch. Curse the fellow; could it be possible that anybody could be so inhumanly cautious?

The watcher with a frenzied snarl moved his finger from off the trigger. It was shaking with the man fever which is vastly more potent than buck fever. There must be no such awful mischance as an accidental discharge into nothing. Deadly sure the very first shot would have to be; with a possible second shot for the native who would be with the man—though that didn't matter a whole lot. It was the other man—*the* man—who was as clever as the devil and more to be feared. Yes, without fail and absolutely the first shot must settle the devil's hash. The shaky finger steadied itself with a quivering effort and began to curl round the trigger once more. The watcher concentrated all his faculties on the edge of that shadow.

And then out of the shadow the man who was as clever as the devil whistled shrilly like an avenging fiend. Out of the foliage mass above the watcher's head with a scramble and a crash fell a black demoniac shape that screamed and wrapped prehensible legs round the watcher's neck and clawed at his face and eyes.

THE WATCHER'S pent up nervousness broke from him in a choked shout—the indrawn, strangled cry of sudden, startled horror. The twittery fingers cramped in a convulsive grip. Both barrels of the shotgun roared into the night. Watcher and screeching incubus fell from the tree to the ground and disintegrated into two shadows, a large bulky one and a small shriveled one. The bulky one lurched to its feet and dashed down the ravine.

Out of that other blackness above the sand patch leaped the long shadow of the man who was the very devil. Two lithe bounds he took across the sand patch, and then fell cartwheeling over a rope that stretched across the *donga* and lay dazed. Instantly the small shriveled shadow scuttled to him and fussed over him with crooning noises and clucks of dismay.

"Shut up," muttered the fallen man dizzily. "Make a light." He sat up. "No, don't make a light—I must be silly. Golly, what a smash I came!"

The smaller figure was anxiously reassuring.

"Nay, *bwana,* a light is safe. Listen, he still runs and he is already far. Moreover in his haste he left his gun lying."

"Even so a light is not safe," the man insisted; and to himself he commented, "A jasper who's careful enough to stretch a rope to cover his getaway on the slim chance of his having to make a break is smart enough to have a couple more tricks in his hat. I've been a fool once to get caught by the rope trick; I don't give him another easy chance with a light. Wonder who he was and why he was laying for me?"

"He was a white man, *bwana.*"

"Huh? What's that? How do you know he was a white man? There are no other white men within a day's trek."

"I smelled him, *bwana.*"

The tall man chuckled; he knew the African claim that white men have a distinctive and unpleasant odor. Then he reproved:

"You are a wise little ape, Kaffa, but also a fool. If you had obeyed my order we would have caught this mysterious assassin who is a white man. My order was to throw stones upon him."

"Yes, *bwana;* and indeed I had a stone as big as a small goat all ready—"

"My order was small stones."

"Yes, *bwana,* small stones was the order. But, waiting up there, I heard the two clicks of his making a gun ready; and that goatherd boy had said no word of a white man with a gun; only that a man waited in the dark in such and such a tree. So I, knowing that *bwana* came without suspicion of a gun, I climbed softly into the tree and—"

"It was well intended, little ape man, though you muffed it. Had I required violence I would have sent Barounggo with his throwing spears."

"Yes, *bwana.* Barounggo would surely have torn his throat out, had he once placed hands upon him. But, *bwana,* it is also sure that Barounggo could never have climbed into that tree."

"True, thou very ape; that was well done. And for the doing and the foolish intention there will be a gift—a new blanket with stripes of many colors. Also we must find a gift tomorrow for that goatherd boy who shouted his news and ran so fearfully away."

The smaller shadow stooped quickly and clasped the tall man's knees to chatter his thanks.

"Shush, shush! Cut it out," growled the tall man. "For service there is reward. It will be wise now to get out of this *donga* back to camp to tell that Masai blood letter what a fight he has missed. And tomorrow we shall come to the *dipty c'mishna bwana* to ask what manner of men are in his district who lie in ambush for people with guns."

LATE THE following evening the tall man's compact little *safari* halted in front of the gate in the barbed wire square that was the official residence of Mr. Sydney Fawcett, assistant commissioner of the West Rudolf district of Uganda. The very black, khaki uniformed Kavirondo who stood sentry at the gate grinned and presented arms, and incontinently left his post to announce the visitor.

The tall man gave terse orders to his *safari.*

"Barounggo, make camp well away from the village, and give to each *shenzi* a portion of meat with his *potio.* They have come well this day's trek. Kaffa, it will not be necessary to prepare a meal; I eat with the *c'mishna bwana.*"

The man Barounggo, an enormous Masai, lifted a huge spear in salute and herded the porters off. Kaffa, the shadow of the *donga* episode, a Hottentot as shriveled and monkey-like as the Masai was big and fierce, grinned and trotted after them.

Assistant Commissioner Sydney Fawcett, who, six months ago had greeted the announcement of this man's presence with the worried query, "Good God, what does that pestilent man want here?" came out into his veranda to wave and call:

"Why, it's Mr. King, no less. I've been expecting you for some days. Come on in, old man, and tell me all the news of what is going on in the farther corners of this district which I govern."

Relaxed in a long cane chair, sipping the tepid whisky peg of tropic hospitality, the man King remarked with affected unconcern, although there was a question behind it—

"So you were expecting me?"

The assistant commissioner chuckled.

"Yes indeed, Kingi Bwana, and by all means I was expecting you. Surprised, what? Wasn't it yourself who taught me how to listen for bush telegraph?"

The level brows flicked once, the wide mouth drew tight and then King laughed with a shamefaced expression that was unusual to his hard angled face.

"Glad you made so apt a pupil. And that, incidentally, explains also a mysterious bird who tried to dry gulch me last night."

"I don't at all know what your curious language means, Kingi Bwana, but tell me about it."

King related the facts of the attempted ambush and wound up with—

"But how the devil could he know so accurately just what road I'd be going?"

Mr. Sydney Fawcett was serious. Killing of any sort shocked the dignity of British law and order; and an attempt to assassinate a white man within a days' trek of the very seat of government was an outrage. So unprecedented an offense that the assistant commissioner ventured to censure even the innocent near victim, as being to blame for luring that kind of character into his well administered district.

"Now, Kingi Bwana, really my dear fellow, you deserve a lesson. You're so bally confident that nobody knows your comings and goings that you've slipped up at last. Look here, old man, I know—even I, government official—know that you're going to some place back of the Assaua River country. I don't know what for—as yet—but I've been waiting for you."

King's cold gray eyes narrowed.

"Well, I'm glad the bush talk didn't have my plans all drawn up and blue printed. But they might easily have guessed. I got hold of a story about some few hundred quills of gold back there. What else ever happens in those back woods but gold and ivory?"

"Well, there you are, my dear man. Quill gold. That meant, of course, that you would be coming here to get a permit to buy that gold from the natives at whatever rate you could haggle me down to; for all of Africa knows that you're not fool enough to try to bargain the natives down to trashy trade goods and hope to smuggle the stuff out of the country."

Quick wrinkles appeared round King's eyes and he pinched his lips together.

"Thanks for the kind opinion," he drawled. "Not but what a wide awake man could get away with it without straining a sinew; but you paternal government fellows are so damned vindictive when you find out."

"Confident King," jeered the official.

King's face hardened to weather stained oak.

"Yep, I guess I've got that coming to me. I've been careless somewhere and the underground has got hold of the talk of my going, though my own men don't know what I'm going for. I eat dust, O most transcendent of pupils; and from now on you can write me down in your official record as the king clam… So then, having accounted for a broadcast of my route, what in thunder d'you think this well meaning gent wanted to bush-whack me for?"

THE ASSISTANT commissioner blew out his cheeks.

"Kingi Bwana, your innocence these days astounds me. You don't mean to tell me that you imagine everybody in all of Africa loves you for being a stiff necked, nosey Yankee?"

"From North Dakota," murmured King. "But I'm innocent no more. I was just getting careless in the security of your law abiding colony. This discriminating gent's gun, by the way, is a Ballard, London, twelve bore hammerless ejector, No. 47029; and he uses Kynoch shells. Seems to be no sort of a fool all round. I'll get some of my witch doctor friends to send out the quiet inquiry about such a man; and I won't bother you about him any more. Now what's this talk that you've been waiting for me?"

"I want you to do a small job for me."

King raised an eyebrow.

"Official?"

"Well—er—semi-official," admitted Mr. Fawcett, and added quickly, "but I won't ask you to write a report and I won't offer to put you on the emergency payroll—I know your stiff necked independence. It's just that you're going there anyhow, and the man is one of your pestilent countrymen."

"Ha!" King nodded with immediate understanding. "A missionary is in trouble again. What's the matter this time? Somebody going to hot pot him, and his society will plague my government to plague your government to plague you? What crowd does this man belong to?"

"It's not that bad this time, friend cynic. He's a 'Sudan Interior' man—he ought not to be so far south anyhow. But since he is, it's my *shauri*. He complains about obstruction, fights with his converts, boycott, petty thieving of mission crops, and all the usual smoke before the fire. His place is at the junction of the Imbobo with the Assaua. So since you'll be somewhere in the neighborhood, I wish you would keep your ears open and let me know quietly what it's all about."

King stretched his big shoulders and relaxed. As long as no official cooperation with its attendant red tape was asked of him, he was glad to oblige. He did not know that the shrewd old governor of the colony had long ago sent voluminous and confidential instructions to the assistant commissioner that if he could but inveigle this masterless man into a little freelance information gathering, King would go to endless trouble, would take all responsibility for his safety on his own easy shoulders, and would furnish cooperation more valuable than any official on the staff.

"Sure," said King. "Glad to oblige. I'm strong for missionaries anyhow; I always figure that converting the heathen to religion with a book is no worse than converting him to civilization with a gun. The heathen don't care much for either; and the book men have a lot bigger percentage of good eggs than the gun men."

The assistant commissioner laughed.

"You are already docketed officially, my Kingi Bwana," he told the other sententiously, "as a revolutionary, an obstructionist, an anti-imperialist, and a stiff necked Yankee. But if you find out for me just what the festive heathen on the sunny banks of the Assaua are thinking about I shall not ask my government to deport you on the grounds of being a menace to the administration."

"Thanks again," said King. "I'll see what I can do to help out my persecuted countryman."

THE VULTURES wheeling against the blue steel sky inspected the *safari* with experienced criticism. They swung a couple of wide circles above it and then set their fringed planes to the exact fractional angle against the wind and with magnificent effortlessness were removed in one vast swoop ten miles from that place, where they wheeled again.

There was nothing to interest them in this *safari*. It was small—barely a dozen men—compact, no straggling. At the head strode a tall white man; by his side trotted a wizened Hottentot; behind them came the porters, treading almost on one another's heels; and the rear was brought up by an immense spear man who saw to it that the endless straggling of the usual African *safari* was nipped before it ever started.

There was no profit for vultures in such a *safari*. They were more interested in their new prospect. The Hottentot pointed to where, pin points in the clear air, they banked in their great circles.

"Village," he said.

The white man shook his head.

"You know better than that, little monkey man. If it was a village they would be there all the time. It is a camp."

"Yes, Bwana, it is a camp—" the Hottentot snatched up dust and slapped his mouth with it. "My head knows, but the words tumbled from my mouth without permission."

The *safari* plodded on. After an hour the Hottentot ventured again—

"A white man's camp and belonging to one who has little experience."

"And how do you judge that, O wise little ape?"

"Natives would not stay so long in one place by day; the birds would have descended to feast upon the leavings. And as for experience—our camps, *bwana,* have no such devil's attendants."

King chuckled.

"That time your head kept watch over your mouth. I guess you're right. And out of your wisdom tell me now this: White men are few in this country; would it be perchance the camp of that white man whom you smelled in the tree by night?"

"No, *bwana.* That man had much experience."

"Right again," said King. "So we don't prepare for war. But we might as well be careful. Barounggo, hold back the *shenzis* a half hour and come in prepared to make a diversion if need be."

The great Masai lifted his spear and barked at the porters. King and the Hottentot went on.

In another half hour the camp became visible. There was a white man's tent, ill pitched and sagging. It was surrounded by an astonishing number of piles of baggage in disorderly heaps, covered over with oddments of canvas and tarpaulin. Native boys in unusual and unnecessary numbers lounged all over the place.

The Hottentot clucked his tongue against his palate.

"My mouth spoke wrong again. It said little experience. This *mzungu* has no experience."

The word in itself indicated the quick African reaction to that indefinite but vital thing, prestige. It meant merely white man, as differentiated from *bwana*—white master.

"Hm. Queerest camp I've seen," grunted King. "The man has men and equipment enough for a huge *safari* with headmen, leaders and whatnot; yet there seems to be nobody to handle things."

As the two came nearer, the herd of lounging boys looked at them with the furtive curiosity of the native, but with no other outward sign. They lounged and lay about in their established indolence; whereas it is customary in the bush for *safari* men—at least those in the direct path—to rise in deference to a white man's coming.

"These cattle," said the Hottentot, "need a one such as Barounggo to prick respect through their hides."

A boy who squatted on his heels near the tent rose and, without standing at the flap to ask permission, ducked within. In a moment a white man came out; and his appearance at once explained everything to both the newcomers.

"Ow, it is a *mon-perea*," murmured the Hottentot.

King advanced to the white man with equal certitude.

"I guess you'll be the Reverend Eli Wallace. Howdy. My name's King. Fawcett asked me to look in on you."

The missionary was delighted.

"An American, by all that is wonderful! Why, what a good fortune to temper my misfortune."

"Mm-hm," assented King. "It does look like trouble around here. Your boys seem to be a good bit out of hand. I suppose you can feed a starving stranger! Then let's sit down and tell me all about it."

"Oh, no," the missionary fussed. "I mean—oh, yes, of course, I can still offer you my small hospitality—David, tell cook boy make water hot, please… But I mean, my boys are good boys; they're my little flock, you know. No, the trouble is not with them—they're good lads."

King brought his frowning eyes back from a survey of the slipshod camp and the lolling natives, and he laughed.

"The good black brother, eh? It's the old argument, *padre bwana*, between your people and we Africanders. My boys are good boys too; and I sometimes even tell them so, but we—well, we camp different. However, let's consider your troubles on the mend from now on, and after some chow you can tell me how they began."

BUT THE Reverend Mr. Wallace was not able to tell King very much; hardly anything, in fact, more than King already knew.

"Fawcett told me you'd been having the usual petty annoy-ances—and I know my obstreperous African well enough to know exactly what you've been up against. But what then?"

"Well, Mr. King, that's about all I know myself. It kept getting worse and worse; and I had to stand for the most hu-miliating indignities till—"

"Yeah, that's just it," King interrupted him. "You stood for it instead of socking some fresh black buck in the very beginning. The African will always try it, and he'll carry it as far as you'll let him. But, hell, it's no use ever arguing with you people about how to handle the African. Well, what did it grow into?"

"I don't really know, Mr. King. There was no violence—I mean, nothing against me personally—though my boys were constantly getting beaten up. And then, less than a week ago the whole village came in quite overwhelming numbers and—well, to make it short, they just expelled my converts; made them pack up everything in my mission house and escorted them a day's march out of the village and left them with threats of dire violence, should they return. Of course I came with them."

"Hm. You came of your own accord? No compulsion or anything?"

"No, I was not molested. But of course I came with my flock."

King's eyes narrowed in introspection.

"Pretty smooth," was his comment. "No violence against the white man. Only an expulsion of certain natives against whom they will swear women stealing and half a dozen different com-munity offenses. Ever have any trouble with the chief?"

"Never, Mr. King. He is a man—Tembe Dawa is his name—a man of the average kind: fat and sensuous with a lot of young wives, and lazy and good natured. His attitude was one of amused tolerance as long as I didn't make an issue of polygamy."

"So? That argues a pretty intelligent coon, if you ask me. Have any run-in with the medicine man? How big a man is he in the tribe? Is he a society man—what mark, and so on?"

"I—really, Mr. King, I don't know exactly what—"

"No, you'd hardly know that, of course. Here, let me ask your boys. You, there—David is your name, isn't it? Come here…"

The man came forward slowly—as slowly as he dared; though, as he felt King's level gaze, he speeded up till he stood, respectful but with suppressed insolence just under the surface of his whole being. He made round ox eyes at the questions about the local wizard and tried to pretend with African stolidity that he knew nothing about the man. King shrugged and turned to his Hottentot.

"You talk to him. Ask him what society the witch doctor belongs to."

The Hottentot addressed the man in a stream of quick, low invective that quickly convinced him that the master of such a servant was no white man to be fooled with like his own master. But he was honestly ignorant about witch society marks and a little nervous that this white man seemed to know about them.

"Ask him," said King quickly, "whether the *ba-tagati* uses the *muavi* poison magic?"

The mission boy's eyes rolled white at the question. He looked furtively round, then nodded fearfully.

"Hm, that's useful," muttered King. And to the missionary, "Apparently you've had no trouble with the witch doctor; at all events, no serious trouble, else you wouldn't look as healthy as you do. So then it sums up. No trouble with anybody, but continued obstruction, culminating in being thrown out on your ear. Gosh, what a wild and mysterious country is this Africa!"

He sat back and blew thoughtful smoke rings from his polished and intricately carved pipe. At intervals he whistled tunelessly through his teeth. What new enigma was this? What trivial circumstance, utterly obscure to the white man, had jarred upon the inexplicable native mind till it had built a mountain for itself that had eventually erupted into open resistance?

NATIVES IN all of Africa were so accustomed to the white interlopers' vagaries these days that they no longer objected to the mere preaching of a new religion. They regarded that as an attendant evil as inescapable as the white man's insensate desire to regulate things and to collect hut taxes. It required something more personal, some more immediate interference with customs or rights, to arouse them to action for which they knew that, in the long run, there would be a penalty. Speculation on so vague a thing was hopeless. King jumped up.

"Tell you what's the only thing to do. I'll go to this Tembe chief's village and prowl around and see what I can pick up."

"Splendid," agreed the missionary. "I shall return with you."

King looked at him through narrowed lids, and then he nodded.

"*Padre bwana,* you've got all the nerve that your people always have and, like all of you, your nerve outruns your horse sense. Man, don't you realize that you haven't come of your own accord just to be with your flock? You've been thrown out—they're smart enough to know how you'd move. Now, both of us know that the African doesn't get that energetic unless something all red and mussy is in the back of his mind somewhere."

The missionary was calmly resolute.

"If there's danger, what about yourself? Besides, my place is—"

"Hooey." King cut him short. "You stick around with your boys here. If you ask me, you've got none too tight a hold on them, and if you leave 'em they'll melt away like that well known snowball. I'll light out in the morning with just my own boys. Besides, I haven't trod on that crowd's toes—not yet. And, anyway, I'm looking for gold to pay me for any risk that may happen along."

The missionary sighed as he looked over his lounging camp and was forced reluctantly to agree.

"Yes, my place is with my flock."

"Sure is," said King. "Just hold 'em down here awhile and we'll have you reestablished in your own mission house in the course of time. These things always blow over—the African can't hold a mad for very long…

"You say it's a day's trek? I'll leave my *safari* here with my Masai; I'll guarantee they won't bother you any and, incidentally, I kinda fancy your own boys may pep up a bit, too. I'll just hop over with the Hottentot and see what I can see. Guess I can get Chief Tembe to supply hut and feed for a couple of days. And, by the way, did you ever hear of any gold along your river?"

"Yes, indeed," said the missionary. "Every now and then some native would offer gold dust for medicine; but of course, I couldn't take any such remuneration for my services."

"Good," said King. "Well, I belong in the other side; I'm the unregenerate trader person who accepts all the remuneration I can get. So that'll make my visit profitable as well as interesting."

The missionary looked hard at King; and then suddenly he smiled and held out his hand.

"And yet, Mister Unregenerate Trader, you drop out of a blue sky and offer to help me for nothing."

King shrugged easily.

"Shucks, *padre bwana*. Your village will pay me with gold for the medicine that you give them for nothing."

IT WAS quite a big village. Some couple of hundred huts showed their untidy round roofs through prosperous looking banana groves that filled the wedge of land between two shrunken threads of yellow river that wound through wide, rain washed gravel beds.

Scars and scoops in the gravel and a twisty pattern of little canals, without forethought or design, indicated native industry. The wind brought the familiar and never to be forgotten effluvium of an African village left very much to itself.

King's surprised comment to himself was:

"Lot more workings than I had any idea. If that coon who brought the rumor down to Nairobi had reported anything like this, there'd have been half a dozen of the boys out on the jump. Looks like here's where I win out for taking the chance."

He strode on down to the village without any thought of misgiving. The petty disturbance against the missionary could be quietly sifted while he entered into the negotiations for what looked like a profitable trade.

But things were somehow not right in this village. At the outskirts King passed what was clearly the mission house, a wattle and mud hut like the rest, but much larger, much better built, with square walls and a peaked roof; a white man's building, in a square of methodically laid out garden.

The wrong thing about this house was that it seemed to be inhabited. If the natives had just ousted the owner and then left it alone, the thing would have been a normal indication of some passing unrest; but if they had taken possession so soon, that looked like a quite unusual determination that the missionary should not come back.

Two hundred yards farther, as King entered the first filthy lane between the straggly huts, there was a scurrying of startled natives, a peering from dark, beehive doorways and a running of quick feet to convey the news farther up.

A man of less assurance might have wavered in his advance; might even have retreated. But retreat, King knew very well, would have meant a fatal loss of that prestige which is the white man's very necessary God in Africa; a loss that would necessitate years of spectacular daring to recover. And prestige, King knew, sheer white man's indomitable nerve, would hold a native mob in check in all circumstances except the one of crazy, screaming war.

He quietly slipped his rifle bolt to throw a cartridge into the chamber, shifted his pistol holster to the front and went on.

Men came running to meet him, surrounded him and kept pace with him, jabbering.

"Tell them," said King to the Hottentot, "that I am neither a policeman nor an assessor of hut taxes. I come to make trade talk for gold with the Chief Tembe Dawa."

The men merely jabbered more. Other men came; men of a different type. These villagers were thin legged, pot bellied Nilotic negroes. The newcomers were of a sturdier build, men from farther east, the sort that hung about Nairobi to hire out as *safari* men, more accustomed to white men and less impressionable to sheer prestige.

A swift suspicion flashed into King's mind; and at the same instant—before he could act on it—came the perfectly planned attack.

From somewhere out of sight somebody shouted an order. A black arm from behind flung itself about King's throat. Instantly a dozen paws clawed at him. Something hit him heavily on the head, and he knew no more…

WHEN KING came to his senses he was in the dark, in pitch blackness. His head hummed still, but was clear; his hard trained constitution was such that he had never known a headache.

He was in a native hut—he could smell that; he was alone and—miracle—unbound. Listening carefully he was sure that no other person breathed within the hut. It was night outside, too; he could dimly distinguish the low oval of the door opening.

This was quite too good to be entirely true; there was some trick about the thing. King was never one to waste time in speculation when action was possible. He got cautiously to his feet—and then he knew.

A drag at his ankle and a clank told him in an instant that a chain held him. He sat down again and felt carefully with his fingers. Not with any hope. The man who had planned this thing was too smart to leave any such stupid loophole.

It was a white man, of course. That had been King's swift suspicion at the moment when he had been knocked unconscious. He cursed himself bitterly for a fool for having walked into a trap. Then he shrugged and composed himself to think the matter out during the hours before daylight. He felt for his pipe. His fingers found the carved bowl. But matches—means of making fire—had been carefully taken from him.

As he ruminated he began to recover his spirits. What had hurt him most was not that he was in a trap—traps could be gotten out of if one had ingenuity and nerve, and the faculty of quick action upon lightning thought. It was a blow to personal morale and confidence to know that he had walked like any tenderfoot into a trap—for nothing can cure foolishness. But reflection brought with it a certain justification.

How should anybody have suspected an unrest engineered by a white man, when the missionary who had but just come from the scene knew nothing of a white man's presence? The missionary, of course, was new to the interior and, being new, was still trusting and knew nothing about the innate secrecy of the black man in all his dealings with the white. But, even at that, this must be a particularly shrewd white man to have hidden his presence—decidedly a clever white man and one who knew his African. King's eyes narrowed. Who might this white man, who knew his native so well, be? And why had he taken this so determined offensive?

As to why, guessing was not difficult. Wherever there was gold, there were presently to be found white men of every desperate breed who would do anything and would dare almost anything to get that gold, and to prevent anybody else from getting it.

As to who, King could only draw a parallel. That mysterious person of the night ambush in the *donga;* that man was unscrupulous enough, knew his Africa well enough, and was bold enough also to have engineered this feat. But, who?

With the thought that he must presently meet this man, a certain grim elation overcame any anxiety that King might have felt as to his own fate. Since he was still alive, there was clearly some reason for it. This man wanted something; he would come to get it. And when he came, well, who could tell what might happen—*if* one had ingenuity and nerve and the faculty of swift action upon lightning thought?

The man came with the early beginnings of morning. Voices jabbered outside, the low oval of the door opening was darkened for a moment, and then King could distinguish the bulk of a large man within the dimness of the hut. He took the initiative.

"My name's King," he drawled in the voice which he used to conceal his readiness for steel spring action. "Squat, won't you, and let's get down to business."

"Business—that's just what I came for." The man spoke a perfect English with only a faint trace of a queer accent that stressed consonants and stretched vowels. He remained standing near the door—too far for King to reach. "It is business that I want to talk with Mr. King, whom—er—I have great pleasure in meeting for the first time."

"First?" asked King lazily. "Didn't I flush you like a baboon from a tree in Lenkoko Donga a few nights ago?"

If this man could be insulted, bluffed, somehow, into losing his temper, many things might be possible.

The man only laughed.

"My dear chap, it hardly matters at this stage of the game, does it, whether you met somebody in a *donga* or no?"

"Just idle curiosity," murmured King "Matter of future identification. Finger prints on that excellent shotgun and all that sort of stuff."

It was a pure bluff, of course; but that idea of finger prints always stood out as such damning and ineradicable evidence. The man's laugh this time was less assured. King noted it like a hawk and, reassured by the man's uneasiness that he was on the right track, followed up his offensive. He was nonchalant, as though no stout iron chain held him to a thick stake in the floor of the hut.

"All right, let's get down to cases. And, so as not to waste time, let's get this clear. You haven't had me speared while I was dead to the world; and I know from the *donga* foozle that a little thing like that doesn't bother you. So there's one of two reasons: First, too many people know I'm here—the missionary and the commissioner, and you've been silly enough to leave too many tracks like shotguns and so on; second, you want something more'n you want my scalp. So cut out all the bluff and intimidation stuff and let's talk turkey."

THE MAN still contrived to laugh; but there was a snarl in his voice. King's close analysis of the situation with its implication of safety to himself was robbing his captor of his expected advantage.

"You are very clever, Mr. King. You analyze the situation very nicely. So clever that I follow your suggestion and do not try to bluff you. I admit that it would be very—er—inconvenient to have any accident happen to you just now. Therefore, since I, too, am not altogether a fool—as I think you will admit in turn—I want to talk business with you."

"Well, I'm in this country to do business." King was carelessly interested. "So come on in and sit down, and spill your proposition."

The man chuckled fatly out of the dimness.

"Really, Mr. King, you do not give me credit for any cleverness at all. This is three times now that you have tried to lure me into coming within your reach; and I have heard too many things about Kingi Bwana to be doing that just yet."

King hid his impatience under a laugh.

"I have already given you a plenty of credit, Mister Whoever-you-are, and my Hottentot has indorsed you very thoroughly."

"Ah, the Hottentot." The big dim shadow was genial. "A good boy you have there. I have heard of him too. He gave us a lot of trouble."

"I hope—" King's voice was steel—"I hope, and for your sake, Mister Whozis, that your gang hasn't hurt him."

"Oh, by no means, Mr. King. He bit and scratched like a small gorilla; but we knew we could capture him. It was out of

compliment to you that we hit you on the head. No, your Hottentot is safe and well—and, as a matter of fact, since it is quite
impossible for him to get away from here, you can have him to
attend to your wants. You see, I am anxious to have nothing
but the pleasantest relations with you."

King laughed out loud. The alert little Hottentot loose in
the village, even though he could go no farther, was a decided
ace in the hole. King considered his predicament practically
solved. It remained only to keep this very wily person from
becoming suspicious and changing his mind.

"Go ahead; shoot the works," he said.

"I am glad you are open to reason." The man drew a three
cornered stool from the dimness of the hut and sat down, still
out of reach. "I am quite sure that you already understand that
we are both after the same thing. We both know what conditions the damned government sticks on to trading gold…

"Well, I'm not a fool. I want to do this trade right, so I laid
low, of course, and got that fool of a Bible thumper out of the
way—and a dashed persistent blighter he was, too. He gave me
no end of trouble—just wouldn't get out until I exerted my
strongest influence with the chief and had him quietly dispos-
sessed. I was smart enough to manage that."

King was non-committal, yet cheerfully offensive.

"You must have quite a drag with the big smoke. Guess you've
maybe come down to sitting in and sharing his mealie beer
with him; that'll put you in solid with any of 'em. Well, that's
your hard luck, not mine. Go ahead, mister, and shoot what
crookedness you're aiming to pull."

The man was still able to force a laugh. From his very patience
King deduced that his own neutrality was a much to be desired
factor. But the man wanted more than neutrality.

"There is no crookedness, Mr. King. Only business. Now let
me talk to you as one trader to another. There is more gold here
than you think; enough to make a tidy little haul for both of
us—if the business is conducted right."

King grunted. The man warmed to his subject. He was eloquent in his exposition of the age-old quarrel between the freelance man who worked for his immediate profit and the government man who worked for a vague, ultimate national profit.

"The right way, Mr. King, to conduct this business, is not the government way. I'll bet you that I can guess to a penny what rate the commissioner allowed you to offer for the gold. I'll bet you he considers it a just rate, making all allowances for distance and transportation and all that; and there'll be a reasonable profit for you in that rate.

"But dammit all, my dear fellow, we traders don't do our pioneer work and risk our lives in these blasted places for reasonable profits or for the good of the nigger man. We take our chances and we want our profit for ourselves and to get out of the country as soon as possible. We're not paid by the government to live in comfortable security and build up colonial jobs for our sons to step into."

"Them's my sentiments," said King. "But—let's hear some more."

"Well, my dear chap, since you understand the thing, that's all there is to it. I propose to trade for this gold in the good old way, the trader way. And, since you are here and, I admit, a serious problem, I offer you a partnership in the trade. We can give Chief Tembe a few loads of gimcrackery and get over the Sudan border before anybody finds out about it, and everybody will be happy."

"I don't trust you that far," said King bluntly. "Why am I a problem? If you can trade like you say—which I don't believe—why don't you grab the loot and *safari* out in a hurry?"

The man was frankness itself and he did not hesitate.

"My dear man, you know what gold weighs. How much can one man carry through the bush, plus his absolutely necessary equipment? Nothing worth talking about. And I tell you there's enough gold, all packed in neat crane quills, for twenty loads.

Now I'll admit that I dare not leave Kingi Bwana alone with no better guards than niggers while I make twenty trips to the place I have chosen as a last base; and I am not taking a *safari* of twenty witnesses with me. To dispose of them would be— In any case, only a fool would trust himself with that much gold and those insolent Nairobi niggers so close to a getaway over the border."

KING PICKED up the broken thread of the man's previous sentence. With silky coolness he completed it.

"To dispose of them in the good old way would mean quite a lot of good cartridges; and some might get away at that. Have you considered poisoning their water?"

This, when the man was just beginning to think he was winning King over. His patience gave out to the extent of showing his teeth.

"You are very smart, Mr. King. And let me remind you that I'm not such a fool as to take any chances with you. Now, either you come in with me; you implicate yourself or—"

In his enthusiasm the man rose from his stool and strode a short walk up and down the hut. Unconsciously avoiding the arc of the wall, he came closer to the chained man than he knew.

King's swift action followed upon his lightning thought. Like a sliding base runner taking the utmost advantage of his length, he threw himself in a long reach for the man's ankle.

His own ankle jerked agonizingly against his leg shackle. His hands fumbled in the dimness round the big man's boot. The latter, surprisingly fast for his bulk, snatched his foot away, kicked the stool over toward King. King received a solid crack on the head for his pains, and the man was out of reach once more.

King felt rather than saw that a gun was pointing at him while the man stood tense, watching. Finding King secure, he laughed nastily.

"Dashed clever, eh? But I'm not altogether a fool myself, Mr. Kingi Bwana. Good Lord, what a stiff necked ass you are! But you'll be all the more useful if you'll see sense. Don't be a fool, man. I'm offering you a small fortune."

"No luck." King recovered his position, squatting against the hut wall and felt at his ankle gingerly.

His drawl was as unconcerned as though he had but lost a point in a game, and as judicious as though it were he who was dictating terms.

"I'm not being a fool. It's you who's a fool; and I'll tell you why I won't throw in with you. Now I'm no supporter of your grandma government; but in this business the government way is right. The good old way has been tried by your kind of trader for a hundred years, and what's the result? Just those fresh Nairobi niggers that you dare not take a chance with. They've learned that there's some white men that's just men who happen to be white.

"No siree! Your British colonial government has pulled plenty boners; but its policy in Africa is right. It's the square deal for the black man that makes the white man stand out as white. It's white man's prestige that let's you and me and the missionary come to this place and keep our scalps. I don't give a hoot whether the next generation of colonial administrators are British sons or Zulu sons. That should be one of *your* patriotic worries. But I'm sure that if you gyp this Tembe village, you won't be able ever to come back; neither will I; neither will the missionary—nor any other white man without a military guard."

"You talk like a damned missionary yourself," snarled the man. "Who the devil wants to come back to this filthy hole, once we've made our haul out of it?"

"Well," said King, "I'm living in Africa just at present; and there's a whole lot of white folks aiming to live here all their lives. And it's only white man's prestige that'll let that little handful do it—especially now, after that fool war. I'm no hairy philanthropist about the future of your colony; but I've got to be free to prowl around and pull my fortune out of this country yet."

"You fool!" stormed the man. "I'm offering you a small fortune out of this trade."

"How d'you know this crowd is so anxious to be gypped?" King asked disconcertingly. "Why should Chief Tembe take up your gyp proposition rather than deal with me on a square basis? I've just got to holler my offer and the whole village will hear it."

The man's laugh out of the dimness was a gurgle of sheer delight.

"You persist in underestimating me, my dear chap. Nobody other than the chief would have sense enough to understand. My very good friend Tembe knows that according to authorized procedure every man would weigh out his gold and get the authorized trade for himself. What would he get out of it? He's no gold digger; he's the fat bellied chief. Whereas, dealing with me, he gets the whole payment and gives his silly people whatever he thinks right. That's the good old way. Trader gets something worthwhile for his risk; chief gets some first class beads and knives and everybody is happy. Furthermore, my clever Kingi Bwana—" the unction in the voice was positive oil of self-satisfaction—"he will deal with me and not with you because I have taken the precaution to marry three of his daughters—native fashion, of course; it doesn't tie me up in any way but these poor fools don't know that and it puts me, as you Yankees say, in pretty solid."

"You filthy polecat!" King's blazing speech came after a long moment of astound and disgust. "You poor white offal! It's your stinking kind that smears the white man in the dirt. You're one of those leper lice who'll stick at nothing to get what you want. Taking a shot at a man out of the dark don't sicken me—heaps of fellers who rate not much lower'n hyenas have done it. But this marrying into a savage tribe is the lowest—"

"That's enough. Shut up, damn you!" The command was an ugly growl.

"It's not enough!" King shouted. "I'm telling you one per

cent, of what you are. You're— Hell, I know what you are. I got it now. I got that funny accent of yours. I'd been figurin' you were the lowest Britisher loose. But I know now. You're not British at all. You're a yellow belly, that's what you are. A Eurasian, a half caste from India or somewhere down the Cape. You've got the tar brush. Sure you'd marry a nigger family; they're your kind. Trouble is you look whitish an' your stink smears all of us."

A choked scream of rage came from the man, and King could see the glint of high lights on the gun. He jeered at both.

"Put it away. Hide it, cur! You haven't the guts to shoot. You'd take a secret shot out of the dark; but you daren't even hook finger over trigger, now. Too many people know I'm here and you're here. Put it up, yellow belly!"

King was damnably right and the big man knew it. With an inarticulate bellow he ducked quickly through the low door opening and his footsteps told that he almost ran.

King sat back against the wall of the hut and panted. Broken interjections at intervals showed his indignation. Then, at last, he grinned.

"Phew! Forgot myself that time. Now he'll stay away and hatch some particularly slick meanness. I was a fathead. I should ha' made to fall in with his game. But, hell—there's a limit! Wonder what he'll do? He's damn right he daren't trek out an' leave me under nothing less dumb than native guards; he knows I'd be outa here like a rabbit. If he'll just lie still and give me a couple hours, I'll be outa here anyhow!"

He fished his pipe from his pocket, swore softly as he remembered that he had no matches; then, caressing the fine carving on the stem with loving fingers, he composed himself with a feline patience to wait for the appearance of his Hottentot. His captor, he knew, would now quite surely not send the servant to wait on his master; but King had great confidence in the wizened little jungle man's native cunning, a cunning that he had been at pains to develop through many years of close training. Of the man's loyalty he was sure.

YET IT was noon before the Hottentot appeared. Like a djinn of fantastic fable diving for its dark hole he ducked suddenly through the doorway and was within the hut. And like a djinn he was miraculous. Instead of the ragged old shooting coat that was his customary raiment he appeared in a wide frocked coat and tight pants of cotton goods that were near white; and in his hands he carried a tray upon which was food, sumptuous fare of rice and curried chicken.

For just a fleeting instant King thought that his captor was mean spirited enough to have swallowed all insults and was still hoping to placate him. Then in the next second he knew better.

"Tell the tale swiftly," he said.

The Hottentot set down the tray and embraced his master's knees.

"*Bwana*, I could not come before. The order was that no man should speak with you till that white man gave leave; and two great fellows stand before this door with spears. That white man is very strong with the chief and his orders are the chief's orders. The chief is a strong chief over his people. That white man lives in the *mon-perea's* mission house with his women; and *bwana's* guns are also there. All this day have I tried to steal them; but I have been caught and beaten. At noon that white man eats food such as this; he had a servant of the Banyan people who prepare it."

"Hm," grunted King. "I was right. He's a Eurasian from British India. But what of the servant?" A suspicion was coming to King. "These are Banyan clothes. Tell the tale."

"*Bwana*, it is all told. That white man ate, and it is his custom after food to sleep like a bush pig. The servant was preparing to eat his own meal of the surplus, but I said, 'Shall this low fellow eat while my *bwana m'kubwa* hungers?' And I took it from him and brought it. I took also his clothes so that I might come saying, 'That white man sends food to the prisoner.' Those great fellows at the door are oafs of this village."

"And the servant?" asked King softly. "He gave you all these things?"

"*Bwana*, he called me ill names and came to hunt me from the cook hut with a broom, calling loudly for his master. So, *bwana*, I ripped him open with his own cook knife and took the things."

King was silent awhile.

"That was ill done, little devil ape."

"Nay, *bwana*, it was well done. The body I stuffed into the wood box and covered with fire wood; and I spread ashes over the place where his bowels fell. No man going to look for him will know."

"It was ill done," repeated King. "The man was but a servant. Yet again it was well done, for now the way is clear. There will be six sticks of tobacco—not for the doing but for the quick thinking."

"*N'koosa, bwana!*" The Hottentot stooped again to clasp his master's knees. "Yes, *bwana*, the way is clear. By nightfall I shall have dug this stake out with this good cook knife and *bwana* will then walk forth to slay mightily with the club."

"You've a fine imagination," was King's muttered answer. "But there is an easier way and a surer. The chief is a strong chief over his people; but no man is so strong that there is not a stronger. Listen carefully, now, thou wise ape. What was it that the *mon-perea's* impudent boy said about the witch doctor of this village?"

"Ow, the witch doctor. *Bwana* asked the question and the boy said that the wizard knew the magic of the *muavi* poison ordeal."

"Good. Take now this, my pipe, and go to this witch doctor. Show him the carving of the stem and tell him that it was carved by Batete the Old One, the witch doctor of the Elgon Mountain. Let him take the carving in his hand and let him read the magic of it. It will be sufficient."

"Ow, Batete the Old One!" The Hottentot's eyes rolled white.

"*Bwana* is indeed the friend of that one. *Bwana* has many magics. *Bwana* himself is *tagati m'kubwa*. His strength is as *ingaga* the gorilla. His wisdom is—"

"Cut out the chatter and beat it," said King gruffly.

"I go with speed."

King composed himself to wait once more—to plan just what he would do when he should be free. That big Eurasian was no fool; he would not be easily caught napping. He had all the guns, too. Planning and careful replanning were certainly in order.

He had plenty of time to plan. The afternoon dragged on. Footsteps came and went past the prison hut. The guards grunted at each other in monosyllables. They were changed. These also grunted. The swift dusk of African evening came. The patter and sniff of prowling dogs circled the hut, broke into shrill yelpings as they caught the alien scent.

It was not till the door opening had faded to a low, dim oval that soft footsteps stopped at the hut. Mumbled words came. Explosive grunts of surprise from the guards. Footsteps went softly away. A figure shrouded in a blanket ducked through the opening. A monkey form hopped excitedly behind it. The shrouded figure silently felt for King's hand; pressed his priceless pipe into it; with it a cold, rough, three cornered rod; silently still it ducked under the door opening again and was gone. The monkey form chattered in incoherent excitement.

"*Bwana*, that was a great magic of the carving. I showed it and he spoke a word here and a word there and men obeyed. All is prepared. The guards have gone. Only it took much time to steal this iron from the house of the *mon-perea*, where that white man now calls in a rage for his servant to make speed with the night meal."

King's blood was racing through his veins. Action at last! His thin, tuneless whistle broke through his teeth. The links of that chain were strong enough to withstand any bare handed wrenching and twisting; but to a file they presented only ten minutes work—and it was a new file. King let alone the shackle round his ankle; he concentrated on the first link. The shackle could wait till later. In less than ten minutes he stood up.

"Come," he said in a short, hard voice.

THE BIG MAN sat in a sagging camp chair in the living room of the mission house and ground his heels into the mat that covered the split bamboo floor raised on stilts four feet above the ground. The only other room was the bedroom, separated from the living room by a split bamboo partition daubed with mud. In the low thatched veranda outside a kerosene lantern hung. In the cluster of servant's huts fifty yards away the white man's native boys cowered from his rage and muttered obscene insults about him to one another.

Suddenly the white man stopped his cursing to listen. Something shuffled gently outside the living room window hole which had never known glass. Something pulled gently at the square of print cloth that made a curtain. The white man put his big hands on the leather strap arms of his chair and pushed himself softly to his feet. The bamboo floor creaked horribly. There was a scuffle at the window, a wild clutch that tore the print cloth from its bamboo rod, and then running footsteps through the dark. With a bellow of rage the white man hurled himself at the window, vaulted through and dashed after the running steps.

At the corner of the house a fist like a hoof hit him full in the throat and sprawled him, choking and gagging, on the ground.

"Fool," said King's very quiet voice. "You caught me once with that rope trick in the *donga*. This one of getting somebody else to do the running away evens us up."

The fist was in the big man's shirt collar, hoisting him to his feet.

"That much for the rope," said King. "Now I owe you something for knocking me on the head."

The fist let go of the shirt collar and smashed against the big man's ear, sending him lurching against the house wall.

"And for chaining me by the leg," continued King with methodical enumeration of wrongs. "And listen, you big hog, don't start getting any idea that this is a fight. If you do I'll let go and split you wide open with my two hands. It isn't a fight. It's just a plain beating up…

"Kaffa, little monkey man, bring that lantern so that I may see the places where I haven't hit him yet—and tell his boys to come and watch how we handle this kind of white man."

The big man, eyes boggling with surprise, tortured with pain, made a desperate attempt to fight back, to use his weight in bull-like rushes.

"What did I tell you?" said King—*smash!* "I'm not fighting with you." *Bang!* "There's some things I don't fight with." *Slam!* "I'm plain beating you up because I don't like you." *Smack!* "And for disgracing the white man—that one's for your first marriage." *Crash!*

And methodically and very thoroughly King proceeded to beat the man while his native boys leaped and whooped their derision and his native women screeched in the background.

Till King could hoist the fellow to his feet no longer.

"There," he said, breathing hard. "I figure a whole lot of white men are even with you now… Hey, there, one of you boys throw water on his face. Kaffa, go get my guns from inside the house; and you yourself carry his guns."

The man sat up, moaning, feeling in anguish at his puffed and cut face, dripping a steady stream of blood from his smashed nose all over his front. An unlovely and most unimposing sight.

"Speed it up," King ordered tersely. "Get a move on before I kick you up. We're going on a visit, you and I. Hey, there, you boys, go and tell Chief Tembe his son-in-law is coming to see him."

The man, battered as he was and blear eyed, stared at the sheer effrontery of the thing. It was not possible that this hard grinning person, having once escaped, and with his further getaway open before him, should thrust himself through narrow gullies lined with hostile huts into the very heart of the enemy stronghold.

But King was quietly going ahead, pushing the man before him, his mouth wide and set, his eyes very cold and hard and narrow.

The Hottentot led the way with the lantern through the filth strewn alleys of the village. Shadowy forms lurked behind every hut. White eyeballs peered. Silence descended as the little procession came. Furtive jabbering broke out when it had passed.

THERE WERE perhaps some hundred and fifty men of fighting age in that village. Half an hour ago they would have rushed screaming to the kill on the order of that big fellow who had married into the family of their chief. Now nobody made a hostile move. Another kind of white man dominated the situation. Quietly he walked, slowly; no gun in his hand—pistol in holster and rifle slung over his shoulder. He looked coolly about him—not timorously to avert attack—easily, almost smilingly.

Many of the natives had seen that kind of bearing before; and those who had not seen had heard of this amazing thing that the white men alone could do. Exactly so was the manner of the white men whose prestige had taken Africa and who with only prestige to carry them held the African millions.

The big, battered man broke under the inexorable progress. He made a desperate appeal on what, to him, were the most powerful of all motivations.

"For God's sake, Mr. King, don't go through with this—this awful humiliation. I'll give you half my share of—I'll give—you can have it all! I warn you, you devil, if you go on you will bring the chief into derision before all his people, he being the father of—of those three women. You'll never get a chance at that gold; not a single quill will you ever see. Good God, man, can't you understand?"

"Shut up," said King. "There's some things more important than quills with yellow dust in them—which you'll never understand. Keep moving."

The little procession came to the center of the village. Chief Tembe had received ample warning. He sat on the ceremonial stool before his hut, a group of lesser chiefs behind him, spear men at their flanks holding torches. He tried to look dignified, but succeeded only in looking fat and surly.

King brought his battered and bedraggled prisoner close into the light.

"Tell your father-in-law," he ordered, "first, the missionary is coming back."

Sullenly the big man obeyed.

"Tell him," continued King mercilessly, "that you are not a full white man." The prisoner stiffened. King laid a hand on the back of his shirt collar. "Tell him, or I'll beat you into pulp right before the whole gang." The man wilted, shuddered, and at last in broken mumbles condemned himself before the assembly.

"You have heard," said King to the chief. "A white man does not do the things that he has done. It is enough."

Slowly the little procession turned and went back through the alleys of filth between the serried huts, leaving, without ever once looking back, the raging chief of a hundred and fifty fighting men.

Not a warrior lifted spear. Not a voice shouted insult out of the dark.

"What are you going to do?" asked the big man very meekly.

"Well—" King squared his shoulders and laughed—"I'm going to take you in to Assistant Commissioner Fawcett."

The man moaned a plea for mercy.

"Shut up," said King. "I'm not going to tell him it was you who took a shot at me. I figure I'm plenty square with you for that. I'm just going to turn you in for marrying native, and he'll probably ship you back to your own country where the white man lost his standing long ago. I may never see any of that gold, but I'll allow that those coons have had a lesson so some other white man'll get a clean break for it—and that's the important thing that *you'll* never understand!"

With his promise of not bringing any charge more serious than miscegenation King caught a sudden wild gleam of hope in his prisoner's eyes. He laughed softly.

"And," he added unhurriedly, "don't get to having any pipe dream, my very clever friend, about pulling off any getaway some night. I'm carrying a strong leg shackle with me right now and I'm just betting you've got the key. You're going to sleep for the next few nights on trek chained by the leg to a stake in the ground. And thanks much for the lesson. It's one of the neatest and safest tricks I've ever learned."

UNPROFITABLE IVORY

KING SAT, an immobile blackness in the shadows overhanging the steep bank of red clay that marked the Sobat River ford. A faint luminosity diagonally below him between the massed darknesses of foliage showed where the clay bank cropped out again on the farther shore between the low tumbled shale cliffs that pinched the river down to a treacherous brown channel for many twisted miles in either direction.

At the foot of the clay slide the long, dim form of a dugout canoe weaved and tugged against the pale reflections of the current. For now there was no ford. The rainy season had just come to an end and the river was reveling in its scanty four months of usefulness that justified the marking of a little blue anchor on the map as the head of navigation at Dawesh, ten miles above the ford.

Navigation meant that during the four months of "high water" a quite crazy sternwheel steamer could dodge the rocks all the way from Taufikia, on the upper Nile, to deliver small assortments of brummagem hardware and Lancashire piece goods among the mud villages of the Sobat Pibor province of the Anglo-Egyptian Sudan, and unload its final cargo of enamel cook pots at Dawesh, where it would take on goat skin sacks full of wild coffee that came down by mule caravan from the Kaffa highlands of Abyssinia.

This month the steamer was only three days late—that was why it was risking the tricky run by night. King could hear the panting labor of its engines that echoed from several bends downriver, criss-crossing up the tunnel of tumbled rock and giant fig trees. Only the glow from his pipe bowl threw into intermittent relief the hard angles of his cheek bones and the straight brows that hung over narrowed eyes in a permanent frown born of long gazing over wide spaces of hot sun and shimmering veld.

The pipe glowed and waned in slow steady puffs. King was not interested in the river boat. He was just enjoying the night while he waited for daylight before attempting to use that dugout canoe. The steamer labored round the nearer bend. Of a sudden, as though a door had been opened, all its confusion of noises surged up to desecrate the quiet of the river.

Voices dominated; and immediately it was evident that the reason for that was an altercation of some sort. The glow from King's pipe brightened almost to a lengthy glare. The level brows lifted once; the eyes changed from somber thoughtfulness to alert interest, and swung downstream. Otherwise he remained as before, a motionless shadow among the shadows, long, sinewy arms hugging muscular knees.

A voice floated from the boat.

"You'll have to lock him up and take him back."

It was a loud voice, dominant, authoritative. Clearly the voice of a man who was accustomed to giving orders and being quickly obeyed by underlings afraid for their jobs. Instinctively King did not like it. He was one of those who felt that the proper sort of man could control his underlings without the arrogant superiority which that voice spread all over the quiet river.

The boat was near enough to distinguish dim figures grouped under the feeble oil lamps of the after cabin deck—no electric lights on this little wood burning river tramp.

Another voice, lower pitched, self-contained, seemed to be expostulating with the loud one. A coarser, less cultured voice; it might have been some officer of the little tramp. Only odd-

ments and snatches of words
came across.

"Why—er—Mr. Fan-
shawe—sort of difficult just
what to do with him—"

The big, authoritative
voice cut in with angry impatience.

"I insist, Captain, that
you take him into custody.
Otherwise I shall report it
to your agents as a breach of
duty. The fellow admits that
he is an American and I am
positive that he is spying
on—"

The big voice checked
itself—it had almost said something. But the captain, faced
with the threat of authoritative complaint lodged at the home
office, was ready to acquiesce in what seemed to him to be a
harsh and not very necessary action.

NONE OF this had anything to do with the silent watcher
on the bank. But all of King's sympathy went out to the under-
dog, whoever he might be, whatever his offense. It could not
be anything so very frightful if the captain was willing to be
lenient.

King shrugged and relighted his pipe, which had gone out
during the watching of these doings on a ship that passed in
the night. The long flare of the match lighted up the brows
frowning low in disgust. What a lot of unnecessarily unpleasant
people there were in the world. How well he knew that loud,
overbearing type. He had had his own dealings with them many
a time and his gorge rose anew at their arrogance. But that
captain seemed to be a decent fellow. Pity that the other fellow
dominated him so easily.

The boat was just about opposite now. The captain was speaking.

"Very well, Mr. Fanshawe, if you put it that way—"

A flurry of forms broke up the dim group. Cries—a scuffle. Somebody fell. A dark form sprang quickly to the rail and threw itself over. A splash. The rest hurried to the rail to peer into the dark water. It was all over in a second. Then the bull voice, furious, roaring, throwing orders in all directions.

"After him! He must be caught! Stop the boat, Captain! I'm positive now he's spying—"

Confusion. Jangling of bells. Snorting of engines. Shouts.

King took his pipe from his mouth. Without turning his head he called softly—

"Kaffa."

Immediately a small shadow—it might almost have been an ape—took form out of the darkness behind him and scuttled to his side.

"Choose quickly two good trackers and put them to follow where that swimmer goes. He must not be lost."

"*Nidio, bwana.* Is he to be caught and brought in?"

"You think too fast, little monkey man," said King evenly. "The order was only that he be followed."

"It is an order, *bwana.*"

The little shape faded back into the darkness. King hugged his knees and smoked.

The boat's engines snorted hugely. Water churned in yellow foam at the stern wheel. Men ran about the deck. The boat's way stopped. It dropped back. The wheel churned furiously. The boat crept forward again.

It was quite a maneuver to push that boat's nose into the dark clay bank. A maneuver of a good ten minutes. A lantern arrived at the bow. Orders flew. A gangplank began to be pushed out to the bank.

King moved at last. He knocked out his pipe and put it back between his teeth. Then he lifted his sinewy length to his feet. An instant shadow bulked behind him. Tall and broad; taller even than King. A pale glimmer of light reflected from a great, two-foot blade of a spear.

"*Umbo, umbo,*" growled King. "Not this time, Barounggo. There is no call here for spear work, thou great slaughterer."

That shadow, like the first little one, melted back into the night.

With a great scuffling and much admonishment to be careful, men straggled across the teetering gangplank. Natives, by their voices; though an excited cockney voice directed them while the big bull voice from the higher rail of the deck shouted orders to hurry.

King—quite needlessly—placed a lighted match to his empty pipe. Men swarmed up the bank to him. King put his pipe into his pocket. Hands pawed at him. In various lower Sudanese dialects they announced their triumphant capture.

"Bring 'im dahn 'ere," yelped the cockney voice.

King suffered himself to be pushed, dragged, hustled down the bank. At the foot of the gangplank he stopped and braced himself.

"I guess this is as far as I'm going," he said coolly.

"Bring 'im along, ye black swabs," shouted the cockney.

THE BLACK men hesitated. The lower Sudanese, perhaps more than any other African, takes a sneaking delight in offering indignity to a white man, if he but dares. Backed by another white man's orders, this gang of roustabouts was encouraged almost to the point of violence. It was only the cold confidence of this long and hard white man that held them.

The cockney was, by the nature of his job, accustomed to handling men and he had plenty of courage.

"Wot the blinkin' 'ell!" he shouted; and with long, ungainly, but expert hops he traversed the teetering gangplank and charged on King, lashing out fast with fists less expert than his feet.

Big, hard hands smothered his. Harder elbows blocked his wild swings. His own elbows were pinned to his sides in an unbreakable clinch. A cool voice said:

"Easy, feller, easy. Who you aiming to tangle up?"

The cockney gasped. This accent was the same; the language was the same; but the easy power of the dim figure that held him helpless was astonishingly different from the man who had jumped from the penalty that the big bull voice demanded. Enough light came from the boat to enable the cockney to peer up at the face that loomed close over his own.

"Blimey!" His hands dropped passive with his shout. "Wot the 'ell! 'Ere, we've copped the wrong bloke."

"What's that? What do you say?" roared the bull voice. "Bring him on board."

King stepped back and shook his head, grinning.

"No siree; I'm not stepping on to your boat just now."

"What the devil is happening down there?" shouted the bull voice. "Who is the fellow? Bring him on board, I tell you."

The cockney looked at King. King grinned at the cockney, head tilted amusedly to one side, legs spread wide, hands deep in khaki breeches pockets. The cockney turned.

"I dunno 'oo 'e is, sir; but—'scuse me, sir—'e ain't the kind you just brings aboard."

"Damnation! Is there never anybody who can do anything? Must I— Here, Captain, bring a light. I suppose I must get him myself. Come along now."

Commotion and scurrying followed. A lantern traversed the deck and came down a companionway to work its way forward, over and around bales and crates of lower deckload.

"Who's all the noise?" King asked quietly of the cockney. He held no ill will against this man.

The answer came in a low voice, apprehensive of even discussing the great man.

"'Im? Why 'e's Mr. Fanshawe. 'E's a big gun, 'e is."

"Huh. Sure goes off like one," grunted King. "But who'n hell is Mr. Fanshawe?"

The lantern was already bobbing along the gang plank. A large figure loomed behind the man who carried it. He strode confidently up to King.

"Let me have a look at the man, Captain."

The lantern lifted and King saw a face that fitted exactly with his conception of that voice. Large, full, strong eyebrows and mouth, a large nose thick at the root, heavy jowled. The face of a man of affairs; forceful, with the confidence born of success— a success due to the will ruthlessly to drive well chosen subordinates.

The man saw King's face, sun burned, hard angled, wary eyed, with the faintest suspicion of a sardonic smile set on a tight lipped mouth. The torrent of ready speech checked for a moment in the man's throat—he was changing his mind about what he had been all set to say.

"Now then, my man, who are you and what are you doing here?"

It was quite a lame beginning after the kind of talk that had preceded it. But then, the man had not expected to see that kind of face.

King's antipathy had set in against this man; against his whole type. He was not inclined to turn a soft answer to wrath. His Western drawl was exaggerated.

"Jest settin' here, when your gorillas horned in on the landscape an' jumped me."

Something about the accent infuriated the big man.

"Well, what were you doing? Don't quibble now. How do you happen to be just here?"

King teetered on his toes and heels and stuck his thumbs into his belt.

"Free country around here, I guess."

Suddenly the man shouted:

"I know. I've got it. You're another, of those interfering Americans. I see it now. I saw you signal to him just before he jumped. I saw you strike a light; and then he went over. You're a confederate of his. By heaven, I'll have you—"

King's head was one side and he nodded judicially, like one weighing an offer; amiably, as though disposed to accept the offer. His grin was wide and engaging.

"Yes, mister? You'll do what? I'm all set an' waitin'. Shoot."

THE GRIN was full of good humor, inviting. But there was a certain cold gleam in those narrowed gray eyes that carried a suggestion that the invitation was for the other to start something. The strong man of affairs received a forceful impression that this very hard looking person didn't like him, and particularly that he was not at all cowed by the strong personality that was good at controlling subordinates. The longer he looked, the less inclined he felt to say anything that might start something.

King waited, almost regretfully. After the awkward silence he said—

"Shucks, I guess maybe you meant you were going to bulldoze the captain into taking me into custody for something or other."

But that made an opening out of the situation. The big man turned on the captain with an irascibility calculated to cover up his relief.

"What the devil are you all standing round like bally images for? Get your men out with lanterns at once and scour the bush for that other rotter. He can't have gone far. We've got something on him that we can hold him for."

The captain obediently shouted orders back to his boat. But King interposed.

"Wait a minute. Easy awhile." His unhurried confidence halted proceedings. "Now supposing you should catch this bird—which I kinda think you won't—but supposing you should, just what do you aim to do? This fellow's an American citizen, I judge from some of your complimentary talk."

"Yes he is, damn him," the big man flared. "But he's not in his own country now, and he can't do what—"

"I don't care what he has done," King broke in. "But I'll tell you exactly what you'll do. You're good an' right, he's not in his own country. But—" King grinned—"neither is he in yours, big feller. Nor is he on your British ship—I don't know just how the law stands on that. But right now he's in Abyssinia; and stick that in your pipe awhile. The skipper knows; you came over the border fifteen miles downriver. So listen in while I tell you just what you can do.

"You'll lodge your charge, whatever it is, through your consul, to the nearest Abyssinian police authority. That'll be at Dawesh. The Abyssinian police will catch him—if they can—and they'll hold him on your complaint." King's voice was full of unction. "Your police at Bahr-Yezdi in your province of Sobat Pibor will make application to the Abyssinian government for his deportation. The Abyssinian government will obtain the concurrence of the American minister at Addis Abeba, which is about four weeks' mail from here; it will then furnish authority, by mail, to your police at Bahr-Yezdi. Then they can come and fetch him. Guess you'll have your man—allowing for routine and official pow-wow—in about three months from now. And the reason I know is 'cause some one tried to pull it on me once."

King rocked on his heels and grinned benignly at the nonplused group. The big man alone had any decision. He was unaccustomed to being thwarted, and this insolent fellow had twice foiled him. He flared into swift anger.

"I'll be damned if I let this fellow dictate to me. There's no silly Abyssinian policeman here. Get your man out after that other fellow, Captain. And we'll take this one along too. Let him talk law to his consul. That will hold him from sticking his nose into my business for a time. I'll take care of the responsibility. Get him, Captain. Here you, coolies— *Sharoof.* Catch him."

Africans are quick to recognize authority. During the few days' run upriver they had observed this man; they knew that he was a very important personage indeed. It was the encouragement they needed. Yelling, as Africans must, they rushed toward King and he disappeared in a dim pyramid of clawing hands and straining bodies from which issued grunts, howls, and the rank, goaty odor of sweating natives.

The white men held off. The big man, as a Cæsar might have done, giving terse orders to underlings; the captain, because the dignity of his position forbade any mixing into a scramble with some unknown on a dark river bank; the cockney—mate, or whatever he was—because he had received no direct order and because, being a man of his hands himself, he appreciated the hardy nonchalance of this stranger who baited arrogant authority so carelessly.

King did not know how many unclean paws clawed at him. He was submerged in a wave of shouting black men. It was an indignity which no white man in a black country can permit, and which no proper white man would condone. He fought viciously. Rough and tumble was an art in which he had a considerable and hard experience. On the other hand, the African, weaponless, is a rather ineffectual person.

KING FELT a big fellow in front of him who held one of his hands in both of his and tried to twist the wrist over. Somehow the other hand was for the moment free. The wrist twister did not know till long after what sudden cataclysm had caused the firmament to explode into stars about his head. An ill smelling arm reached over King's shoulder and wound itself round his throat. He dragged it down and got the full heave of his shoulder under the armpit. That one cartwheeled out of the mob and arrived in the dark water with a splash. Other hands clutched at him. He ducked, twisted, struck.

One cunning paw from behind devoted all its efforts to trying to dig its fingers in between King's lower ribs in that excruciating, tearing hold. King kicked upward with his heel. That one fell off, howling.

Knees, elbows, fists; everything that King had he used. His own grunts of effort were drowned in the yelps and screeches that they evoked. Presently only four dim figures pawed at him. A hard fist, cracking like bone upon bone, downed one. The others stood off, shouting still, egging one another on to go in once more. But that was all the courage that was left in them.

King stood, breathing deeply. The yammering of the natives died to frightened clucks. The white men faced each other. King was full of truculence. The exhilaration of fight overcame all caution. He jeered his scorn of the three.

"I suppose people who'll set their niggers on to a white man will all jump him at once. All right—I'm waiting."

But it was to the credit of the others that they came of a race that did not ordinarily fight in gangs against a lone opponent. The big man thrust forward. He had courage enough, though personal fisticuffs were still far from his lofty thought.

"Who the devil are you, to talk that way to me? What do you mean by it?"

"Name's King. And I mean just what I say about any white man who'll set his niggers on to another white man in Africa."

The big man was quite unable to understand the enormity of his crime. He was too unfamiliar with the situation of the white man in a black man's country. What his next move might have been remained unknown; for the cockney gave vent to a sudden yelp.

"Crickey! Not— Lumme, 'e must be that Kingi *bwana* bloke. 'Ere, Capting, sir."

He whispered excitedly with the captain. The latter drew the fuming great man aside and talked earnestly with him. All three locked around as though expecting they did not know what force to be lurking in the shadows. The cockney pointed suddenly.

On the brow of the clay bank, a black silhouette against the pale sky, stood a great naked shape leaning motionless upon a huge spear. Only the fringes of monkey hair garters at elbow and knee fluttered in the thin, downriver wind and a single tall ostrich plume swayed and nodded in ominous beckoning.

The Sudanese deckhands chattered quick noises to one another and clustered at the gangplank. The white men had no means of knowing what might be behind that looming shape.

The forceful man who dominated his several hundred subordinates in his perfectly organized offices back in civilization somewhere, felt suddenly that he lacked something. Here was wanting a civilized something which had always been at his elbow to back up his authority. His imperious will was suddenly an empty thing. Not he, but this tall, cold man with the narrow eyes held the situation in hand. Furious words choked unborn in his throat and he trembled with the thwarting of his will. But he suffered the captain to lead him back across the gangplank to the boat.

The cockney lingered a moment. He was two handed man enough in his own right to appreciate a brother human. He came close to King and murmured:

"Lemme give you the orfice, cully. Don't you go runnin' afoul o' that bloke.'E's a ruddy Proosian hemperor around 'ere."

With that he quickly skipped across the gangplank to be in ready attendance on the great man who, aboard ship again, felt that intangible civilized something that bolstered his authority to be comfortingly present once more. He recovered his assertiveness sufficiently to stamp the deck and to grate between grinding teeth that he would square up matters yet; that he would call that ruffian to account.

But for all his ravings, the gangplank pulled back to the boat; the boat's nose pulled back from the clay bank; and the boat snorted on its slow way. King grinned widely to himself.

"Looks like some one's been speakin' evil of me somewhere. Gotta admit a bad reputation *is* a help. Now let's take a look at that other fellow."

He ascended the bank leisurely. The little ape shadow scuttled to him.

"*Bwana,* he hides in a bush clump two spear throws from here. One man watches; he will signal the jackal call if he moves."

"Good. Bring a lantern and come along."

Approaching the bush clump, King called out:

"Hey, there, feller, if you've got a gun don't pull any wild stuff. This is a new deal."

The fugitive ran out from his hiding as though catapulted. He sprang aside in sudden surprise to see how close to him a dark spear man had stood all the while; then he came forward with open hand.

"American? By golly, this is like a miracle from heaven."

"Hm. That'll all depend," said King noncommittally. "But come on in anyhow and wrap in a blanket while the boys dry out your clothes; you can't sit wet in this climate. And don't you know enough not to jump out of boats in these rivers? A fifteen foot croc could have grabbed you off just as easy as nothing."

IN THE tent King took stock of the stranger. He stripped down to a clean, athletic looking youngster with a readily smiling face and honest open eyes. He was silent while he robed himself in the blanket King gave him; embarrassed, not knowing what to say to the quiet man who seemed to know just what to do and whose arrangements all clicked off like clockwork.

To King he did not seem to be any frightful criminal. He handed the wet clothes out of the tent, noting as he did so that the youngster carried no pistol in a hip pocket—nothing, in fact. To the skinny brown hand that took the clothes through the tent flap he said—

"*Kaffa, lete moto chai.*"

"A cup of hot tea with a dash of rum in it will be just about right for you. Now then, feller, squat and tell me what it's all about. What have you done that they wanted to pinch you for?"

The youngster grinned up into King's face.

"I hadn't any money to pay my passage. I bluffed it out and ducked the steward till a little way back there; and then that big fellow got suspicious."

"Come clean, feller," growled King. "If I'm going to lend you a hand I want to know the yarn from the inside. If you've got no money, what the devil d'you want to steal a ride to this hole for? If all you did was to be broke, what was that big noise so interested for? He's no river tramp official. Come across with all of it."

"Honest, mister—er—"

"King's the name," said King, watching the other. It meant nothing to the youngster; he was very new to all this country.

"Honest Injun, Mr. King. I know nothing about that man, except that he's a swine. And I'll tell you, straight, why I came down. I got out of college last year; and—my name's Weston, by the way—and my dad gave me a year to poke around before getting my nose down to the desk. I'm interested in glyphs, so I came to Egypt. Then in Khartoum I lost nearly all my money, so—"

"Street of Beni Hassan's Mosque, I'll bet," interjected King. "Confess, now—and when you woke up your money belt was gone, no?"

"Well—er—yes. Only I came out of it on the steps of the mosque and I couldn't describe to the police which house it was."

"Yeah, and the police couldn't guess 'cause somebody was due to get about a third of it. Go on. And—"

"And—well, some little time before I'd bought a map from a Greek showing the location of some buried ivory across the Abyssinian border near Dawesh."

"Humph!" grunted King judicially. "What college was it that taught you all the things you know?"

The boy became suddenly abashed. Here, in the presence of this man who positively oozed experience and common sense, his enthusiasm about a map of buried treasure looked to him like the very acme of youthful gullibility. But he had a certain defensive excuse.

"But, Mr. King, he had a tusk with him, a small one; and he couldn't come back himself because there was a judgment against him for debt, and in Abyssinia they chain them to their creditors till the debt is paid. I checked up on him at the Greek consul's in Khartoum. The consul said it was true the man had come from Dawesh and he, too, knew about there being some ivory near there. There was another Greek—a trader who—"

"O-ho, the Vertannes cache," King murmured. "Well, go ahead."

"Well, then, I was just about flat; and I didn't dare cable dad—he's a deacon and a pillar of the church and all that. But I had enough left in the hotel to buy passage as far as Taufikia; and I had to save a few piastres for outfit at Dawesh; so I took a chance at bumming the ride from Taufikia on; and—" he suddenly grinned whole heartedly—"by golly, I nearly made it, didn't I?"

KING'S EYES disappeared between thin slits of lids

and his mouth spread across his face in a silent line. This young-ster was all right. King could understand him exactly; it was not so many years before that he would have done just the same thing; would have gone out on the same harebrained hunt for the sheer glorious adventure of it. This kid was the right kind. King was all for encouraging him, as he himself would have appreciated encouragement during his own hard beginnings. In point of years there was not much more than a decade between them; but King felt himself to be a grandfather in experience. He pointed an admonishing finger at the other.

"Now listen, young feller, to one of the things your econom-ics prof at that college didn't teach you. You thought ivory was worth a helluva pile of money, didn't you? Well, son, you can buy ivory at Khartoum right now for about a dollar a pound—if you know where to go. That's average for soft Egyptian. If it should happen to be hard Ambriz or Gabun, that would add maybe fifty per cent. Scrivelloes—billiard ball stuff—might double it. On the other hand, it might be French Sudan—ringy—and that would cut it right in half.

"So there's more to buried ivory than just a map. You don't know where those teeth came from. Ivory will travel the length and breadth of Africa for maybe half a century, as currency, before some trader gets to ship it out.

"Now it happens that I've known about this little cache for months, same as the Greek consul. I haven't gone after it because it's only the big loads that pay a profit. What with cost of *safari* and buying information and hunting up clues and all that, this little pile wouldn't cover costs. There's only half a dozen tusks at best—call them fifty pounds apiece, if you're lucky—and there's no nourishment in that. Still, if you've got a map—a real one—that would save a whole lot of running around and you'd maybe pay a dividend. What was the name of this Greek who saw you coming?"

"Petropoulides—a short fat chap with a limp."

King nodded.

"Petropoulides? That old fox may have got hold of something. You see, the yarn is that this other Greek was hoping to pack his teeth out through Abyssinia, rather than pay Sudan duty; and the local chief wanted to grab his tithe; so the Greek buried it and then he up and died. Quite likely brother Petropoulides inherited some information. Mebbe we'll go look-see if we can snoop around and pick up the trail some time. But that isn't so important right now."

King frowned into far distance through unseen tent walls. There was something in all this affair that he, who liked to understand all things, did not understand at all. He brought his gaze back and cocked a questioning finger at the man who huddled in his blanket.

"Now what d'you figure a large buzzard of this Fanshawe man's caliber was so interested in you for—you being an American? And why should I be a confederate of yours—I being an American? What's he got such a mad against poor old Uncle Sam for? Do you figure that Fanshawe is after your half dozen tusks of ivory too?"

The young man's eyes opened wide.

"Gosh, I don't know. He sure was a lot more vindictive than my couple of pounds passage money warranted; and he wasn't an officer of the boat."

King grunted and looked again into distance. Whatever high value the youngster might place upon the glorious adventure of hunting for buried treasure, King was quite sure that no such ephemeral lure had brought that other forceful man, so obviously a man of large affairs, on a long and uncomfortable trip to Dawesh. And why should such a man be so insanely prejudiced against Americans? Why so insistent upon catching and holding two people just because they were Americans?

The thinly introspective eyes opened the veriest trifle at the upper lids; hard little lines began to grow at their corners. Here was a mystery—that in itself was something to lure investigation. Further, the mystery was directed at him; impersonally, perhaps, on account of his nationality; but—a deep, perpendicular line grew between his brows and his lips formed a thin horizontal to it—that man had made the thing acutely personal by setting his black men on to manhandle King; in the presence of other white men, too; and much worse, in the presence of his own *safari*, who, of course, had watched every little move from the bank above. For that, in Africa, there was no forgiveness.

And at that King's smile began slowly to break, the wide mouth first, then the eyes in narrow slits, then wrinkles all over both sides of his face.

He turned purposefully to Weston.

"It's none of my damn business. I was just sitting looking at the scenery when that big noise came and made a blot on it. It makes me nervous that he should be mad at poor old Uncle Sam. Mebbe we'll go look-see if we can snoop around and pick up that queer trail first—just sort of en route to your ivory."

The youngster was full of enthusiasm.

"Say, Mr. King, it's swell of you to offer to help me find that stuff. I'm beginning to see that I'd have a pretty thin chance in this country—even with a map. And if it's not worth very much and it's going to be expensive—anyway, if we do find it, of course, we'll have to consider it a fifty-fifty proposition. And if I can reciprocate any way—I mean finding out whatever you want to know about this Fanshawe—"

King grinned delightedly.

"That's fine. But I guess you'd better keep outa that bird's territory for awhile. And we can mebbe write off my share of your ivory to the sheer joy of having made this good Mr. Fanshawe's acquaintance."

KING WAS snooping. He was at the little outpost town of Bahr-Yezdi. Young Weston had been left at the last camp just across the Abyssinian border line with the great Masai spearman in charge of safari. So King knew that everything would be exactly as he had left it. With him was only Kaffa, his wizened little Hottentot—because Kaffa had the inquisitive observation of a monkey and nothing moved that he did not instantly note and watch.

King's method of snooping was to stalk into the office of the local assistant superintendent of police. The official's greeting was almost a description of the visitor.

"Why, hello and hello again, you long Yank. I thought you were bothering the local powers somewhere down in British East— Boy, two whisky pegs bring! Come in under the fan and tell us what ill wind blows you into my peaceful bailiwick."

King put his pith helmet on the desk and stretched his length gratefully under the swinging palm leaf *punkah* that was pulled by a Sudanese boy through a hole in the wall.

"I'm snooping," he said ingenuously.

"You would be. What mess are you stirring up now? For Harry's sake, Kingi *bwana,* don't go bringing any trouble into my district. We're all peaceful and quiet just now—except of course these slave runner blighters; and there's some talk about native uprising down Mongalla way. But everything else is all nice and comfy."

King raised one eyebrow.

"You haven't heard any particular howl about me—I mean, not recently?"

"I told you we were all peaceful here."

"Well, then," said King with certitude, "the boat hasn't got back from Dawesh. I kinda thought it might have passed me."

"With whom have you been having trouble on the— I say, you don't mean Fanshawe?

King nodded, grinning at the other's consternation.

"For Harry's sake, Kingi *bwana*—I mean for your own sake, don't go having trouble with Fanshawe. Why, man, he's a power in finance. He's president and majority stock holder of the United Kingdom Construction Company and he's a director in half a dozen other big things in London. He pulls weight even in Imperial politics. He may be knighted any day. A complaint from him could make almost anybody's desk in Africa uncomfortable. And I tell you, he's merciless. 'No excuse for inefficiency' is his motto; and everything that doesn't go his way is inefficient, and out goes the man. Don't you be fool enough to run foul of that man, Kingi."

"Hmph! Sounds like considerable eggs." King filled his pipe with methodical care and puffed luxuriously. "What's this U. K. Construction crowd do?"

"They're engineers on a big scale. Roads, bridges, harbor works, anything; nothing is too big for them. The rumor is that Fanshawe went into a rage and fired half a dozen men quite high up and came down here personally to look into some big irrigation contract that—"

The policeman stopped, feeling that he was perhaps verging upon official secrets. King grinned at him from under his level brows.

"Shucks, you're not telling me anything. I know all about that deal. That's the big irrigation dam project in Abyssinia. Your people have been wanting to build it for the last twenty years so you could have the water to irrigate another couple million acres of cotton here in the Sudan and control prices over the neck of Egypt if she gets too fresh—cotton being Egypt's chief revenue."

The policeman laughed, though constrainedly.

"Really, Kingi *bwana*, you ascribe motives to us that—"

King waved the objection aside with his pipe.

"Aw, be yourself, chief; you know there's nothing can be kept secret in Africa. I know as well as you do that the Abyssinian Government has dodged letting your people have that contract 'cause a smart Russian military expert scared 'em by saying that a dam like that would mean heavy concrete and that concrete could mean gun emplacements, and that the work would necessitate a good road all the way in from your Sudan, and that artillery could travel on a good road; and then he showed 'em the map of Africa and pointed out how much of it was already

colored pink; and he reminded 'em about the French raid on
Fashoda; and—"

"Kingi *bwana*, you have the suspicious mind of a Machia-
velli."

King lifted an eyebrow.

"Suspicious hell! None of it's my own bright reasoning. That's
the last twenty years of Afro-European politics. Your people
aren't the only ones in it; they're all playing it up there in Addis.
There's agents from every country in Europe, all telling the king
that none of the others is after any good. And quite aside from
that, there's fifty million dollars' worth of work involved in this
irrigation stuff, and that's worth grabbing off too." King paused
a moment before continuing.

"But what's this U. K. Construction crowd poking around
for? That American syndicate, Simon L. Green Company, has
just about got that deal all sewed up since they were able to
prove to the King that America wasn't interested in territory;
and all they wanted was the job, get the money and get out."

The policeman was piqued.

"Not quite true, my Kingi diplomat." And then he shut suddenly up, closer than a clam.

King almost grinned.

"It's pretty nearly right," he said. "I happen to know all about
it because I took the survey party in last season. A good bunch
of boys. Peterson, their medico, just about pulled me out of the
long dark hole when I was running a steady hundred and four
malaria; wouldn't give me a bill, either; all a home team together on foreign ground, he said. Well, that crowd has got their
draft contract all agreed to and they're waiting with a gold
fountain pen. It's only final details now.

"Hell, this Fanshawe man, big as he is, even if he could cut
the deal from under them, underbid them or something, he
couldn't cut in on it. He can't argue the Abyssinians out of their
fixed policy of twenty years—there's too many other European
diplomats would all gang up against him, each one rooting for
his own crowd."

KING WAS talking to cover up his thoughts. This long winded rambling speech was not like him. He hid behind a screen of furious pipe smoke while quick suspicions raced through his mind. The policeman too sat silent, vaguely uneasy that perhaps he had let slip something about the great man's doings that he himself did not know any better than by the tea table gossip of the little white community at Bahr-Yezdi. Though he himself was in the dark, he had a professional appreciation of the diabolical aptitude of his visitor for digging information out of the dark mazes of African intrigue.

King made a move to go.

"I suppose it's all right if I camp in the government rest house overnight before I light out tomorrow."

The policeman was relieved.

"Oh, certainly, by all means. There's a secretary of the big man's occupying part of it just now with a lot of baggage, but there's plenty of room. His Nibs is an honored guest at the D. C's house. But listen, Kingi *bwana*, for my sake, if not for yours—get out before he comes back. If you get into any argument with him, the whole district will be hounded till we've offered you up as a burnt sacrifice."

"Don't worry," said King gravely. "I'm a busy man. Tomorrow isn't coming nearly soon enough—but thanks for the warning."

King needed to think. What deep affair had he stumbled upon? He installed himself in the rest house, told his Hottentot to run away and pretend he was a monkey—which meant that the little man's natural curiosity would lead him to pry into everything everywhere—and then with great deliberation and precision he filled a pipe. He needed to take counsel with himself.

This much was patent: The man Fanshawe was interested in the big dam contract. He was deeply interested; otherwise he would not have undertaken such a journey himself.

Well, who would not be, in view of a fifty million dollar turnover—quite aside from any possible imperial policy that might be involved. He was interested in rivalry with the American concern that was on the point of closing the deal; otherwise why the suspicion against two stray individuals just because they were Americans? And why such a frantic—for a man of his caliber, undignified—fury against Americans? Clearly because they might be agents of the rival concern who might spy out what deep plan he was working upon to snatch the big deal.

And there stood that blank wall of the question, "Yes, but how?"

King thought of every business possibility. He twisted the thing inside out. A subsidiary company under another name? A holding company with foreign capitalization? Some deep maneuver of high finance with a camouflaged incorporation in innocuous Finland or in soldierless Monaco?

None of them would hold water. The question remained unanswerable. King consumed many pipefuls and tasted none of them. There was only one thing to do. To accept the accusation that the big man had hurled and to become a real spy on his movements. To take up the trail and to camp on it unseen, as King knew very expertly how to do.

The thought came of course that it was none of it any of his business. King was no employee of the Simon L. Green Company—he'd be hanged if he'd hire out as anybody's employee. He was not interested in the Abyssinian people's obsessions about European aggression. He had no quarrel with the imperial policies of any European government, Fanshawe's or any other. But—

That Fanshawe… What an autocrat of big business! What a demigodling of money bags—ready to catch and lock up in an African jail a harmless youngster on the off chance that he might be a business rival! Well, that, of course, was big business.

But then, again, those Simon L. Green boys. That had been a good trip with them. And Peterson, the doctor. That had been expert and tireless nursing that he had given to King—without it, he might easily have slid from malaria into the dreaded black water fever. Well—King nodded to himself with a tightening of the mouth—if those American boys wanted the big contract, he, King, was all for them. After all, they'd put in the work.

HE STRETCHED his corded arms above his head and creaked the sinews of his shoulders, cramped from long and motionless cogitation. He lighted a fresh pipe and his expression slowly changed back to his normal one of smiling thinly out at the world. He called for his Hottentot servant. The little man came and, at a nod from King, squatted in a corner. With his wizened black face and bright, restless eyes peering out of a ragged khaki shooting coat of his master's that swept the floor, he looked more like a dressed up monkey than ever.

"Well, little wise one, did you have a good day playing in the bazaars?"

The little man contorted his countless grinning wrinkles to look solemn.

"Yes, *bwana.* No man knows anything about that great man, except that he is a very great man."

King had given him no instructions about the great man; but that was the shrewd little bush dweller's value—he knew how to do things without detailed instructions.

"If no man knows his doings," said King appreciatively, "that in itself is a mark of greatness."

"Yes, *bwana.*" The little man contorted his wrinkles to look preternaturally wise. "But I know, *bwana.*"

King chuckled. He had counted upon some light upon this tangle.

"For knowledge there is reward in this world," he quoted the maxim.

"Yes, *bwana*—and I have no tobacco. That great man, *bwana,* prepares to make safari."

"That may well be guessed."

"It is indeed so, *bwana:* any black savage might guess. But this great man prepares to make safari into Abyssinia."

"That is good guessing."

"No, *bwana:* that is true knowledge—from the tally of his baggage."

"Ha, you have then made talk with his servants?"

"No, *bwana.* His servants are black men from Cairo, speaking Inglesi and very proud. They know nothing; they do not even know how to read the tale of the different baggages. But I have seen it all. It is in the bottom room of this house."

"A good reading of the tale is worth perhaps a small piece of tobacco."

"Yes, *bwana*—only for a very good reading, a bigger piece. Now this great man's baggage reads that he makes a small safari, of not many days. It reads that he does not make safari among the savages of the south where the white men go to hunt game; for he has cartridges for but one small gun; neither has he goods for trade with the naked peoples. Moreover, that man, having gone in the boat to Dawesh, it is clear that he makes preparation for his small safari into Abyssinia."

"Hm. That is a reading that shows craft, thou bush imp; but that knowledge is worth not a very big piece of tobacco. We must follow that man's safari into Abyssinia."

"Yes, *bwana,* not a very big piece. We must follow. Only—" the imp squirmed his body and screwed his face into a wrinkled mask of gnomish gloating—"only in the bush, Nama, the great snake, who is very wise, does not follow his prey but goes to that place first and waits for it."

"Ha!" King's judicial calm was stirred. "What do you know, imp? What secret hides beneath all this talk?"

The Hottentot writhed and cackled in shrill appreciation of his own astuteness.

"Keh-heh-heh-heh! It is the custom, when one makes safari into Abyssinia, to carry a gift to the chief into whose district one goes."

"And don't I know it!" murmured King to himself, remembering the great Ras Gabre Gorgis' craze for carpets—horribly bulky things to carry; and Ras Masfan's childish delight in strong perfumes. "Well, what do you read from the gifts?"

"*Bwana*, among the great man's baggage are four cases of wood set aside for gifts. They contain a food in pots which is eaten by white men who are rich and which those Inglesi speaking servants—who are all great thieves—steal for their own unworthy stomachs. It is a very good food. I have seen such a food before in Abyssinia."

"Ha! What is the name of this food, apeling? And where in Abyssinia have you seen it? It might well be a clue."

"I do not know the name of that food, *bwana*. But those servants are very stupid thieves, and if one more pot be counted against them they will receive no greater a beating. So—" the imp shape writhed again within the sagging old shooting coat and handed to his master a round earthenware jar, sealed over the lid with tape and the pretentious seal of Desbrosses Frères of Paris, and containing *paté de foie gras*.

King let out a whoop.

"O prince of bush imps! This is verily a marker for the road. This is a knowledge worth six sticks of tobacco. Although—" a doubt came to him—"is there perchance any other?"

"Nay, *bwana*, do we not know? The Betwadet Haillu takes weeskee; Lij Zakhiel takes cartridges and women; Ras Hapta Mariam takes all three. Who is there left amongst these hill chieflings except the Fitaurari Yilma, the old general of King Menelek, who has no teeth?"

"True, O wisest of many apes. Yet, the Fitaurari is but a little chief. What so great a business can so great a man have with so small a chief?"

"That, *bwana*, is a knowledge that is not written in the tale of those baggages."

"Hm. Four days trek up the hills from Dawesh. What the devil! He'll have to come back here to get his stuff. The D. C. may give him a fast launch back to Dawesh—or he may trek from here. But good Lord! The contract is practically tied up. What can he do? How can he steal it?"

With quick decision came energy.

"Little man, the trail leads first to Dawesh. Since that man went there, knowledge must exist in Dawesh."

"Yes, *bwana*, first to Dawesh and then, armed with knowledge, to the Fitaurari. It will be a good trail. For two more such pots of this food—three in all—the Fitaurari instructs a female slave to attend upon all the wants of the giver. Moreover, for the loss of two more pots will the beating of those proud servants be none the greater."

"Out, scoundrel, out!" shouted King. "We have no time to waste upon your pilfering; no risk to waste upon your getting caught. It is an order. We go at once."

"Yes, *bwana*—" the Hottentot was immediately attentive— "we go at once. There is no delay. Two such pots are in my pack bundle."

KING ASTONISHED young Weston by the fierce energy with which he swooped down upon his camp across the Abyssinian border and ordered, quick-quick, up and on the trail to Dawesh. The youngster was too much of a greenhorn to be astonished at the speed with which camp was broken and got under way. The big Masai growled fierce orders to the porters. Each man knew which articles went into his load. There was none of the endless argument about trying to disclaim something from one's load and shove it on to another. Loads were packed; nothing was left out; the safari was away before the youngster knew exactly where they were going.

"Dawesh," explained King. "Didn't your map say your cache was somewhere along the old caravan trail? Well, it's a coincidence, but I've got a strong hunch that this Fanshawe bird is getting all set to take that same trail."

"That's no coincidence, Mr. King. That makes it pretty obvious that he's after that ivory, don't you think? Golly, d'you suppose that means perhaps there's more'n you thought?"

"I wish I knew just what he's after," grumbled King. "I'm hoping mebbe to dig up some dope from a wily Syrian Jew trader who's lived in Dawesh ever since it was invented. I guess anyway he'll be able to tell us whether friend Petropoulides stole a map somewhere or whether he just drew it."

The youngster was full of gratitude.

"I sure appreciate all the trouble you're going to, Mr. King. I only hope there'll be enough to cover expenses."

King smiled with a tight lipped benignity.

"That's all right, young feller. I sorta hope to be killing more than one bird with one stone. Mebbe this Fanshawe buzzard will be one of them."

In Dawesh King went straight to the group of beehive wattle and daub *tukuls,* connected by twisted passages, that constituted the trade store and residence of Yakoub ben Abrahm. An anomalous odor, half of divine coffee and half of ill cured leopard and serval skins and other assorted foulness, stifled the dim warren. Old Yakoub rubbed his hands together as he raised quick, bird-like eyes up to King out of a tangle of grizzled face hair and greeted him with half apprehensive friendliness.

"Come in, come in, Meester Kingi *bwana.* It is seldom that you honor my poor house."

"That's 'cause I lose money every time I come here," said King cheerfully. "Come on, gimme some coffee and let's talk trade."

The hands washed themselves silkily.

"Trade, Meester Kingi, I can always talk. And you know that for you and for your friends my prices are the lowest and my services are free for the pleasure of doing business with one whose word is my contract."

"Hooey," said King. "What about that American I sent up to you to outfit for going out leopard hunting?"

The hands flung out deprecatingly.

"You want to throw that up against me? I tell you, Meester Kingi, that man was ordained to be swindled. You don't know what money he had. That man's function in the world is to pay high prices to poor men who serve him. How could I make my prices to you if I did not make a little profit from the strangers that the good God sends? Tell me your needs and see the price I make for you."

"I'm not buying," said King. "I'm trading. I'll trade you information for information. You've tried for five years to find out who's the big chief amongst those lower Sudan Nilotic tribes who controls the gold dust that filters down to Khartoum. Well, I'll trade."

The old man put a quick hand on King's sleeve and drew him down a crooked passage to a smaller and darker hive that smelled more terribly than the first. His shrewd little black eyes shone.

"You tell me that, Meester Kingi, and I will make a profit that you—you are a child yet in trade—you will die with envy. What information do you want that you offer me this?"

King laughed.

"If you can see any fortune in it, you old wizard, it's all yours. I could never do anything with those drips and drabs that come downriver. Here's what I want— But this is not for bazaar gossip, Yakoub."

The trader laid his palm to his beard. "By the sacred books. Sit here close and tell me."

"All right. Now listen. There was a man—Fanshawe—on the last boat. *M'kubwa sana,* a big man all round; money, influence, everything. He's proposing to make a little trek up the trail."

The other nodded.

"Yes, he was here. He made a big stir and gave orders to everybody and he held long conferences with the English consul here. Tcheh! if I had known. But that is the trouble with these rich Englishmen. Their consuls and their commissioners all run to their help and make all arrangements for them. A trader gets no chance, for their consuls know the prices. Well, it is past; he has gone back with the boat. Where does he want to trek, this great man?"

"I think—" King chose his words carefully—"to visit Fitaurari Yilma."

"Ah, the old Fitaurari? That is four days on the caravan trail—for you, three. But—" the trader was surprised—"what does he want of the old man?"

"That's what you've got to tell me, Yakoub. You've been here for I don't know how long. Nothing has ever happened that hasn't come to you; and you've never forgotten anything. Now tell me what you know about the Fitaurari? Everything—every little thing. So we can perhaps piece out why this millionaire wants to visit this little chief. And so you'll earn the gold dust information."

THE JEW sat and clawed his thin fingers through his beard while his eyes dimmed in far back memories.

"The Fitaurari, henh? Old Yilma? Well, now, let me see. He was a general of King Menelek. He gained great favor with the King at the time of the Italian defeat at Adowa. His reputation was very brave and he was a young man of brains; he took many prisoners with his own hand; and Menelek gave him twenty thousand lire out of the indemnity.

"That was a long time ago. And then—and then what? There is not much. He remained a member of the king's councilors, and since he was clever he was the speaker of the king with the foreign ministers who all came to the country after that victory. And then there was some disagreement about something and the king was angry with him and he came here to his estates to live.

"That was before the World War; and since then, nothing. He has never gone back to court. He has enough money but no influence, and he has just grown to be the old Fitaurari living in his jungle estates out of the way of everything. There is nothing about the old man to make a business for your millionaire. What business is he interested in?"

"He is—" King shot out a compelling forefinger at the other—"remember, Yakoub: on the sacred books you promised."

The Jew bowed.

"On the sacred books."

"Good. He's interested in big engineering. Anything. Bridges, dams. I suspect that he's interested in the big irrigation dam up on the Abbai. I have a hunch he's hoping to steal the deal from the Americans. That's all I know and I'm guessing at that. Now think, Yakoub. Remember everything that ever happened with the Fitaurari; or anywhere around here. What has there ever been that could help this man queer the deal before it's all signed up? And if he did, how in hell could he grab it for a British concern?"

The old man clawed his beard, and slowly a dim light began to grow in his eyes. He nodded, and then nodded again as events began to piece themselves out. Softly he began to chuckle and to nod with a deeper conviction.

"Yes, yes, that would do it. Yes—*aie!* but they are clever, those people. That was why that consul—yes, surely that was it. But the Fitaurari, he is not in it at all—unless at the end. Oh, yes, yes!"

He thrust eloquent hands at King across the table.

"Listen, my friend, and I will tell you a story—a rumor it was, even to me; but in fits in now here to make a whole piece. *Aie,* how deep are the ways of diplomats. Yes, those people should be traders.

"Listen, now. Menelek the Lion, he was the creator of unified Abyssinia—but he was a fool. A great fighter, who brought all the big chiefs under his rule; a shrewd man, but ignorant of all things outside. After Adowa he thought he was a king like those of Europe and he made treaties with all those diplomats, from which Abyssinia is still suffering; for diplomats are traders, too; treaties are the profits of their bargaining and they never let go of them."

King's face was alight. His mouth was set bet but his eyes a-sparkle as he followed every word of the old trader. He could see where the trend was; he required only details. His pipe was cold between his teeth; he only nodded to the other to go on.

"So old Menelek made treaties for everything outside of his hills. You know his saying: 'Our mountains are our defense.' He signed away his boundaries, his sea coast, everything. He was a fool. Only inside his country he would sign away nothing. For twenty years—you know that too—the British engineers have known that they would need this irrigation. Ah, they are clever, those people. That is no secret. But there were others; other European diplomats who were at the king's ear and they were afraid of the British. So old Menelek would never sign."

The eloquent hands drooped, expressive of lessened emphasis.

"That much is in the history of international intrigue in Africa. You know it yourself. From here commences the rumor. There was appointed to Dawesh a British consul. There had been a consul before this one to take care of the caravan trade into Sudan. But this one—Townleigh his name—he was too clever a man to be wasted by his government in such a job. A man of charm, of much persuasion—often have I sold him supplies at almost no profit. He made a long visit to the capital to discuss trades and tariffs and so on. But the gossip was that he went, in the guise of an unimportant consul from the interior, so that the other diplomats would not interfere. He went to talk, not tariffs but treaties, with the king."

The old Jew bowed his head and laughed in long cackling chuckles. He could appreciate just such cleverness.

"*Aie, aie!* Yes, to talk treaty; that was the rumor. Then Townleigh came back and looked to be well satisfied; although word came that he was to be recalled and another consul sent to fill his place. So the very secret rumor then was—listen to this, my friend—the whisper that came to me was that he had persuaded the obstinate old Menelek and had a treaty in his pocket."

"By God!" It burst from King like a gun shot. "A treaty would do it. An old Menelek treaty would give unbreakable prior right. That's how the French got the railroad and the Italians got the wireless station and— But what happened then, Yakoub? What became of the treaty, if there ever was one? Where does the old Fitaurari come in?"

The eloquent hands shrugged ignorance.

"Who can say, my friend, if there ever was a treaty? The whisper that came to me was so secret that it did not come until long afterward. But it was at that lime that Fitaurari Yilma, councilor of silly old Menelek, had his so serious disagreement with the king and was banished to his estates here. And then— consider this, my friend—one of the many sicknesses of this country overtook Consul Townleigh, and he died. It was unfortunate; for he was a man of great charm. He died before the new consul arrived."

KING SUDDENLY reached his fist across the table and shook it under the old Jew's nose.

"Damn you, Yakoub!" he grinned. "You're doing this on purpose, just to see if you can get me going. Come on, shoot the works now. What became of the treaty?"

The old man threw up his hands.

"My friend, I have never said there was a treaty. It was a rumor, a whisper, a breath."

"Damn your whispers and your breaths. What happened after this Townleigh died?"

"After that," said the old man, as one concluding an argument, "there was some confusion—before the new consul came; and then came the World War and there was nothing else but confusion. But a whisper came to me that before the new consul came, some little things were stolen—not things of any value; for the watchman was an ex-soldier and faithful.

"Maps, the whisper said. The Abyssinians have always been afraid of maps. The Kitchener survey almost caused a revolution; and then Germans and Frenchmen who came as traders were always making maps—that was before the war. And then later again a veriest breath of a whisper came to me that the stolen things had been taken to Fitaurari Yilma. Might it not be?" The Jew completed his question with outflung hands and shaggy eyebrows that lifted into his low hanging hair.

King's narrowed gray eyes looked across the dingy table into the other's bright black ones. Both men nodded in slow unison many times. The Jew thrust out a dark skinny finger and ticked off items against his palm.

"Consider, my friend. Fitaurari Yilma, bold, intelligent. Councilor of the king in his foreign dealings. He disagrees with the king; a disagreement so strong that he is banished; he returns to his estates. Townleigh, the clever consul, also returns. He dies. Papers are stolen—maybe a map; maybe—who knows what? The papers go to Fitaurari Yilma. Then comes the great war and all is confusion. Now comes an American firm about to get the coveted contract. No country in Europe today can afford to let fifty million dollars' worth of work slip out of its hands. Does it not all fit, my friend? Does it not make a whole piece?"

"And so—" King completed the train of reasoning—"the great man Fanshawe goes to visit the little hill chief Yilma. Yes, by golly, it all fits; fits like a jigsaw job—every piece. If such a paper exists it would be recognized, even at Geneva, as prior right. It would be the one card that's left to Fanshawe to play; and it'd be the winning ace, too. But why would the old Fitaurari have hung on to such a thing? Why wouldn't he have destroyed it?"

The Jew shook his head.

"Never. You know the old law; the man who destroyed the seal of Menelek must lose the hand that did it. And now that the great king is dead the thing has become almost sacred."

King nodded.

"Yep, you're right. He must still have it—and I've got to get it."

Sudden energy came to him. He jumped up from the table; his eyes glinted hard and he breathed hard through his nose.

"Yakoub, you've done me a service. I've got no time now. Got to go like the devil. If that man went back on the boat and started his trek from there, he'll be well on his way. I'll come back and give you full details of the gold dust."

Yakoub bowed.

"I am well satisfied to wait."

At the door King stopped.

"And write me a letter to the Fitaurari, will you? I don't know him; I may need a recommendation. I'll fetch it as I go by."

Twenty paces down the mud road he turned and dashed back.

"One more thing, Yakoub. You know Petropoulides. He sold a map for some buried teeth. I want to know, did he invent it or is it worth looking for?"

The trader threw out his hands.

"My friend, you are surely not wasting your time with such play."

"No, no, Yakoub. I have a boy whose life's first great adventure this is. A good lad. A little encouragement is good when one is young."

The Jew laughed out loud and turned to enter his dark doorway.

"Run away, Meester Grandpapa Kingi *bwana*. You do not fool me. You would rather run after a profitless treasure hunt than settle down to business and make some hard money out of this gold dust. As for the map, it is possibly good. That fellow was 'Poulides' cousin. He died right there in Yilma's village. The teeth must be close by. 'Poulides never went to get them because Yilma demanded the old Abyssinian law of each right tusk for the king; and what would then be left for him? But for you it is different. Run along, Meester Kingi, and play."

LIKE A whirlwind King swept into his noonday camp.

"Up, up! Away! We've got no time to lose. Three days hard going to your teeth, young feller. Your map seems to be all right. But we've got to move. Fanshawe is on his way."

Weston was all excited.

"Have you had news, Mr. King? How could you get news here? Are you sure he's after the ivory? How do you know he's started? Come on, I'm all ready!"

King grinned at the thrill that the other was getting out of it all. Watching this keen youngster, shepherding him along, he lived over again the exhilaration of his first days when things were new and the fascinating unknown lurked around every corner.

And for that matter, as the shrewd old Jew had taunted him, he had never outgrown that same thrill; he was just as keen as eight years ago when he had been new. It was alas for him that, with experience, there remained fewer unknown things. But it was his delight not to disillusion the suspense of the other.

"I don't know a thing, young feller, No news. But I'm giving Fanshawe credit for being no kind of a fool to waste any time right now. We've got a shorter leg to go—just about due north by the caravan trail—while he'll be making a long slant from our left. But he's got a good start. Come ahead. The Masai will bring the porters along; they'll overtake us."

Passing the trader's store, King stopped for his letter of introduction. The Jew, smiling, handed him a sheet of notebook paper, without envelope. Upon it he had written only a single laconic line in the intricate Ethiopic script.

> This man is King, my friend. Whatever he will tell you will be true.

King nodded soberly.

"You're a good egg, Yakoub."

The eloquent hands pushed away thanks.

"No, no, Meester Kingi. It is only very difficult for me to write this terrible language. So I make it short. Go quickly now. Only just a minute— Hey, there, boy. *Bocklo amta.*"

Out of one of the beehive *tukuls* a servant led a mule, saddled and ready. The Jew inspected girth and reins. He signed to the Hottentot to take charge.

"They told me the young man was very new. He will lie down and die on the hill trails at your rate of travel. Go now, my friend. And for the sake of my gold dust which you owe me, take care of yourself."

The caravan trail left the river immediately outside of the town and within a mile struck the first slope of the series of wide shelves which rose in steep steps eight thousand feet up to the main Abyssinian plateau. In the heavier jungle where the sun filtered thinly, the slippery clay path had not dried out so well after the rains and the going was not too good.

King was consumed by a restless urge to push on. Now that he had found out what the prize was and how much it could mean, he could understand why the angry financier had dismissed less successful subordinates and had come so far afield to handle the delicate negotiation personally. And, while he couldn't like the man, while his whole soul rebelled from the ruthless system, he had an uneasy respect for the will that had carried the magnate to his lofty position, and had now brought him so far out of his normal sphere. That kind of will would trample through to the end.

With each rise where the down mountain winds had thinned the vegetation along the brow King scoured the long ridges to the left of him with his prism glasses. He was sure that the man would have wasted no time.

The day passed; the night; the next day of hard travel. The going was slower than King had hoped. Three days the trader had confidently allowed him to make a trek that normally consumed four. Yet the village of Fitaurari Yilma remained two full days' distant.

It was not till the third afternoon that Kaffa pointed to a far ridge that swept up to meet the hogback along the spine of which the caravan trail crawled.

"Men travel in that jungle," he announced.

KING BROUGHT his glasses to bear, not on the jungle, which was impenetrable, but on the sky. Yes, there was a concentration and a distinct dip in the wide circles that the vultures swung high in the blue. The birds did not drop and the concentration moved slowly up hill. So whatever it was, was alive and traveling; and men, because vultures do not follow moving game in the jungle. King judged the distance critically.

"That would be about the right direction for the Bahr-Yez-di trail," he said to Weston. "Whoever they are, they'll reach the meeting with this trail before we do."

"Then they'll be ahead of us. Gosh! Can't we hurry, Mr. King? Here, you take the mule, won't you? Perhaps you could get there first and—and do something or other."

The suggestion was vague enough. A party of unknown numbers was approaching. Yet the boy had a vast confidence that King, should he get there first, would contrive to do something or other. King had no such confidence; his frowning regard of the ridge was anxious. But he grinned and uttered a simple strategy of the trail:

"No need to hurry. It'll be getting on toward dark. They'll camp at the first good place. We'll hold back, and if we come up with them after they're all unloaded we'll have a good hour's start before they get going again, I don't care who they are."

It was another anxiety that bothered King. If this should be the Fanshawe party, how many others might there be? How many white men? If the deputy commissioner and perhaps the police superintendent and one or two others were accompanying so important a personage, it would complicate matters.

But reflection dismissed that thought. This business for many reasons would have to be kept as far as possible from any official complications. King's more cheerful mood was indicated by a tuneless whistling through his teeth as he strode along. He was busy upon the devising of plans to gain more than one hour's start; for his business with the Fitaurari, like all business in Africa, could not be conducted in a hurry.

Only one comment did he make as the steep miles dropped behind.

"Hope to all hell it is the big noise's party and they're not ahead of us."

They came to the joining of the trails. A mess of tracks showed that the other party had already passed.

"What do you read, little bush dweller?" King demanded of Kaffa.

"Mule caravan, *bwana*. Two white men who do not know how to travel; for there are at least fifteen servants to eight, or maybe ten, pack mules; and two riding mules of good quality."

"Hmph! Sounds like our crowd, young feller, no? I'm glad it's mules—it'll take 'em two hours to load up again. They've passed long enough. Let's go on and say hello."

The camp was as straggly and as distraught with confusion as only an African camp can be. Aimless yelling of men cursing the mules, hammering of tent pegs came downwind long before it was in sight.

King threw a look over his shoulder to the Masai, and the jabbering of his porters ceased. He approached softly, warily taking stock of the camp as he came. He was looking particularly for the caravan leader, whoever he might be, who had been appointed to conduct the august traveler; for on this man's initiative much would depend.

It was still daylight on the high hills. King at once distinguished the big form of Fanshawe standing moodily watching the aimless blundering of four men with his tent. A little way off the secretary essayed to help some more men with his own less pretentious tent. To one side a native who wore shoes was importantly directing two other natives in the erection of a cook tent.

"Hai-a, these Frangi travel with a city," muttered Kaffa.

Near Fanshawe a native, very raggedly dressed, stood to smart attention awaiting orders. King's smile was full of joy. That one would be the caravan leader, probably an experienced sergeant of the King's African Rifles, detailed to the job and dressed up—or undressed—for the occasion. Good! A soldier would do anything under orders, but would have no initiative at all.

The soldier pointed and Fanshawe turned quickly to see King approaching, Weston behind him, screened by his height. For a moment Fanshawe was merely surprised—he had seen King only by lantern light before. King spoke:

"Howdy, Mr. Fanshawe. I've got to congratulate you on the good time you made. You sure had me worried."

THEN CONTROL slipped from Fanshawe before he could recover from his surprise and catch himself. First he paled; then the blood surged back to his face and rage swept over him.

"You! The man on the bank! The American spy! I knew it! I—how the devil did you get here?"

King's wide grin and careless assurance if were maddeningly suggestive of a mild derision for anything that the other might be able to do; and to that egocentric contempt for his power was a thing unaccustomed and not to be borne.

"Curse you!" he shouted. "You ruffianly scum! I'll—Mr. Jepson, here—damn you, why aren't you here?—here are those two American bounders who have been following me."

The secretary came and stood rather ineffectually beside his fuming employer. King's chuckle was full of appreciation. He saw the justice of destiny here. The forceful driver of men, by the very fact of his dominance, had crushed all initiative in his close employee.

To the driver it was infuriating to the point of murder; but there was that cold something in King's grin and in his stance that made the big executive feel strangely impotent.

King still grinned. He could stand the man's abuse. He held all the cards in this game, he felt.

But Weston was younger.

"We don't have to take that," he cried, striding up to the magnate. "See here, mister, cut it. I've listened to as much of that as I'll take from any man."

For a moment Fanshawe looked at him in astonishment, with a sort of incredulity. This boy! This impertinent nothing! Why, he had held the fortunes of hundreds of such youths in the hollow of his hand. He had hired them and fired them by the score at a time. He had merely to press a button before his mighty seat and snap a few words to an underling and the deed was done.

And now this one stood upright before him and—

"You!" The word was almost a scream of triumph, as the big man lunged forward and swung a heavy, open hand. The boy blocked it rather clumsily with his elbow, staggered under the weight of the blow, recovered and landed a glancing swing on the magnate's face.

To the big man that was the completion of release. The blow swept away the ingrained inhibitions of dignity. Gone were the carefully nurtured conventions against ungentlemanly fisticuffs. The primitive man was released.

He roared in his throat and launched another annihilating swing, this time with closed fist. The boy managed to block it again—and then King's hard shoulder thrust in between them.

"Lay off, kid," he grunted. "We can do this without any rough stuff."

But neither was outraged dignity to be easily thwarted from battering, pounding at the thing that had so insulted it; nor was hot young blood willing to stand back. While the big man snarled against King's stiff elbow planted in his throat, the boy panted:

"Lemme go, Mr. King. This is my affair. He can't talk that way to me; and—if he wants that ivory he's got to damn well fight for it."

King held stiff for a long half minute; and then slowly he drew back and shrugged. It was good for a youngster to fight for his convictions and for his rights. Even if he lost, the right kind of youngster wouldn't lose the former; and King felt grimly confident that he wouldn't lose the latter.

HE DREW back. Immediately the big man lunged forward again and swung with furious intent. This was going to be no contest of skill against weight. Neither man knew anything at all about boxing. It was going to be a contest of nothing more than give and take and give again; stamina and plain nerve. Well, the kid had an advantage in the former; the big business man was softer, older—though by no means too old to annihilate the younger one if he but got him right. As to nerve, well, the end would show.

Within the first minute the younger one went staggering and down from a ponderous smash on the side of his head. It was to the big man's credit that he took no advantage over the fallen opponent. The boy rose, shaking his head, and moved warily round. His elbow blocked another swing and he grunted as his own fist collided comfortably with the other's face.

After that it was hammer and tongs; toe to toe, slug, clinch, wrestle. The youngster went down again. He came up and bored in. The big man staggered from a neat punch in the middle of the face. He roared and hurled a barrage of swings at the other. The youngster stopped some; took some; gave a few. Wrestle, clinch, slug. Blood showed on both faces.

Whatever the big man's ideas had been about chastisement, this was a fight. It was crude, hopelessly inexpert, woefully without skill. But King, standing on widespread legs and whistling thin discords through his teeth, nodded appreciatively. The conclusive factor of nerve was showing up. He was a good kid.

King beckoned the Hottentot, who with all the other camp boys stood gaping at the battle between their white masters.

"Make camp a hundred yards up the road; and quick-quick make hot water."

"*Bado kidogo, bwana.* It is a pity that the young *bwana* does not kick that other in the stomach as we do a mule that fights the halter."

"Away!" ordered King. "Hot water, and plenty of it."

The big man fell suddenly. The youngster stood drunkenly and dripped blood over him from a well battered nose. Fanshawe got up and bored in to clinch, push, grunt. Gone was his fierce rage that clamored for punishment. He was fighting, and he knew it.

So did the youngster. Ponderous swings came in every now and then that his inexpert elbows did not know how to block. His own blows were more frequent; but with each swing that cracked against the side of his head they were less effective. He went down again. And in a little while again. He rose each time more slowly. But still King nodded to himself. The important thing was that the boy rose.

It was when the youngster was shaky on his feet and dim eyed, weaving uncertainly on weak knees that King pushed his shoulder between the fighters.

"All right," he grunted to Fanshawe. "Your weight wins."

With one arm he supported the boy who pushed feebly to get past him. The big man's temper still held him. He was in the grip of a totally unaccustomed and enormous emotion. To fight, to beat, to batter, were the only impulses that he knew.

King pushed him off with an open hand against his chest.

"Snap out of it, big feller," he growled. "You win this lap. But I'll take a bet with you that we win the next."

The big man only stared at him owlishly; and then, like an ox that does not understand, he moved away. King led the youngster away.

"Come on, kid. You don't have to fight any more. You've done aplenty to that man—more than you or I will probably ever know. You've done him a heap of good. And, kid, you've done yourself proud. That was the best fight I ever saw lost."

IN THE camp which was already taking shape in the fast growing dusk under the skilled direction of the Hottentot and the gruff orders of the Masai, King led the youngster to warm water and advised him to strip clean and wash down.

"Nothing like a warm sponge to refresh you," he said. "And you're going to need it right soon."

Himself, he went to rummage for medicine kit and find that most useful of all camp medicaments, surgeon's tape. He helped the youngster wash up his cuts and bruises and made neat patches with tape where necessary.

"You're a mess," he told him with deep appreciation. "I don't know whether you know it, young feller, but this has done you a heap of good, too. Stretch out now and take a rest while you have time."

He called the big Masai to him and issued a curious order.

"Those boys who are putting up the tent. Tell them to roll it up again. Pick two men who are strong, who can carry a tent and a little food. Tell them to eat their *potio* swiftly."

Then he lighted a pipe and chose a spot on the edge of the hill where he could sit hugging his knees and watch the last of the sun paint the clouds crimson and amber and pale green, and throw the hilltops into blue-black silhouette against the swiftly darkening gray. Such things stimulated thought; and he needed thought.

The Hottentot came and announced supper. King was immediately on his feet and calling to Weston to up and get it while it was hot.

"Good Lord," the youngster mumbled. "I don't wanna eat. I'm so sore that I couldn't chew a mouthful."

"Come on, come on," said King. "You're going to need it. You've had a good and plenty beating up and you'll need your strength."

"I'll be all right in the morning, Mr. King; honest I will."

"In the morning," said King decisively, "you're going to be a long way from here. Time, young feller; it's time that's going to count. We need all the start we can get."

Weston groaned.

"Gosh, Mr. King. If that fellow's half as sore as I am he won't be starting for a week."

"Don't you fool yourself," said King. "If that man knew we were getting ahead, sore as he is, he'd heave himself up and come right on our tails. Don't ever make any mistake about Fanshawe, young feller, or any of his kind. He's all kinds of dog and he's swelled up so he can't see the little humans that run around about his feet. That's big business. But he's got the stick-to-it-iveness that put him up where he is; and he'll be hotfoot on our trail."

King called the Masai.

"Barounggo, I place a responsibility upon you. We go as soon as it is dark—Kaffa and the young *bwana* and I, and two strong men to carry tent and food. The rest stay here and make fires and noises of camp. The responsibility is that no fool of ours goes into that camp to smoke tobacco and to gossip the news of our going, and that no man from there comes here."

It was a large order to keep two groups of natives apart throughout a night; for Africans on *safari*, like animals, sleep fitfully and are restless; and gossip of the road is all the recreation that they know. But the Masai drew a line across the path with the point of his spear.

"It is an order," he said simply. "No man crosses that mark."

Half an hour later the little party stole out into the farther dark, leaving behind them the chatter of natives round bonfires; and beyond the fires, outlined in bronze highlights, the grim figure of the great Masai leaning motionless on his spear.

King was light of heart and full of glee at his strategy. "It's going to be tough going," he chuckled. "What with rocks and roots and all in the dark. But if we—if you, can keep going like the devil was after you, we'll reach the place where your ivory is by morning. I don't know how early Fanshawe will find out; but I guess he won't oversleep, and he'll kill his mules to come on. But we'll be at least half the day ahead of him."

Weston groaned, but clamped his teeth down on it.

"I'll do my damndest," he said.

King smiled in the dark. He was a good kid. And a stiff test of everything that he had—whether in a football game or in a race or in a fight or in just a forced march—was wonderfully good for the right kind of youngster.

"Might be the making of a regular outdoorsman of him," he muttered to himself, "and steal him away from that desk that his dad promises him."

And that, to King, was the epitome of human existence.

THEY WON through this time, too. Late morning saw them in view of the first straggling huts of the hill chieftain's village. King was deeply seamed about the eyes and mouth, but his stride was as springy as at the start. The Hottentot, wizened, shrunken, too black for the grime to show, looked exactly as he had looked twenty years ago. Weston and the porters were exhausted. King gave the little man instructions.

"I go to see the Fitaurari. There is a place here where four tamarind trees make a good shade. Find it and make camp. Give each porter a dash of rum with his *potio*." And to Weston:

"I've got to go and make my official visit. You go on and rest up. I'll come along whenever I can."

The *gebbi*, the so-called palace of the Fitaurari, was a rambling cluster of forty or so round *tukuls* in various sizes and conditions of repair. They were grouped together on a hilltop and surrounded by a stockade. King knew the conventions. To the head man, or chief steward of the household, he gave an immediate present of money. That opened the way to hospitality. King was conducted to a dim, cool *tukul* and provided with water to wash in and strong black coffee.

Presently a slave brought flat pancakes of sour bread and a dish of furiously peppered stew. King was in a fever to get to the chief and get down to business. But here he was not the lordly white man in a country ruled by white men. He was a foreigner in the last independent kingdom of ancient Africa. It was an hour—and a joyful surprise at that—before the steward came to conduct him into the chief's presence.

The Fitaurari sat in what must have been a chair, but it was so draped with carpets that one could only guess. A gold embossed shield of rhinoceros hide with a long curved sword in a solid silver sheath and a spear hung on the carpeted wall behind him. These were the insignia of his rank. He was a man in vigorous old age, with white hair and flowing beard, and a keen, strong face.

"*Thena'yisth'a'l'enge*, may God give you health for my sake," he greeted King. "Give me joy by taking a seat, Amricani, and tell me the news of the road."

"I come as a poor man, Fitaurari," began King bluntly, "bringing no gift to recommend me; only promises."

The old general smiled.

"Yet this letter. The Jew has robbed me in many a business, yet never has he put pen to words that so compromise his judgment. Surely that is a recommendation. Tell me then these things that he guarantees will be true."

King told him the whole story from the beginning, in detail; his hopes, his fears, his suspicions, and his anxiety about what might now happen.

The old general heard him through, nodded slowly, smiling from time to time, nodded again.

"So the old wizard knew?" he murmured when King had at last finished. "I have thought that he knew these many years, but he has kept the silence of wisdom." He laughed a short, hard laugh. "Yet, *getha Amricani*, you have made a long journey in a great haste for no cause."

King's heart sank. If the old man were going to pretend that there was no such document, the argument would be endless. But the ex-general's eyes grew fierce.

"Never will I give up that paper to any Inglesi. Have I borne my banishment these eighteen years and have I grown old in the jungle here for the principle of that paper that now I shall surrender it?"

"Fitaurari," said King earnestly, "I don't know about the principle of that paper. Whether you are right or wrong is not my affair. But this thing is now a matter of money. There is enough in that business to make many men very rich. That man will offer you much money to buy it; more than you will believe."

"I am old," said the Fitaurari calmly. "I have lived. My son will have my many hundred miles of estate. He may not have so much money as you say; but by holding this paper, as I have held it these many years, I insure at least that he will be a chief amongst his own people, not a subject. Let your Amricani people do this work. I am well content."

"But, Fitaurari," King urged, "this is a paper that can give the whole work to the Inglesi without further talk. This man is a man of much power; he has brains, he has force of will. He will produce argument to show you that conditions have changed in the world; that the principle no longer exists; that it is only the business that he desires. He will persuade you."

The old chief laughed.

"I have grown old in my principle. I have heard these arguments given twenty years ago before the Lion, my Lord. Given by the Inglesi and by the Taliani and by the Russki and by the Ferenchi. Twenty years ago they bade me tell my king that no one of them desired any more land in Africa. And then they all went to war together and when it was finished they took all the land of the Germani who lost the war. I am proof against persuasion."

KING FELT that the bigoted old man was rooted in his conviction of many years; but he knew what things had been done, what incredible cleverness had been brought to bear on business deals involving very much less money than this irrigation project.

"Fitaurari," he said, "You are proof. Good. Yet tell me how many men are there in your household who are proof against much money? How many men, for much money, would steal that paper? Do you think you could keep it hidden from all your household for one whole day? And for very much money—you know your own land, Fitaurari—how many men do you think would swiftly mix for you the black coffee which is the end? Who would then get the paper?"

The old man remained silent. Once his eyes grew fierce and he cast a backward glance at the weapons on the wall. King put the thought into words for him.

"Yes, but the penalty that the thief would pay would not bring back the paper."

The old man nodded somberly.

"What would you have me do with this dangerous thing?"

"Destroy it, Fitaurari," King urged. "While it exists it is a danger. Think. Have you a single means that will guarantee that it will not be stolen? Destroy it before it is too late."

The general of King Menelek shook his head vigorously. Almost reverently he quoted the law.

"'The Seal of Menelek, Lion of Judah, King of Kings, the Chosen of God. He who shall dishonor it, his hand shall be cut off at the wrist; his land shall be taken from him and be shall be outcast.'"

"Then give it to me," said King boldly. "I place my hands in your hand and give you my word that I shall respect the seal."

The old man looked at him out of his fierce old eyes for a long time in a brooding silence. Then:

"Give it to you?" he murmured. "This paper which you say is worth so much money?"

"Worth much to the Inglesi," said King. "Worth nothing to me. If I could by airplane carry it to the Amricani company before the business is signed, they would pay money in order to keep it from the other man. Since it will take three weeks of travel to get to the capital, and by that time the business will be signed and finished, they may in their generosity give me a small present to avoid argument."

The ex-general nodded in understanding.

"'When a battle has been won,'" he quoted, "'the chief who comes up afterward receives no spoil.' But—" he voiced a doubt—"if you expect no payment from your own side, how do I know that you will not sell this paper to that man who will offer so much money?"

"Hell!" shouted King. "Fitaurari, my hand in yours and my word. Besides, as you are an Abyssinian and have your reasons, I am Amricani and have my reasons."

The old man nodded again. His burning eyes bored into King's. His head swayed rhythmically with his thoughts.

"And the Jew wrote that whatever you would tell me would be true. That is a good recommendation. Tell me truly then, Amricani, what will happen if this paper falls into the hands of this Inglesi who comes prepared to pay much money for it?"

For the moment King was tempted; but in the next moment he answered steadily:

"I can tell you only this, Fitaurari. If that Inglesi gets the paper my people will lose that work and his people will get it."

The old man brooded over that reply. Suddenly he became fierce. He shouted as though remembering an old battle cry.

"And I tell you, *getha Amricani*, as I told Menelek my king— but he would not believe me—I tell you that if that Inglesi gets the paper, my people will lose this land and his people will get it."

With a quick decision he clapped his hands. A very black slave appeared. The man appeared to be deaf, for the general took a long silver pin and scratched with it upon a board smeared with bees' wax. The man read and went into an inner room.

He came back with a cheap japanned tin box and knelt, holding it before his master. With torturing deliberation the old man hunted through an immense bunch of keys till he found a common stamped out thing that must have had a thousand duplicates in the land. He opened the box and rummaged through a collection of trash and folded papers.

King's heart stopped as the old man apparently didn't find the paper. Perhaps the coveted document had been stolen long ago. The old man, with maddening reminiscence, unfolded several crackling old papers and glanced through them, refreshing his memory as to their contents.

King's effort to control himself from manifesting eagerness and to keep an immobile face was immense. He pictured to himself the back trail with a furious man flogging a mule along the steep slope. How far back, was the excruciating question? But he forced himself to examine with great intentness a rent in his sleeve.

"Ah," exclaimed the old man suddenly. "Behold!"

After all this effort, all this mental anguish, it was a disappointingly unimportant looking little thing. An eight by ten oblong of parchment, stiff and brown with age and dirt.

THE OLD MAN lifted an eyebrow at the slave, who immediately disappeared. Slowly he unfolded the crackly skin, and King's heart jumped to recognize the close written maze of Ethiopic script and above it the great three-inch black seal of Menelek, with the king's own inexpert initials scrawled across it. The old man read it carefully through, pondering long thoughts of the dead past. King's jaw muscles showed how his teeth bit upon each other.

The old warrior ruminated, looking at King from under shaggy white brows.

"A paper worth much money, you say? Hm-mm!" Then with an access of fierceness once more, "But I say, a paper worth the lives of many Abyssinian men! Take it, Amricani, and guard it with your head. Let your Amricani people do this work; so that it is at last done and so that the importunities of those others come at last to an end."

King took first the hand that held the portentous document.

"Fituarari, you do me a favor that I can not—"

But the old man cut him short.

"Tscha-tscha! It is not so; I do nothing for you. I do a favor to Abyssinia—and to myself. For when that man comes with his arguments and with his money and with his importunities, I shall be able to take oath by the head of Menelek that I have no such document. And no other man of my people knows of this thing; for those who knew have long ago died."

And at that evasion the old man chuckled. It was just that form of specious truth that appeals so strongly to the Oriental in the complex Abyssinian heredity.

"And so when my servants accept bribes to search out and steal that which I have not, the only loss will be to the briber."

The logical sequence of that thought followed through. The old man laid his hand on King's arm.

"And you—will you expect me to protect you with a guard of my soldiers from that man who will do so much to gain possession of that paper?"

King laughed his hard little laugh.

"I've been protecting myself all around Africa pretty successfully for many years, Fitaurari. But I don't like trouble when I can duck out of it. I offer a plan which will at least cloud the question in uncertainty. No man knows, you say, that you have such a paper?"

"But it is already being talked throughout my household that a white man has come to ask for something."

"Good. Give me, therefore, something. Give me this, Fitaurari. I have a young man, a boy, who has foolishly bought a map from Petropoulides the Greek showing the location of those elephant teeth that his cousin buried before he died."

"Ah, a map?" The old man's face clouded in angry reminiscence. "I have often wondered where that fellow hid the things. He died; otherwise I would have I exacted the tribute that the law stipulates—each right tooth for the king."

"Yes, I know the law," said King quickly. "But it is also the law that the trader or the hunter may pay the price of each tooth according to its weight and may keep the teeth. Therefore, Fitaurari—this is a good youngster, though lacking experience—I will pay the tribute of each right tooth in money. Do you, therefore, summon your secretary and instruct him to write out a permission for me to take up those teeth out of your village. And so will there be a reason for my coming."

The old chief shouted his sudden laughter and clapped King on both shoulders. He laughed until a coughing fit choked him. This was a subterfuge better even than the other. It capped the story and made a perfect alibi. Though nobody might believe the story in its entirety, it was on the face of it palpably true and the proof was forthcoming. And no man more than an Abyssinian loves to brazen out such a situation.

"Go, go!" the old man wheezed. "There will be no profit left for you in that ivory. But I have sworn to that obstinate Greek to collect the king's lawful tribute. I accept it as payment for the paper. Go, my friend. You are a man of my own heart. The permit will be sent to you."

A N D   S O King came to his camp in the tamarind grove, jauntily; full of silent laughter. King very different from the man who had dealt so cleverly with the old general. The tent was set up. Weston had eaten and was rested.

"What!" shouted King. "Haven't you dug it up yet? My land, how'd you ever hold off that long?"

To which Weston replied only—

"Hunh?"

"Man alive," said King. "Didn't your map say tamarind trees? Four of them in a rough square; the only ones in the whole village? Or didn't you know these were tamarind trees?"

"Good—good Lord! You mean to say—" the youngster's eyes popped wide—"you mean to say this is the place where—Golly, and I've been sitting here like—"

Gone was the pain of his bruises; forgotten the stiffness of his grueling journey.

"Lord almighty, where the heck is that map now?"

"D'you have to look it up?" derided King. "Gosh, at your age, young feller, I'd have been able to draw it by heart." And for that matter, so he could now. "Diagonal the trees, it said, didn't it? And dig at the point of intersection."

Weston rushed to look for string, mule rope, tent rope—anything. He limped from one tree to another—and never knew he was limping.

King squatted, hugging knees, looking on at it all through a screen of pipe smoke with a huge satisfaction.

"I think I've got the place," the youngster finally called. "This is where the lines cross to a hair."

Then King got up and joined him with a pretense at nonchalance. A shade of annoyance crossed his face.

"Shucks," he muttered. "Hate to overlook things like that. I've forgotten to bring along a digging tool. Never mind, a couple of hunting knives have dug up many a loot bigger'n this."

It was hard work digging in the stiff clay soil with hunting knives. But this was too absorbing a play to let the native servants do it all while one just watched. King sweated and scrabbled in the dirt with Weston, and whooped just as loud as the boy did when the first long, hard brown curve showed.

Man and boy, they scrambled with one another to scratch it out and bring it to the surface.

"Wow!" shouted King. "A forty-fiver! That's pretty good, young feller, as they go nowadays."

"I've got another," came the youngster's muffled voice, groping deep in the hole.

In another minute he wriggled his shoulders out and heaved up another slim shape. King shouted again.

Six tusks they exhumed in all; of a fair size and apparently of hard ivory; though that would have to be determined later. Then King, grubbing in the lower dirt with the last reluctant hope of the born treasure hunter, whooped again.

"Whee-ee, there's—I think there's another one."

Like a terrier he scratched, his head and shoulders deep in the hole, his long legs splayed out over the flat ground to balance himself. In a moment he came up, sand in his hair, one eye painfully screwed, but grinning delight through the other. His hands hugged a seventh long, shiny tusk.

Weston pushed him away in a frenzy and preempted the hole. Shortly his voice mumbled triumph. He threw the tusk out and dived back into the hole before King could get to it. This was the most intense excitement of his life. King sat back and let him win the most out of his thrill.

Ten tusks there turned out to be in all; the wily Greek had contrived to collect more than anybody knew. Like boys having unearthed the pirate's treasure the two men laid them out side by side in a shiny row and admired them. They grinned at each other through sand specked eyelashes, spitting grit from between their teeth and shaking sand from their necks. This was one of the times, when the world was a good place to be in.

And in this position Fanshawe found them.

Disheveled, dirty, caked with sweat and dust, he had rushed down from the palace gates to prove the thing that he did not believe. He had not seen the Fitaurari yet. The old chief was exhausted, word had been sent out. He begged the visitor's indulgence; would he mind coming later in the afternoon? But the story was out that the earlier arrivals had come to get a permit to dig up buried ivory within the very confines of the village and were even now exhuming a vast treasure.

Like a charging bull Fanshawe thrust his way through the circle of gaping natives. And there the proofs of the incredible story stared him in the face. Long and curved and glistening brown in the sun.

Weston shouted his triumph. Having fought and lost, and won again, he was ready to forgive bygones.

"We beat you to it, Mr. Fanshawe. No hard feelings, I hope. Ain't they beauties, though?"

Fanshawe looked, spluttered, choked. Incoherent words burst from him.

"Is—is that what—was that what you came to get?"

King's steely eyes met his; but his wide mouth grinned beneath them.

"Well, what the devil else was all the scramble about?" he demanded; and then rising and confronting the man with an assumption of suspicion, "Sa-ay, what were you so hot after? What else is there around here?"

Fanshawe gave vent to a noise like the throat rattle of the wretched mule that had dropped dead under him in his mad race to get here. He turned, and battered his way through the crowd once more to insist upon seeing the Fitaurari and proving again the baffling thing that he refused to believe.

King grinned after him.

"Wonder what he thinks he can get out of the chief?" he asked ingenuously of Weston. "What I've seen of the old boy, he'll get damn poor satisfaction."

The Hottentot had to add his acute observation.

"What audience does that man hope to get in this land of Abyssinia, coming without a gift in his hand?"

"Make no mistake," King muttered half to himself. "That man has plenty force. Why should he not see the Fitaurari whom I saw without a gift?"

"Nay, *bwana*," said the little man. "Three pots of that food have we presented upon our arrival here, as an earnest of gifts to come with our caravan; and a female slave has already brought milk and a goat."

"Out!" shouted King. "Get out. Bush baboon, you disgrace me with your philanderings."

"Nay, *bwana*," the little man defended with an immense seriousness. "In this land of Abyssinia it is necessary to a white *bwana's* dignity that his servants have also their servants."

To which very truth there was no reply.

After that there remained only the question of division of the spoils. Weston was insistent upon his former proposition—fifty-fifty.

"Gosh, I owe it all to you, Mr. King. All I had was the map. I'd never have got here at all on my own. I can see now what a job it's been."

"Well," said King in fatherly manner, "there won't be any profit in that stuff at all if we split. And—I turned a little business with the chief there that'll about make me quits. I've had a hatful of fun out of it, kid; and that's worth quite a lot too, isn't it?"

"By golly, yes." Weston said. "Me, too. I've never had such a good time in my life. This—say, the way you do, Mr. King, this is living."

King's grin was pure beatitude.

"Take a tip, young feller. You'll get a lot more for that stuff in New York than you will here; and—maybe if you give your dad one of them whole he'll stake you to another trip."

To the youngster it was an inspiration.

"Gosh! You're dead right on that. And—I'll just have to have another trip after this. But—if you won't split—Say, you don't mind my asking what kind of business you put over, do you? I mean, do you honest to God make anything out of it?"

King's grin this time was free from all care. He lighted his pipe and puffed deeply.

"To tell you the truth," he explained. "It wasn't really any of my *damn* business. A matter of a little contract for Uncle Sam. As a matter of fact, by the time I can get it to that crowd, I don't expect they'll give me a whole lot more than a nice thank you. That's big business."

THE WITCH CASTING

KINGI *bwana* was experiencing a new sensation. It piqued him. In fact it more than merely piqued him; it nettled him. The thing was so entirely novel; it struck at an emotion against which he—so carefully poised in most things—was unguarded.

It required a grunted observation of his wise little Hottentot head-boy to bring him to a realization that he was letting himself give way to a foolish vanity.

The other two white men whose camp he was visiting had both gone into their tent; gone together by deliberate design, King thought—or rather the one had gone in and the other had deliberately followed him. Kaffa the Hottentot, who had carried the lantern for his master, huddled like a monkey in a blanket in the dim outer fringe of light; motionless, oblivious of the doings of the white lords, a creature only, without soul, ready to come when called and to go when sent—as a good head-boy should be.

Yet Kaffa in the outer circle had the acute ears of the ape that he resembled, and—wise as an ape—he had been a close intimate of his master's doings for sufficient years to have gained a rudimentary understanding of English.

Without moving, looking into the empty night, he grunted his observation.

"Those white men are as the swamp tortoise—fools who will not accept wisdom."

King continued to sit in
the luxurious hammock
chair under the African stars,
also motionless. But he felt
a slow flush creep over
himself. From his face to his
neck it went, and spread then
uncomfortably over his
whole body, even down
inside his mosquito-boots. It
had required just that remark
of his servant to show him
that he was resenting these
men's brusk disdain of his
experience. He burned with
shame at his unguarded pet-
tiness; and he was immea-

surably glad that his servant's shrewd remark had brought him
to himself.

Yet to the servant he said quietly, still without moving:

"It is ill to speak so, unasked, of white masters. One tenth of
your pay for this month is fined."

"Yes, *bwana*, it is ill," murmured the Hottentot meekly.

He knew that he had transgressed. He knew, too, that by
meritorious service he could win rewards during the month
well overbalancing the stiff fine.

King relighted his pipe and, calmly master of himself once
more, set himself impersonally to analyze this unaccustomed
thing.

Americans, these men were. King, crossing trails with them
at the last little outpost settlement of M'bandele, had joyfully
come over to their camp to ask eager questions of home whence
they had just come and to offer his experience of whither they
were going. Most men in East Africa would have absorbed that
knowledge with thanksgiving; and to most men King would

not have given it. But to these two from home he was willing, even anxious, to offer such information and advice as they might need.

And they—or at all events one of them intimated by his cavalier aloofness that when he needed anything out of King's experience of Africa he would ask for it.

This was a quite new experience in Africa for King.

The first man came out of the tent again and let himself wearily down into the adjoining hammock chair. This was Chester C. Howard, large framed, pale faced, tired eyed, and much too young to be legitimately so worn out after a day's trek. An invalid, King judged him to be; a tired business man perhaps, come to Africa to do some hunting in the wholesome outdoors and to give mind as well as body a rest from the frenzied fight for dollars.

This one had been inclined to be more cordial. He had listened attentively to King's proffered information about the hinterland. He sat silent now, drawing a breath every now and then as though on the point of speaking, and then letting it go again and shifting uneasily in his chair. He seemed to find difficulty in coming to a decision.

King leaned back and blew silent smoke rings at the stars, his narrow eyes apparently closed in peaceful enjoyment, but taking in every move of the other.

Decision came to Howard at last. He sat upright and set his shoulders in his overloose coat. He drew a breath again and held it. He had to force himself to say what he wanted.

"Mr. King, I was about to say just now, er—I wanted to ask you, whether you would throw in with my party and give me the benefit of your knowledge of that back country."

King remained as he was, head thrown back in his cupped hands; he lifted one eyebrow to the stars.

"I don't think you need me exactly, Mr. Howard. Mr. Gerardi seems to know his way about pretty well."

The other, having come to his hard won decision, clung to it still.

"Oh, yes, by all means, Dr. Gerardi has safaried extensively in South Africa and in Rhodesia; but he doesn't know that Uganda-Sudan border country. Er—if your fee—forgive me if I put it crudely—I'm fortunate, I suppose, in that money doesn't—what I mean is, from what I've heard of you, Mr. King, I'd be glad to pay you whatever—"

At this juncture the other man came out. He bulked large in the dim triangle of the tent flap. A well set up man with an easy confidence in his hearty manner. He took the third chair and spread his robust legs before him in comfort.

The invalid still clung desperately to his decision.

"I was just telling Mr. King, John; er—I was asking him if he'd care to join us."

The other laughed in loud good humor.

"That's a hell of a compliment to me, Chet. Anybody would think I was a new born tenderfoot."

"No, no, I don't mean that, John. You know I don't. Only, your knowledge of that border country is, on your own admission, hearsay; and you've told me yourself that the big thing about hunting is to know where to look for game. Now Mr. King here—"

The other laughed good humoredly again.

"Good old embarrassed Chet. Heavens, you can't make me mad by getting another man to take a lot of the responsibility off my shoulders. I'll be only too glad to get some more time for shooting. But suppose you talk to him about it in the morning. As your physician, I think your medicine and your camp cot are about due."

The invalid subsided. He was clearly, and quite properly, under the dominance of his friend, physician and expedition leader.

"I suppose you're right," he acquiesced. "I'm not properly on my feet yet. You'll excuse me, Mr. King, won't you?"

His loose clothes flapped about him as he went obediently to the tent. King prepared to go to his own camp. Dr. Gerardi was heartily apologetic

"Sorry you couldn't settle your business tonight, old man; but I don't have to tell you what a lot of details would have to be talked over. We'll be seeing you in the morning, I suppose. I'll send a boy over for you when Howard is up. Good night."

The voice was cordial and the confident dark eyes were smiling. But King felt that there was more of triumph in the smile than cordiality.

He returned to his camp with long thoughtful strides. There was something queer there. Once he muttered to himself—

"The devil you'll send a boy for me in the morning!"

He knew that by the next morning the invalid's decision to hire his services would have been very thoroughly changed for him. If the little Hottentot pattering ahead of him with the lantern had any thoughts he kept them wisely to himself.

In his own tent King saw his face in the little mirror that hung on the center pole. A thin vertical line between his brows, eyes very narrow, mouth compressed hard and drawn down at the corners. He looked at it in frank astonishment; then he laughed at it.

"Shucks, what a fool I am," he grunted to himself. And retrospectively, "What a fool that doctor is too; I wonder do I look to him like I want to steal his job of millionaire herding."

He laughed again, genuinely this time, and he stretched his long corded arms above his head till the shoulder sinews cracked. For him the incident was closed.

OF COURSE, no boy came over in the morning to call King to any discussion. By morning the rich man had changed his mind about the need of that much extra experience. Or rather, his tired mind had been changed for him; and King didn't altogether blame the doctor either; he himself in charge of an expedition would have resented the sudden inclusion of a rival.

He shrank from drawing attention to himself, as though begging to be sent for; so he stayed within his own tent while the other safari packed up and got under way.

A safari departure was no uncommon occurrence at the little mud and corrugated iron village of M'bandele; yet the complete population turned out, as it always did, to stand around and comment and gossip and—the native boys—to scramble for discarded tomato cans.

Kaffa, the Hottentot, and Barounggo, King's big Masai porter driver, stood together and submitted the safari to expert discussion; Kaffa, shriveled, amazingly wrinkled, huddled in a gaudy blanket; the Masai nakedly immense, dressed only in a twist of leopard skin loincloth and monkey hair garters at knee and elbow. He leaned on his great spear and laughed deeply in his chest at the little Hottentot's acid comments.

According to the little fellow's reasoning these people had offered insult to his master by not leaping to engage him. Loyally, therefore, he disliked them. Furthermore, they had cost him a fine of one-tenth of his pay. So presently he was the center of an admiring group who tittered and slapped their thighs at each sally of keen and crude native wit.

At last everything was packed and bundled, and in not too long a time; the doctor man had certainly traveled before. King came out of his tent then. There was no room left now for misunderstanding or embarrassment. These people definitely did not want him and the matter was closed. Any feeling about the thing would have been absurd on either side.

Most particularly these were Americans, countrymen of King's. Friendliness was therefore almost a rite. Among the dwellers of this outpost village were sundry British-Indian halfbreeds, a Greek trader or two, and an English-Africander sergeant of police. Anything less than extreme cordiality between compatriots far from home would have been most unseemly.

So King came out and shook hands all round and wished them luck and passed on the last word information about water holes; and natives shouted farewells and told the safari porters scare stories about lions in that back country; and everybody laughed and waved; and the Hottentot giggled inordinately; and the big safari departed with the proper eclat.

It was not until evening, until the safari was a full day's march distant, that the Hottentot raised a sudden outcry. He had lost his most precious possession.

Every African boy—every one, that is, who hopes to work for a white man—treasures above all things his letter of recommendation; for without one it is difficult to get any save the most menial jobs at manual labor.

Every house boy, tent boy, head boy, safari man, has a greasy scrap or two of worn paper that sets forth his recommendations above the signature of some forgiving past time master. The smart ones have several such. The too smart ones carry a whole sheaf of them—neatly typed on stolen official stationery by Eurasian clerks—bearing the carefully done signatures of generals and famous travelers and governors of colonies. It would astonish the ghost of Colonel Roosevelt to know how many absurdly young boys he had personally employed. These clever ones wait at the ports and the outfitting stations for the ever increasing tide of rich travelers who come out every season to do their Africa.

No such letter had Kaffa the Hottentot. He had never had a master other than King; never hoped to have another. But since every good boy had at least one such letter of recommendation he felt his dignity to be incomplete without a similar witness of his worth, and so had begged King to give him one. Now he wailed its loss. But complacently he besought his master:

"But *bwana* will give me another one, yes? For, barring that matter of having spoken disrespectfully of those two white lords, I am indeed a very good head boy."

"There have been times," said King, "few and long ago, when you have been not worse than a well trained grass monkey. But I will give you another. Though how can a man not a fool lose such a paper?"

"True, *bwana*, a wise man does not lose such a paper. But, *awai*, I have suspicion that it has been stolen from my bundle."

"Huh," grunted King. "Who in this place could steal anything from so wise an ape as Kaffa?"

The Hottentot wriggled in his blanket and then assumed an expression of preternatural innocence, whereat his master immediately regarded him with suspicion.

"*Bwana*, it is ill to speak ill of any man—I have learned. Yet I have suspicion. That boy Umbobo, whom *bwana* dismissed for thieving, was in this village."

"Umbobo, hey?" King was interested. "Why, that slick scamp could steal anything; and he knows how to plant his loot with every bush chief along the road, and how to gouge it back from him too. But—" suspiciously again—"why would he steal your paper? Why don't you take Barounggo and beat him and get your paper back? What is all this outcry about nothing?"

The Hottentot was the very embodiment of a wistful monkey.

"Alas, *bwana,* he was here. He is now gone."

King began to see light.

"Gone where? Tell me truth now, imp."

The Hottentot's artless innocence was that of a wizened ape.

"I think, *bwana,* he must have gone with that safari; for indeed I saw him talking with the great white lord of whom it is ill to speak ill; not the sick one, the strong one whose hair is smooth like the chi-m'panze and whose eyes are keen and set close in his face—"

King was forced to an effort to keep an immobile face at the cunningly uncomplimentary description. The Hottentot looked everywhere in the air except at his master's expressionless face.

"I have suspicion, *bwana*—I am afraid that that evil boy stole my paper in order to take my name and to—to—" He could hold that innocence no longer. He writhed in fearful effort; but the giggle burst from him in shrill falsetto.

"Keh-heh-heh-heh—in order to gain employment with that white lord. Keh-heh-heh-heeh-heeh!"

"Phew!" King whistled. "That boy will loot himself rich out of that outfit."

And then suddenly he knew; and on the instant, with a sudden movement, before the Hottentot could leap out of reach, he shot a long arm out and had the boy by the scruff of the neck.

"Devil's whelp!" he shouted. "Bush baboon! You gave him that letter. By wicked design you gave it to him."

"Nay, *bwana.*" The imp squirmed under King's two hands in the air. "Not so. I did not give it to him. By the great rock snake, I swear it."

That oath with the Hottentot meant truth. King let go of his neck. The boy writhed again and stretched it ruefully from his blanket folds like a tortoise. Then he giggled again and quoted with sententious virtue:

"In the wisdom of my people is a true saying. 'The head-strong-man runs his head into the unavoidable snare of justice.' Keh-heh-heh-heh, those white lords ought to have taken *bwana* who has experience of such things."

King reached quickly for the graceless scamp again; but he had already scuttled out of reach. To have chased him would have been derogatory to white man's dignity.

"Tell truth now, scoundrel," said King. "Or you can go seek service with your paper. How did that Umbobo boy get that paper?"

The Hottentot scuttled farther.

"Nay, *bwana*, I—it was but justice for the insult to *bwana's* knowledge—I rented it to him. He is a great thief, but he is honest; he will bring it back."

"For how much?" demanded King grimly.

The Hottentot twisted in desperate abashment, like a boy who must confess a mischief before omnipotent authority. He stood on one leg and scratched himself in an extremity of nervousness with the toes of the other. Unable to meet the boring eyes of his master, he mumbled at last—

"For one-tenth of the amount of my month's pay, *bwana*."

"So?" said King evenly. "Bush imp. It is therefore justice that I fine you another tenth."

DEPUTY COMMISSIONER FAWCETT, dining on his veranda in all the solitary formality of evening dress, rose with alacrity to meet the tall figure that loomed suddenly up out of the dim veranda steps.

"Damn those boys," he grumbled. "Why didn't they tell me you were here? But I was rather expecting you to come and make serious *indaba*."

King relaxed into a cane chair, stretched his khaki breeched legs luxuriously on its long arms and lighted his pipe before speaking, ignoring the little matter of his unannounced presence.

"Serious stuff? My conscience is clear of anything that your fussy old government can bother me for."

The commissioner chuckled; he was immensely pleased.

"What, what? Have I been getting something that you haven't heard yet? That begins to be news in itself, my dark and devious Kingi."

King blew smoke at the ceiling.

"Lots of things you ought to hear before I do, you with all your official sources."

"Ought to, yes," said the deputy commissioner dryly. "But this isn't your trouble, my dear chap, though it's going to be."

King was vehemently positive.

"Nothing doing a-tall, Dipty *bwana*. I'm free and guiltless and I'm going Rudolf side to meet a Palestinian friend of mine from Abyssinia to whom I owe thousands of sacks of dust gold—if he's smart enough to build a trade."

The deputy was equally positive.

"All the same, it's going to be your *shauri*, old man. First of all, though this has nothing to do with it, there's been a man hanging about here for some days, waiting to see you. A native. That's how I knew you were coming."

"That's pretty damn good official deduction." King grinned. "Wouldn't he tell established authority what he wanted, and go away?"

The deputy chuckled again.

"He wouldn't even tell me he wanted to see you. But he has three cicatrices on each shoulder and a row of six across his chest. So—"

King let his long legs quietly down from the chair and pushed himself upright. Then to cover that movement he rather ostentatiously relighted his pipe.

"And so," continued the deputy slowly, "I thought he might be some *tagati* man from that old witch doctor friend of yours at Elgon Mountain. Batete the Old One, they call him, I understand; and he carved that pipe bowl especially for you?"

King sat all the way up.

"Fawcett, *bwana*," he nodded softly—"you're learning so much about dark and devious Africa that you won't be any damn good as an official presently."

The deputy flushed with pleasure at the back handed compliment.

"Well, my Kingi, it was you who taught me how to listen in. But I'm officially handicapped; those fellows won't talk to my men like they do to you."

"I must go see this *tagati* neophyte," said King. "His news is probably vastly more important than this trouble of yours that I'm not going to mix into."

"All the same you will, my cocksure Kingi. And this time I have no hesitation in asking you. They are your compatriots, not mine."

"Huh?"

King stood up and paced the veranda with long silent steps.

"Who is in here at all—except—?"

The deputy nodded.

"Millionaire safari. They're up in the Dodinga country, beyond the big thorn swamp. A deuce of a place to get to. I'm really sorry for you, old chap, because speed is an important factor and all round the swamp is a long way."

"Good Lord!" groaned King. "Why should I have to mix into their troubles? They didn't want me from the start. I met them going in two months ago. And they ought not to be having any bother anyhow; the leader man knows African travel aplenty. Why don't you wire Kitgum to send a police sergeant? He can work around the western end of that filthy bog and get into Dodinga country all sweet and pretty."

The deputy laughed. He was quite sure of his ground.

"Kitgum is two weeks farther away than you can make it through the swamp; and you know how these smoldering native troubles can suddenly flare up into tragedy. I have two native policemen stationed up there as it is. They send a rambling and quite incoherent report about black magic and witchcraft, from which I can make out only that a white man is sick from some queer thing that looks like a magic killing. And if you're going north anyway, it won't be more than a couple of weeks out of your way. And since they're your own silly people, and—"

King could see himself being overwhelmed by sheer mass of argument. He sprang to his feet and made to go away.

"Oh, shut up!" he shouted. "Why did I have to come along? I could just as well have gone to the Rudolf water by way of Lokri and Naura. Witchcraft, you say? Is there any connection, d'you suppose? Where can I see this young *tagati* man?"

"I fancy—" Fawcett, who was growing to be very wise, smiled—"that if you just go outside my gate and stand in the dark he'll jolly well appear in quick time. And I'll have some dinner warmed up for you."

Fifteen minutes later King stood silently in the veranda again. He nodded morosely.

"You were right. And it clicks. There's some fool of a witch doctor up there who seems to be horning in on white man affairs. So Old Batete sends to remind me of favors he had done in the past."

Fawcett nodded, too, with understanding.

"And he knows that, while we have to keep shuteye on native spellbindery, if they start fooling with white men it will jolly well bring a bee's nest about the ears of the whole brotherhood. So that's two reasons for making this thing your *shauri.*"

"What a mess," grumbled King. "I wonder whether this *tagati* can get a message to my Palestine date to meet me somewhere else? Sometimes they can."

The deputy commissioner nodded in sober agreement.

"Yes, sometimes they beat the telegraph; and it's too often to be guesswork. Some day I'm going to find out how this mysterious communication is done."

King laughed shortly.

"If you do—which you will not—you'd know the dim beginnings of all the queer things in Africa which no white man will ever know. Me, I'm glad enough that sometimes I can get them pulling for me instead of dead against. You, Dipty *bwana,* you'll never get them pulling for you; for the simple and unchangeable reason that you're an official of the white man's government that insists upon trying to make the black man in his own country do things the way the white man thinks is right in his country."

The deputy laughed in turn.

"And that is the reason, my Kingi, why you can do this thing better than a policeman from Kitgum; and plain brotherly love for your own troublesome people practically forces the nasty job on to your shoulders."

KING WAS in the middle of the great swamp and in vile humor. No brotherly love for his countrymen sweetened his disposition. He cursed them as he grumbled:

"I knew it would be a filthy job, and it's twice all of that. I'd let them go hang and get themselves stuffed full of spears like a porcupine, only that commissioner fellow would jeer me for the rest of my life that his crowd never let their own people down; and they're plenty ready to high hat us as it is. Barounggo. Hey, Barounggo, get those men spread out more, and prod any fool in the tail who isn't careful."

Swamp did not mean by any means an endless morass. It meant, rather, muddy pools and soggy paths intersected by oozy runlets between higher ridges of dry ground covered with a dense shrubbery of all the thorns known to Africa and inhabited by mosquitoes and huge gray leeches that knew how to search out the lace holes of high boots and swell up like red striped gooseberries.

In this maze one of King's men was lost, a stupid *shenzie* who with the animal dumbness of the African porter had disregarded the strict instructions to keep together.

Some men would have gone on, leaving the native to follow, excusing themselves on the perfectly sound ground of the health—and possibly the life—of the whole safari. King knew how a man might be incapacitated by any one of a hundred different accidents and might lie for days before crawling things in their myriads would finally submerge his ever weakening struggles.

King's consideration for his fellow humans was of the practical kind that made him stay in the swamp and search for the lost man; but that, at the same time, grimly promised itself that if the man were not pretty deathly sick from his hurt when they found him, he would be so from the very proper beating that would be his due for getting stupidly lost.

Kaffa the Hottentot shouted directions to a *shenzie* to work out toward the left and to search in the direction of a scraggy sentinel tamarisk tree. The man made his slow, unwilling way in the direction indicated; and there he suddenly stood shouting, waving uncouth arms. Others scouting in far flung line scrambled, splashed, pole vaulted toward him. King came up to them as they stood in a bovine semicircle, heads stretched forward in fearful fascination, eyes rolling.

Splay footed tracks led to a brown scummy pool; web footed tracks came out of it. Kaffa the Hottentot could read that story like heavy face type.

"Look, *bwana*. Here that fool stood to look. *Awai*, what a madness he must have eaten! Here it rushed forth and seized him. Rearing high, it seized him by the hand—for see, his both feet still show. Here he struggled, screaming.

"For ten minutes he struggled, for it was a small one. But in the end it was stronger than he and it pulled him in. And that all happened just four hours ago."

King nodded as he followed the sign reading.

"How do you place the time, O wise little ape?" he wondered.

Kaffa giggled, delighted to show off his astuteness.

"Four hours ago, as *bwana* sat to eat, the marsh plovers rose with a great screaming at this place. For ten minutes they screamed before they settled. It came to me just now that the spirits of this evil swamp, who must be many and strong, caused the birds to rise in order to cover up the cries of that man whom they had marked for their own."

King nodded again, soberly, with set lips. Here was just another of those mischances, seemingly fortuitous combinations of circumstances, under which the dark gods of Africa exacted their toll.

"That was a good reading," he told the Hottentot. "For that one-half of your one-tenth fine is remitted. Barounggo, make those *shenzies* understand that there is no profit in staying to hunt that crocodile for blood payment; and ammunition is getting low anyhow. Give them instead out of No. 3 pack a piece of red cloth to hang up for his ghost; and then up packs and trek; and one inch of spear point in the rump for him who straggles."

It was a little thing, a piece of red cloth. Yet in that kind of little thing lay the secret of King's phenomenal speed of travel that left so many other safari conductors wondering. His porters knew he was a merciless driver when it was necessary or convenient to his desires and that the very practical persuasion of a spear prick would be the immediate penalty for any disobedience of orders or shirking of the hardest kind of work; but they knew, too, that in really important matters, such as the proper propitiation of the host of spirits that haunted their dark lives, their master was lenient and gave in to them.

So that in two more days the safari came out of that swamp, whole and well, into the higher rolling plain country of the Dodinga tribes.

A NEW worry was now on hand to drive the vertical furrow deep between King's brows and to send him toiling up every other outcrop of tumbled rock—uncomfortable lion roosts, in the heat of the sun—to scour the undulating skyline with prism glasses.

He had an appointment with his friend Yakoub ben Abrahm the trader. He owed him certain information, promised in return for a previous trade. That appointment had been for a place many days' march to the east. Was it possible, then, that word had somehow been conveyed—by signal drum or smoke or whatever hokum the witch doctors practised—to the other man to edge his route over and meet north of the big swamp?

The thing had been known to happen. King's hope was that the mysterious signals of the African "underground" had this time worked for him instead of, as a white man, directly against him.

And this time they had. News at the first little cluster of thorn fenced huts was that a white man had arrived at a village half a day's journey distant. King's hope rose almost to conviction. This should surely be his appointment; for white men were not frequent in that country. He hurried on. He wanted to meet his friend, explain the change of plan and beg a few days' indulgence while he went on to the scene of the other white men's trouble.

The first distant look at the little encampment told him that this was indeed his trader friend and no other. A disgraceful tent stood in lopsided disarray; oddments of cloth fluttered from its guy ropes, dish rags and clothing; baggage lay about in confusion; porter men lolled.

At King's halloo the man himself appeared. A patriarch out of a scriptural print. Unkempt, grizzled hair hung over his high forehead in wisps, a beard with the first silver threads beginning to show grew up to his cheek bones. Eyes black and alert as a bird's peered from under tangled brows as from the thatch eaves of a roof. A great eagle nose thrust out under them.

The man threw both his hands heavenward in querulous complaint.

"What is this, Meester Kingi? What do you do to me? A black man comes to my camp many days ago and tells my servant that another black man tells him that you do not come as agreed but come to this place. No letter, no sign of recognition, nothing. Is this the way to do business? But I know you have dealings with the devil, so I came. And now what?"

King pulled one of the protesting hands out of the air and pressed it.

"Sorry, Yakoub, old grouch. This was important and none of my own doings."

But the other was not yet ready to be mollified.

"There is always something important with you that is none of your business; that is why you are not long ago rich. But I tell you, my friend, you do me a wrong. I am no wild safari runner of the wilderness. I am a trader, a man of the settlements. I do not like this. I am afraid of these people with their naked-ness and their wicked rolling eyes and their weapons. Ha, here is your great fellow, Barounggo, with his frightful spear; he makes one feel safe. But come in, come in. A black man out of nowhere came and told me you were coming; so there is a stew of young kid with red peppers and garlic. Come in, and you shall tell me what new madness it is this time that claims your attention and wastes my time."

King laughed in contentment over the ready meal.

"And yet, old cynic, you believed that black man who came four hours ago. Although four hours ago we had just reached the first of the villages; and no black man has outrun us that fast."

The Jew was immediately suspicious of a trick.

"How do you know he came four hours ago?"

King grinned as delightedly as his own Hottentot might have done.

"It is four hours ago that you must have started this good stew that you remembered I liked. I wish your man could teach my Kaffa how to make it. But Kaffa says your people put snakes into it; and his people of course are children of the great rock snake."

The Jew snorted.

"Your Kaffa is a child of the seventh hell. But all that is not business. Tell me the reason of all this troublesome wandering in the desert."

King told him briefly while he ate, and produced in conclusion his own excuse to himself, that the British deputy commissioner would hold it against him if he did not go to the help of his own people.

THE JEW looked at him intently. And then he threw out his hands in a gesture of helplessness and cackled shrill laughter.

"And that is what you want me to believe for the whole reason? Listen, my friend, and I shall tell you about yourself. That reason, yes, it is a part of it; for it is born in those Englishmen to condescend over the rest of us, even when they like us. But I know your people too, and I tell you this: The best way to cheat an American is first to persuade him that you are from his home town; and the farther away you are from your home town, the wider you are ready to increase its boundaries; till finally in the wilderness you embrace your whole country. Yes, yes, I know, I have dealt with many of your people. You are all children as yet. I know because we too—" cynicism gave way to more sober introspection—"my people too are in the same manner clannish. We feel that we, scattered over the earth, must help each other. You do it because you are very young; we, because we are very old. *Aie, aie,* yes; it is in your country that we find understanding. Tell me more of this madness that you undertake for your people."

King told him as much as he knew and hazarded—

"I suppose that this physician man, feeling that he knows everything about Africa, and being naturally a rather conceited and overbearing sort of a cuss, has contrived to tread somehow on the toes of the local witch doctor quite heavily; and so the wizard has just set about praying him to death."

"You don't believe in that yourself," said the other quickly.

King's eyes narrowed and looked into distance.

"I don't know, Yakoub; I'm hanged if I know just what I believe in Africa. With natives, maybe, yes. You know the old theory that the native must know about it first; though Old

Batete swears that that isn't necessary. But that's neither here nor there. There are other things; things that even the medicos know exist, yet they don't know anything about."

"What things?"

King shrugged, somberly frowning.

"Many things. As just one possibility I'll mention poisons. I know almost nothing; but I know this much, or this little. There's a root the witch men call *acca*. Thoroughly boiled it is harmless; but parboiled it is poison. They dry and pulverize crocodile gall; and that's a poison: A splinter from a tree they call *ujungu* is poison. There's a striped beetle called *isi-bunu*. An infusion of that in hot water is poison. And there's half a dozen other deadly secrets of the same sort."

The Jew looked at him with the fixed eyes of a bird fascinated by a snake. Softly he muttered:

"Truly, my friend, you have dealings with the more hidden devils of Africa. And you think then that—"

He left the sentence unfinished. King took it up.

"I don't know what I think. I don't know how any of those poisons work. Medical men say that there's no such thing as a slow poison; but I'll make a guess that any witch doctor knows a dozen poisons that our medicos don't; and I'll guess further that many a wizard knows how to administer some of his poisons in small doses and to wrap up the whole process in a hokum of mumbo-jumbo about magicking his victim to death. So this white man, whatever sickness is eating him, may well be wasting away from something a darn sight more practical than evil eye."

The Jew clawed sensitive fingers through his beard the while his troubled eyes roamed about and around his shabby little tent, as though looking for something, searching for some escape out of this dark entanglement. Suddenly he shot the question at King:

"And you, my friend, you propose to thrust yourself into this black business that is none of your business? To go to pit yourself against the one most secret, powerful thing in Africa which the white man has never been able to eradicate? You who know a little something of these evil currents that flow under the surfaces?"

"Gosh, I got to go," said King. "The deputy commissioner said the man was already taken with the mysterious sickness before I came away; and I don't know how slow or how fast these things work. The man may be wasted past all help already. But I've got to go and see."

The Jew nodded, quite dismally; and with conviction laid down his opinion.

"You are very foolish, my stubborn friend, and very brave—which is a result of foolishness. And when you have trampled your way into this morass what do you propose to do?"

King's wide shoulders shrugged with a nervous irritation.

"Gosh, I don't know, Yakoub. I'm all in the dark. I've got to go and try and find out just what it is that's happening and who's involved—and then ferret out who is the wizard who's doing the mischief and then—those fellows often have antidotes to their various hokums—to see if I can twist his tail somehow and make him call it all off."

The Jew sat still, nodding, staring into a darkly prophetic future, his slender fingers combing his beard. Snatches of sentences mumbled between his lips.

"Foolish, princely foolish. Just that little thing—to smash into African witchcraft about which we know nothing except that it is bad, and secret, and revengeful. *Aie-aie* what a business. There is no profit in such a foolishness."

Suddenly the hands flung upward in a gesture of despair; the shoulders shrugged up to the ears; the thick eyebrows disappeared into the low tangle of hair and the lips drew down in a sour grimace.

"I don't like it, Meester obstinate Kingi. I have always been afraid of these meddlings into the dark undercurrent of Africa. We shall probably both be drawn into that current along with your other foolish compatriot who has already meddled, and we shall sicken of something that we do not understand. But—"

The gesture and the deepened grimace finished the sentence. King laughed with quick relief.

"But, Yakoub, you don't have to mix into this mess. You just stay right here for a week, maybe two weeks—the water in this village isn't bad. And when I come back I'll take and introduce you to the various chiefs who control these little collections of gold dust, all exactly as I promised, and you can organize whatever business you think you can. All I ask is that you excuse my appointment with you and give me a couple of weeks' extension."

The hands descended from the air, but the Jew's expression remained one of extreme disgust.

"All you ask?" he grumbled. "When you are already committed to your Kingly foolishness. What use. Besides, you are too foolish and too obstinate for me to let you shove yourself into this black business all by yourself. I must be along to restrain you; otherwise you will never come back to lead me to my gold dust."

King laughed again; this time throatily with a quick warmth of feeling. He tried to be firm.

"Yakoub, you're a good old grouch. But I can't let you run into this danger on my account. I—I'll be all right. You just stick here and—"

The hands pushed the suggestion away with the extremity of impatience.

"*Na, na,* don't talk more foolishness. It is not on your account; it is for my gold dust. And—" with a sudden resumption of birdlike alertness—"for gold, my friend, throughout all time my people have run into dangers that have made history. Who am I to expect any easier fate?"

KING WAS traveling light and fast. Only his Hottentot and two strong porters accompanied him. Himself, he had been looking upon this trouble of the two misguided Americans as not much more than an unpleasant tangle requiring for its straightening out a knowledge of native character, a little strong arm work perhaps, and maybe a present or two to soothe the ruffled feelings of some local wizard. It was the dark forebodings of the trader, more sensitive than himself to the under surface of trickery, that had rendered him uneasily anxious to get to the scene of the doings, whatever they might be, as soon as possible.

He left the big Masai and the rest of his safari with Yakoub. His last instructions had been:

"Barounggo, this man is worthy of regard. See that he travels in comfort, and beat some order into those boys of his so that they may know how a safari should be."

And Barounggo had lifted his great spear in salute and growled:

"*Nidio bwana,* it is an order. It will be three days, maybe four, traveling with these untrained savages, before we come up with you. But upon arrival the safari will be as *bwana's* own."

King did not know just what he might find at the white men's camp; what queer trickery might be going on, shaping up, as the deputy commissioner had said, for a magic killing. At best he expected to find this Dr. Gerardi mysteriously sick from some ailment that quite baffled his own medical knowledge.

But he found only surprise. Almost a pleasant surprise.

The camp was all in good order; well set up in the shade of two immense baobab trees. A good pool of clear water formed a pleasant oasis of green bush and ferns. The thorn boma round the camp was strong and high. Native villages were not too close. Game tracks were plentiful. The doctor certainly did not lack experience in African ways.

And the man himself—to King, in his preconceived expectation, he was almost a shock. Big and strong and in the best of health, he greeted King cordially and without a care on his mind.

"Hello, Mr. King, how are you? If we had known when we met you a couple of months back that you had business in this part of the land we might have joined forces anyway. I heard you were headed this way only a couple of days ago, so I expected you would drop in."

And that in itself was almost a shock again. The man heard that King was coming. That meant that he was at least in not unfriendly communication with the native gossip that so often preheralded news of importance in their own little affairs. If he had been marked down for any sort of magical vengeance he would have been surrounded by a dense blank wall of ignorance of everything that happened anywhere; he would have met only empty bovine stares in the villages, porters would have deserted, hunters would have been impossible to find, even chickens and eggs would not have been forthcoming. Aloofness and fear would have been in the atmosphere. Yet this pleasant camp seemed to have plenty of everything.

King was on the point of blurting out the cause of his coming, the mysterious report of trouble that had come to the deputy commissioner. Only that cordiality of the doctor's gave him pause. The man had been cordial in the same expansive manner when they had first met two months ago; on that occasion he had quite definitely influenced his wealthy friend to give up the thought of employing King. The smile, too, in those compelling, too close set eyes, was not as truly impersonal as the casual words of greeting tried to imply.

King decided to keep his information to himself for the present. Clearly he had been mistaken in his premise. There was nothing the matter with this man; no mysterious sickness ailed him. The trouble must be with the other one—though how that mild mannered invalid, so completely under the influence of his physician, could have roused the malignant antagonism of some black magician was another mystery. That one was not to be seen; sick, possibly, in his tent.

King inquired after him. The doctor laughed easily

"Chet? Oh, he's having the time of his life. This open air stuff is just what he needed to set him up. He's out somewhere with a couple of the trackers. You'll see him at dinner—you'll stay, I suppose, and take *potio* with us?"

And there was another blow to the conviction that had brought King hotfoot to the supposed rescue of his compatriots. Chet Howard out with the trackers? The man who used to be so exhausted after a short day's trek? In that case neither could he be, wasting away from any mysterious ailment.

There was mystery in the sheer lack of mystery. Could it be, King wondered, that the two native policemen had become stupidly panicky about some ineffectual mumbo-jumbo and had thereupon sent in a baseless report of spellbinding built largely out of their African imaginations?

But then there had been the corroborative report brought to him by that disciple of wise Old Batete who could foresee a universal trouble in any meddling with white men.

Those two policemen would have to be interviewed. But they, King knew, were stationed at the head chief's village of the Doginga tribes, two days' distant. To the doctor's invitation to stay long enough to take dinner he replied:

"Sure, and thanks a lot. I guess I'll be staying around here a few days. I've got to wait for my partner to catch up. We're not hunting; so we won't be spoiling your sport; we're on a gold dust deal a bit farther east. I'll make camp across the other side of the water hole, if it's all the same to you."

And the doctor said:

"Oh, good indeed. It will be nice to have company for awhile. And there's any amount of game around here anyhow; you won't be bothering us, meat hunting. Come around about sundown then, yes?"

KING, AS he thoughtfully selected a camping place, wondered just how much of all that the doctor had meant. The man was cordial—not effusive to a stranger, but friendly to a coun-

tryman in a far land—completely at his ease, and astonishingly well. But—

King did not know, but what?

Kaffa, engrossed in camp preparations directing the two
shenzies in clearing off bush and stacking up a thorn boma,
shrilly abusing their clumsiness, busy as an ant, found time to
stop near his master and, speaking into the distant air—

"That great white lord whose eyes are like the black mamba
but of whom it is ill to speak ill is not glad that we are here."

That was King's own vague suspicion; though he could not
as yet place his finger upon any definite sign to justify his impression, unless upon the Hottentot's acute description of the
man.

"In what sign do you read that, O impertinent monkey?" he
asked.

Kaffa, wriggling his toes in the dust, gave his observation.

"There is no sign, *bwana*. Only—the word came two days
ago that we were on the road and on that day that white lord
was angry for all day and beat his servants for no cause."

"So?" King stared frowningly across the far rolling plain, feet
wide apart, thumbs in his belt, squinting into the sun. Quite
inconsequentially he said:

"Let the *boma* be a strong one. There are lions somewhere in
that rock *kloof*."

"Yes, *bwana*," the Hottentot agreed. "I too have seen the
zebra sniff and toss their heads and trot away." And equally
inconsequentially he added, "The witch doctor of this place is
a lion man."

King continued to squint narrow eyed into the sun. He was
forced to a hard little laugh.

"So you know why we are here, most cunning of imps?"

The Hottentot shuffled uncomfortably, as though detected
in a crime almost of eavesdropping. With his bare toes he
scuffled up a pebble and with a quick jerk of his ankle threw it
at a shining skink lizard.

"No, *bwana,* I do not know. That is, not exactly. I know only that that *tagati* disciple of Batete the Wise One brought word that there was a witch casting. He did not know what kind of a witch casting, only that it was a strong one that was making a trouble for these white men; and we know, Barounggo and I, that it is *bwana's* fate that where trouble is there he must go."

"Huh," was King's grunted comment to that observation of his henchman. "So Barounggo knows also?"

"Yes, *bwana,* Barounggo knows." And then with a sudden rush of candor, "And the *shenzies* also know. They would have run away; for the word was that this was a strong witchcraft. But we know that *bwana* is himself a master of wisdom and that he has a strong protection from Batete against all wizardries. So Barounggo said that he would not put spear to any man who thought to run away, but would break him like firewood over his knee. So they came."

King remained silent, interested only in the doings of the distant zebras round that rocky hill. It would be impolitic to express any surprise; though these occasional disclosures, like stolen peeps through a dark window, never ceased to amaze him about the tortuous reasonings of the black man and the intense emotions and fears that went on right under the white man's nose all unbeknown to him   by most white men never even suspected. King therefore said only in a quite impartial tone:

"That was good. There will be a strong ox for Barounggo's father when we next come into his country. It is a promise."

"Yes, *bwana,* it will be remembered," said the Hottentot. "And I, too, am a very good servant—but there is more to that tale. That man in the swamp, that *shenzie* who got lost, he would not believe that *bwana* had a protection against the wizardries, and he was hoping that in that place he could hide and we would not look for him and so he would escape. But when the spirits of that place gave him to the crocodile it was clear that the protection covered all of *bwana's* doings. So the rest of the *shenzies* are now without fear. Only the *shenzies* of that other white man, the wise old one who comes after us, they would like to know whether the protection covers them also."

This time King could not refrain from a thin whistle; and he covered it immediately with a tuneless continuation of disharmonies through his teeth. Would he, or any other white man, ever understand the weird twists of black man's thought? And with what a casualness came these rare and priceless gems of information!

"Those men are covered," he told the Hottentot evenly. "That is why I left Barounggo in order that the spirits might know. I see no witch casting in this place against these white men. But we will stay a few days; and if your eyes are like the snake that does not sleep and your ears like the Semmering gazelle there may be a very small piece of cloth for you."

"Yes, *bwana*," said the Hottentot. "It will be remembered."

KING STROLLED over to the other camp for dinner, prepared to be surprised at the condition of the man Howard. But, at that, he had underestimated. Howard, like the doctor, radiated good health. He was brown and cheerful. His loose clothes had filled out considerably during the two months in the open and the real bulk of the man showed beneath. He was full of enthusiasm.

"This is just what I needed, this open air stuff. I was running all to pieces. But this life without any business worries, and this climate!" He laughed and flexed his arms and drew a deep breath. "Gee, I feel like twenty years old. I can do anything."

The man was full of confidence; and he was grateful too.

"I owe a tremendous lot to John here. I would have cracked up in harness; but he persuaded me that a few months of these backwoods where I couldn't get any mail or telegrams or damned telephones were imperative if I wanted to keep my mind; and he was dead right. I feel as husky and carefree as any native."

The doctor murmured a conventional disclaim of the enthusiastic tribute. But Howard was not to be denied.

"Oh, yes, John, you know I'd never have broken away if you hadn't almost hypnotized me into it. I owe it all to you. I'd have been just about dead by this time; .and now look at me; I've forgotten all about business and I can go around just like any black man who has never been sick in his life."

The doctor laughed, a little uneasily, King thought.

"Chet is having such a revulsion from civilized worries that he's going native," he explained.

"Sure thing," boasted Howard. "I can sleep on the ground and paddle around barefoot, just like when I was a youngster."

King sat up alert.

"Say, but you can't do that," he said quickly. "You'll be getting yourself full of hookworm; and while tsetse fly isn't bad here you can't take chances with sleeping sickness. The doctor can tell you that better than I can."

"Yes," agreed the doctor. "But Chet is getting to be very obstinate."

King remembered their first meeting when the doctor's wishes entirely controlled his patient. The doctor found it necessary to explain the change.

"With his health Chet is getting back some of that don't-give-a-damn determination that put him where he is in business—and that, incidentally, brought him to the verge of a nervous breakdown, because he wouldn't listen to me or to anybody else."

"Well, I listen to you now, don't I?" said Howard. "And you admit that there was never anything organically wrong with me; it was just my nerves all shot to pieces. And it's your theory that a white man in good health and condition can do anything that a black man can do, and usually do it better."

"Don't you ever fool yourself," said King. "No white man can do things that a native can do with impunity. They've been building up a resistance for generations that civilization has been losing. And the first instance of that is drinking water. Don't you ever get thinking that you can drink out of the same contaminated puddle that a native can."

And then it came to him suddenly that it was the doctor who should be telling his patient these things. And the doctor said quickly:

"Yes, I've told him that. He's careful about water; but he does everything else; he goes hunting with them without a gun and all that sort of foolishness."

"And why not?" was Howard's confident retort. "Other white men have gone after big game with a bow and arrow. Why shouldn't I be as good a man as they?"

"Yeah," said King with rasping cynicism. "But you take it from me—and I'm telling you what I know—those white men have made good and certain that there's a sure shot with a heavy rifle standing just outside of the moving picture."

"Well—" Howard laughed, full of bravado in his health and returning strength—"these natives don't have any guns and moving pictures handy, and if you'll come out with me tomorrow I'll show you that a white man doesn't run any danger greater than a native does."

King weighed the proposition.

"I'll come with you," he agreed finally. "And I'll watch. I won't hunt with you, 'cause I never take chances just for the fun of taking them. I gave that up ten years ago when the hurts didn't stack up with the profits. And I'll carry a gun, because I go no place in the interior of Africa without a gun."

Howard laughed at him, not ill naturedly but with a certain condescension. He had thought that King, the Kingi *bwana* of whom he had heard so many tales before he ever came into this hinterland, would be a daredevil who would try anything once.

But King only smiled, wholly impervious to banter. He knew what he knew and he did what he did for his own coldly calculated reasons, and ridicule was not going to tease him into taking a dare.

"I'll come with you and I'll carry a rifle and I'll stay near an easy tree to climb," he promised.

"Oh, come now," Howard jeered him. "There's a million times more kick to it with the primitive weapons. It's man with his nerve and skill against brute; and man's intelligence in addition gives him the advantage."

"Yeah, I've heard all that before." King nodded quietly. "In the moving picture titles—But I've been the man with the gun three paces to the right of the camera."

"Pshaw," said Howard. "The natives go out on their nerve and their skill; and John here will tell you that dozens of scientific tests have proven that physically, in muscular strength and agility and in reaction to brain impulses, a white man is always superior to—"

"Gosh," the doctor interrupted. "If we get on to that argument we shall be shouting at each other all night. Time for your tonic, Chet."

To King he said:

"A little medicine and a lot of sleep. That has been my invariable prescription for the tired business man; and I stand on my results." And to his patient again, "If you are going careering round again tomorrow with your native hunters you'll need a clear eye and steady nerves."

Howard was reluctantly acquiescent.

"Oh, all right, I suppose you're right, John," he admitted with surprising meekness. "It's results that talk, and I'm certainly feeling fitter than I've been in years. I'll come round for you tomorrow, King, and you'll see how much finer sport it is without a gun."

King went back to his camp on the farther side of the water hole and stalked with long strides in front of the fire. Up and down, down and up, thumbs hooked into his belt, pipe stuck at a stiff angle into his tight mouth, eyes glinting thinly under brows that met in a perpendicular furrow. Plenty of sleep was a good prescription when it could be taken conveniently. On the other hand, it was useful to be able to do without any of it sometimes.

King did not know why he was bothered. There was nothing wrong with that other camp. There were two white men in the best of health and on the best of terms with each other—on the part of the one man the regard for the other was almost idolatrous. They were also on friendly terms with the natives, as was evidenced by the hunting parties.

This was no demoralized camp, oppressed by a sinister atmosphere of magic mumbo-jumbo, taboo to the natives, white men wasting away from some mysterious poison, as King had pictured to himself.

And still something was not right. As yet it was no more than a feeling to King. Laboriously he went over every detail, trying to find something, some irregular point in the seemingly harmonious whole to which he could attach the vague disquiet that he sensed and the native policemen's report of a magic killing in the offing.

On the face of it everything was normal. And was quite contrary to all the established villainies. Villains lured their victims away into desolate places in order to kill them. Here the doctor was well and had nursed his patient back to vigorous health. Everybody was happy and nobody was sick.

The camp was in every way normal. A wealthy sportsman, happily rich enough to afford his private medical adviser, had come to Africa for a much needed holiday to recuperate shattered nerves and to regain his health; and under the close control of that quite obviously clever physician had done both.

This Howard was a little unusual in his obsession about hunting with primitive weapons. But there was nothing new in that. Other people had done it before with perfect success though perhaps with not quite such a crazy disregard of personal safety.

The only irregular thing about the whole situation—and it bothered King—was a persistent groping in his mind to try to fit the doctor into the role of villain. Why, he kept asking himself? Was he being unconsciously prejudiced by the Hottentot's shrewd description of the man as one having eyes like a black mamba? Or by the doctor's not very well concealed desire for isolation with his patient?

King was angry with himself for having suspicions for which he could find no reasonable base. And where anyhow in all this did the story of a witch casting come in at all?

King shivered in the chilly night air and kicked some more wood on to the fire. The booming roars of the lions that had greeted the nightfall from the far rock *kloof* had long ago ceased, and low throaty moanings and muttered grumblings signified that they were hunting closer to the water hole. Inside the *boma* was a good place to be at such a time. King retreated moodily within and woke a *shenzi* to pull the ready thorn pile into the opening after him.

HOWARD CAME around with early morning, full of vigor and impatience. The man had talked loosely enough the night before about native methods; but his appearance surprised King.

He was dressed only in a shirt, the shortest of shorts, British fashion, and light sandals. His muscular legs were criss-crossed with countless little scars in all stages of healing, the results of thorns and sharp grasses. King judged that the man must have been quite an unusual athlete before the lure of making dollars caught him. For weapons he carried only two light throwing spears and a longer heavy thrusting weapon. A boy behind him carried a bundle of replacements.

"You certainly go the whole hog," King commented critically.

Howard laughed.

"I've never believed in half measures either in work or in play. Let's get along. It's quite a hike to the nearest village where I have a young fellow who supplies the other hunters."

"Doctor not coming?" asked King, methodically inspecting

the chamber and magazine of his rifle and buckling his heavy automatic pistol round his waist, while Kaffa collected the civilized impedimenta of fieldglasses, light lunch and water bottle.

Howard shook his head with a pursing of the lips.

"He's strong on the theory of white man's—trained man's, of course—physical superiority over the black man. But he's like you; he hunts with a gun. All set? Let's go."

They talked a little on the way. Howard was full of a nervous tension. His mind was unwilling to dwell on any subject other than the sport in prospect. King had seen enthusiastic hunters before; but this man was a maniac.

At the village a group of about a dozen natives squatted in the sun in front of their *boma.* A superior sort of man, young for so much authority, counted them off by name and gave them their directions. Howard's boy translated.

King sensed rather than saw that Kaffa was attracting his attention. The Hottentot, casually drawing patterns in the dust with his naked toes and scratching himself with all the restless energy of a monkey, kept his eyes fixed in one direction.

King saw that they were focused on the too young director of proceedings. Casually, therefore, he took critical stock of the man. Upon first survey there was nothing unusual about him beyond the fact that he wore more bits of cloth and dangling ornaments about his person than the underlings. But in the next moment King noted that his amulet pouch, suspended by a thong under his left arm pit like the rest of them, was made of the hairy tuft end of a lion's tail.

All the argument and shouting of Africans left to their own sweet wills hampered affairs. Howard seemed not to mind the wordy delay. He was hunting native fashion; and native fashion the whole business progressed. King in ordinary circumstances would have picked his men, would have given terse orders and would have started. But he kept silent; he was not participating in this hunt; he was only a looker on.

After a wasted hour agreement was finally reached as to where to hunt, and the party straggled off in single file at the long lope of all native hunters the world over. Kaffa, trotting behind his master in the rear, found opportunity to ask at last—

"*Bwana* saw it?"

King strode on without turning his head.

"That was well observed, little man. The fellow is probably a *tagati.*"

"Yes, *bwana.* So I, too, thought. A disciple of a lion man."

"Watch him," said King.

He strode on after the line of spear men, his mind busy again with the baffling problem. The circumstance of a young neophyte of a witch doctor accompanying the party might mean nothing at all. All would-be sorcerers had to show their fitness and courage before they were accepted as ready for the more personal and frightful ordeals which formed a necessary part of their initiation into training. Yet this was the first direct contact with witchcraft in a situation that was singularly devoid of witchcraft.

The party headed for a tangle of thorn bush and high grass through which ran a rain scoured gully. As they approached it the noisy chatter died down and the spearmen spread out in a ragged line along the leeward side of it. Howard was tense with excitement.

"This looks like a good place where we might flush a leopard, don't you think?" he asked eagerly of King.

"For your sake I hope you don't," said King. "There isn't much getaway cover beyond this patch; and a leopard, rather than break into the open, is likely to turn and fight through."

Howard only laughed gleefully at the suggestion. It was easy to see how the thrill of personal encounter gripped him. The man was of just that type; big, strong, aggressive. Whether in business in the fight for dollars or in sport, it was the joy of pitting his wits and his brawn against the other side that keyed up every nerve. That was why he had won so well and why the winning had so taxed his nerve forces.

Just now he stood breathing fast, eyes wide and shining, his lips, as he let out a short laugh every now and then, curling up almost in a snarl. So must primitive man have looked when he went out with his primitive weapons to battle or to the chase. So looked the black native hunters waiting for the signal to advance against whatever that brush patch might hide.

The young *tagati* man whistled piercingly through his fingers. Immediately every native let himself go. Howls, yells, whistles broke out; spears brandished; the line crashed into the thicket. Howard yelled and leaped forward with them.

The strategy was the usual native one of driving whatever game there might be into the steep sided dry water course and then to bottling up the ends and closing in on whatever might not have climbed out at the other side.

King moved along the thicket edge and found for himself a tall anthill from which he could look down into quite a stretch of the *donga.* He had seen this kind of thing often before; but never a white man in it.

The first signs of startled wild things were, of course, birds. With squawks and screeches they flew high to safety. A flock of guinea fowl raced to the *donga* edge and sailed superbly across. Came a pause before the slower land creatures arrived. Then a spotted serval cat soundlessly appeared, slunk down and—wise beyond most beasts—climbed daintily up the farther bank and melted away.

A pair of great wolfish looking silver-backed jackals stood looking back with red tongues lolling and then they too dipped down. Other beasts all along the line, with the always astounding silence of wild things, found their way down the *donga* sides. Quick forms showed along the gully bed. The bottom grasses waved; bushes rustled; a great scuffling and scurrying was apparent.

Wisely the shouting natives did not come too close. Their

yells died down. They were separating into two bands to climb down the ends of the *donga* and converge to the final rush.

Black panting forms appeared at King's end, eyeballs staring, necks craned forward, spears gripped in tense fists.

With them was Howard, eyeballs similarly staring, neck craned. He saw King on his anthill, waved a delirious halloo and plunged down a steep incline as recklessly as any of them.

A BEDLAM of howls and yells broke forth and the party charged up the *donga*. King, cautious and poised as he was, felt the glowing primal urge to yell, too, and to race in with that hunt. Instead, he smiled thinly and clicked back the safety catch of his rifle. There was no telling what thing might be down there.

With a whoop a wild black form hurled a throwing spear into a bush that moved. Something screamed. Half a dozen spears followed it. Husky throats howled success and charged on.

The white form of Howard was conspicuous. Charging with the rest, he whooped with them, hurled spears with them, yelled with them at spurting blood.

The howls of the other party became apparent at the other end of the gully. A tremendous agitation of the shrubbery between. King sat with ready rifle. Not that he expected any devastating leopard form any longer—a leopard would have showed itself before now. But there was no telling what danger might still be there.

And danger there was. With an angry squeal a gaunt wild pig, dashed from cover and immediately shrieked out its life in piercing agony. Other shrieks indicated a whole herd. The hunters out-shrieked them. Here was meat indeed.

Furious grunts came as a great slate-colored boar crashed out directly in front of Howard. King could see its wicked teeth champ as it tossed foam bubbles aside. Howard whooped and flung a light spear. It struck. The boar squealed its rage and ducked back into cover. In another instant it squealed again and with two spears sticking in its sides charged furiously out, directly at Howard.

It must have weighed all of a hundred and fifty pounds, and one slash of its tusks could have ripped a man wide open from knee to sternum. To shoot into that mass was impossible. King held his breath; for tragedy hung on a hair balance.

But superbly Howard dropped his throwing spears, gripped his heavy lance in both hands and bent to meet the shock. The charging brute impaled itself, reared high with the spear waving in the air, and fell over. A dozen other blades flashed into it.

Howard leaped high and screamed his kill. Black forms leaped and screamed around him. Swiftly converging forms and darting spears marked the end of the drive. Uncouth leapings, howlings, waving of weapons announced triumph.

But there was still ceremonial to be performed. Rites that surround every phase of life for the African to propitiate or to avert the ghosts of slain things that haunt his imagination.

Sharp blades quickly gashed throats to let the still warm blood run. Black men bathed their arms, their thighs and their foreheads in the thick welling liquid. White man Howard bathed and shrieked with them.

King looked down on it all, very still, very serious, with the beginning of understanding in his eyes.

"Good Lord, just like one of them," he muttered.

Kaffa, still too, like a watching creature of the wild and quite as frightened, understood.

"No, *bwana*," he whispered. "Not just like one of them. He *is* one of them."

King let minutes pass while he watched the orgy. Then explosively—

"And that, by God, is the witchcraft of this thing."

"Yes, *bwana*," said Kaffa with conviction. "He is a lion man."

"Who?" said King sharply.

"The witch doctor of this place, *bwana*. A man who can turn himself into a lion can surely turn a white man into a Dodinga savage."

"Rubbish!" said King. But he could perceive a dim connection to the truth in the Hottentot's ingrained conviction. He continued to sit on the anthill, hugging his knees and gazing down at the screaming mêlée below, seeing nothing of it all.

Howard climbed out of the *donga*, his excitement all gone. He was pale; he looked quite used up. Rather shamefacedly he was wiping the ritual blood from his forehead and arms with handfuls of grass. His manner was that of a man, come back to his senses after a wild outburst of emotion, who knew that he had been making rather a spectacle of himself. He was almost apologetic.

"There's a tremendous kick in that sort of thing for me," he explained. "I used to be a gun crank; but gunning took up so much of my time that I was neglecting business, and I had to cut it out altogether."

King nodded without speaking. Howard forced the subject.

"But gunning went stale on me. There's no sport in slaughtering animals with a gun. But there's thrill in a bow and arrow; and a spear is even better. To tell you the truth, I don't understand how a man with the experience of Kingi *bwana* still sticks to the rifle."

King's answer was laconic.

"Shoot only for meat myself," was all that he said.

He could understand easily how any man might grow weary of precision killing with a modern rifle—he knew more than one big game man who had come back as a camera hunter pure and simple. He could understand—he thought—how a man in whom the hunter instinct was strong might be bold enough to revert to primitive weapons, though still retaining the insurance of a gun in case of necessity; he knew such men too. He could understand—almost—how a man of nervous temperament might be so obsessed by the need of a new thrill that he might forego the insurance of a gun. But none of that explained at all satisfactorily how a man might go stark screaming primitive along with his weapons.

He left Howard with his chattering blacks, and struck off on a detour to climb a hill for the ever enthralling purpose of looking over new country and filing away in his photographic mind geographical details for possible future use.

But he filed away little. He was absorbed in other thoughts. So absorbed that when, nearing camp, a reed buck flashed up and skimmed over the grass, he snapped up his rifle and scored a clean miss. A second shot was necessary to bring down the meat that he knew his two *shenzies* expected.

"It is an omen," said Kaffa lugubriously.

"Rubbish!" snorted King.

But the Hottentot knew better.

"Nay, *bwana*, it is truth that the happening of any very unusual thing is never by accident but it is a sending from the ghost world to warn of a worse happening to come."

And surely enough, come it did.

The lions were bad that night. In country where game is plentiful for the reason that it is far from the usual route of white men's safaris, lions, too, are plentiful for both of those reasons. And, quite logically, are also correspondingly bold.

M A N Y A tenderfoot has quaked the night through in his blankets, feeling quite sure, even in his inexperience, than any lion could easily spring over the hastily constructed six or eight foot thorn fence of a camp *boma*. He has argued the case on the logical basis that if a cat can jump four feet with hardly an effort, a lion surely ought to be able to do six. And he has bolstered his argument by pointing out the discrepancy between the miserable camp protection and the strong, tall, regular stockades of thorn bushes round every established native village.

And of course he has been right. A lion can hop over a camp fence, seize a donkey, or a pig, or a man, and spring back into the night as easily as a cat can do the same thing with its kitten. And lions have done it often enough.

It is only the innate suspicion and caution of the cat tribe that restrains a lion—or any other animal—from forcing a barrier, however flimsy. Animal instincts, or hereditary memories, or whatever the naturalists like to call it. It may be true that a human child does not dread the fire until it has once been burnt. But it is none the less true that the season's new grouse or rabbit or deer whose progenitors have been shot over are much wilder than the same animals in virgin country.

So also lions who have had experience—or perhaps whose parents have had experience—that out of such low thorn barriers surrounding the man smell there are likely to come sharp reports, long flashes of light, and stinging lead, are vastly more cautious than others in faraway districts that have had no such experience.

In this camp it was necessary to keep a good fire burning within the *boma* and to see to it that the man on watch kept moving about. It is when all has been still and dark for a long period that a lion, watching with that feline patience, will make up its mind that it is safe to make its devastating dash.

As it was, King was kept awake by the ominous circling moanings and snufflings that came too close and he was forced to shoot out into the night at vaguely moving shadows more than once. At the third shot a furious snarling evidenced that something had been scratched, if not worse. And after that there was peace.

Only Kaffa's voice, muffled out of his blanket, proclaimed his conviction—

"Tomorrow if we find that wizard, the lion man, it will be seen that he has received a wound."

"Fool," said King, "so do your brother apes talk in the trees."

But he remembered circumstantial stories, not out of ancient folk lore in Europe; but stories of Africa today that made the same claim.

But the little matter of prowling lions at night was not the presaged ill luck of which the Hottentot had been so sure. It was concerned only indirectly with a much worse happening.

The misfortune came to light in the morning when Kaffa, according to his master's invariable rule, was cleaning the gun used overnight and was preparing to bring it for inspection along with the shells for the new load.

Kaffa scuffed in sudden alarm through the packs. He threw things in every direction, picked them up again and looked under them, opened each impossibly small package and container, before he came to his master in the greatest agitation.

"*Bwana*, the evil has befallen. The cartridges are gone."

"Hunh?" King whirled, then stood and screwed his eyes in swift thought.

"While we were out yesterday—this is serious—that boy Umbobo from the other camp."

"Nay, *bwana*. Umbobo is honest. From me he will not steal. Besides, those *shenzies* were left on guard. It is the witchcraft of this place. It was foretold; and the lion man sent his people to cause *bwana* to shoot away all the cartridges in his gun."

"Fool," grunted King. "Those *shenzies* slept like oxen; or they went visiting in the village the moment our backs were turned; or they squatted by the hour at the *donga's* edge and made monkey talk. They did everything but stay on guard; and from them we shall never extract the truth."

"Nay, *bwana*, those *shenzies* have been trained by Baroung-go; they would never dare to disobey. And as for truth, it is a wisdom of my country that a hot spear blade under the armpit is a great magic for bringing out the truth."

King gave vent to a bitter little laugh.

"Kaffa, little ape, I have often said that civilized man in a savage country suffers many disadvantages on account of his inhibitions—which phenomenon you will not understand. For the present say no word to any man about this loss. But go to the other camp and talk with a snake's tongue to this Umbobo. Perhaps your wisdom will discover something. This is a matter that requires thought before action."

To be without ammunition in the middle of Africa was

serious enough; King knew, of course, exactly what guns the other safari carried. He had known within half an hour of their first meeting. They were not of his caliber. He knew that Yakoub would be coming along within the next day or so with some kind of antiquated gun. He still had his heavy automatic pistol with a belt containing a string of cartridges.

So it was not a matter of starvation in the midst of plenty. The serious aspect of the thing was that this queer plot, whatever it was, that haunted this place had now included him, the interloper, in its field. And it was evidence of what King had almost begun to doubt—that there was a deliberate something going on inimical to white men. He knew enough of Africa not to have to be reminded of the deputy commissioner's warning of how these dark underground unrests could flare into sudden disaster.

Whatever was sinister in Africa, wizardry of course was at the back of it. King's lips set very hard and his jaw muscles swelled. He would have to go and see this witch doctor and would have to show him that his tricks could rebound upon himself. A difficult enough undertaking; for a witch doctor, like a high priest among his own people, could not be attacked without the frenzied hordes of his people coming to his aid.

Still King had made African wizardries his special interest and he hoped that he knew of methods of approach less drastic than strong arm. He would have gone to see this lion man long ago, but that the sorcerer exercised his subtle sway from his residence in a *juju* grove a full day's journey distant; and King was waiting for Yakoub to arrive and keep his clever old eyes on things before he should absent himself.

KING WENT round the water hole to the other camp—just to snoop around, as he expressed it to himself; to help his Hottentot ferret out whatever might be discovered. Not for a moment would he permit himself to harbor his insistent suspicion that possibly that very clever doctor who desired his absence might have something to do with his mysterious loss.

The doctor was as cordial as ever. If he had any guilty knowledge, his boldly open eyes and ready smile concealed it wonderfully well. The other man, Howard, was out.

"Gone off somewhere or other," the doctor said carelessly. "Making a day of it. He has got a new excitement quite a long way from here. Some young buck who is making his manhood ceremony is going to pull off some new crazy method of hunting and Chet has gone to see the stunt."

More seriously he went on:

"You know I'm getting to be a bit worried about that chap. He's so reckless about his sport—always was; he used to play polo like a wild man and he hurt so many ponies and riders that at last his club wouldn't play him any more. Then he fell for this new bow and arrow stuff; until business caught him up; and he went for that with bull enthusiasm, till the mental strain just about got him. Now he is back to play with the same intensity. What I'm afraid of is that he'll be getting himself all clawed up some day, and I'll have to patch him up."

King was very subtle.

"You've known him quite long, I suppose?"

"Oh, yes. We were in college together."

"Then you might almost have guessed he'd go off like this," said King accusingly.

The doctor laughed.

"Heavens, how should I have guessed? I never saw so much of him. I was hardly in his class. He always had a fair amount of money and he could play; while I had to study like a dog and to work besides to pay my way. Then I traveled around a good deal, working for an Austrian scientist, a Dr. Holzmann, for very little more than experience. And I had a job with the South African Free State government. In the meanwhile he went into business and in a few years made a spectacular fortune. I saw very little of him till he called me in as his medical adviser; and he was not playing then. I've pieced all his furious history out since we came away."

"Hmh," was all King's ungracious comment to so much personal information. "Was that Dr. Franz Holzmann? A white hunter whom I know took him out some years ago from Dar-es-Salaam when all that country was German East Africa."

The doctor shot a quick glance at King who was absorbed in an extraordinary business of blowing smoke rings through one another.

"Why, er—yes, I suppose that must have been the same man," said the doctor shortly.

King grunted again, even more shortly, and took his leave. He had found out nothing at all about his stolen ammunition; but in its place he had found—he thought—one tiny hook upon which to fasten his vague misgivings.

On the following morning Yakoub ben Abrahm came in with the rest of the combined safari. King, as he made him comfortable, and while Kaffa scurried with hot water in a five-gallon kerosene can for the refreshing bath after travel, watched the orderliness of things with critical amusement.

The big Masai strutted officiously and growled orders. The trader's tent and the cook tent sprang up smartly, with straight walls and taut ropes. Baggage was stowed neatly under the fly eaves. *Shenzies* went to gather more thorn bush to enlarge the *boma*. These men had been very properly drilled.

"That was a work well done, Barounggo," King commended.

The Masai lifted his spear in salute and grinned proudly.

"Yes, there is a certain ease, almost a symphony, in travel," said Yakoub, "when that great fellow of yours conducts the music with his spear."

King was glad to have the Jew with him. He wanted to discuss many obscure things, to throw the light of the shrewd old trader's observation upon the darkness in his own mind.

Carefully and methodically he related all the happenings of the last few days, all his vague misgivings and almost groundless suspicions, and then propounded the question that baffled him.

"But why? I ask myself. What would be the motive? I mean, if this doctor has brought him here for any purpose—to get money out of him, let us say, as the natural suspicion—why has he brought him at all? What can he do here that he couldn't do at home? The man has grown well and strong here."

The Jew screwed his face in a grimace while he reviewed out of his own experience all the amazingly involved and twisted things that men would do for money. From time to time he nodded slowly as possibilities opened themselves up, and then clawed sensitive fingers through his beard as difficulties obstructed his theories. At last he chuckled over a quick pointed finger at King as his reasoning ran in an unbroken chain.

"My friend, you are very clever; you do many things that few men can do; but in matters of money you are a small child. Listen to me, Yakoub ben Abrahm, and I will teach you some of the possibilities about money.

"Let us consider a great deal of money, such as would make a long journey worthwhile. Consider a rich man, sick of a nervous breakdown, a little bit off from his mental control. What might such a man do?"

"I've considered all that," said King. "Such a man, grateful, as this man is grateful; a little off balance, as this man was off balance, might be persuaded to pay his doctor a quite unreasonable fee—or to marry his nurse; or to donate a fortune to the church. He might do anything. But why would he have to come here to do it?"

YAKOUB SMILED like a benevolent devil who knew the very depths of human avarice.

"I have said much money. Let us consider a million dollars. Do you think a man sick and off balance might be persuaded to write a check for a million dollars?"

"He might if he were crazy. But even so, he would have signed it. It would be cashed. There is still no need for bringing him here."

"Ah." The Jew leered a worldly cynicism. "But, my very simple friend, there are always many difficulties in the way of collecting a million dollars—or half a million, or a quarter million. Consider. Our rich man recovers his senses. He feels that the fee that he has signed away has been exorbitant. If he does not feel so of his own accord, there are always many people to persuade him so. Lawyers. All rich men have lawyers, cold blooded and perfectly balanced, who look after their financial affairs—who would quickly tell him that he has been fooled; who would arouse his anger by showing him that his ill balanced condition has been taken advantage of; who would persuade him to let them take steps—injunctions upon banks and all the legal tricks that earn fees for lawyers—to recover the greater part of that exorbitant fee. You think that is possible, no?"

King nodded.

"The man is of nervous temperament, a strong man, proud. True, he might be so persuaded."

"Good. Our doctor, too, fears this possibility. He persuades his mind sick patient to come away for his health. Perhaps on the voyage, working upon him alone, he persuades him to write a check for much money. Perhaps the rich man then—dies in Africa—"

Quickly outflung hands stopped King's response to the thought. With saturnine logic the Jew continued his deadly argument.

"The man dies, not under any suspicious circumstances, lost in the wilderness alone with his physician. But before witnesses who have seen him regain his health, under the eyes of British native police, as a result of his own very foolish method of going hunting."

He ceased and peered at King with questioning eyes through his wisps of straggling hair.

"By the Lord, I believe you're right, Yakoub." King expelled a long held breath. "You're the very devil, old friend. Only a devil could think of such things."

Yakoub cackled a dry laugh and laid down an axiom.

"For much money, my friend, many men have become devils. And it is for you—" the swift finger pointed compellingly at King. "You have dealings with the dark devils of Africa. It is for you to find out by what witchery a man may be persuaded to go looking for danger in his hunting."

King remained in frowning silence. Carefully he reviewed the facts as he knew them and the shrewd interpretation that the trader put upon them. Then very softly he said:

"It fits. It all fits. I don't see a hole in it anywhere. And as for the man's crazy hunting, being the man he is, I don't think it would need any very great witchery to swing his sporting instincts that way—and our clever doctor man would know that too. But we must have proof. I must go and see this witch doctor."

"Tell me something of this witchcraft," said Yakoub. "What sort of wizard is this lion man?"

King shrugged his shoulders doubtfully.

"I don't know whether that counts so much; but they are like the leopard cult of the West Coast. A lion man establishes the idea that he can at will turn himself into a lion. Same as the old werewolf belief. Lycanthropy, the scientific gents call it. Mixed in with the surrounding mess of hokum is the strong fact that these wizards can persuade their followers that they can actually turn them temporarily into lions or leopards or wolves or whatever it is. The method is probably hypnotism, suggestion, hystero-epilepsy—call it what you will. But it is proven fact that people of a certain nervous temperament can be made to believe that under certain conditions they become the animals of their cult; and they go out and behave like those animals. You've probably seen hyena men in Abyssinia slinking around after dark, fighting with the dogs for dead things."

The Jew shuddered uncomfortably.

"Yes, I have seen. But those men are crazy, afflicted with some horrible madness of this dark land."

"Not a bit of it. They're not crazy. Their original hereditary conviction of its possibility and the enormously suggestive ritual that they go through beforehand makes them believe that for the time being they actually are animals."

The Jew remained dubious.

"You think such unholy things are possible?"

King was positive.

"I know it's possible. Science knows it's possible. It's just a little extension of the principle that if you get a man in a certain mental condition and tell him a thing often enough he will begin to believe it. There's no more magic in it than in advertising."

The Jew was unconvinced. Coldly practical, a man of material business, of purchases and sales and profits and losses, so new an idea of the vagaries of the human mind required time to assimilate.

"So I suppose, my obstinate Kingi, you are going to thrust your head into this lion man's jaws in order to do what you may for your countryman who does not want your help?"

"I'm beginning to wonder whether the lion man is much more than a hired hand in this thing," said King. "But I'm going to see him. Evidence is what we need. Something more than guesswork. I'll start right away. His place is a day's march away. I'll take Kaffa and Barounggo. We'll *boma* some place overnight and I'll surprise him with an early call."

The Jew shook his head.

"You do not surprise those devil dealers. They know."

Long after King left, he remained standing, a lugubrious figure framed in the tent flap, shaking his head over the profitless effort of such folly.

THE JUJU grove of the witch doctor stood deserted and silent. The usual litter and claptrap of African sorcery lined the approach. Bones of various sorts—the leavings of lions' kills—impaled upon stakes. Wisps of colored cloths wound, Maypole fashion, round denuded tree boles. Woven grass curtains festooned across paths to obstruct evil spirits. The witch doctor's rather pretentious hut stood in the center, surrounded by a stockade of poles capped with lions' skulls.

King carefully refrained from the customary white man's brazen trampling over all tabus, arousing thereby antagonism. He knew that a witch doctor, whether rightly or wrongly, had established around himself a certain cloak of mystery and that human vanity was a force with which to reckon.

So he sat down and lighted a pipe while he sent Kaffa to follow a maze of carefully marked paths and to call from without the stockade what he knew the wizard knew very well—that a stranger sought interview.

His reward was, if nothing else, a saving of much time. A young *tagati* neophyte quickly came down the wooded knoll and led King along other paths, carefully holding aside grass curtains so that they might not be touched by the uninitiate. King was ushered within the skull crowned stockade into a roomy circular hut and found himself alone in a dim, smoke filled room with a figure entirely shrouded in a tanned lion skin.

"I can tell you nothing about that white man who is bewitched," came an ungracious voice from beneath the skin.

King was not surprised that the man was already familiar with his object; the thing was pretty obvious. But it was of interest that the man admitted the other to be under a spell. King was wise in the ways of witch doctors; he knew their dignities and their conventions.

"I bring a gift," he said. "A tribute to knowledge that I desire to consult and perhaps to buy a release from a spell."

"I can give you no release," said the voice. But a dark hand emerged from under the skin to receive whatever it might be.

King placed into the open palm a small jar of luminous paint such as is sold to sportsmen for spotting their rifle sights for night shooting. Beneath the shuffling of the lion skin he could hear the soft unscrewing of the cap; some more shuffling and a succession of grunts. This thing was a great and most useful magic to any wizard; and it betokened, moreover, that the giver knew that a certain amount of hokum was legitimate to all magic.

The lion skin was thrown aside and the man showed himself; a native in sturdy middle age with a strong face and fierce eyes, which were, however, just now friendly. King was glad to think that diplomacy had perhaps removed the need of hostile methods against that determined looking face.

"*Jambo sana,*" said the wizard. "This is indeed a gift of one who has understanding. I have heard that there is such a white man. If you are that man, show me the thing that speaks for you."

King handed the man his pipe with its intricately carved bowl that had been done under the direction of the old wizard of Elgon. The man bent with it over the tiny fire that was cooking whatever it was that stank. He peered at the pattern, felt the convolutions of the carving. He looked up over it and asked an unexpected question.

"Do you know what things this says, white man?"

It was noticeable that he did not address King as *bwana*—master. Had King exacted that established tribute of respect, that would have meant the end of all negotiations.

"I know some of the things," said King. "Some, no white man may know."

"Some, I do not know," said the wizard. "For he is of another brotherhood. But the things are good. I will therefore speak truth, as to one who understands.

"I tell you, therefore, in truth, white man, that I have sent no witch sending upon that other white man. It is ill to deal with the affairs of white men."

"Yes, it is ill," said King. "For the commissioner *bwana* of all this district is a man who begins to have understanding too. Yet the word came that there was a witch casting."

The wizard grunted angrily.

"Those two black men who take the white *serkale's* money to interfere with other black men are fools. By their foolishness and because I will not pay tribute to them, they would bring the *serkale's* trouble upon all my people. I have already seen to it that they shall lose, each man, a cow, taken by lions. It is just; for I do not deal with the affairs of white men."

"Yet that white man does things as the black men do them," said King.

The wizard came closer, confidentially.

"Am I the only one," he asked in a tone full of meaning, "who can do a magic? Are there no small magics among the white men? Look, you who have understanding, I can look into a man's eyes and tell him, 'Lo, upon the rising of the next moon over the tree tops you will be a lion', and forthwith he will go forth and slay like a lion. That is no very hard magic. It is but making a pattern in the soft thing that is a man's mind. Among my young men are already three who can do it. Is there no white man who knows how to plant the seed of a thought in a man's mind and then, by a careful watering with words, make that seed grow? That is a little thing that is not even magic."

King nodded. He felt that this wizard was being candid with him.

"Yes, I was beginning to think so. I wanted to be sure that he had not bought a witch casting from you."

"I deal with no white man," complained the wizard. "There is only trouble in it. How should I know why that other white man has told the foolish one that he is a great hunter and that he can do all things as the black men do them? What affair is it of mine that he has spoken that seed into his mind and has made it grow? What should I care why that other white man is the foolish one's enemy and wishes to destroy him? What business is it of mine that the foolish one is even now in the plain behind this hill looking to do a lion killing with shield and spear? I have no dealings with the affairs of white men."

"Hunh?" King jumped up and caught the other's arm in a sudden grip. "What talk is this?"

"It is a true talk," said the wizard doggedly. "What has it to do with me? This place is the home of many lions."

"What wizardry do you talk here?" snapped King. "Out with the truth."

"There is no wizardry, white man. Yesterday one of my young men who would be a *tagati* made his manhood test with shield and spear; and the foolish white man came all the day's journey to see that thing done. Today that foolish white man goes forth with shield and spear to show that he can kill as a black man kills, and my young men go to watch that sport. What has it to do with me who kills or who is killed? I have no dealings with the affairs of white men."

"Good Lord! *Now,* you say? Where? Exactly where?"

"How do I know exactly where he may find his lion? There are many lions in the plain. But wait and I will cast the stones for you; and if the conditions are favorable for a seeing I may see what will be. Though for white men—"

But King was already gone. Shouting to Barounggo and Kaffa, he raced over the brow of the *juju* hill and anxiously swept his field glasses over the plain beyond.

I T WA S a typical African plain, rolling ground with low hills covered with long grass and patches of bush and interspersed with clumps of tall umbrella spreading acacias. The hunt—or the tragedy—might be going on anywhere, under one's nose almost, screened by the first low hump of ground. The only hope was to go, to climb each hill, to survey as much as might be and then to race to the next hill. And above all to pray for time. And time, if lions were as plentiful as the wizard implied, was the least likely kind of luck to expect.

King cursed himself for an easily hoodwinked fool that he had no suspicion of the suave doctor's careless remark about a new excitement that Howard had gone a long way off to witness. What a crafty planting of an alibi that had been. In his heat he promised himself some heavy conversation with that doctor man whose eyes were like a black mamba's.

Together the three men trotted. King's impulse was to race; but hard common sense told him that grass covered plain and hills to be climbed called, not for any excited sprinting, but for dogged plodding. The first low hill was a blank. Only peacefully waving grass and brush patches met the eye. A small herd of Grant's gazelles and another of hartebeeste grazed quietly. Their manner was unhurried, confident. No lion scent there.

The three toiled on. More than a mile to cover to the next hill. Slow going. That hill too disclosed no man figures within its horizon. Barounggo pointed silently with his spear at a farther knoll. There, blending marvelously into the sun flecked background, beautifully posed in lazy grace, a magnificent male lion lolled, licking a paw like a great cat. That too was quiet and at ease. No hunting here, nor any man smell downwind.

So downwind King struck. The next knoll, too, was a blank. Only peaceful beasts at their ease. But Kaffa pointed above the flat horizon of acacia tops. King nodded critically.

"They're watching something. But what? Those birds are circling easily and without excitement. Whatever is going on isn't violent—as yet."

A good mile again to that hilltop. Nobody who has not tried to run, urged by anxiety and the need for haste, across bunch grass the roots of which stand up in stiff hillocks with rain scoured trenches between, can understand what a breath taking grind that is. But the little hill was reached, and beyond it the panorama of yellow grass and brown thorn patch and green mimosa scrub stretched pleasingly.

King yelled. Barounggo roared. Kaffa whistled through his teeth. Together the three raised all the uproar that their lungs permitted to attract attention. But only the circling birds took any notice. They shrieked in answer and flapped higher. The far silhouettes of men, black against the sunlit grass, paid no attention. Their full senses were taken up with serious business.

It was a spread out line of men, some twenty of them, like skirmishers, all armed with spears and big oval shields of ox hide. They faced the hillock. The eye caught their contrasting black against the grass at once. Next it flashed to another figure, not so differentiated, facing the black line, some seventy yards away. This figure's brown shirt and khaki helmet cover merged better with the grass; but it was easy to see that that one, too, carried spear and shield and that he was advancing slowly, tense, with weapons poised.

Between the solitary figure and the farther line was something upon which the attention of both was concentrated. The three men on the hill knew instantly, from the strained position of the men, what the something was. But it was only when it moved that their eyes could pick it out from the perfect blend of its surroundings.

It was the black tuft of tail that first attracted attention. In quick sweeping strokes, with short intervals between, it lashed over the grass tops. Then the rest of it could be seen. Its mane was flared out and its head held low as it crouched with wide spread front paws.

It was easy to see that the beast was angry, vicious from having been hunted by men, harried into its present position. It gave out two coughing grunts and plunged forward in a short rush and then crouched again and lashed the grass.

The white man, with superb madness, poised with long spear lifted as the beast charged; and then, as it crouched, he advanced slowly again.

King yelled and raced down the slope as fast as his winded condition would let him, bitterly cursing the fact that his rifle had been left in camp because there were no cartridges for it. At that elevation and distance, he might have overshot the man and possibly have hit the lion.

His pistol, as yet, was useless.

The lion made another short rush and crouched as before. King's heart came up into his mouth and he yelled again and raced on.

Howard, if he heard him at all, paid no attention. He dared

not permit himself to divert the littlest fraction of his concentration from the angry beast in front of him. Inch by inch, on
soft shuffling toes that felt for the ground, he advanced, his
great shield held with its rim just below eye level and his right
hand grasping his long spear with point low.

The technique of this thing was to judge time and distance
to a hair and, as the lion rushed in on its final charge, to lunge,
full armed, knuckles up, and to take the beast in the chest,
meeting weight with weight so as to plunge the blade deep into
the vitals. The proper stroke at chest center would reach the
heart.

Howard plainly knew how the thing ought to be done. He
had seen a young *tagati* perform the supremely dangerous stunt,
and without doubt he had asked questions and taken instruc-
tion. His pose, as he faced the most perfectly equipped killer
of all the great carnivora, was excellent.

Unhappily for himself, in this hunting mania that obsessed
him, he was overlooking—or perhaps his attention had been
carefully diverted from—a small but very vital factor. However
true might be the doctor's thesis—however well bolstered by
scientific tests in American universities—that a white man's
muscle quality was better than a black man's, that his reflex
responses were faster, the inconspicuous but enormous fact that
Howard was overlooking was that the plain matter of skill in
spear handling comes with the years of constant practise that
a black man gives it.

LONG BEFORE King could arrive on the scene, the
distance between lion and man reached its minimum limit. The
lion coughed, a furious *hough-hough*, and charged in. Howard
lunged, gashed only its shoulder and the next instant disappeared under swift batting paws and a roaring, tearing five
hundred pounds of beast.

The skilled native technique in this position—provided that
the hunter still survived—was not so desperate as it might seem.
A man who retained his senses could cover with the big shield,

head under and legs drawn up, like a tortoise, clinging desperately to the hand grip to avoid being turned over; in the meanwhile looking for an opportunity to use a short heavy stabbing spear that had been held within the shield in the left hand.

Howard was down and lay inert, whether by luck or by design, covered for the most part by his shield. The lion stood over him and tore indiscriminately at whatever it reached.

King wrenched his pistol from its holster and raced forward. Barounggo's voice growled at his side:

"Let be, *bwana*, let be. This is my work that is known to me."

His great form outstripped King's. The lion, as the huge black man bounded toward it, held down the shield with one wide spread paw and lifted its head to roar defiance and warning. The big Masai, charging in with great spear balanced for stabbing as though to hurl himself bodily upon the beast, swerved suddenly so as to get behind its tail. The lion scuffled round in two short plunges and reared up on its hind legs, front paws wide apart, to meet this new menace.

Then the Masai struck. Not a lunge in this position, but a full arm downward stab—in the center of the chest, just where the mane began to give way to the lighter colored, short, abdominal hair. The long three-foot blade slid in as though through soft butter. Right up to the close binding of brass wire that held it to its shaft.

The lion gave an immense twisting bound high in the air, away from the thing that stung it so excruciatingly. Landing erect on all four feet, it still tried with splendid courage to charge at the man. But its front paws turned under it. It slid over them. Its white tuft of chin plowed a furrow in the dust while the yellow eyes still glared defiance. Then it rolled on its side and stretched in a series of quivering jerks.

Other men came running. There was shouting and confusion and crowding. The Dodinga men looked at the great Masai spear, tugged tentatively at it, clicked guttural approbation at the power of the stroke. Barounggo, helping King to pick

Howard up, affected a vast unconcern. Over his shoulder he admitted carelessly:

"A fair stroke. A not bad stroke. Hey, fellow, be careful there how you draw that blade. Twist it not, or I twist your neck."

"It was a man's deed, cleanly done," said King shortly. "There will be suitable recognition to your father. We must get this man swiftly to the witch doctor's house. There will be water."

Howard lay quite unconscious. Claw tip punctures in a row behind the ear showed where the lion had slapped him with a force almost sufficient to break his neck. The shield rim had probably broken the force of that blow. His left shoulder and upper arm were slashed to the bone in three separate wide gashes. His right leg below the knee, where it had protruded from beneath the shield, was scored in ribbons by the rasping hind claws of the beast. Nothing seemed to be broken.

The wizard came out of his hut as the mob of jabbering men approached.

"So the foolish one has not been destroyed this time," was his only comment. "Why do you bring him here, white man? I have no dealings with the affairs of white men. Yet it was made known to me that you would come; so I have made preparation."

He gave low, quick orders to some of the young men and sent them scurrying for water and various leaves and a frightfully unsanitary gourd containing some sort of pungent ointment.

"For the sake of the gift, white man, I will make a spell that he may live. Ha, that lion was a young one; or he would have known to slay with the first blow."

King found the wizard to be quite expert in helping him to wash and put a temporary dressing on the wounds.

"He will have fever," said the wizard. "He must be made to drink the thing that I was already preparing for him over my fire when you first came."

King knew that the wizard was talking for the gaping natives to hear; and he knew enough not to show anything but belief. He came to a swift decision. He was going to take a heavy responsibility upon himself. To gamble a man's life against— against he did not know just what. For a wounded man a physician was the first and obvious necessity. Yet that physician had had this same man under his care before when he was sick and weak. The man had certainly recovered his health. But King could not be sure— But what?

If those things, the motives that the Jew suggested, were true; and if the mental suggestion that the witch doctor said was no magic at all was so; if the same physician should nurse the man again, would he recover this time? It was a wonderful chance for a man to die surrounded by white men witnesses of his own foolhardiness. Or, if the man recovered again, would he not perhaps go out and next time do some completely fatal thing?

All these considerations raced through King's mind. On the other hand, his own experience of many years in the bush had perforce taught him quite a deal about field doctoring; his own medical kit was quite complete. The man was strong and in good health. It was even possible that King had more actual experience with lion wounds than the physician. And some of those witch doctors had a very keen knowledge of herbs.

Boldly therefore King decided. He drew the witch doctor aside.

"Do this thing for me, Wise One. Give me a place under a tree where I may make a camp. I will send for my things. Do you let the word go out that this is a tabu; that this happening is among the things unspoken. So that that other white man shall know nothing of what has happened, nor shall he know where my men have gone. Let his servants say that they know nothing; and when he asks among the villages let men say, 'They have gone to such and such another place.'"

The witch doctor looked long at King and then looked away while he cogitated; and finally he said:

"For the sake of the good things that the carved pipe says,

and because you come to me as one having the understanding, and because the doings of that other man brought blame upon me, I will do this thing. The word shall go out and there will be a wall of ignorance about that man."

And the thing was perfectly possible. It had happened time and again and would happen often again. For their own mysterious reasons, African communities have decided that some happening or other, or all happenings connected with some custom or other, should be kept secret from white men; and forthwith the thing has been a blank wall of mystery which the white man might know to exist but which he would be utterly unable to penetrate.

Once again the dark and devious things of Africa were pulling for King instead of directly against him.

HE GAVE instructions to his two henchmen to go with all speed and to break camp as quietly as possible; to get away, if they could, without the doctor's knowledge. Or if they could not, to tell him that their master was moving along on his own business. They would, of course, not be expected to know anything about Howard or his doings.

The wizard sent one of his young *tagati* with them.

"To make the servants of that man eat ignorance," he said.

And King told him—

"For these doings I shall make a writing to the commissioner *bwana* of the *Serkale* that will speak things of you as good as the carving of my pipe."

There was nothing to do for Howard but to fight the fever, which both men knew would come, by keeping compresses on his wounds and his head. King set a man to swinging a pot of water wrapped in a wet cloth hung from the limb of a tree. Howard moaned presently and feebly opened his eyes. Mumbled questions came from his lips. But the witch doctor said:

"See, my spell has snatched him back from out of the very belly of death. Sleep is now good for him. Much sleep. I do now a magic that will make him sleep for the passing of a whole sun."

He laid an inexpressibly grimy hand over the sick man's eyes and went through a performance of mutterings and rolling of his eyes; but all the while he was gently, very smoothly, stroking Howard's face and cheeks and pressing lightly upon his eyeballs with his finger tips. And presently the sick man's mumblings became very tired and then passed away and he slept.

During the course of the following day the safari arrived. Everything had gone splendidly. The doctor had been away—out hunting. The *tagati* man had very properly frightened his safari men. Villages along the way had been warned of the silence. The word would go out to all surrounding villages.

Only the sheer accident of the doctor's wandering a day's journey over the empty plain and happening upon that precise spot would discover the new camp.

Yakoub, in something of consternation, propounded the very question that King had weighed with himself and quickly decided—

"What if the man grows worse, beyond the skill of amateur doctoring?"

"Time enough to send for the professional then," said King sturdily. "He won't go away in any hurry because he must, for the sake of keeping face, make a show of looking for his companion."

And he explained all his reasons for taking the grave responsibility. Better that the sick man recover under other hands.

"And maybe we can argue with him quietly about his crazy hunting while he is weak and receptive and work a little magic ourselves."

The Jew nodded agreement.

"Yes, yes, you understand these things, you who have made a study of deviltries. But that doctor, he should be apprehended and held. He is a master devil."

But King, strangely enough, defended the man.

"We know nothing about the doctor, friend Yakoub; we only suspect. We have built a theory to supply a motive. Till Howard regains his senses we know not a single thing."

Yakoub's eyebrows disappeared into his hair as he peered at King and combed his fingers through his beard. It was not till a long time that the slow nods of understanding came.

"Yes, yes, doubtless—it is true, in a court of law he could bring suit. Yes, you have a great foresight, my friend."

Kaffa came into the tent, swollen with importance and mystery and with something under his blanket. King nodded to him to unburden himself.

The Hottentot squatted, still hiding his treasure. With the gloating of a schoolboy detective, he delivered his news.

"*Bwana,* that white man of whom it is ill to speak ill, but who has evil eyes, owns a box, a small box of metal, very strong and with a lock that is fitted by no key but opens with a magic spell of numbers. The boy Umbobo did not know that spell. But, having spoken of the matter of cartridges, he came to me with much excitement as we were breaking camp there and said, 'Lo, that box has grown heavier, and there are things in it that rattle not like paper.'"

"Ah-h-h," breathed Yakoub. "We are arriving at something more than only suspicion, it seems."

"Therefore, *bwana,*" continued the Hottentot with unholy triumph. "That boy Umbobo stole that box and—behold, it is here."

He swung aside the blanket, with a movement as dramatic as that of a monkey who might have performed the miracle of laying an egg, and disclosed a small steel dispatch box.

"Ah-h-h," breathed Yakoub again.

KING SAT on his cot edge, silent, frowning down at the thing that contained who could tell what infamy—or perhaps innocence. Slowly he bent down and lifted it by one brass handle; shook it. Dull, solid thumps came from within.

"Cartridges?" asked Yakoub excitedly. "In packets?"

"Don't know," said King shortly. "Might be. Might be any-thing else. Papers mostly."

"Ah-h-h," Yakoub's eyes glowed like coals under the dark recesses of his brows. "Papers! Letters perhaps, that throw some light. Evidence. Perhaps—" his voice sank to a dry whisper and he clutched King's sleeve—"perhaps checks—for much money?"

King remained darkly silent.

"You can open it, perhaps, without damaging the lock? Or must you break it?"

For a long time King made no answer. At last, he growled sourly:

"We have no right. We know nothing. We are not police-men."

The Jew gaped at him for a full searching minute this time before he nodded; and then he said:

"Ah, yes, yes. Not till Howard is recovered. He is his em-ployer. He can take the responsibility."

King remained in dark rumination. Then in a voice hard with obstinacy he said:

"It is possible that neither does Howard want to know. He is—was, his friend."

Yakoub peered quickly at King with the wary suspicion of a hawk. To every impulsive suggestion of his the other had raised coldly logical objections; and now he was branching into a guesswork of another's emotions.

King, with very hard set lips and working jaw muscles, went on to dogged decision.

"I think it would be better for everybody if that box were to be utterly lost."

The Jew gasped a grating noise that was no speech and sat back and stared at King in amaze.

"But, my friend, you are insane. That box contains perhaps, evidence of—"

Suddenly he cackled shrill laughter and flung an accusing finger at King's face. Wagging it in high triumph under his nose, he screamed:

"*Aie,* I see it. You can not befool me, my friend Kingi. I know—yes, yes. We would do the same. So exactly would I do for one of my people. You would save the face of your compatriot. His employer knows what he knows. It is his business; and a lost paper more or less will make no difference. And you do not—what is it?—you do not wash your dirt before the strangers in the land. *Aie,* my friend, my very good friend, you do not put your American bluff over me."

King got up in confusion. But his determination was hard set.

"I'm taking responsibility enough," he muttered. "I may as well take another."

To Kaffa:

"Take that box. I do not want to touch it. Take it and let it be completely lost so that no man may find it. It is an order."

"Yes, *bwana,*" said the Hottentot mournfully. "It is an order."

HOWARD'S RECOVERY was as fast as might be expected. His naturally robust constitution and his great reserve force all tended to a quick recuperation. King sat with him for long hours at a time, "working magic," talking quietly, rationally, about men and things; about hunting, of course; anecdotes, methods, customs, general practises, habits of animals, and so on.

Till Howard smiled wearily one day and said:

"Why not save up some of your stock of stories for a campfire some time? I know I've been a goat all right."

And on a day not much later, after a long silence—

"Just how much do you know, Kingi *bwana,* man of circumspection and mystery?"

King looked straight before him.

"I *know* nothing. Only that you were carried off your feet by a swelled head about your hunting prowess."

"Hmh. And how much do you know about my fr—my physician, Dr. Gerardi?"

King still looked doggedly at the horizon.

"I *know* only one thing—that the Dr. Franz Holzmann under whom he studied was a leading European expert on mental phenomena and that he came to Africa and gave some exhibitions of hypnotism in Dar-es-Salaam, and that he wrote, among others, a book called, 'Hallucination: Its Analysis and Induction'."

"Hmh." After another long silence. "Well, I guess I'm well enough. Let's send for Dr. Gerardi and let him know where we are."

So the silence was lifted and a messenger went to lead the doctor to where his patient was convalescing. But the news that came back was that the doctor, instead of packing up safari and coming with speed, packed up with speed and went in the opposite direction—the fastest way out of that country.

"Hmh," was all that Howard said, and flushed under his pale skin.

"We can overtake him," said King pointedly. "If you want to overtake him."

"In how long?"

"Plenty of time. He's got six weeks of going round west of the swamp to Nairobi. I've just got to go east to introduce Yakoub among some of the Atbara tributary chiefs. But we can still short cut him and catch up before Nairobi."

Howard smiled slowly, a hard little smile while his big fingers tensed in his lap.

"Yes," he said. "I'd like to catch up. In six weeks I shall be strong enough. Is it possible for us to start tomorrow?"

"Sure, why not? We'll rig you a hammock until you can walk."

"Splendid. Now tell me, what can I give this good witch doctor—and your Masai fellow too? They've both saved my life."

"Oh, some gimcrackery or other." King laughed. "And you

can give Barounggo a cow for his father; he can't own anything under their patriarchal system."

Suddenly Howard laughed too.

"But I'm a pauper. I've got nothing in all Africa but a torn shirt and a pair of shorts—and the friendship of Kingi *bwana.* But I tell you what I'll do; and don't you argue me about it, because I'm a weak man and sick. I'll send out for this sorcerer the biggest assortment of magic gadgets, illusions, er—hallucinations—that Chicago can produce; and for your Masai fifty head of good stock. And I'll hire you, you damned proud Westerner, to bring the things out and deliver them."

A slow grin began to break over King's face. It spread till his eyes disappeared in their slits and his mouth cut a gash parallel with them.

"Well," he agreed. "It'll be a holiday for once with no helpless tenderfoot to lead by the hand. And I guess I'll have earned it; because, take it on my sacredest oath, it's going to be one big safari man's chore to get this outfit out of here and feed us and all those *shenzies* on no more ammunition than Yakoub's piece of galvanized pipe." He twisted a rueful face. "I was a fathead over that box; but I thought I'd be able to draw on your battery."

Kaffa, squatting in the sun in ready attendance upon his master, expending an immense energy over the useless polishing of his cook pots, caught the word ammunition, and with it the look on King's face.

He fell to squirming and hiding behind his own shoulders while he looked all over the landscape with an expression of agonized virtue; till King demanded—

"What ill thought eats you up, apeling?"

The little man writhed.

"*Bwana,* in the matter of ammunition, a few cartridges we still have."

King was skeptical.

"Hunh? Where have we a few cartridges?"

"*Bwana,* that box that was heavier than it used to be."

King was quickly stern.

"Kaffa. It was an order."

The Hottentot twisted in an extremity of confession.

"Yes, *bwana*, it was an order. It was obeyed. I took it to a steep place in a far *donga* and threw it down, though my heart was water within me. But the spirits of that *donga*, who are good spirits, broke that box when it fell; and, looking down, I saw that cartridges speckled the rocks. So—since it was an omen—I went down with a great difficulty, though I was afraid of the spirits; and in three hours of searching I collected one hundred and thirty and seven cartridges. But four of them are bent and will not fit in the gun, and I have been afraid to mend them with the hammer."

King's frown was still on his face. Howard, wincing under his own contorted efforts to keep a straight face, said—

"And for that supreme imp I shall send out a specially tailored full bandmaster's uniform."

So it was that many days later King paraded through Deputy Commissioner Fawcett's headquarters with a jaunty air and with a well fed and contented safari; and Fawcett had them in to dinner and congratulated Howard on his physical condition. And Howard laughed and flexed his big arms and said that there was nothing like open air travel in that East African climate to build a man up fit to fight for his life; and it had all been a mistake anyhow about that witch casting yarn; the wizard, in fact, was a very good fellow who had no dealings with the affairs of white men.

And then they went on their way swiftly to reach Nairobi before six weeks should pass.

But when King, on his way back, met the deputy commissioner, that wise person said with a blank seriousness—

"Oh, by the way, I heard that one of your people got badly mauled by something."

And King brazenly replied:

"Why yes, I told you. A lion clawed him up quite a lot."

"I don't mean that one," said Fawcett, straight faced. "I mean the doctor man. They tell me he got into Nairobi a frightful mess, his clothes in rags, bruised and limping, and with a broken jaw or something."

King's face tried to express concern, but the light in his eyes was one of a very pleasing reminiscence.

"Sounds like something surely must have lit right into him," he said, and he rolled the words in his mouth as though they tasted good.

The deputy commissioner quite needlessly shook hands with him.

"Old humbug—" he laughed—"come on in to dinner."

KING STOOD teetering slowly on his widespread legs, his thumbs hooked in his broad pythonskin belt. He frowned ruminatively down at the man who sat expectantly at the table with a heavy gold banded fountain pen poised over an open checkbook.

The difference between the two men equalled all the disparity between the tropics and the north pole. One was tall, angular, lean with the long drawn toughness of a strenuous life, burned to mahogany brown and dressed in the shirt, breeches and high boots of the African outdoors. The other was slight, anything but strong, gray at the temples, dressed even in Kisumu—less than one degree from the equator—in the meticulous City of London business garb of one to whom correct clothing was synonymous with ordinary decency.

The Londoner waited to sign away money. But King hesitated, looking, narrow eyed, through checkbook, table and floor into the deep hidden possibilities of something he did not know. The abstract frown focused upon a concrete annoyance and deepened to a scowl. As he teetered thoughtfully on his long legs one of his new looking boots creaked ever so faintly. King threw his weight upon it and worked his ankle.

"Durned thing screeches like a Hottentot cartwheel. Anything in the whole wide veld could hear it a mile. And those noises are the devil to locate and oil out."

The squeak of the shoe was of more immediate importance

than the checkbook. King's attention came back to the suggestive weave of the fountain pen top. His frown was one of discontent.

"I don't like your proposition, Mr. Smythe. I hate to jump off into what I don't know."

Smythe tried out his pen point on the edge of a check stub, shrugged slightly and smiled as one who knew his ground, saying—

"I have been told different about Kingi Bwana—quite a lot different."

A faint gleam came into King's eyes, and the frown lightened almost to a grin.

Smythe pushed his argument with calculated persuasion:

"I am a business man, Mr. King. My proposition is quite definite. I want you to go to a certain place and fetch me a report of conditions in that place. All I insist upon is secrecy. If your report proves what I hope it will prove, there will be money enough involved for business rivals to go to any lengths in order to get that information. Secrecy is therefore imperative."

The grin that had been struggling against King's frown split his face like a crack in hard wood. He looked down at the other man in slow amusement.

"In Africa, Mr. Hamilton Smythe, there are no secrets."

"This one is." Mr. Hamilton Smythe snapped out his conviction, as if annoyed at the other's obvious innuendo against his lack of business acumen. He continued persuasively, "And I don't mind telling you that if you make good on this thing, your future with my firm is assured." The gold banded fountain pen executed preliminary curlicues over the checkbook. "Name your own figure, Mr. King."

King grunted. He had made his decision.

"I'm not looking for a future with anybody's firm, I don't care how assured it is—but I'm broke enough to deal with you. My terms are flat expenses and a fat bonus if I deliver the goods.

Nothing if I fail. But I make one condition. I have a little obligation of my own to settle—a long standing promise to a friend. If your affair doesn't interfere with that, I'm your man."

This was a most cavalier manner of accepting a job in which so much money was involved that other people would go to any lengths to find out about it. But the financier was the more anxious of the two. He bit back his annoyance and shrugged agreement.

"All right. Your private affairs can not interfere with my project. I make a condition too—that you leave at once with my sealed instructions; and I take your promise that you will not open them until you are a week out on the Karamojo trail. Now—how soon, and how much?"

King made three long steps to the door.

"If I hustle I can get out of here by tomorrow night. And you don't want all Kisumu to know that I cashed a check of yours. I'll send you a boy, a Hottentot who looks like a dried monkey. His name is Kaffa. Give him a sealed bag containing cash. About five hundred sterling will be enough."

The door closed behind him and only the faint creak of that new boot advertised his every second stride down the passage.

Another door opened silently and a man entered. He and Smythe looked at each other questioningly. The newcomer was pleased.

"Well, you landed him."

The financier voiced exasperation.

"So it seems. But I'll tell you, Jim, if you hadn't been so insistent about recommending him as being about the only man in East Africa who could do it and who wouldn't doublecross us, I would have sent him packing. I never heard such independence; and what kind of arrangement is that! Nothing on paper, no contract; and I'm to give five hundred gold cash to some African boy. All on a loose say-so as he slid out of the door."

The other nodded.

"A square dealer is worth all of that, my business friend."

The financier snorted.

"Well, I suppose we've got to trust him. And in any case he couldn't develop it without finances, and he might as well come to us as to anybody. There's a certain safeguard in that."

The other man nodded again.

"All you've got to worry about now is whether anybody else has got on to your secret."

"Never." The financier was positive. "Not a chance of that, I'm certain. This thing is a closed secret; the one man who found the key to it is dead."

The other laughed crookedly.

"There's a saying in Africa—" he began; but the financier cut him short, angrily.

"Yes, yes, I know it already. There are no secrets in Africa. But this one will prove the rule. I tell you nobody has ever been up into that country. It's unknown. The only surveys are aero maps."

The tall man nodded thoughtfully.

"I rather wish you had told him there was a chance of native trouble. Those people up there seem to be quite untrained to any knowledge of machine gun retribution for white man killing."

The financier was positive again.

"Not for a minute. He would have wanted to take a fighting party along; and that would immediately double or treble the chance of one of them selling out on us. If he is the man you say, he'll fight through. And why would I give him so much money if it isn't to pay for taking his chances? If he doesn't get through the secret will still be there, and we can try again with another party, being only five hundred pounds to the bad."

"He'll get through," the tall man said with assurance, "and you'll get your report, or your money back. He's a quixotic fool. He didn't even stipulate the size of his bonus, did he?"

And at that supreme lack of business acumen both men laughed.

THE FOLLOWING day for King had every right to be a considerably busy twelve hours. Just now his legs and his left arm formed a long tripod over the quite inadequate table in his stuffy hotel room, and he frowned over a map while he drew wandering, tentative lines upon its surface in a general northward direction.

The room was stuffy because Kisumu at that season on the equator was not the coolest place in Africa, and the Jew had insisted upon closing the window that opened on to the wide, screened veranda. King grumbled about the heat. But the Jew, who had been watching the progress of the wavering lines with the intentness of a discontented bird, shrugged his shoulders up to his ears while his heavy eyebrows disappeared into his tangle of hair.

"My good simple Kingi, I tell you again you are a child in matters of business. That Kingi Bwana should want to trek into the far middle of nowhere is nothing; all men know that he is loose footed and harebrained. But if a whisper should go abroad that Kingi Bwana and Yakoub ben Abrahm, the trader, were preparing a safari together—oho, that would be altogether another kind of a talk. Fifty people would prick up their ears; and ten of the worst of them would immediately get ready to trail behind."

"Well, it will be plenty trail," grunted King. "A good six weeks of hard going."

The Jew's ears and brows disappeared again.

"Six weeks, yes, if this new silly thing that you have tangled yourself up with doesn't take us another six out of our way."

King was immediately apologetic.

"Gosh, Yakoub, old friend, I know you've been patient. I'm ashamed to take on the job. I've been promising you this trip for a couple of years now. But be reasonable. I told him I'd take up his proposition only if it didn't interfere with my long standing promise to you. And he wants me to go by Karamojo; that's pretty near halfway in our direction. And this thing pays half our safari expenses; and when we're both so flat broke that's more than a little reason, it seems to me."

It was the last item that reconciled Yakoub, though he threw out his hands in querulous complaint.

"Reasons, reasons, you have always reasons for all the profitless things that you do. Even if it is no better than that your friend, the commissioner, asks you to go and smooth over some silly native trouble for which the government pays you no money."

King was immediately serious.

"That's a long and a deep matter, friend Yakoub. It goes all the way into the white man's future in Africa; into the coming time when he can no longer hold the black millions by machine guns but only by the careful and consistent policy of the square deal. The white man's burden, my grouchy cynic. That's not a sentiment; it's a religion."

"Your religion, maybe; not mine." The Jew's brows disappeared and his nose came down over his lips in a smile of unalloyed satire. "My religion, my dear Kingi, is business. And now that we are at last partners in a business, you and I, I tell you you will not need to worry about the future of the white man in Africa. If those little ingots are any indication and if your witch doctor can show you how to find this so mysterious place, there will be money enough for you to go home and buy that ranch in your wild and woolly Yankeeland. Money, I tell you—"

A crisp knocking low at the base of the door interrupted. King knew it to be the battered silver toe ring of his Hottentot, and he called—

"*Ai!*"

The man came in, huddled even in that tropic temperature in a blanket of brilliant red and orange stripes. Swathed in all that cloth, he looked smaller than he really was, shrunken, a veritable ape with all the wisdom of the ages peering out of the bright black eyes in his wizened face.

"The talk was of much money," he said softly. "It could be heard without the door."

He made a simple statement, implying nothing, suggesting nothing. But King looked accusingly at the Jew, and the Jew amazedly at the little Hottentot. He combed sensitive fingers through his beard and nodded in thoughtful appreciation.

"Yes, I was talking too loud. But how did that little devil know that we didn't want to be heard?"

"Much money is here," said the Hottentot. He produced a strong canvas bag, like those used by banks, from under his blanket and laid it on the table. "Five hundred pieces of Inglesi gold."

King's only movement was that of his eyes, which flashed to the bag and its seal.

"And how, wickedest apeling, did you satisfy your curiosity so surely?" he asked quietly.

Under his master's accurate diagnosis of his motive, the Hottentot squirmed; but he twisted the myriad wrinkles of his face into an expression of sententious virtue.

"Bwana told me only to fetch a bag that would contain money. That other bwana who is rich made so much talk about giving the bag into my keeping that I knew it must be much money. How can a man take proper precaution about carrying much money if he does not know how much? So I took the bag to Abdul Huq, the Banyan money lender, who knows all things about all the moneys; and he, by the sound and feel, said it was gold, and by weighing the bag he knew the pieces would be five hundred."

The Jew nodded in Mephistophelian delight.

"A good lad, a smart lad. And I suppose there is no man in Africa but Kingi Bwana who has a servant who would not run away with all that money and become chief of his tribe. How is that miracle done, my Kingi? I, who handle money—alas, only sometimes—must know that recipe."

"The square deal," said King shortly; then to the Hottentot with severity, "And how, O most foolish apeling, did you think that the Banyan would not contrive to rob you of so much money?"

"Nay, bwana." The Hottentot was confident. "Barounggo stood beside me like the father of death anxious to strike, and the Banyan trembled so that he with difficulty weighed the bag."

A grim little smile played about King's mouth. He could visualize that money lender under the shadow of his great Masai spearman.

"It was well done, O wise apeling. There will be tobacco for both. Tell Barounggo that we go out this night—secretly. Let all be ready."

"*Nidio, bwana.* All will be ready."

King turned again to the Jew, his eyes twinkling.

"The recipe works, my friend, eh? Even in Africa—sometimes. Come along to Koomer Ali's to lay in some trade goods; I guess your just being along won't stir up ten bad amen to follow us."

KING PUT on a heavy pith helmet and led the way to an oven-hot section of the town where the streets were narrow and dusty and the house fronts were whitewashed with lime. An odd mixture of half the races of the East moved listlessly in this African setting. Natives of India predominated; noisy, chattering Zanzibar Arabs, negroid of feature and truculent; Chinese, of course, and halfbreed brats who contrived somehow to survive, hatless, in the vertical sun rays.

The trade store of Koomer Ali the Banyan was a rambling half block of ground floor filled with a litter of all the gimcrackery that might delight any savage heart. For the discriminating buyer there were stocks of better goods. Like an old fashioned country store, it was a meeting place for half the upcountry outfitters of East Africa. Among the loungers a group of three were looking over trade goods with a carelessness so studious that King whispered to his companion:

"They quit talking the minute we passed under the window. It seems that Yakoub the trader can't go shopping without at least three of the worst men in British East sitting up and taking notice."

One of the men was an old-time Africander who had hunted and traded his way from the Cape to Cairo, doing anything and everything. A big, capable looking fellow he was; his name, Van Vliet, suggested Boer extraction. There was some story about his having skipped from the Rand on account of a shortage in the sluice box returns of one of the gold mines down there. But that story was whispered only when Van Vliet was somewhere else.

He had come up into East Africa and had disappeared after a time under suspicion of selling liquor to the natives. The local police had utterly failed to get any direct evidence, and the district commissioner had employed King to make the suspicion a certainty. It was then that the man had skipped. Now he was back again, cool and confident.

One of his companions was a refugee from Portuguese East Africa. King knew him too. Dago Lopez he was called, and he had a reputation for an ungovernable temper and a lightning skill at throwing a thin, heavy bladed knife—which was why he was not just now in Portuguese East. A fit companion for any desperate venture, if he could be controlled. And Van Vliet was quite competent to do that. The other man was a stranger— a thick, wide shouldered man with a battered face and the shapeless ears of a not very skilful pugilist.

The other loungers in the store conversed in low tones, pretending to be at ease. Not that Van Vliet was a brawler, a senseless trouble seeker; he was much too calm and collected for that. The condition was no more than a certain unease in the air, the sort of tension one might expect around some celebrated gang leader when any startling thing might happen at any moment.

But Van Vliet was in a good humor. His bold eyes roved over the room without any hostility; the corners of his mouth, just visible above a curly brown beard, worn untrimmed in Boer fashion, were turned up in a smile of mild contempt at the discomfort he knew he inspired.

King, immersed in a meticulous testing of trade cloths, paid no attention to the three who were the center of attention. To him it was more important to select a good grade of honest materials rather than the showy, shoddy kind for native trade.

Van Vliet laughed sardonically at a meticulousness so different from his own methods and raided his voice.

"Too much trouble, Yank. Altogether too much trouble. Take it from my experience; instead of so much fuss over quality like an old wife, give 'em lots of cheap color and a flask of square-face to close the deal."

The remark in itself was not particularly offensive; but it drew more than the intended rise from King.

"You know damn well I don't sell liquor to natives," he snapped. The emphasis was all on the I and the inference might be taken as anybody wished.

Van Vliet only laughed and shrugged noncommittally. His good humor, as he conceived it, held good. But his thickset companion took up the innuendo with a heat even more surprising than King's.

"Oho, what is this? A blinkin' missionary, what? A long nose? Mebbe yer'd like ter preach us a bit about niggers an' whisky?"

King gave him no more than a glance. His eyes were directed coldly and narrowly at Van Vliet while he ostensibly answered the other man's challenge:

"I'll preach you this much, my bucko. It's a pretty poor sort of white man who'll swindle a naked African over a piece of cloth; and it's a worse one who'll sell him liquor. And both of those mean a whole lot more than you'll ever understand."

Van Vliet only laughed in easy amusement. But the other man took the whole insult upon himself. He ripped out a short epithet of just two staccato syllables, snarled a broken toothed grin of confident pugnacity and commenced to sidle in, soft footed. Thin flanked and heavy shouldered, his wary poise and the quick, shifting little eyes in his battered face were evidence that he was no amateur at argument.

King moved only his feet; spread them a little farther apart and shuffled them gently to feel the floor under his boot soles. That was all.

The whole altercation was so sudden, arising out of nothing, that the storekeeper and the other men stood appalled.

Van Vliet's voice rose in unhurried warning—

"Look out, Johan, you can't take chances with Yankee King."

The man hesitated. The name conveyed an impression which he misunderstood.

"Oh. Oh, indeed. A Yankee gunfighter, yes?"

King stood very still. Only the elbow that had been leaning on the counter lifted clear; the other hand still held the cloth he had been examining.

The man clung to his delusion. It seemed to him that King was in a most unfavorable position to reach for a weapon. His own advantage was clear.

"Well, crummy—" he grinned wolfishly—"if he fights a gun, I'll oblige 'im."

His hand tugged at his hip pocket. The slowest gun-fighter in the world could have drawn and fired while the man still fumbled. But King never carried a weapon within the purlieus of any law-abiding British colonial town. His eyes gaged the distance between them, his legs gathered under him for a dive at the man's feet. And then in the same moment Van Vliet became an astonishing tornado of action.

"You blasted fool!"

His voice roared its fury while he was still in the midst of his leap. His hand closed over his henchman's fumbling fist. With one great wrench he tore fist and pocket and gun out all together. The same movement carried that arm over his shoulder; he slipped his hip under the man's body and whirled him cartwheeling off his feet to crash on the floor. The impetus of the flying body slid it to the very threshold of the door.

The whole extraordinary episode was over as suddenly as it had begun. Van Vliet stood smiling sardonically at the awe-struck onlookers. He slipped the confiscated gun into his pocket and his smile broadened to a grin of pure bravado. He nodded curtly to King.

"I'll be seein' you, Yank," he said and swung out to the door. "Come along, Lopez. Lug that fool out."

KING LOOKED after the trio with amazement and a slow, dawning relief; but his expression was mostly of the former.

"Now what in thunder did all that mean?" he asked aloud. Then his astonishment culminated in a shout. For Yakoub, the peaceful trader, was quickly wrapping up a shiny little black automatic in a silk handkerchief and stowing it in an inside breast pocket.

"Shooting," said the Jew, "in these so lawful British towns is more dangerous than not shooting. Still, the need looked to be desperate."

King dropped a hand momentarily on his shoulder. Then he cackled a short laugh.

"For a would-be gunman, my good Yakoub, your holster arrangements are as bad as friend Johan's. I'll have to show you sometime." His mind went to the mystery of Van Vliet. "Why, do you think, didn't he want trouble? I mean, why didn't he want trouble just then?" King cogitated the matter, narrow eyed. "He's tried it himself before now. I wonder. He's nobody's fool, is Van Vliet. Used to work for the DeWet outfit down in the Rand. Three hard *hombres,* those. Wonder if they're peddling liquor back country again?" Eyes and mouth hardened. "That'll mean hell breaking loose somewhere. By golly, I ought to crab that beastly game."

But Yakoub threw his arms round King.

"No, you don't. Not this time. You don't push your nose into other people's trouble. You belong to me, my imbecile Kingi. I have your promise. We have a business together. Money is our object, not white man's burdens."

King stood irresolute. Then he grinned down at Yakoub.

"Damn my old promise. But it's been on my chest too long. And—"he laughed a hard little laugh—"me too, I'll do anything for money these lean days. I'll make my promise good to you as straight and as fast as the trails between the water holes will let me—if there are any trails up there, or any water holes. Nobody I've ever met could tell me. You're starting on consid-

erable safari tonight, friend Yakoub. Come along; there's plenty
to do before we melt out of this burg."

S U C H   A plenty there was to do that it was going to be a
miracle of swift organization if they could get away by nightfall;
almost as great a miracle as "melting out" of a small frontier
town where a dozen astute people were furtively watching for
a safari start.

Kaffa the Hottentot came and stood on one leg while he
scratched the inside of his knee with the toes of the other foot.
King knew by that hesitant attitude that something more than
direct statement was on his mind.

"Bwana, there is a boy," began the Hottentot, looking all
round the room with the faraway disinterest of a monkey
trained to do an act, "a Basuto boy from Pemba's kraal near the
Witwaters Rand. He is a big boy and strong and his name is
Umfoli."

King knew that this was circumlocution. There was something behind all that preamble; and he knew that it would come
out sometime. He only grunted disinterestedly.

"He is a very clever boy, bwana. He understands the Inglesi
tongue; and his master, who knows no other tongue, pays him
very much money therefore. Twice as much as my pay. If I knew
the Inglesi I would be worth—"

King fixed the crafty little imp with a steady stare; and the
imp quickly glossed over that line of suggestion with something
of real interest.

"That boy is the servant of the evil white man who would
have fought with a pistol in the shop of Koomer Ali the
Banyan."

King grunted again.

"Hmh, it didn't take that one long to get abroad."

Yakoub nodded sagely.

"No secrets in Africa, my Kingi. Except—" he smiled with
smug satisfaction—"the secret of our little business together."

"That boy—" the Hottentot looked directly at King for the first time—"that Umfoli heard his master talking with the other more evil white man. The talk was that the more evil one would come tomorrow to bwana to make an *indaba* about sharing in the business that bwana has with Yakoub Bwana."

"*Adonai!*" Yakoub jerked galvanically straight in his chair, his eyes staring, clawing at his beard.

A straight vertical cleft in King's forehead formed a T-square with his brows. His eyes looked through the Hottentot and beyond. He muttered questions half to himself, half for Yakoub to hear.

"Just how much does he know, I wonder? He's got his nerve, all right. I'll bet he's working a bluff on his guess that we're together. Hell, he can't know anything. We're going on the barest hint ourselves."

"Yes, bwana," said the Hottentot innocently, "he can not know anything. Even I do not know bwana's business."

Both King and Yakoub were moved out of their concern at this disclosure to shout with laughter at the cunning little Hottentot's betrayal in one breath of his perfect understanding of English as well as of his inordinate curiosity. Kaffa writhed in abashment and quickly covered up again.

"That boy, bwana, that Umfoli wanted to leave his master who is evil and desired to take service with bwana. And a boy who understands the Inglesi, as has been shown, is very useful."

"Has he any more information?" King wanted to know.

"Nay, bwana." The Hottentot screwed his face into a maze of disdainful wrinkles and clucked a noise of derision. "He is but a Basuto. What knowledge he had is now mine. Only, since he knows the Inglesi—"

"Then chase him," snapped King.

"Yes, bwana." The Hottentot screwed his face into another pattern of wrinkles and chittered like a monkey that is being tickled. "It was known to me that bwana would so order about a Basuto; so I had Barounggo beat him and hunt him from the door this hour gone. But, as has been shown, bwana, a servant who understands the Inglesi is most useful and—"

So then King knew what had been the basic motive underlying all this long story. Very gravely he reached for a scrap of paper and fished a pencil stub from his pocket.

"Tell Barounggo," he said as he scribbled, "to make ready for immediate departure with his men. And to you I will give a letter of recommendation, a very good letter, to take to that white man who has need of servants who understand the Inglesi."

The Hottentot's eyes became saucerlike as those of a nocturnal lemur, and he wailed the lost-soul noise of one and fled.

King turned back to Yakoub.

"That man had his nerve all right." He meant Van Vliet. "We've surely got to melt out tonight."

So that night Kingi Bwana and Yakoub ben Abrahm the trader, the furtively watched pair, performed the miracle of melting out of Kisumu town on safari.

King's little ruse had the virtue of simplicity; and, since nobody had ever done it before, of novelty. No one had ever done it before because no one had ever had African servants who could be trusted to carry out a quite responsible job without the supervision of a white man. King and Yakoub alone, with only shotguns under their arms, strolled out with the sunset in the direction of the big western *donga* where guinea fowl might be found scratching in the slanting sun rays, or perhaps parrot pigeons in the umbrella acacia tops.

Nobody could go out on safari with shotguns and nothing else. So nobody followed the two pot hunters. King and Yakoub therefore trudged quietly on.

The slanting rays dropped horizontal, shooting mile-long sword blades of fire along the grass. They hung so for shimmering minutes, as if resting on the parched herbage, then they tilted suddenly, pale searchlight beams against the already graying East, and as suddenly were gone. Yellow grass, brown ant-hills and dusty green acacias absorbed the gray sky, drank it up and blended with it. They were all at once black shadows. Stars punched glittering holes in the black blanket above. The astonishing equatorial night was upon the two men.

They trudged quietly on. There would be no lions so close to Kisumu. Jackals and gaunt, striped hyenas were the largest beasts likely to be met. A leopard, possibly; but a leopard would probably be prowling closer to the hut fringe of the town, hoping to lure a frenzied dog just a little bit farther out than its more cautious fellows and snatch it before the rest could join the attack. The open veld was before the lone white men.

Fifteen miles farther on a ghostly tangle of orange glowed in the sky, resolving itself into the under side of acacia branches illumined by a fire as yet hidden in the tall grass.

King whistled the *phwee-ee piu-piu-piu* of the little banded plover. Immediately dark forms rose up in the glow. A tall shape strode toward them. Red light flickered on the outlines of a great naked figure and glinted from the blade of an immense spear.

"*Jambo, bwana,*" boomed the figure. "All is well?"

"Ha, Barounggo. It is well. And here? Everything all right? All the men?"

"Assuredly, bwana. How else would it be?"

The little Hottentot came running, querulous, complaining.

"*Awo, bwana,* it is late. We thought that a lion—that is to say, a leopard perhaps, or some ill spirit hunting by night had— All is ready, bwana. The tents are set and the coffee is waiting."

A F T E R   T H E toilsome night a lazy morning would have been excusable; and under his usual conditions of lone travel King might have been tempted to linger. For he had long ago reduced safari needs to the irreducible minimum. But on this trip he was tied down to the speed of his slowest man. He was up at an uncomfortably early hour to inspect by daylight his goods and gear and the men who had started out on safari without his personal supervision.

First the packs. Every one was opened and its contents laid out in a pile beside its canvas wrapping. Nothing was missing, and the mathematical nicety of the weight distribution was a tribute to the organizer. King only nodded, without saying a word. But Kaffa the Hottentot, who had been waiting for that nod like a dog watching for commendation of its trick, grinned all over his shrunken face.

Then the men. Barounggo marshaled them in line—ten of them. He himself stood, a great monument of ebony nakedness, not covered so much as ornamented with a short leopardskin loin-wrapping and with monkey hair garters at his knees and elbows and his single black ostrich plume nodding over his head. His long Masai spear stuck upright on its butt spike in front of him.

He dwarfed the other ten, though they were no collection of thin limbed porters. Shenzies they might have been by heredity and occupation, bearers of burdens upon their heads. But they stood forth now as spearmen—*askaris.*

They constituted King's careful precaution in jumping off into country he did not know; and in themselves they constituted a minor miracle of manipulation with native habit and tradition. Shenzies existed in plenty for safari portage; and *askaris* for the purpose of guarding those Shenzies; but it had been Barounggo's labor for weeks to select and train a little troop who, having been graduated to the dignity of shield and spear, would still condescend to carry burdens. The ten were Barounggo's pride and joy of achievement and he growled abuse at them accordingly.

"Baboon, is it thus that you hold spear with toes in place of fingers? And thou, Bushman. Shield in your jungle was doubtless a toy of woven grass; is oxhide too heavy for you? Hey, fellow, fourth in the line, roll not your eyes like the tree galago of the night. This is the *bwana sana* who inspects. His one word to me is death."

The troop shuffled their feet and tried not to look self-conscious. The big Masai watched King out of the corner of his eye. King nodded. The Masai swelled his great chest.

"It is well, fellows. Today you do not die." To King, with nonchalance, but loud enough for all to hear:

"Cattle they are, bwana. Spearmen all they claim to be from their youth up; yet the ghosts of my fathers have wept that I have the handling of such. Feet have they and no hands. Yet this alone may be said for them: They will not run away."

And at that excoriating analysis of them the ten men swelled their dark chests.

At his tent flap Yakoub stood, unkempt from his exhausted sleep, his hair twisted in horn-like spirals, his beard a tangle; a veritable satyr of the woods in benevolent mood.

"It is a miracle, my Kingi. This recipe of the square deal works wonders. No other white man in Africa has such servants. I am converted to your application of the white man's burden. I shall make it a rule from now on."

King only grunted.

"A means to an end," he lied to cover any show of sentiment. "I'm working this way for money. Get a move on. We've got to cover ground today. The faster we get to Karamojo, the sooner we can get through with the Ham Smythe job and away to our own little secret out of which you promise me so much money. And the sooner we get to see the old Wizard of Elgon the better we'll know whether he can give us any dope about that unknown country up there."

Yakoub agreed.

Ground, accordingly, was covered. The porters, under Barounggo's driving and the shrewd implication that they were not merely beasts of burden but fighting men of strength and spirit, made marches that were astonishing for safari travel.

Yet King frowned when, during the second day, topping each low rise of ground, he brought his prism glasses to bear upon a haze of dust that persisted behind.

"There's a safari behind us," he told Yakoub shortly. "Forty or fifty men, I should judge."

He had taught Kaffa the—to a native—quite difficult feat of looking through binoculars. The Hottentot screwed his face into agonized contortions behind the eye pieces, looking above the dust and around it rather than at it, then lowered the glasses and scratched his head for a moment.

"Safari," was his verdict. "Middle big safari, for the dust is not great. White man safari, for the vultures are not many." He looked up to study King's expression.

King frowned and grunted dissatisfaction.

Another day went by, the miles fell behind; but still that persistent cloud of dust hung over the horizon, the safari just below vision, even from the low, rounded hilltops of the rolling country into which they were coming.

KING SWORE angrily.

"There's only one white man I know who can drive a safari of that size to keep up with the speed we're making."

He stopped and considered awhile. His face set like rough cement work. He told Yakoub:

"You go ahead as fast as you know how and make for the wizard's *boma*. Kaffa knows the way. Sit until I come. I'm going back to make sure about those people. I'm taking Barounggo. Kaffa, I expect the men to make as much distance as if Barounggo were behind them."

The Hottentot instantly threw out his chest in ape-like imitation of the great Masai and screamed frightful abuse at the porters. They grinned cavernously at him.

"Buffaloes," he screamed at them, "Cattle of the fields, move! Run with speed! Or, look, I borrow the spear from the Masai. In the spear is a magic. With it any man can drive cattle as does that great one."

At which Barounggo looked with the enormous indifference

of a mastiff, and the men guffawed. But the Hottentot knew his own methods of handling porters.

"Listen, goat men, beetle eaters. The friend of bwana is the Old One, the Wise One of Elgon. Let me not have to tell him that bwana's cattle dawdled on the way, or he will make a witch-binding upon you that will be remembered by the grass monkeys who will be your descendants."

And at that the porters covered their mouths with their hands and took up their packs with alacrity.

King swung back on the trail to meet that persistent cloud of dust. He had determined on one very definite thing—this trip with Yakoub. He had promised it for more than a year. It was a secret between himself and the Jew, this thing Yakoub had found out—a hint, rather, of a venture that might develop into vast possibilities. And nobody was going to intrude into the secret for which his friend had lived in anxious and patient expectation for all the months during which King had been called to half a dozen profitless deals.

The Masai strode grimly behind, muttering some rhythmic recitation deep in his throat with a reiterated chorus of *sghee, sszee,* which in the ideophone of his people represented the stabbing and swishing of flung spears.

"What foolish daydream do you chant, old blood-letter?" King wanted to know.

"I sing my ghost song, bwana. They are fifty and we are two. Yet it will be a good fight while it lasts. Though I think that with my ten whom I have been training we might have made some headway against those Shenzies."

"So talks Kifaru, the rhinoceros who charges blindly at each new scent. Do you think that I am a fool as well as you? There will be no fighting. We come only to look."

"If bwana so orders. Yet that but means that the fighting will be later. I will train my ten with the heavy stabbing spear."

King only grunted and strode on. As the dust of the safari began to come nearer he was careful not to top any skylines over the low hills. And when the confused clamor of African porters on the march began to be heard he looked about him to select a tall anthill well covered with scrub.

The safari came slowly on, three white men in the lead, the porters straggling out for a quarter-mile behind with some twenty spear armed *askaris* among them.

"See, bwana," the Masai whispered, "that is no honest hunting safari with so many *askaris*. There will be fighting, as I have said. I smell trouble. Lumbwa dog eaters are they all—twenty men. Yet with my ten who are Wa-Kuafi we could make a slaughter."

"Shut up," King told him, and he trained his glasses on the group.

His guess had been right, of course. The white men were Van Vliet and his two ill favored companions. How they had found out anything was a mystery to King and a blow to his conceit; for he had been desperately careful. Yet there was no room for doubt that they were following his trail. But it was not the knowledge that these men were obviously hoping, as the Hottentot had reported, to share in his secret business that infuriated King. He swore through set teeth and his hand closed hard on his rifle breech as he recognized among the porter loads some twenty very familiar wooden cases.

"Squareface," he gritted. "Damn 'em! Twenty cases of trouble for some poor naked fools!"

He would have liked to open fire at long range from his shelter and obliterate these three menaces to black men and white alike; and he cursed the inhibition that restrained him. He growled to Barounggo:

"We have seen enough. Come on. From now on we must travel with speed and secrecy."

The Masai's eyes were eager, and he spoke softly through pinched lips:

"A throwing spear, bwana; a light throwing spear balanced close to the blade will be a good weapon. I will make me such a spear. And those ten, I will train them also to the throwing spear. Only twenty *askaris,* and Lumbwa men at that; the rest are cattle. Look, bwana, thus shall the battle go."

"Peace, murderer," King told him. "Here is not even cause for a fight."

But to Yakoub, when he caught up with him later, he said:

"You were right. Yakoub the trader and Kingi Bwana can't go out together without at least three of the hardest cases in Africa following on their trail. They mean to crash in on our secret, and they've come prepared to fight for it. That's what comes of having a reputation as a shrewd business man."

The Jew's eyebrows disappeared in his tangle of hair; his hands outflung, he nodded sour, smiling agreement almost as if more pleased at the implied tribute to his astuteness than troubled at the complication.

"And," he appended, "of Kingi Bwana's having a reputation for knowing how to discover the secrets of the land—even if he doesn't know how to profit by them. Never mind, let them follow. Who are they? Three bad characters. It is nothing. But Yakoub and Kingi together—the Jew and the Yankee—that is a combination. We shall outwit them."

"By golly, if we don't outwit them," said King, "we'll have to kill them off like the rats they are. Come ahead, let's go. Move. Speed. Get distance."

A THIN haze far away to the left began to assume wavering outlines that came and went as the mists drifted. Later in the day a pale gray cone hung in the sky, ghostly, standing upon a chill purple fog of nothing. A cool wind drifted down from it.

King broke away from the Karamojo trail and headed toward the mountain flank. In a sheltered valley at the foot of a long blue ridge nestled a thorn *boma*. Like the nucleus of a spider web, this isolated huddle of huts was the center of countless faint paths that came to it from all directions. But the most extraordinary feature of it that immediately arrested attention was its condition of dilapidation. Thorn *bomas* in the more accessible regions of East Africa are nowadays not intended for defense; their purpose is protection from wild animals. But it seemed here as if even the lions and hyenas knew that the home of Batete the Wise One was something to be treated with awe.

Fat cattle grazed around it. Naked herd boys gazed owlishly. The porter men clustered, wide eyed, at the gate. Barounggo, with immense disdain, but with spear gripped tight, prepared to follow his master within. But King knew the courtesies of calling upon wizards. He told his men to wait, and went in with Yakoub.

Inside the *boma* were several round, thatched huts; and in the center stood another decrepit thorn fence, hung all round with cattle skulls and colored rags and snake skins—all the regular appurtenances of sorcery.

Three low stools, each carved out of a single trunk, stood in front of the central hut in a patch of sun. Upon one of them sat a shrunken ancient. He might have been sixty years old, or eighty, or a hundred. His face had reached that condition of desiccation in which age could mark it no further. His limbs were wrapped in a monkey-skin cloak.

But he was no senile antique. He was alert, and waiting.

"*Hau, jambo, Bwana Kingi,*" he called in a voice astonishingly strong for his appearance. "*Jambo sana.* It is a long time since my eyes have been glad. See, the stools wait. And let your Shenzies enter. *Potio* is ready for them in the outer huts."

King had long ago given up wondering just how the old sorcerer gained his apparent foreknowledge of events. It might have been the blackest kind of magic, or it might have been no more than a system of native runners. Bush telegraph was a mystery recognized even by the government.

"*Jambo,* father of wisdom," King greeted the old man. "My good fate has fallen on this day. You are well? Your house is well? Look, I bring a gift. In the nighttime the wind that comes from the ghost mountain is cold. This is a blanket from my own country. It is woven by hand and it will shed rain."

It was no cheap trade goods that King presented to the old man, but a gorgeous, lightning striped, genuine Indian blanket that he had long set aside for just this purpose.

The wizard's face remained an immobile net of furrows. Only the keen old eyes glowed. He dropped his ingrained habit of preternatural knowledge.

"There is no white man in the land but the *bwana m'kubwa* who would think of that. Sit, bwana; and this man, your friend, let him sit too. It is enough that he is your friend. The women shall bring maize beer and we shall talk."

T H E   TA L K wandered throughout all the little unimportances that are of import to the dwellers in the wilderness. Gossip of the road and of the town: of people's comings and goings and dyings, of the movements of game and of the mealie crop and of the next rain. King knew it was necessary and he went through with it. It was hours before he could bring in his inquiry about the country up north where he wanted to go.

The wizard became silent and thoughtful. Automatically, as if from habit, he drew an odd assortment of cowry shells and colored pebbles and bones from a pouch and threw them fanwise in the dust. With a lean finger he sorted them and traced lines between. Hesitantly he began to talk.

"So? It is up to the People of the Amulet that bwana would go? So indeed? That is bad. They are a far people and a hidden people. Few people are left hidden in this land. It is a pity that bwana knows about them."

The old man nodded his head stiffly many times, moving his pebbles and bones almost like chessmen as he cogitated. Decision was difficult. He looked up squarely into King's eyes.

"It is a pity. Yet—if it were any other white man in all the land I would weave a net of lies for his feet. But if Kingi Bwana wants to go, who am I to plant the weeds of difficulty in his path? He will rend a way through many mats of weeds and in the end he will get there. I will, therefore, tell him truth and bwana will see those people and will do the thing that he will know to be right."

The old man was talking no mumbo-jumbo of his craft now. This was a confusion of words with a meaning behind them. King sat silent, waiting. Yakoub clawed nervous fingers through his beard.

"This is the truth, bwana. Even I, Batete, whom men call wise, do not know that country. I know only that the people are the People of the Ancient Amulet. This is the magic of that amulet: That whosoever shall see it, it shall tear his heart in twain that he can not take it away with him. This too I know: The people beyond the Toposa, between them and the hidden people, are an evil people, strong and war-like. And this last thing I know. The road to the hidden people goes by the mountain country of the black Christians, very steep and difficult. He who does not know that the mountain is the road goes to the left, which looks as if it should be the road; and at the end of many days he loses himself in the swamps that guard the country on that side. That is all that I know."

The old man relapsed into silence.

In a low tone Yakoub addressed King:

"The black Christians. He must mean Abyssinia. And the Hidden People—that must be the strip of unclaimed territory along the Sudan-Abyssinian border that we hear about. But what is this amulet thing? Have you ever heard, any so queer story?"

King shrugged first a dubious negative and then nodded in slow reminiscence, reluctant to break the spell of hidden romance that had settled on them. He whispered only to Yakoub:

"Something once long ago; a fairy tale that might connect. But the place sounds like where I figured it would be. Those rivers must rise somewhere in that mountain country."

Suddenly the wizard spoke out of his muffling robe:

"Blood is on the trail of bwana. Much blood."

"So said Barounggo," murmured King. "Tell me of that blood, wise one. What do you see for me?"

The wizard remained hunched under his blanket and moaned. His voice came painfully:

"I see only blood. White men will die." He twisted his body and appeared to strain himself to effort; then he relaxed. "But my snake does not show me the faces of those men. Many black men will also die. There will be much blood."

He relapsed into stertorous breathing. King muttered to Yakoub:

"Cheerful, isn't he?" Then his teeth set hard and his jaw stuck out at an ugly angle and he grunted, "Well, if one of them is going to be me, there's going to be others too."

The wizard spoke again:

"Let bwana now go and let him send his men to me. Because bwana is my friend of old I will make a magic for those men that their hearts may not melt in that blood—the strong magic of the lion dance. Let bwana go and send his men to me."

King knew that this was dismissal; and he knew better than to try to stay and witness the spellbinding that the wizard would make over his men.

"This is a great thing that you do for me, wise one," he said in genuine appreciation; for he knew that such a witchcraft would be infinitely more efficacious than any exhortation or leadership or promise of reward. "Wise one, I go. But make speed with the magic; for there is great need."

ANOTHER TWO days passed. No cloud of dust followed behind. But King was by no means satisfied. It didn't mean a thing, he grumbled. Van Vliet was nobody's fool; he was just hanging back a bit; he wasn't so easily scared off. And the old wizard with his gloomy talk about blood… King didn't believe any of this pretense at prophecy—or, at least, he said he didn't. But this was Africa. He had seen things and had heard

things that required a lot better explaining away than just laugh-
ing them off as native hokum.

King shrugged savagely at his own gloominess. He could
positively feel that something was about to happen after listening to that old man. But there to the left was the trail to Karamojo, and in his pocket the sealed letter which had become
such an incubus. He told Yakoub to supervise the making of
the *boma* and chose himself a flat rock where, with an expression
of martyrdom, he sat down to break the seal.

And in that same place and position Yakoub found him when
he came an hour later to call King into the finished *boma* for
supper. King sat very still, gazing into distant nothingness
through the dusk haze, whistling, as was his habit, thin disharmonies through his teeth.

Yakoub knew that sign. His face lost its customary expression
of genial cynicism and he came quickly closer.

"Trouble?" he asked.

"Plenty," was King's answer.

"Well—"Yakoub shrugged—"fifty per cent of a partnership
is for the purpose of sharing the profits; the other fifty is for
sharing the worries. Tell me this so unpleasing secret."

King grinned wryly up at him.

"Yakoub, old friend, I'll tell you a truth that we both know;
and we've both been so cocksure of our smartness that we've
forgotten it. Listen to it again: There are no secrets in Africa!"

"You mean—our business? It is the same? This Mr. Smythe
knows too?"

King nodded.

"All I wonder is how he got on to it. Gosh, I thought I had
stumbled on to something new. I thought that this was really
a dark one. Consider it again and tell me if I was a fool.

"I came out of Beni Shangul in Abyssinia—and that's full
of gold; only old Shogh Ali won't let anybody work it without
an army. I worked south amongst a lot of crawling little Atbara
tributaries that haven't even got names. I fished a man half dead

out of a mountain stream and, stripping him for first aid, I found those little ingots. And all hell and a bluff at torture wouldn't scare a peep out of him about who or where or what. And he had the guts to laugh when my bluff fell through.

"I tried to prospect it up. But that river ended in a hole in the ground; subterranean from somewhere higher up. I tried other streams; but the mountains were fierce, just about perpendicular. And where they fell away into the plain miles away west there was peat bog, morass and, lower down, swamp in the flat, empty desert, just like the witch doctor said. Hellish country. So I pretty near died getting across to the White Nile at Mongalla and I figured there must be a way in from the south."

"My friend," said Yakoub with serious conviction, "I will tell you this about gold. You were not overconfident; you had every right to think this was a new thing. But gold is a queer material. It is devilish and magnetic—but only in large quantities. A few gold pieces can not talk to one another. But where a man has a large accumulation of gold, other gold tells it telepathically: 'Look, I am here, in such and such a place.' But usually the message comes only to my people. What right has this Mr. Smythe to know?"

King was able to muster a crooked laugh at this queer whimsy that had so much of cynical truth in it.

"Well, he knows all right. Only he doesn't know any more than general location; no more than I did till the old wizard gave us the straight dope."

The Jew quickly reviewed this new angle from his viewpoint of a business man. He grimaced sourly.

"I will tell you this also about gold, my Kingi. When you have none of it, a very little of it makes you its slave. You have taken this Mr. Smythe's money, five hundred paltry pounds of it, and now you are tied with a chain. But—" his alert mind considered the thing from the viewpoint of business; and, like the financier, he quoted the inexorable law of business—"after all, we can not develop our finds without capital; and if this Mr. Smythe has felt that the thing is so great, there will be enough money for us not to worry.

"Only this time, my simple friend, you will let *me* talk to the capital. You are a child, I think I must have told you, in matters of business. From now on I, who am your partner, look after your negotiations. You have nothing to worry; I will yet make you rich in spite of your foolishness. Your Mr. Financier Smythe knows no more than general location, hunh? Very well, we have a starting place from which to begin the discussion that we shall have, this Mr. Smythe the financier and Yakoub the Jew."

King got up from his dejected position and stretched his big shoulders till the sinews cracked.

"Friend Yakoub," he replied wholeheartedly, "you take a load off my chest. Let you do the negotiating and me do the easy work of just getting there. That's a good partnership. Let's go eat."

AN HOUR passed. The meal had been finished, the pipes lighted, and King laughed in carefree enjoyment of nothing at all. The night was warm; the food had been sufficient. They had reached the water hole before the evening-drinking game had polluted it. It had been a good day. King leaned his head back in his folded hands, stretched his legs to the top of a pile of duffle and blew smoke rings.

Behind in the shadows, their masters having eaten, the natives chattered over their *potio* of parched corn and fresh antelope meat and with African carelessness stole dry thorn sticks out of the *boma* for their crackling fire, leaving gaps that a leopard could easily crawl through. Everybody was contented.

Suddenly came the Hottentot's voice:

"Bwana! Men approach!"

King dropped his feet from the duffle pile and reached for his rifle which always stood ready to hand against the tent pole. But these men had approached very carefully indeed; and they knew how to approach—as they had to know—very thoroughly, taking the risk of the outside darkness.

"Just as you were, Yank. Take it easy and make no mistake."

Van Vliet stood framed in the opening of the *boma*, watching over his rifle. He had timed his arrival exactly, counting on the general relaxation after dinner and knowing that the last thorn bush would not be dragged into the *boma* gate until bedtime.

The man Johan and Dago Lopez sidled in past him. They were well rehearsed. Johan helped to cover the party with his rifle, and Lopez stepped forward and removed King's rifle out of reach. Then with business-like deliberation he searched both white men for guns.

"Alla right," he reported.

King had no inkling as to what might be the move. So he put a match to his pipe and waited.

Van Vliet came forward.

"We're goin' to talk, Yank," he said with a determination which showed he understood to the full that any talk between them would have to be forced.

King was uninterestedly resigned.

"Well, since you insist on being social, I'm listening. But why all the armed escort?"

Van Vliet grinned at him in enjoyment.

"I know you, don't I? All East Africa knows that your business is *your* business. An' d'you think I didn't spot those two klipspringer that winded you an' acted up that way? I sent a man over immediate, an' he picked up your trail exact where you'd been watchin' us."

"Oh, pshaw!" King laughed as if caught out in a game.

He put his feet up on the duffle pile before him and put another match to his pipe.

"I'll hand it to you, Van. I'd hoped you wouldn't notice them, or that you'd put it down to hyenas or something. But I might have known you'd be taking no chances. I always told Yakoub you were nobody's fool. What's on your mind?"

Van Vliet nodded in acknowledgment of what he knew to be his own worth.

"We're goin' to talk, Yank. An' you're jolly well goin' to listen."

"All right," said King, as if it were he who condescended. "Make it snappy 'cause I don't like your friends."

"Damn your hide—" Johan lurched forward.

At the same time a sharp hiss of intaken breath came from Lopez. But Van Vliet's growl stopped both of them short.

"Easy there, you two. I'm runnin' this. An' you, Yank, you're not winnin' anythin' with insults. We haven't come for trouble; we want to arrange this thing nice an' friendly. So you just sit tight an' listen."

"I'm always friendly on the front side of a rifle," said King, blowing huge puffs of smoke into the night and watching all three men warily from behind its screen. "Go ahead and say your piece."

Except for Van Vliet's careful watchfulness, the scene might have been a friendly visit of passing safaris. King at ease in a canvas chair tilted back, throat, nostrils, and cheekbones thrown into yellow relief by the lamp. Yakoub in another chair, passive, humped up like a brooding bird, only his bright black eyes taking in every move. Across the table in the paler outer circle of light, three men framed against the warm velvet blackness.

Only one unusual thing indicated tension. Just as insect noises, warned by a mysterious telepathy, fall silent when there is a jungle killing, the chatter of the natives out of the dark behind the tents had ceased.

Van Vliet put his proposition with commendable brevity.

"Fightin' won't pay any of us. We make you an offer to join up with your outfit an' split even."

"Split what?"

"Ah-h-rgh!" Van Vliet's patience did not hold out well. "We

know what you're out for. An' you know I'm workin' for the DeWet company."

"Yeah, I know." King was exasperatingly supercilious. He knew that in any argument the one who lost temper first lost opportunity with it. "But what interest have the DeWet people with us? They hired you and your two gangsters to peddle gin to the natives."

"Damn you, Yank! Easy there, you two. I'm boss here. Come off actin' innocent, you. I tell you we *know.* DeWets have been watchin' your boss, Ham Smythe, for weeks. Their London agents have reported every time he breathed an' batted an eye. They've been in this game long enough to know when somethin's movin' on the quiet."

King suddenly threw himself back in his camp chair and astounded everybody by shouting with laughter.

"DeWets! Oh, of course, the DeWet crowd would know. Do you hear that, Yakoub? DeWets have been watching him for weeks. Ho-ho-ho! He thought he had a secret—a secret in Africa, the poor fool. Land sakes, this is funny. And we thought you were interested in us; Yakoub and Kingi together. This is good for our conceit. So DeWet sniffed a rat in all the elaborate precaution and put a watch on Smythe. Ha-ha-ha, what a secret!"

And at that Yakoub, too, saw the irony of the situation and he crowed aloud with acrid laughter.

VAN VLIET regarded them both with dubious anger. Here was something that he did not understand, and the tension was beginning to wear on his nerves. Even more so on the others.

"Aw, he's makin' a monkey outer you," snarled Johan.

Lopez shifted suddenly like a black leopard in the dim outer fringe of the lamplight. His hand stole down to his boot top.

"What the hell you got to laugh at?" growled Van Vliet.

"Ho-ho," King chuckled exasperatingly. "The joke, my dear Van—but I know you won't believe it—the joke is that Yakoub and I started out on this trip on a deal of our own. We've only just learned that Ham Smythe is in on it."

Van Vliet stood angrily suspicious. He could see no joke in that situation without understanding a great deal more about it. But Dago Lopez was quicker to attribute a foul explanation.

"Ha, you don' work for heem no more. You don' foola me. You doublecross heem an' you go for yourself."

"Why, you filthy—" King pushed his chair away and rose to his feet. It was an interpretation that had never entered his mind as possible, and the insidious foulness of it enraged him.

"Easy there!" Van Vliet's rifle pointed squarely at his chest. "An' you drop that, Lopez. I told you there'd be no knife play, you fool."

Lopez glowered till Van Vliet's will dominated him. Then he shrugged and his teeth glinted white out of the darkness. He offered the olive branch to King on a basis of give and take among equals.

"Alla right. Then we onderstan' one the other. We doublacross DeWets an' we go weeth you. So we alla mek planty moch more. Hunh, Van? Joost lika we talk before. Ees good."

King was master of his indignation again. He was very deliberate. His move had brought him closer to his rifle. His words were chosen and distinct.

"Well, I'll tell you, Van Vliet, I might make a dicker with you—if I was drunk or doped. I'm not proud. I'm not ashamed of anything that creeps or crawls or stinks. But your partner, Lopez, there—"

"*Morte de Deus!*" Lopez screamed in ungovernable rage at the sudden twist of insult. The light glinted on a venomous arc as his hand flung back over his shoulder.

"Drop it!" shouted Van Vliet.

The agony of apprehension in his voice was astonishing. He jumped blindly for Lopez. But he was too late. Lopez's arm was already in the swing of his throw.

"*Sszee!*" shouted the voice of Barounggo the Masai from the farther darkness.

A thin shaft of yellow light swished past King's shoulder. Lopez's arm twisted spasmodically in its down swing; his knife spun high, turning glittering somersaults in the air and fell somewhere out of the light circle.

In that instant of confusion King made one enormous bound and snatched his rifle; and when in the next instant Van Vliet and Johan recovered their wits King had them covered.

"Ve-ery careful, you two," he warned them. "In this bad light I'm apt to be jumpy. Take their guns, Yakoub. So. Now you can look to Lopez, you two."

Lopez's dim form was writhing in the shadow. He was snarling in furious pain and rage.

"There was no order to slay," said the voice of Barounggo, "so I but transfixed his arm. *Hau*, it was a good cast. A good spear, a light spear; swift as the snake of the night—"

His voice began to break into a rhythmic chant.

"Shut up," snapped King. "Still, it was well done. Guard now those two white men. Here, Kaffa, bring the light and let's see how much damage was done to his arm."

Lopez was sitting up, gritting his teeth, his arm awkwardly stiff with a thin shaft protruding from his biceps, the narrow blade ten inches through on the other side.

"Hm, a nice clean hole," commented King coldly. "Better than you deserve. A knife, Kaffa." He ripped the shirt sleeve.

"Now clench your teeth, Dago. This is going to hurt you more than it does me."

With a quick jerk he pulled the blade clear. Lopez yelped once. Then King said calmly—

"Water, Kaffa."

The Hottentot was well experienced in the requirements of camp surgery; already he was there with a bowl and the iodine bottle and bandage.

The little operation was completed with methodical dispatch. Lopez stood sullenly muttering and holding his arm. King motioned him over to join the other two. Then very carefully and meticulously he lighted his pipe, making time to think. A half minute was sufficient.

HE TURNED to the three prisoners. He knew exactly what to do. His eyes smiling narrowly over the lantern were belied by the hard, incisive voice:

"The other way round again, eh? Now I'll tell you three crooks what you'll do. You knew enough to come here after dark. So you'll know enough to go. But I'm holding your guns—no sniping out of the night— No, don't yelp yet. I know well enough that taking a white man's gun from him in the African bush is murdering him.

"You'll find them in this place tomorrow, if nothing eats you up tonight. But that's your funeral that you brought on yourselves. My advice is that you climb a tree right quick—a good thorny one—and I hope to holy Pete it hurts you plenty. Or you can make a thorn *boma*, and that's another sweet job by firelight. Got matches? All right. Git."

He motioned with his rifle. The three men, looking at that thin smile shadowed in hard hewn lines by the lamp, knew that King would not relent, although they were receiving a vastly more generous deal than they would have given. But Van Vliet was a man not often thwarted. He held too hard a grip upon himself to fly into any sort of ungovernable rage; but there was cold venom in his voice as he pointed his last threat at King:

"It's you or me, Yank, from now on, and so I'm tellin' you. You can't leave me out of this deal, whatever it pans out. An' I'm not talking partners any more. You've had your chance. There's just one of us two is goin' to win."

The man was courageous enough, standing there covered by the rifle of the man whom he threatened. But he knew King as well as King knew him. He was perfectly assured that that rifle would not go off unless he were to make a direct physical attack. And he knew King much too well to make any such attempt as that.

King's face in the flickering lamplight was a mask of hard corners and thin slits. A bitterness soured the set grin; a bitterness caused by the knowledge of his own inhibitions which prevented him from removing with one clean shot what he knew to be a menace of treachery and trouble and bloodshed.

"All right, old-timer. You or me. There'll be a whole lot of people, black and white, a whole lot better off when you're through. And that goes for Dago Lopez and your gunman too. And let me tell you this again like I told you before: Yakoub and I, we're going on our deal alone. Now skip. Footsack. And I hope the lions get you before I do."

Sullenly the three men went from the *boma*. Their footsteps sounded awhile. Then the night swallowed them.

King was full of an exhilaration that was extraordinary in the face of a threat of death left by a man whom he knew to be infinitely cunning and dangerous and whose capabilities he was grudgingly forced to admit. He bustled about the final preparations for the night and his voice glowed with an astonishing satisfaction.

"All right. Get a move on there, everybody. Get that thorn tree pulled into the opening there. See that it's good and high. All fast for the night. Barounggo, let two men watch together by turns."

Yakoub stood thoughtful, troubled, while King went about, whistling in the greatest good humor, attending to the last little precautions and inspections for night in an open *boma*.

The muffled clatter of the delayed tin plates of supper died down. Uncouth yawning noises came from the natives behind the tents. The snap and crackle of sticks added to the all-night fire. A soft clapping of hands and a rhythmic stamp of feet betokened the Masai getting ready to chant the delayed song of his deed before his troop:

"*Hau*, it was a good cast.

A fair cast, a clean cast.
In the dark stood that one.
Where is he?
Ow, he is gone.
A light spear, a swift spear.
Whence did it come?
Out of the dark it flew.
True and straight.
As a snake it stung."

King knew that that would go on for an hour. All the details, all the action, even the impelling thought, would be given poetic expansion. He grunted to himself.

"Probably keep us all awake. But he deserves it. It was good."

Yakoub still stood thoughtful and troubled. King in his high spirits rallied him on his depression.

"I'm afraid," said Yakoub, "that those are three poisonous snakes allowed to go loose. Yet what could one do?"

"They are," said King cheerfully. "And one can't do a thing. That's a rule of the outer places. The poor fool who has inhibitions always loses out against the other fellow who has none. We can't cut their throats, but they'd cut ours the first minute it suited them; and that's all to their advantage. But do you know what advantage we have gained out of this night?"

Yakoub shook his head dolefully.

"I see no advantage that makes you so cheerful. Only that your religion of the square deal applies to three clever and quite unprincipled enemies."

King laughed happily.

"Not so, my mournful friend. Consider. Twice now Van Vliet has interfered to save me from harm; both times to save my life. Is it because he loves me do you think? Or is it—tell me if I'm not right—is it because he doesn't have any hint of where this gold is. The DeWet people who hired him knew only that Smythe was on to some big secret. So they hired a hard, bad gang who knew safari work to follow whoever Smythe might hire, to wipe them out of competition and steal the secret. So that's all to our advantage."

"I see," said Yakoub. "Our advantage is that we are followed by three ruffians who have no inhibitions and who have come prepared to steal the secret at any cost."

But King's cheerfulness was proof against misgivings.

"Not so, my doleful Yakoub. Our advantage is that none of them—not the three hard guys nor Smythe nor the DeWet company—know anything about the location of that secret. Only we. And that's a real secret this time. And that is to our very great advantage. You said yourself that we'd outwit them, or we'd have to—" King's face made three hard horizontal lines—"outfight them."

WITH THE morning not a sign was to be seen of the night's visitors. Kaffa the Hottentot was already up and had made a circle of stones and oddments of lion claw ornaments and bits of skin that he had taken from the Shenzies. Inside of it he danced and genuflected and chattered with an intense solemnity.

"What, can you tell me, is that completely mad devil doing?" Yakoub asked of King.

But this was a new manifestation of his servant's many queer-nesses, even to King.

The Hottentot finished his incantation and stepped out of his witches' circle.

"I make invocation to Atto Happa, who in my country is the lord of all lions and leopards and beasts that slay," he explained.

"And what for?" King wanted to know.

"But that is plain, bwana," the Hottentot told him. "Surely in order that the beasts, if they have not already slain those three, may yet do so before the sun becomes too hot for hunting."

"Hm, I hope your Atto Happa delivers the goods," King grunted. "It would surely save a heap of trouble for a lot of people. Did you hide the rifles as I told you?"

The Hottentot screwed up his shoulders and leered like a distorted black gnome.

"Assuredly, bwana, did I hide them. First having stuffed all oily places with sand, I shoved them down an ant-bear hole as far as Barounggo's spear would reach. A father of the mission told me that the gods help men who help themselves; and thus have I done my share toward earning the favor of Atto Happa."

King considered the matter, frowning.

"Pretty drastic," he muttered. "But Van Vliet won't overlook anything so likely as an ant-bear hole. I only hope there are plenty of them and that he'll dig them all before he comes to the right one. It'll win time for us; and time is what we'll need if we're going to shake him."

KING SCOURED the horizon for dust as the days passed. Dust there was, lots of it, rising slowly behind or eddying away to one side. But it was intermittent and traveled this way and that in slow, low-hanging drifts or in tumultuous spurts— animals grazing peacefully upwind or dashing in wild stampedes as some taint in the air alarmed them.

Dust there was, too, before them; once a quite heavy cloud. King inspected it anxiously through the glass; they were getting beyond the confines of the Toposa tribes where the natives were, as the witch doctor had said, strong and war-like.

"Wildebeeste," King announced with relief. "I can see the tick birds. Probably zebra with them. It'll be good trail smudge."

He hurried the little safari along on a long slant to get in front of that grazing herd, and for half a day he held that position, letting the countless hoofs obliterate all other tracks.

Twice he was able to do that. In spite of grumbling among the porters he insisted upon making the nightly *bomas* far from water holes, carrying the minimum supply requisite for camp. Cooking fires were screened. No smoke was made by day.

These were days of hard and uncomfortable going. Not for a moment did King relax vigilance or permit himself to under-estimate the ability and the persistence of the man who followed. But Yakoub, observing all these precautions that seemed to him sufficient to baffle a bloodhound, found it in himself to be more optimistic. The farther they went, the nearer must be their goal. To him it was irresistible to speculate upon that mysterious country of the Hidden People.

Who might they be? Why did the witch doctor so darkly insist that it was a pity that anybody should know about them?

King, with a certain hardness in his voice, was able to elucidate.

"Huh, that's an easy one. There's never been a savage race in the history of the world which hasn't claimed it was better off before the white man came. Which I'm not defending one way or the other. But that crowd behind us with twenty cases of trade gin is a pretty big argument."

The Jew, with his keen mind trained to balance the hazy profits of future prospects, could no more refrain from the fascinating game of computing from the eagerness of others the possibilities of vast fortune lying waiting for them, than could King from computing, by the movements of birds and game, the location and distance of the next water hole.

But King's guessing was concluded with each successive evening. Yakoub's was interminable. That mysterious amulet which would tear at one's heart strings—what could that queer thing be? What could so rend a heart because it could not be taken away, but some wonderful jewel? Surely a jewel. Sacred, of course, and its origin wrapped in legend and folk lore. That, too, would be fascinating. Yakoub had a hereditary veneration of ancient tradition.

And about doing the thing that was right—what could the old wizard have meant by that? What mysterious power could an amulet, however ancient, have to make practical men of the modern world—a Jew trader and a Yankee adventurer—do some enigmatic right thing?

Again King was able to elucidate. A little self-consciously he explained—

"That's really one of the biggest compliments I've ever had handed to me; and it's a direct intimation that the old principle of the square deal sometimes pays a dividend."

The Jew's eyebrows made an inquiry; his two hands were busy attending to the rifle that he had learned from King's example to carry himself. King elaborated on the details of his African diplomacy.

"The old witch doctor of Elgon earns his name of wise one. He knows that the square deal as the white man, or as the white man's well meaning government, may see it is not always the way the African sees it. My pull with him is that I've often consulted him about the queer native angle. So he didn't attempt to hold me up on information, but said that he'd lie to any other white man, only he'd tell me because he knew I'd do the right thing for those people; and, putting it that way, don't you see, the wise old bird knew he'd have me tied up under an obligation."

Yakoub nodded. He trudged a long distance, nodding in silence. At last he said, as if musing in understanding, oblivious of King's presence:

"Yes, it is so. We too, we know it. A few governments have from time to time tried to do the square deal for my people; but, alas, it has not been as we have seen it."

Those were exciting days, days—since all things are relative—of good going.

A pale purple haze began to show across the horizon to the northeast. King inspected it at long range with interest. Yakoub was immediately full of excitement; but King only shrugged with exasperating apathy.

"May be only mirage. We'll know more by tonight's camp."

With that night's camp the haze was no nearer. It remained a pale discoloration in the immeasurable distance. King got out his maps and, after a brief survey, announced:

"Yep, that's our mountain of wealth all right; look, there's nothing at all marked on the map, and I see that there's swamp country away to the left of the haze."

This was all quite enigmatic; for the map was truly a blank, marked across a large expanse in thin, wide spaced type. The haze was no more than a smudge of pale color, and as far as the eye could see to the west was nothing but parched brown grass and patches of mimosa scrub. Yakoub's shaggy eyebrows and his shoulders together put the question.

King pointed again, high up to the evening sky.

"Water birds going home to roost; look like ibis or spoonbills. And see, here's the Abyssinian plateau marked all along the East. The thing that isn't marked must be some sort of unexpected outcrop. That'll be the 'unclaimed territory' that so exercises the diplomats up in Adis Abbeba; and there will be our Hidden People. That'll put some extra pep into all our shoe-leather, eh?"

KING GRUNTED with disgust as a tall, nude figure stood suddenly in hard silhouette against the sky over a low rise. He had hoped—almost—to get through to the now visible goal without running into any of these people to whom the old wizard had given the reputation of being evil and war-like.

He knew better than to display any sign of hesitation. Ostentatiously he lighted his pipe.

"There'll be more somewhere," he muttered to Yakoub. "Probably lying down in the grass. This one is only to distract our attention; he's too durned unsuspicious looking without even a spear in hand. Hold your ten men here, Barounggo. I'm going ahead to make *indaba*."

Barounggo, his nostrils wide and twitching, eyes rolling white, head bent forward eagerly, dared to demur.

"They will not run, bwana. It is not fitting that a white lord speak with naked savages through his own mouth."

King nodded and signed to Kaffa to stay back. With the Masai he went forward. The tall, nude figure saw no more than a pitifully small safari of two white men with a couple of ser-

vants and ten porters. Therefore, as King approached, a score
of spearmen sprang from the grass and stood barring the way,
looking quite pleased with themselves over their unintelligent
trick.

All of them were tall and quite naked. Straight limbs and
mops of hair marked them as a tribe distinct from the potbel-
lied and broad nosed Nilotic peoples. More of a Sudanese type,
these. The Sudanese had ever been aggressive and troublesome.
In itself their move was not hostile; but King knew well enough
that natives so unafraid as to stop a white man meant no mere
peaceable conversation.

With no people more than with Africans does "front" carry
so much weight. King spent a deliberate minute looking them
over; then he greeted—

"*Jambo.*"

Barounggo took the word from his mouth and relayed it.

"The *bwana sana* says *jambo* to you naked people."

A hesitant chorus of "*jambo*" came from the group.

"Tell them," said King, "that we desire to pass through this
land."

The Masai relayed, not as asking a favor but as stating a fact.
The men laughed. One of them, distinguished by an ivory ring
above his left elbow, said boldly:

"The men of the village of Nabu of the Orugniro people own
this land. They do not let strangers pass."

So there it was at last. Unfriendly and boldly unequivocal.
King was torn between the two policies of front and the square
deal. His ingrained principle won.

"Tell them I will give a gift for the meat we take in passing
through the land. But we pass."

Barounggo passed on the word in his own way.

"Listen, naked monkeys of the grass. It is I, an Elmoran of
the Masai, who speak. We give a gift, a small gift, to show that
we make no war in passing through your empty land."

Throughout all East Africa the name of the Masai was synonymous with ferocity and slaughter. The Elmorani, the trained
lion slayers, especially, were known as a super-fighting breed.
And Barounggo, as he stood and offered his lordly insult, enormous, threatening, hair garters and ostrich plume flying in the
wind, great spear flashing in the sun, looked fiercely belligerent
enough to give anybody pause. The bold front was not without
its effect. But the Masai was only one, and they twenty. The
Nabu village headman, as he seemed to be, muttered with his
fellows. Then insolently he compromised.

"The strangers' safari may pass. But the gift that we take will
be a proper gift."

King did not like the word take. He nodded to Barounggo
but said nothing. Barounggo flung up his hand as a signal to
the waiting porters and said no word. The headman of Nabu
village of the Orugniro people instantly accepted their silence
for weakness, to which his African response was immediate
belligerence.

"We will take," he enumerated, "for each man a piece of cloth
to divide among his women, and for each man a gourd of salt
and an iron cup to drink *pombe* spirit and five spearheads." And
as King stood marveling at the man's rapacious insolence he
added to the list, "And for each an iron spoon and his own
length in red wire and—"

He hesitated for sheer lack of other things to imagine. What
he had listed was already half a safari load. King put an abrupt
end to his vain hopes by saying:

"So? Then we go through without any gift."

He stepped resolutely forward. The Nabu men yelped rage
at their sudden disillusionment. Barounggo whistled a shrill
siren note through his teeth. The Nabu headman shouted his
fury and flung his arms around King, as being the less dangerous looking of the two, to hold him.

King hesitated not an instant. For all his principle of the
square deal and his acceptance of the white man's burden theory,

he knew that no white man could submit to manhandling by a native and continue to live in Africa. He jerked his right arm free—his left clung to his rifle—and hit his assailant with all the force of a short jolt full in the face.

The man dropped, half stunned. Blood in frightening quantity gushed from his smashed nose. Barounggo shouted his throaty fighting roar and whirled up his spear.

King swung his rifle to cover the rest of the men.

To the black man, trained to the idea of fighting only with weapons, there is always something awe-inspiring about the white man's unarmed fist; the force of a blow that can knock a man down and cover him with blood conveys suggestion of superhuman strength.

The Nabu men bunched together, startled, gaping at the one who howled on the ground. Some lifted their spears. The Masai's great weapon was already poised at ear level, full arm length, quivering, eager to hurl itself forward. They knew spearmen, these people. It was certain that the first man who moved would go down with that terrible blade sticking out a foot through his back.

They hesitated—just long enough.

AT THE Masai's first signal the ten porters had dropped their loads and had quickly unrolled a long bundle of canvas. At his whistle they rushed forward, each man with shield and spear, shouting his best imitation of the Masai *sghee sszee.* Closer, they made an irregular half circle, crouching, dancing in on high-stepping toes, like the Elmorani lion killers. Behind them screamed the Hottentot, hurling abuse, and Yakoub with nervous rifle.

The defenseless little safari had suddenly transformed itself into a war party of armed *askaris.* The Nabu men stood inactive. One by one their raised spears sank. The stricken leader mumbled inarticulate agony through his fingers while blood ran appallingly over his hands.

King slung his rifle over his shoulder and put a match slowly to his pipe.

"So," he said, "we pass. Tell them that the gift we give them is a proper gift. We give them their lives. They do not die. They may take this man who thought he was a warrior and may go to their village, swiftly."

Barounggo planted his spear in the ground and swelled his chest. A speech was necessary to convey this message with the proper measure of obloquy and insult.

Sullenly the Nabu men helped their headman to his feet and withdrew. The last sign of them was a silhouette, as before, of the leader on the skyline, a tall figure who shook his spear and screamed.

Sheer front had won again. The porter-*askaris* strutted and bragged to one another how each one in detail had held his spear, how he had shouted, how ferociously scowled. It had been their first test as fighting men and they were confident and jubilant.

To Barounggo King said:

"It was well done. Their drilling was good. They shall receive, each man, a blanket."

But to Yakoub:

"I don't like that. That spear waving and screaming over the hill isn't healthy. Let's get out of here as fast as we can move; and let's hope their village is far."

Yakoub was full of the exhilaration of victory over what had been a bad and dangerous obstacle. He had a cheering thought to offer.

"At all events, if those other white men—if we have not outwitted our murderous friends—when they come they will find an angry enemy holding the road behind us."

To which King repeated his pessimistic formula:

"I don't know. Van Vliet is nobody's fool. Come along there. Let's go. Trek!"

THE NEXT two days were the hardest going that Yakoub had ever conceived in a bad dream. Or, for that matter, quite the worst that those luckless porters had known. King drove them mercilessly. There were no revivifying little rest periods under the shade of a spreading acacia; no comforting lounges at an easy pace while the bwana stalked meat.

Meals were a meatless menu of parched corn as many times a day as any hurrying individual felt inclined to stuff a handful of it into his mouth.

Travel continued till well into the night, King and Baroung-go deploying ahead, more for the purpose of giving confidence than with any real hope of spotting any crouching beast. *Bomas,* when finally scratched together, remained fireless, men in couples sitting awake with orders to report to King instantly every scuffling, snuffling noise from without—which they did every ten minutes, or each time that an insect stirred.

When Yakoub was exhausted, King, who was tireless steel, and Barounggo, who was cast iron, took him on either side and marched him along, stirred to effort by the cheering fact that the purple haze was changing to a closer blue and the blue to a patchy brown and green.

The porters grumbled, as is the prerogative and inalienable right of African porters. What was the need for all this fearful running away? Were they not fighting men as well as porters? They had chased away the people of this country once; would they not do it again? They could reason no further than that. This haste was without reason, they grumbled to one another. They required a rest; they were men, not cattle. They would rest, they exhorted each other. They would put their packs down and eat a meal. They would go no farther.

But they did none of these things. Kaffa the Hottentot, pattering in their rear, told them grim stories out of his imagination of the things that the Masai had done to other porters who had proven unworthy of their salt; and with infinite craft he added—

"But those were just Shenzi porters, not fighting men."

So the fighting men complained in bitter chorus, but they plodded on.

The patchy brown and green resolved itself into an enormous spur that jutted out from the main mountain wall and fell away in broad, steep terraces to the plain. There were no foothills; no gradual breaking up of the plain into hillocks and gullies that led to steeper hills beyond. Abrupt and solid the mass towered till the haze of its upper blue lost itself in the blue of the sky.

A wide ravine of gray terraces cut a gash into this formidable barrier and disappeared into black shadows high above. To the far right was the haze of the Abyssinian plateau. To the left the level plain that stretched on in the direction where the water birds flew.

"Looks like our road to the promised land all laid out sweet and pretty for us," said King. "Once we get well into that gully I'll feel better. It's a safe rule that plains people won't go into the mountains at night."

So camp was made that night on a broad terrace where a little trickle of water flowed from the rock and was a nectar that could be appreciated only by people who had strained out through a cloth the countless crawling things of turbid water holes that thirsty game herds had never permitted to settle and clear up since the beginning of all time.

The great ravine continued interminably up the mountain flank, alternately easy and difficult going, as one scrambled up the rise of the ragged limestone terraces or walked along the flat. Green bushes began to appear in clumps in gladsome relief from the dusty thorn scrub of the plain. Euphorbia trees and wild figs, of course, meant monkeys.

A cooler air current began to drift down. Ferns clustered in moist places; presently orchids. Brilliant butterflies and startlingly brilliant birds flashed amid the greenery—all the joyous, teeming life of mountain country rising out of a burnt-up tropical plain.

To offset the country that improved so cheerfully with each hour, the going grew frightfully worse with each step. The sides of the ravine began to pinch in—craggy walls of sliding shale. The ascent was laborious—not scrambling any more, but climbing. Each V-shaped gash on the skyline, promising relief from high above, led only to more craggy ridges and other V-shaped gashes.

"How much farther?" Yakoub panted. "Hours, will it be; or perhaps days? Does this lead some day to some place, or does it go on into the heart of a lost forever? If your little ingots did not promise so much in our promised land, I would just as soon die here."

King stopped to wipe the perspiration from his heavy pith hatband. The best that he could offer was:

"The main Abyssinian plateau is eight thousand feet up. This may be a part of it. Still, I'd say it was the road to nowhere, and I'd quit, except that the witch doctor told us. And look there! Evidently it was the road to someplace once upon a time."

Kaffa was behaving in a surprising manner. Like an inquisitive monkey he had been scrambling in the lead, poking into every hole and corner, turning over stones to flush shiny brown lizards, after which he darted with simian agility. These, split open and broiled on little sticks, were as great a delicacy to the Hottentot as are snails to a Frenchman.

Suddenly that impudent, godless little ape had thrown himself flat upon his face, knees doubled under him, head in the moist dirt, beating the ground with his hands and chattering a monosyllabic stream of prayer.

ALL THAT could be seen to occasion this performance was a mound of stones in the middle of the gully floor; an ancient cairn, moss grown and water worn, but distinguishable and obviously the work of human hands. King grinned.

"That's the only thing the little devil is afraid of. Heitsi Eibib, the Hottentot god of good luck and fertility and half a dozen other things, fought around and died a whole lot and was re-

incarnated again; and he is buried all over the landscape in inaccessible ravines under rock piles."

Yakoub nodded understandingly out of his knowledge of ancient things.

"Yes, yes, a very common belief. In Palestine in the hills overhanging Acre are such cairns. There is argument as to whether the Jews brought some heathen superstitions about the death of the Babylonian Baal out of the captivity or whether they are more recent."

The Hottentot assumed an incongruous command of the party. Very carefully he piloted the porters round the ancient cairn so that no profane foot should defile a single stone. When every man had passed safely he chose a smooth boulder and, crawling on his stomach, pushed it on to the pile.

"O Heitsi Eibib," he muttered, "give us fortune and plenty of cattle."

Barounggo, standing by in enormous solemnity, could understand that prayer; for the Masai, a herd-owning people, live, in curious anomaly to their bloodthirsty character, almost exclusively on dairy products.

He leaned over and with precise care spat upon the stone. At which the Hottentot, instead of becoming infuriated, clucked approval. He knew that such was the Masai equivalent of calling down the blessing of the high spirits.

After that he was full of enthusiasm and a strong confidence for anything that might come. When the road grew worse he scrambled ahead, calling loud encouragement to the porters, promising them all manner of good things—meat in plenty and corn, and milk to steep their corn and honey to sweeten it.

"Is that an omen?" Yakoub asked with less than his usual cynicism. "The promised land flowing with milk and honey?"

And King, engrossed, swearing, in keeping his rifle sights from getting bumped, opined as he clung to a root with one hand and swung his leg up to a ledge—

"If it's true that all good things are hard to get, this country will sure have to be good."

The climb became worse. Sheer cliff with a thin waterfall tumbling down the center barred the way. But Kaffa, climbing like a baboon, found a foothold to ledges yet higher. The rest scrambled up with the help of a rope. The packs were hauled up.

Enormous ferns made wet screens across the way so that it was impossible to know where the gorge twisted; and one fought through a wall of matted greenery to find one's face close up against a wall of slick, lichen-grown sandstone.

The steep sides began to open out, to slope away, giving promise of ending, only to break up into other dark gorges that crawled tortuously up and forever up.

A single compensation was the climate. The dead, dry heat of the plain was left far below. A warm, wet wind filtered down the slope. Honest green foliage was there. Things lived.

CAMP WAS made high on the side of a cliff like a swallow's nest. And for that the compensation was no *boma* and no lions. King ordered the Hottentot:

"Open up pack No. 6. The wind of the night blows chill. Let each man receive the blanket that was promised."

Which comfort, artfully given at just the right time, was one that only naked men could properly appreciate.

The next steep, V-shaped gash in the far sky was really the

last. Toiling through its boulder heaped bottom, they came suddenly through the last forest edge and there was no farther ridge.

The climbers saw before them a short half mile of treeless, wind blown, grassy slope. The last ridge through which they had come towered on to a jagged lipped crater from which, as if drawn with a pencil, a straight black wall of old lava cut across the green plain. Through the wall was a space where some last convulsion had obligingly split a gap; and beyond it nothing except white cloud against blue sky. This was over the top.

"Whew!" King mopped his brow and stood to survey the scene. "Looks like we've arrived. And—" his nose wrinkled to the cool wind and sniffed luxuriously; he nodded this way and that—"this is good country. Look, there's goats, and there's fat tail sheep. There'll be a village through that split in the wall. I'll admit to the world these people are sure hidden. Let's go."

As they crossed the grass land a small white figure detached itself from a grazing herd and ran swiftly through the gap in the lava wall. King snapped his glasses up to cover the runner.

"Hm, clothed in pants and a shawl. Something like the Abyssinian costume. These are no savages. Wonder whether they keep hidden behind the point of a spear? Keep going; I'd just as soon meet them in that defile as out in the open. There's a lot of diplomacy behind a solid front and no way to wiggle around."

But no resistance met them in the narrow passage. Like a rough hewn coal mine cut it diagonaled through the black lava. A fall of immense blocks at the end obstructed the view. King was cautious about turning into that narrow outlet. It was just the place for a spear or a club to be waiting.

But no weapon was there. King poked his head around the corner. All that met him was a magnificent, breathtaking scene.

A wide green valley opened up before him and sloped away to lose itself in a velvet haze. A silver ribbon crept down its middle. Other little ribbons joined it from the hills on either hand. A jumble of round brown roofs straggled across the fore-ground. Terraced fields, square bordered by irrigation ditches, showed yellow under corn, rufous under grass, speckled white under cotton.

A prosperous scene of peace and plenty. But King stretched his long arm and pointed out to Yakoub, not the huts or the fields or the scattered flocks, but a dirty smudge that marred the far distant landscape.

"The slope is too gentle for a landslide there," he whispered.

"And so what?" Yakoub caught at his arm.

"Diggings." King uttered the magic word.

A group of white clad figures was coming from the collection of huts. A deputation they seemed to be, for no sun flashed from spear points.

"Looks like peace all right," said King. "It's a sure rule. In good country you find good people, until somebody comes along and spoils them. Let's go on down."

The group of men, upon closer approach, were seen to be tall with dark, intelligent faces and keen black eyes; more Abyssin-ian in color and feature than African. And they greeted in Amharic:

"*Thena-yisth-al-enye*—may He give you health on my account."

Both King and Yakoub knew enough of that terribly involved language to understand and to know at the same time that these men spoke with a throatily aspirated accent. King, with ap-prehension, asked at once if they were Abyssinians; for a law of that country is that all minerals belong to the imperial gov-ernment and may be mined only under jealously granted con-cessions that very often cost more to procure than ever comes out of the claim.

They lifted a leaden load from his mind by telling him that while they spoke a patois of Amharic, they were strangers. And that load was a gossamer thread compared with the weight that lifted itself as King and Yakoub simultaneously nudged each other and pointed with their eyes to circular disks of red-yellow metal engraved with crude characters that each man wore suspended by a string at his throat.

The deputation with grave courtesy invited King and his safari to accept the hospitality of their village.

They had never seen white men; but they had heard rumors of them now and then from bold young men who went over the difficult mountain trails to trade with Abyssinia. White men, the rumor ran, were very wise and had all sorts of new and wonderful knowledge. Would the white visitors be their guests?

King looked at Yakoub, and Yakoub looked at King. This was beginning to be a fairy story; it was too good to be true. Courtesy and kindliness like this in Africa? Verily a promised land after their labors.

AS THEY walked on down the rich valley both men had the same horrid thought, and it burst from both of them simultaneously. A hideous thought that was quite unthinkable. Imagine these people in the hands of that Van Vliet gang with their gin-trading tactics! It was such traders who had ruined all of Africa.

In the village they were shown into a round hut with a thatched roof. Young men brought water in earthen bowls and—miracle—soft cotton cloths for towels. Presently a meal would be ready for them and the father of the village would eat with them and would learn knowledge from the white men.

That, said King, speaking for his group, would suit them exactly. They wanted to see the chief, or the king or whoever might have the say-so about things, and they hoped then to come to some agreement about a trade.

But they had no chiefs, these people; no king. The head of the family with its dependents was the headman of his village and also its priest; and the headmen all gathered in council from time to time under the headman of the big village fifteen miles down the valley.

Yakoub nodded in perfect agreement and understanding. Here was the pure patriarchal system perfectly adapted to an isolated people who had developed the arts of peace in their favorable environment rather than the arts of war. Truly these were an exceptional people to find hidden in almost the last lone little strip of Africa that hadn't been gobbled up by contending European powers. It would be a pity if they should fall in with the rest of Africa.

Suddenly Yakoub grabbed King by the arm. Enlightenment had burst upon him.

"I know what he meant. I see it now. The Wizard—it was a pity that we knew about them—these people hidden from what the conqueror races call the benefits of civilization."

King nodded agreement. He knew that section of history as well as Yakoub. There was a routine schedule—first missionaries and hymn books, then traders and gin, a fight, then soldiers and guns; and presently another section of the map was colored the same as the nearest adjacent section. True, it would be a pity. Still, how was a country to be exploited without the influx of white man's methods, his machinery, his capital, his brains?

The discussion was still going on when a young man came to say that the meal was ready. With quickening interest they followed him. The attitude of the patriarch would indicate much as to what sort of trade arrangement might be made about whatever it was that came out of those diggings. The young man led the way to a hut that was quite a building, though composed of the same materials as all the rest—a large, round, thatched structure of adobe surrounded by a court paved with flat stones which in turn was surrounded by a circular adobe wall.

They were about to turn into the open gateway when the young man, with a suddenly shocked expression, told them that that was the *Xjehaver-beth*, the tribal prayer house. The patriarch's modest house was next to it and was no different from all the others.

The patriarch himself was a venerable old man, white bearded like a high priest of some ancient cult. He greeted his guests with grave dignity at his door and conducted them without any preliminary conversation through a short passage into the dim interior of his house. This room, like the outside, was circular and up through its center ran the single supporting pole of the whole roof structure. Doorways hung with white cotton cloth led into a series of cubicles between this inner and the outer wall.

Along an arc of the room wall was a built-in bench; before it, a curved plank table at which the members of the family already stood at their places—stalwart sons only, no women.

Both the guests realized that this meal was something in the nature of a ceremony; some sort of initiation before acceptance on a friendly basis. Silently they sat at the places given to them. Immediately two youths entered, one carrying a bowl of water, the other a towel.

The old man ceremoniously dipped his fingers, wiped them and muttered something in his beard. The youths came to Yakoub, who sat next. Abstractedly he went through the self-same rite—dipped, wiped and muttered in his beard as of long familiarity.

Suddenly his eyes dilated. He looked round wildly, as if coming out of a dream. Then he gave a loud cry.

"But this is orthodox of my own people. The washing of hands. These people are—" He turned to the old man—"you are Falasha, the Strangers, of course. Why did I not guess it at once? '*Xjehaver-beth*', the house of Jehovah. You are Jews!"

The old man smiled benignly and shook his head.

"Falasha we are, but we are alone. We have no people. A few of us there are in Abyssinia. From them we have also heard this rumor that there are more of our people in far countries. But that can not be. We are alone."

"But no. But listen! This is a miracle. Let me prove to you—

how can I begin? Look, I know your rites and your ceremonies.
I will tell you them all. I—"

The old man bowed to the torrent of excited speech. But he
had to interrupt.

"First, you must break bread in my house. Afterward we can
talk."

That was another rite; and Yakoub knew the ceremony of
that one, too. Then his waves of words loosed themselves upon
the wondering patriarch.

KING LEFT them talking about things that he did not
understand and went outside to weigh this new angle in his
mind. He knew the story of the Abyssinian Falasha—one of
the most stupendous and incredible dramas of all the world's
nations. How a Hebrew scholar traveling in Abyssinia only a
few years ago had suddenly came upon these "Strangers".

A few scattered groups of them, living among the Abyssinians, speaking their language, burnt by generations of sun and
exposure to their color; but remaining rigidly exclusive units
among themselves. Their ancient language was lost; only a few
distorted words remained. They knew nothing about themselves,
whence they had come or how; only that until the accession of
the new emperor of the land they had been persecuted for the
faith that they clung to with iron tenacity. Before that, a blank.
But—this was the miracle—they had retained practically intact
the forms and ceremonies of the religion they had brought with
them, nobody could guess how many thousand years ago. And
when the scholar told them the news of coreligionists all over
the world they refused to believe the wonder.

Lack of communication in Abyssinia, absence of roads and
appallingly difficult travel had delayed any serious investigation
of them. The scholar had immediately dedicated his life to them
and was engaged in collecting funds for their amelioration. And
now here was this new outlying group, more isolated than any.
The Hidden People.

King had heard theories. One savant traced in an ancient

record hewn in stone that at the time of the captivity in Egypt a large band of Hebrews had escaped and fled up the Nile and eastward; the reigning Pharaoh had sent soldiers after them, none of whom ever came back. Another professor claimed that the caravans of Solomon came to Ethiopia to seek gold and took back the vast riches that went to the building of the great temple.

Ever since those ancient days the story of gold in Ethiopia had persisted. And that brought King right down to the immediate present. Gold there was in Abyssinia, plenty of it. The hereditary prince of the Beni Shangul district in those western mountains paid a colossal tribute in links of beaten gold. If there was gold in these lost hills, what would be the attitude of these hidden people toward its exploitation?

And the more King thought about that and about all the ramifications of the matter—his partner Yakoub included—the less he liked it. His thin smile puckered his eyes as he looked out across the prosperous, peaceful valley. Exploitation—a gold strike. What would those things mean? King fell to whistling his long, mournful discords. Then he shrugged his misgivings from his big shoulders and lighted his pipe.

When King wanted to know more about the diggings down the hillside, they were evasive. When he asked about the engraved disks that they all wore at their necks, they did not understand.

"The root of all evil," King murmured to himself. "And they don't want it to attract any evil here. I wonder, I wonder. What did the old wizard of Elgon mean about doing the thing that is right?"

IT WAS not until evening that Yakoub came away from his conference with the patriarch, and at its conclusion they were both changed men. In the patriarch the change was easy to see and to tabulate. He went about as a man in a daze. Unbelievable things had been proven to him. A miracle in the shape of an untidy man had come from the almost legendary outside world and had blasted the traditions of generations. He was numb, he did not know yet whether from access of joy or from apprehension.

With Yakoub the emotion was not so easy to analyze. He was extraordinarily elated, at the same time vaguely troubled; full of zeal for what might be done with these people, and in the next moment apathetically hopeless against impending disaster. He himself did not know just what was in his mind.

The only definite information he had was that they were to go down the valley the next morning to the big village to be presented to the chief patriarch, the keeper of the amulet, who was learned in the ancient traditions and could adequately discuss these new wonders.

"Were you able to get anything out of the old man about the diggings?" asked King. "They froze up on me like clams when I tried them."

But that was a question that Yakoub had found no opportunity to intrude into the whole afternoon of discussion.

The little journey down the valley was a delightful Springtime hike in the country after the recent toil and sweat and eternal vigilance of safari. Here everything was so peaceful and secure that Barounggo and the porters were left behind to rest and feast after their labors. Only the little Hottentot trotted behind his master and chattered his comments upon the good country through which they passed.

And good country it was. The same rich soil as in the main Abyssinian plateau, the same all-year-round climate; so that crops grew and ripened, not according to season but according to time of planting and irrigation. Here the ripened grain and the new green shoots could be seen alongside of each other in adjacent fields.

In a circumscribed area round each of the little villages men plowed with a crude contraption of sticks shod with iron, or harvested grain with sickles; women spun cotton yarn on whirling bobbins or click-clacked at hand looms. Everywhere the

natives dropped their work and came to look at the white men
who had superior knowledge about these things.

"*Aie, aie.*" Yakoub sighed. "What these people need is development. A little leading by the hand and showing how; a better
plow, a finer loom, a more efficient kiln. They have the material and the mind; all they need is teaching."

"Yep," agreed King. "A little agricultural and mining machinery would make quite a place out of this valley."

"Yes. But, my dear Kingi—" Yakoub threw out protesting
hands—"in time, of course, in time. They must advance slowly
and with care. You would not want to see a sudden commercial
development spring up among these people. You would not
want, for instance—" and here the fear that had been gnawing
at him came out and he groaned at the prospect—"if, for instance, those three ruffians should have followed us! You always
said how clever is that man. If they should come and discover
that there is gold—good God of my fathers forbid it!"

King nodded darkly. Such a contingency would indeed be a
dire catastrophe to this fair valley. But still, he thought to
himself, if gold existed in anything like the quantity that they—
to say nothing of the big business concerns which were on the
trail—had hoped, how was it to be developed without machinery, without capital?

T H E B I G village came as a startling climax to the beautiful, hidden valley. The slope eased gently down to the surrounding terraced fields of green and russet and gold, to the irrigation
dikes that glittered in the sun, to the brown clustered huts.

There was the immediate prosperous, busy foreground; and
beyond it the world vanished. The silver ribbon of river reached
the same place and there it, too, silently disappeared. It was a
beautiful painted landscape; but the artist had suddenly died
and had done no more than smudge in the neutral blue-gray
background.

Their guide who had conducted them down the valley turned
King and Yakoub over to a graybeard who greeted Yakoub with

deference. It was astonishing how instinctively these people had accepted Yakoub in their minds as the leader of the expedition. The old man told him that the high patriarch had summoned the patriarchs of the other villages to a council which would confer far into the night over the astounding things they had heard and that in the morning the assembled sages would see the doctor of knowledge who had brought this great news and would discuss these important things further. In the meanwhile he was at their service.

"I want to go and see that," said King, pointing to the blank cessation of the landscape.

And it was just that. The whole valley fell away over an abrupt cliff. Far down, hundreds of sheer feet down, the treetops of a wide terrace looked like small green umbrellas. Beyond the terrace was another enormous leap into nothing. The flanking hills of the valley suddenly resolved themselves over this edge into mountains that tumbled away in a confusion of precipices, down and away to an indistinct aero map of brown plain.

The little river that passed quietly through the middle of the village took one immense, smooth, emerald leap over the edge, churned itself in midair into a splendid white plume, plunged through the green umbrella tops and disappeared. The lip of the next terrace was a waterless black wall.

"It goes into a hole in the ground," explained the old man.

"Ah," breathed King. "That's the river I prospected up 'way down there in that hellish plain; the subterranean one."

As if to substantiate the fact, a man came running to King. His impetuous approach was in marked contrast to the grave, shy advance of the rest of these people. He embraced King's knees and, taking his hand in both his own, placed it upon his head. King looked at him sharply.

"Oho, so there *is* a way up somewhere," he deduced. "And this is the rogue I couldn't scare into betraying it. Good lad. Is it well with you, wanderer? And have you any more of those little ingots?"

And that brought up the paramount question once more. King turned to Yakoub.

"Here, you've become the boss of the outfit; it's you who's the little tin godling. Ask about those diggings. Maybe they'll tell you something."

But the old man replied to that query with a staggering readiness that implied truth:

"Those diggings? Yes that is where we get a red earth that we melt with charcoal and it becomes iron for our plows and tools."

And to that story he clung. King would have pressed him for information about other workings. But Yakoub demurred irritably:

"What is the need of such an anxiety, my dear Kingi? Tomorrow after the conference, perhaps. *Aie, aie,* who knows? Who can tell what is the right thing?"

There was another weighty conference of doctrinarians. King was left out of it. These were matters beyond his ken. He was left to wander about at his own devices. Everywhere everybody was friendly and courteous. Whenever he stopped to watch some little activity or household chore he was asked in; he was offered milk and a cool drink made of honey and water flavored with a pungent herb.

And they asked questions—interminable questions. They wanted to know things. How did the white men do this? How did they make that? What was their custom of performing something else? Had they come to teach them their wisdom from far lands?

King nodded reflectively, very soberly.

"All chips off the same old block," he ruminated. "Always want to learn something." He had met Falashas in Abyssinia. They were all the same. Knowledge was their thirst and their hunger.

A messenger came running. The other white man, the learned doctor, was out from the conference and summoned him.

"They're going to show us the amulet," Yakoub grunted.

He stood with shoulders humped up to his ears, arms hanging listlessly, eyes dully apathetic—a picture of extraordinary dejection rather than of the keyed-up excitement that might have been expected from so portentous a disclosure.

The chief patriarch, who stood with him, a benign old gentleman bearded up to his eyes and with his hair an unkempt replica of Yakoub's, only snowy white, scrutinized King with shrewd appraisal. He shrugged in acceptance of a course contrary to his judgment.

"Since you insist," he addressed Yakoub, "that you may do nothing without his sharing in it, and since you are a brother in our faith and stand surety for him, he may see this thing that has been hidden since the beginning of our people. Come, then, to the House of the Amulet."

THE HOUSE was a shock to King. He had been picturing a temple at the least—the most elaborate building that the community could produce, surrounded with pomp and ceremony, decorated with the best of the arts and crafts that the people had to offer and jealously guarded by a vested priesthood.

But the House of the Amulet turned out to be a windowless, round stone hut with thatched roof, very much like the rest of the domiciles. Its most outstanding difference was that it stood at the little river's brim closer to the lip of the precipice than any other. The high patriarch produced an enormous iron key from under his white robe and calmly prepared to unlock a not too sturdy door.

"Hm, pretty darn casual about their sacred amulet, aren't they?" King grunted.

The old man seemed to understand the sense rather than the words. He smiled in benevolent enjoyment of a surprise.

"Not sacred—only secret," he said, and pushed open the door.

And the surprise was a crushing disappointment. King had formed no idea of what this amulet might be. A symbolic figure perhaps, he had thought; some ancient thing of mystic design enshrouded in a golden casket. Or an idol of some sort. He had vaguely speculated before he had seen these people; but he knew now, of course, that they had no idols.

The only light came through the single door. King could see that the floor of the hut was paved with irregular stones and that—at the door at least—they had been worn smooth by the treading of countless bare feet. In the center of the hut, upon the bare stone floor, was a massive raised dais, also circular; a sort of altar it might have been, for the top was roughly flat.

But it was empty. Nothing stood upon the altar. No image, no object of veneration. Alone it stood there, solid, ponderous, uninspiring. And the hut, too, was empty; the walls cold, bare stone, devoid of the least attempt at decoration—no niches, no shrine, nothing. It began to come to King that this altar must be it; this thick circular mass must, for some curious reason, be the ancient amulet. And, yes, those fat round disks of gold that all the men wore at their necks were clearly replicas of this great lump of something; and the lump showed here and there faint traces of worn, square cut characters.

King's eyes were becoming accustomed to the interior dimness. He could see that light glinted off innumerable bright surfaces with sharp edges, apparently hacked out indiscriminately with a chisel. The thing seemed to be composed of a metal of some kind. There was no attempt at design.

Suddenly King cried out and leaped forward, then checked his leap in sudden awe.

"Almighty Pete!" His voice was hoarse.

The light glinted yellow from those sharp chisel cuts, the same as it did from those replica disks. Slowly King approached and ran his thumb along some of the shiny grooves. It was not possible—that whole solid mass. But there it stood, ponderous, huge, winking malignantly from its many facets.

Yakoub suddenly whooped, too, and plunged forward with a great cry. But his emotion was vastly different.

"Those marks—the characters! I can read them. God of my fathers, they are Hebrew!"

Crying, muttering, he pushed King fiercely to one side out of the light and knelt over the worn surface, peering, feeling with his fingers.

But the ancient surface had been cruelly hacked over. With vandal carelessness great slivers of the metal had been gouged out. A letter here and there was intact; fragments of others. Hebrew they were. Yakoub knew them. But any inscription that might have been had long ago been chiseled away.

The ancient patriarch stood by, stroking his long beard and smiling with benign understanding.

"A great weight of evil lies there, my brother, is it not so? Grief and sin and warfare, if men but knew."

"You don't know how this thing ever got here, I suppose?" asked King.

The old man shook his head.

"It has always been here. Our people have no knowledge of its coming. This is our secret. The Amulet of our good fortune, if we use it wisely. From time to time, when we have need, we cut pieces from it and melt it into small ingots, and our young men take these to trade over the mountains.

"Phe-ew!" King whistled through his teeth. "There must be a couple of tons of it. What a miracle—what a story! Hebrew characters. Maybe Solomon's ancient miners. Maybe—who knows? And they've chiseled it away for fifty dollars' worth of trade a year. How many hundreds of years? Gosh! Yakoub, old man, I take it all back. Africa is full of secrets that only a wild romanticist would ever believe. What a piece of loot—if any one could ever get it away."

"But you can't, my dear Kingi." Yakoub was clawing at his sleeve and croaking in an agony of apprehension. "We can not exploit this thing. Kingi, old friend, listen to me."

WITH THIN slits of eyes and a twisted smile King harked back to the beginning of this quest.

"Wise old Wizard. He had the right dope. 'And the magic of that amulet is that whosoever shall see it, it shall tear his heart asunder that he can not take it away with him.' He was right. It would need an expedition and an army."

Again the old patriarch seemed to sense his meaning.

"Look," he said, "how wise were these ancient people who fashioned this thing. As long as it is secret it is an amulet of fortune. As soon as the secret might be noised abroad it would become an amulet of evil and death and war."

That thought gripped Yakoub with a sudden terror. He moaned:

"He is right. How terribly right, conceive of a trader safari getting into this valley."

"And look again," the patriarch continued with religious fervor, "how wise were those ancient ones. If an enemy should come with force to bring evil upon us for the sake of this thing, my young men with strong bars would roll this evil to the edge—but a little distance—where the water goes down into the belly of the earth; and so would the evil be removed from the face of the earth and returned to the earth whence it came."

"Golly!" King was aghast at the prospect. "What a crazy idea! What a colossal crime. Or—" he was darkly reflective—"would it, after all, be a crime *for these people?*"

That was a question that was going to be put to the test with a suddenness as starkly dramatic as the issue itself.

In the open air once more, King remained moodily, almost morosely, thoughtful. He sent long, coldly appraising glances up and down the flanking hills, and nodded affirmatively to his own thoughts. He told Yakoub:

"It's a likely enough place. Any of those rocky ridges might show a surface vein a foot wide. But it would take machinery." He harked back to a picture of ancient activity. "Those old-timers, whoever they were, must have cracked out the ore with fire and wedges and broken it up with hammers by hand and just washed out as much as they could pick up with their fin-gernails. No mercury, no cyanide; they had nothing except patience. What a job it must have been to make that great lump.

And what for?" He turned to his fascinating estimate again. "A little mill, a four-stamp mill, could be dragged in somewhere, somehow—and there's water power."

But Yakoub clutched his arm again with an access of horror.

"But Kingi, my dear Kingi, a mill—you couldn't bring such a thing upon these people." An almost religious anguish worked in his face. "Machinery, people, outsiders, a gold rush. Old friend, you can't do such a thing."

King's face was very hard as he visualized that picture. It was a long and a dark vision. He muttered scraps of words to himself.

"Wise old wizard. We'd see that amulet and we'd do the right thing, eh? Yakoub, you're a weak bellied and sentimental— Hey, look there. There's a commotion about something."

Voices were calling excitedly to one another. There was a running and a scurrying.

People huddled in groups. A woman's voice broke high in a thin wail. A man ran to them and almost dragged them to the house of the patriarch. A young man with his white robe tied about his loins was panting out news that appalled the old man. King's face immediately set hard with apprehension. He recognized the young man as a runner from the village at the upper end of the valley.

"Tell it over again," he ordered, "quick, and miss nothing."

The young man gasped out dire news with telegraphic brevity.

The great black man had sent him, he said, and had promised him death if he delayed. The great black man had been uneasy because of a trouble they had had with a naked people on the plain and he had posted a lookout on a high place to watch the road. And now an army of the naked people was coming up the mountain.

All thought of golden amulets and speculations as to their evil potency vanished.

"How far?" King snapped the important question at the runner.

They were yet very far, and the way was, as the white men

knew, very difficult. The great black man was going terribly about preparing to give them war and was driving the young men of the village to hunt up their unaccustomed weapons.

The patriarch stretched tremulous hands out to King. It was noticeable how in his mind the leadership of things in this crisis had reverted to King. The patriarch spoke hesitantly, as one who had not gathered his wits from the disrupting shock of an unprecedented event.

"But what is to be done? It has never happened before. We have known those people from afar; there has never been any trouble. We have nothing that those naked people can use; nor have they anything that we require. Thus has there been no cause for war."

The old man unwittingly spoke a great basic truth about the bedrock cause of all wars. He did not blame the white men as being instrumental in attracting this catastrophe. He only wondered helplessly what cause should now have arisen.

Yakoub yammered at King's side.

"*Aie,* that this should now come! Kingi, we must—you must prevent this thing. This secret must be kept. It would mean ruin. Go, my friend. Go quickly. I will come as fast as I can. Do this thing for me."

King's face was all hard angles.

"I will," he grunted savagely. "I've owed you this secret for two years. I'll keep it tight for you against those bandits." To the patriarch he said, "Gather your young men, as many as you have, with whatever weapons they have. Send them as swiftly as may be. I'll keep your valley inviolate somehow."

"Alas," the old man wailed, "our tools have always been better than our weapons, and so we have been prosperous." And there he spoke another great truth.

King turned impatiently from him to Yakoub.

"Bring the reenforcements as soon as you can get any sort of weapons into their hands." He took in a hole in his belt. "I'm going to be up there in four hours or bust."

To the patriarch again:

"Old man, quit wailing and give me a herald or an officer, a deacon—somebody with authority to collect up the young men from the villages as I go. Let him run after me. I can't wait."

FOUR HOURS to traverse fifteen miles would seem to be a lot of time for a strong man. But fifteen miles over rough country, and uphill, is different from marathon running. And then there were those villages to be stirred up.

The little Hottentot trotted tirelessly behind, his keen mind busy with just one thing. Those naked people—was it reasonable that they should make a very troublesome war on account of a broken nose? Did they suddenly decide that the white men's little safari was worth looting? Or had they heard about gold? And if so, what use would they have for it and why had they never tried for it all these many years? None of these questions could be fitted with an answer.

"Something more is behind this, bwana," he insisted. "Some new thing drives them. A magic gives them courage, for, as we know, they are not over-brave."

King only muttered:

"Hanged if I know. Anything can happen in Africa."

And he hurried on. His heart, which had been in his mouth as he drew nearer to the head of the valley, expecting to hear howls and yells and all the uproar of a savage battle, began to subside when he was able to discern the wall of black lava in the distance and the village below it not yet in flames. A decrepit ancient told him that the Great Black One was beyond at the head of the mountain pass, having threatened, bullied, and in some cases beaten, every man who was capable of carrying even a stick; and he had taken all of them with him. King hurried on, sick at heart.

The Masai met him in exactly the opposite frame of mind. His eyes showed rims of white round his dancing black pupils; he breathed enormously through wide nostrils; a corner of his lip fluttered at nervous intervals to show a flash of strong eye-teeth. He greeted King boisterously:

"*Hau, bwana.* That was a swift journey. And indeed I promised death to that runner, did he dawdle. Look, bwana, thus shall the battle go."

King stopped his eagerness.

"So snorts the buffalo. Tell me first swiftly how many are they and where?"

The Masai strode ahead to show. A couple of miles down the lower gorges a glimpse could be caught now and then of a naked figure scrambling over some bare spot. King watched them with moody intensity. The Hottentot was right. So troublesome a foray, requiring a vindictive persistence so foreign to African character, needed to be explained by something very much more compelling than a smashed nose.

"I have had a man counting all day," Barounggo told him. "A hundred men they must be. *Wah,* it will be a good fight." He was eager to disclose his plan of battle. King knew that the great fierce fellow was steeped in experience; he was willing to listen.

"Thus shall the fight go, bwana. Here where the gorge is narrow and the sides steep I have gathered great stones high up. See, I have posted the men of this village on the flanks in hiding. They are willing, but of weapons they know nothing. When the word is given the stones shall roll and crush those naked ones. Those that break through, I and my ten shall charge upon with shield and spear and shall slaughter them."

King considered the matter frowningly. The great Masai had chosen about the only plan that held out any hope of success. Still, the odds were frightful.

"And what," he asked, "if, let us say, as many as fifty break through?"

"That, too, is foreseen, bwana." The Masai was ingeniously pleased at his own generalship. "The men of this village, having rolled their stones, the half of them shall run swiftly to stand at our backs. If we prevail and drive these naked ones back, the remaining half shall roll more stones. If they prevail and we ten should fall, then—" the strategist paused with the instinctive dramatic sense of his people before he disclosed the single flaw in his strategy.

With meticulous care he fished a tiny horn from somewhere about his waistline; he drew a plug from its end and tapped out a pinch of snuff on to his spear blade; he sniffed it with keen appreciation and then continued:

"If we should fall, bwana, then the affair will be the affair of these people to settle. For us it will have been a good fight."

"Hm." King grunted his only comment to the plan with but a single flaw and went on down the ravine a little way to inspect the possibilities.

The situation was desperate enough, and the issue would depend entirely upon just one thing—how well the invaders would stand up under the combined effect of surprise and organized resistance. If well led—or well driven—their numerical superiority in spearmen was going to be a frightful advantage.

RETURNING FROM his inspection, King regarded the darkening sky with an anxiety that slowly lifted.

"They can't all of them reach this gorge before dark, and they won't fight at night. That will give us a chance for reenforcements, such as they are."

He made one alteration in the Masai's crudely ferocious plan. This heroic shield and spear stuff. He remembered that some great general, speaking of a similar berserk charge, had said, "It is magnificent; but it is not war." He ordered, therefore:

"Let men build here a barricade of stones in this narrow place; and immediately on either hand let a second relay of boulder rollers stand in readiness."

There followed a night of waiting as miserable as any King had ever known. Voices sounded far down the lower ravine—shouts and calls; fires winked derisive eyes. King kept anxiously awake, assuring himself that no stealthy attack was being planned. Barounggo, with grim gusto, held a strip of hide between teeth and big toe and stropped incessantly at his great spear blade. His ten porters—red eyed fighting men now—took example from him and followed suit. King made an opportunity to ask the Masai what he thought of their courage for the coming fight. Would they stand?

The big man laughed easily. "Nay, bwana, did not the Wizard of Elgon make a magic for them, the great magic of the lion's teeth, that they might be brave? How can they then fail?"

Shortly before dawn Yakoub arrived. With him were something less than a hundred men from the lower villages, determined enough in demeanor, but woefully armed with a miscellaneous collection of agricultural tools. The best weapon was a heavy sort of cane knife. A few fish spears were there too, serviceable but hardly strong enough for war.

King marshaled the knifemen in a solid body to support Barounggo's *askaris* behind the barrier. The fish-spearmen he sent up the steep ravine sides to help the stone rollers. And then the patriarchs drove him to frenzy by calling their people to them en masse to spend the remaining hours in loud prayer and exhortation.

Almost with the first daylight a watcher on the ravine side called—

"One comes!"

King and Barounggo shouted, ordered, pushed the men into the positions that had been assigned to them. King put Yakoub in charge on one flank of the ravine.

"Your job will be to see that none of your gang shows himself before I whistle the order to roll. Surprise is our advantage. And you'll act as a sharpshooter wherever you see need."

Barounggo had gone a little way down the ravine to see what might be seen of the advantage. He called now:

"Only one comes. He bears the crossed sticks of a herald."

King immediately climbed over the stone barricade and

ordered a whole mob of his heterogeneous force to follow him
and to stand massed in front of it as a screen. He beckoned to
Yakoub and to the bearded elders to go forward with him to
meet this herald.

"I guess they have a right to listen in," he muttered, "since
it's on their ground."

The herald swaggered up the last slope of the ravine. A tall,
burly fellow he was, as big as Barounggo, but with this difference: While the Masai was decked out in all his savage glory
of garters at elbow and knee, leopardskin kilt with tail flying
behind, black ostrich plume nodding above his head, this man
was naked for war.

He came with a curious rolling gait, brave enough in the face
of he knew not what. He strode up to the little group and guffawed in their faces. His eyes, rolling, bloodshot, traveled to the
huddled mob in front of the barricade, and he guffawed enormously again.

King was glad enough to note his apparent scorn of the
defensive force—so much greater would be the surprise.

But Barounggo took the scorn ill.

"Cease thy yawning, baboon," he growled ominously, "and
speak thy message."

THE MAN stared at him with an exaggerated insolence.
Then he tossed his head and mouthed his message. Magnificent
physical specimen as he was, he seemed to have an impediment
in his speech.

"My message is this," he mumbled, "and it is well that the
ancient ones of the Hidden People hear."

And from that he rambled on into a grandiloquent and rather
incoherent speech full of repetitions and vain boastings. So long
was it and pointless at times that King wondered whether the
whole thing were not a clever subterfuge to gain time. Only
the man did not look to be that clever.

The gist of the long palaver was that the people of the Nabu
villages of the Orugniro had a quarrel with the white men.

Blood had been shed; only a little, it was true, but a little was enough. Now, therefore, let the Hidden People deliver up the white men and their servants and their goods to the men of Nabu; and there would be peace between the Hidden People and the men of Nabu and the friends and allies of the men of Nabu.

It was to the everlasting credit of the elders that they showed no hesitation. They flung up their hands and lifted their shoulders to their ears and told each other, rather than the insolent herald, that the thing was quite impossible; the white men had eaten their bread and were moreover—or the one of them at least—their brothers.

The Masai could never brook insolence from any of the many peoples whom he considered his inferiors. He looked hungrily at King. King nodded shortly. Barounggo took a single great stride forward and flashed his spear before the eyes of the herald. His voice rumbled from deep in his belly:

"The answer of the white lords to the naked grass apes of Nabu is this blade. Observe it well, fellow. It is the word of an Elmoran of the Masai that within this day's sun it strews thy bowels in the dust as a pack cord when the day's march is done. For such offal as make friendship and alliance with the monkey people of Nabu there is no answer."

The man gaped at this ferocious outburst with vacant wonder. Then he guffawed again and swung on his heel to go. Barounggo's great arm shot out and gripped him by the shoulder to twist him around. The man lurched unsteadily as he turned and almost fell.

And then King suddenly knew, and his heart went cold. That knowledge explained everything that had been a mystery before. It explained his rolling walk, his vacant laugh, his rambling speech; it was the foundation of his recklessness. It was Dutch courage. The man was drunk.

A drunken savage was no very formidable person. But what chilled King's blood was the knowledge that natives can not acquire that kind of intoxication on muddy mealie-beer, and that on the march they could not carry enough of the stuff to get drunk on at all.

"Oh, the clever, clever devil," he was forced to admire. "Oh, the cunning beast! He won them over in spite of the trouble we left. He knew from the very start. 'A piece of cheap goods and a bottle of squareface'. Swine of hell!"

Yakoub was at his elbow. As yet he had not understood; but he was racked with apprehension.

"What—what is it, Kingi? What have you found?"

"Van Vliet is back of them," snapped King. "That explains everything. Thirty loads of trade goods and gin. That was the price. A big drunk jamboree all together, and good friends all round. A strong alliance with twenty *askaris* and three rifles. He knows how to handle the African, all right."

Yakoub fell back, stunned. His mouth sagged open and his face twitched. For agonized seconds no sound came from him, though his beard's convulsive trembling showed how his throat worked. He clawed at King. Incoherent noises came. Then broken words:

"God of my fathers! Even this. Were not the naked ones enough? And now these three, of all the wicked men in Africa. The abomination of desolation. The end of all things." He dragged at King's arm, sobbing inarticulate things.

King pushed him off roughly.

"All right, all right. Get hold of yourself. We'll stop them. I promised you, didn't I?" His face was as grimly fierce as the Masai's. Through grinding teeth he muttered, "Him or me, huh? Well, here's the showdown."

He roared at Barounggo:

"Get your men lined up there. Throw that mob back over the stone barrier. Up the hill with your side, Yakoub. Hold your shots for white men only—and keep behind cover. Van Vliet is nobody's fool with a rifle at any range. Move, everybody, move."

Swiftly he told Barounggo what he knew to be his true surmise. The Masai understood it at once. He grinned wolfishly.

"Oho, so those naked ones have drunk the white men's bravery out of a bottle. Good. It will not last."

He looked critically at his men and his mob of reserves.

"Let bwana attend to those white men," he growled. "Leave the others to me. It will be a fight. Hear their monkey clamor. They come."

King had a sudden inspiration. Quickly he imparted it to the Masai.

"Take your ten a little way down; fifty paces will be enough. So, when they see you they will halt and mass up. Then will I signal the stone rollers."

THE MASAI grasped that strategy at once. Quickly he led his little force of spearmen and lined them across the ravine. Silent, their scowling black faces peering over their big oxhide shields, they were quite formidable enough to give pause to the first comers of the naked men. Their enemies stood and chattered. Some laughed; some shouted insults; some leaped in the air and flourished spears. It was quite apparent that all of them had been stimulated to fighting pitch by something more potent than mere words.

Others came up behind them and added their yells. They pushed from behind. More came. They filled the gully—fifty of them. More kept piling up behind. They needed just that little something to rush them to the charge.

Then King whistled.

A rattle like machine gun fire commenced on either hill. A snapping and cracking of branches that grew with appalling swiftness to the boom and crash of artillery, the thudding vibrations of which shook the ground.

The naked men huddled in momentary panic. The front and rear fringes could run; but the center was too close packed. Before the mass could disintegrate the avalanche was upon them. A great advance boulder crushed a red swathe through the mass of black bodies. Then the rest of the horrid carnage was blotted out by a cloud of flying dust and rubble out of which came shrieks and smashing thuds and more shrieks.

A small group of frightened men who had been in the front of the mob was left marooned before the hurtling dust cloud, looking back at the death they had escaped. With a roar Barounggo charged down on them. His spearmen followed splendidly. There was a fierce minute of flashing spears; and when the dust cloud began to settle the Nabu men saw over its top only the cowhide shields and the black faces of nine men. One sprawled on his back.

Coolly Barounggo picked up the fallen man's shield and spear.

"That one died like a man," he growled. "Here are weapons for whosoever can use them."

He threw them behind him and, filled with the exhilaration of battle, prepared to charge down over the mangled mess before him at the scared mob beyond. King rushed down upon him and physically pushed him back.

"Back, fool, back! They are too many. Over the barrier. We don't catch them that way again. They will think twice—or their white allies will think for them."

No white men were seen as yet, but it was immediately evident that brains were behind the attack. More men appeared from lower down and massed beyond the rock barrage area. Wary caution was injected into the advance. The men came in short dashes like skirmishers, watching the ravine sides. More stones thundered down, but the damage to the active single runners was slight.

A white face appeared. It was Dago Lopez. He directed operations, ordering little groups of men when and how to run the barrage. He waved an arm and shouted with cool effrontery:

"You see we come after! Now you weesh you share your doublecross weeth us, no?"

King, looking over the top of the barricade, could have shot him down with both eyes shut.

But Lopez for some reason was without a rifle. Some accident must have happened to it—easily enough in any safari travel and particularly during the rocky ascent of the ravine. King felt himself to be held down by that cast iron code which drew an extraordinary distinction between those finely graded emotions, cold blood and hot. And Lopez, while he was in no way bound, knew that King was, and traded insolently on his knowledge.

King cursed his inhibition, as he always did, and promised himself release as soon as action should become sufficiently hot. There was no sign as yet of either Van Vliet or Johan. But King drew no comfort from that.

"Much too smart to take any risks in a rough and tumble spear fight," he grumbled to himself. "He'll show up when he's good and ready. And it'll be in some desperately mean place."

Action came in a rush. Some forty men had run the barrage. Among them were some of the safari *askaris*. Yakoub on his bank moved his men back and sent rocks hurtling against them. Their position became unbearable. Yet they themselves were too few to attack that defended wall. One, barely missed by a rock, yelped and dashed back to the main body. The rest, in a wild demoralized rush, followed him.

Had they been naked Africans alone, that would probably have meant the beginning of a long sit-down-and-do-nothing till some orator should stir up sufficient courage for a renewed charge. But Lopez cunningly sent spearmen to scale the ravine banks and to drive back the stone rollers.

King groaned. A determined resistance on the slopes might have held off the invaders indefinitely. But he knew that these villagers with knives and sickles could never hold out against spearmen. At that stage he would have shot Lopez without compunction in order to eliminate the brain behind the maneuver. But Lopez most craftily was well concealed behind a rock and only his voice was in evidence.

Closer came the mob of invaders as the men on the ravine flanks were driven back. Close enough for a charge. One tall fellow, brave enough—or drunk enough—to be reckless, shouted his war cry and rushed in. In a howling wave the rest followed.

The barricade disappeared under a black confusion of arms and heads and spears, shouting, straining, stabbing. King sprang up the ravine bank to a flanking position from which he could command all of the wall. Wherever he saw a black shape apparently gaining a foothold on its top he used his rifle. The relay force whom he had stationed closer up the ravine sides rolled their rocks with horrid effect. That charge was breaking up in another shambles.

A shower of smaller stones and rubble clattered past King from above. A white clad body hurtled down and was lost in the black turmoil before the wall. A small avalanche of naked men rolled, scrambled and leaped upon King and swept him from his precarious footing.

The ball of humans, all clinging together like fighting bees, rolled down the slope and thudded full on to the end of the wall.

From the invaders came triumphant howls. The white man was down. The attack took on renewed impetus. King, blinded by dust, choked by a black stomach pressed into his face, could see nothing. He retained sense enough only to know the position in which he was. Struggling, clinging, he put all his effort into trying to roll the man mass over to his own side of the barricade. Somebody shrieked in piercing agony in his very ear. The mass lurched over. They bumped heavily. King did not know which side. He could only hope.

Hot blood gushed into his eyes. It filled his nostrils. The weight above him relaxed. He was dragged to his feet, but not instantly stabbed.

His hands found cloth—somebody's white cotton robe. He wiped his face clear in it. His rifle was somewhere under the stamping, milling feet. Cursing, he dived among straining legs, fighting, pushing. He found the gun and pushed himself up to the surface of the raging human sea. He cursed again; he could feel, rather than see, that his rifle breech was choked with dirt. That was bad. Time and at least a few inches of space would be required for cleaning it.

STANDING PERILOUSLY on the top of the barricade, the Masai raged to stem the attack. Shield held low to protect his legs, ducking down, leaping high, he avoided with amazing skill the spears that thrust up at him, and he drove his blade down, shouting:

"*Ssghee!* That for thee, ape. *Hau,* a good stroke! *Sszee.* Eat spear, fool!"

Three of his men, roused to a frenzy of emulation, leaped up beside him.

"*Ssghee!*" they shouted. "We, too, are men. *Sszee!* The song of our spears is death."

The attack was breaking up at the foot of the blood spattered wall. Lopez had seen King fall. He felt secure. He darted from his position behind his sheltering rock. If that terrible man on the wall could be stopped the attack might yet win over. Lopez ran up behind the struggling line, his knife poised over his shoulder; he was watching his chance.

The Masai shouted a greeting.

"Guard my feet, fellows," he growled down. And to Lopez, "Ah, the little dark one, the juggler of knives. Look, I give thee a mark."

With reckless bravado he swept his shield aside and exposed his full chest. Lopez snatched at the offer and hurled his knife with all his vicious force. Barounggo ducked as easily as he had ducked under a hundred whizzing spears.

"A poor throw," he taunted. "A child's throw. But look, little dark one. A light spear! A spear balanced close to the blade! Thou knowest it already! I give it thee!"

Lopez squealed in terror and turned to bolt.

"*Ssszee!*" shouted the Masai with the delight of one who hunted a rabbit.

Lopez rushed on for several paces. Running, he bent lower, and yet lower; his arms spread out clutchingly; his knees sagged; his face slid in the gravel. And so he lay. The thin shaft stood yellow from the very middle of his khaki shirt.

"*Hau,* a good cast," said Barounggo solemnly.

Then he snatched his great stabbing spear again from behind his shield and drove down among the milling arms and faces at his feet.

And still there was no sign of the other two white men. The attack on the wall broke up. The defenders shrieked victory. But King called Barounggo to him and showed him an inevitable development. The spearmen on the hill had all but dislodged the village people and in a little while more would be in a position to climb down and attack the defenders of the wall from the rear. The way had been shown to them, and they had fighting intelligence enough to follow on even without a leader for awhile. And those two other white men must be showing up somewhere soon.

The barricade was a red splashed and tumbled boulder pile. On both sides of it lay contorted bodies and men who moved painfully and moaned—more, of course, on the attacking side. But there was a mob of howling spearmen, blood drunk now, quite numerous enough to make a holocaust of the poorly armed villagers. Retreat was imperative.

"To the lava wall," said King. "How many of your ten have fallen? Choose quickly five others to take their place. We will hold this place while the rest run."

The lava wall could be scaled, of course. But it was rough and difficult. Men standing on its wide top, armed with heavy knives—or even clubs—would have an advantage over climbers.

The Masai had his little troop already filled out; and he added five more sturdy knifemen to their number. King told off bearers to carry the wounded back immediately and passed along instructions to the rest to be prepared to run when the signal was given.

The Nabu men were now divided into three groups. The main body massed a little way down the ravine, inactive for the present, howling rage and threats, lacking only the initiative of a leader; and the two smaller troops of skirmishers who climbed slowly along the steep ravine sides, driving down the stone rollers, shouting enthusiasm at their success.

King called Yakoub down to him. In quick sentences he gave him instructions:

"Give me your gun. Take mine, and for Pete's sake get all this dirt cleaned out. Take all these men and run like hell. Get them lined up along the lava ledge and beat into them it's their last chance. Away with you!"

KING WAS able to turn his attention to the ravine sides. He was in a fever of apprehension. On one side—the side where he had been—the spearmen had won to a flanking position; they awaited only another frontal attack before climbing lower. On the other side, a steeper slope, they were not so well advanced.

King was cold under the anxiety that Van Vliet and the other ruffian would show up at any minute with some ingeniously devilish plan of campaign that they must have been preparing while Lopez led the frontal attack. Only some heaven-sent accident had held them off this far; but that sort of luck could not continue indefinitely.

High up the ravine side a spearman shouted in glee. He had driven a wretched village youth to a ledge where he could retreat no farther; and now he prodded at him with his spear, trying to pin him to the cliff side. In clear view they stood; the white clad figure flattened against the sliding sandstone, the naked black one clinging spiderlike, stabbing upward.

King threw up the rifle he had taken from Yakoub and fired. With enormous deliberation the naked figure let go all his holds. His spear clattered down the slope. Slowly the man pushed off from the cliff backward. His legs buckled under his weight; his body toppled, sprawled through a swift fall, and crashed on through the bushes of the lower slope like one of the boulders that had preceded it.

Shrill yelps greeted this new angle of the fight. King turned his attention to the men who had won a flanking position. It was a sickening business, this picking off of men like flies from a wall; but it was desperately necessary in order to let the remaining defenders draw off.

A panic grew among the spearmen who had so hilariously hunted the villagers a moment ago. Some contrived to scramble to safety; and those King let go. Some in their desperate anxiety slipped and fell. Some found hiding places. Demoralization was established sufficiently to cover a retreat.

King and his little defending party raced for it. Behind them the Nabu men, inspirited by the flight and quite thoughtless as to its cause, came howling.

As the last man passed through the narrow gap in the lava wall Barounggo swelled his chest with a great laugh of confidence. He told King:

"Let these men go to help that herd on the top, and let bwana go to direct them without fear. This place will I hold alone against all who come."

King, racked with anxiety, grime caked, sticky with blood, could not but envy the man's supreme exhilaration in the sheer joy of fighting. He knew that that narrow passage was an easy place to defend; but he was much too inherently cautious to withdraw all other help, however badly the spears might be needed on the wall.

To Barounggo's disgust he posted five men before the exit. Behind them, at the head of their peaceful valley, old men lifted their hands to heaven and prayed. Some were engaged in helping wounded men who had been hurriedly deposited on the grass King, with ready rifle, waited. The Masai took his stand before the fallen lava block that made the last twist in the passage.

A clamor sounded in the runway, discordant and booming with refracted sound like an ill tuned loud speaker. The Masai laughed and tensed his great shoulders.

Caution is bred of well balanced thought. Africans, fighting, do not think. Urged only by the instinct of the chase, the Nabu men raced into the passage, jostling, shoving, giving tongue. A tall figure without a second's hesitation bounded round the last corner.

The Masai spear licked out and down. The man sprawled, clutching at his middle.

"One," shouted the Masai.

Another man coming saw the trap. He was unable to check himself; he bounded high in the air. The great spear reached him before his feet touched the ground.

"Two," shouted the Masai.

Shouting and frenziedly pushing men choked the turn of the passage. King saw that the position was well defended. He scrambled up to the top to see what went on there. Yakoub, with a great sob of relief, scuttled to him over the broken surface and gave him his rifle. King was equally relieved to feel it in his hands.

At the outer entrance to the passage, not twenty feet below, naked men pushed and milled like cattle at the entrance to a pen. Only a few essayed to climb the craggy wall. They fought bravely enough, these men, but with desperate stupidity. Under a clever leader they could still be dangerous.

"Three," came the voice of Barounggo, exulting at the passage end. And in the next instant, "*Arwhoo-oo!*" he yelled with surprise and pain.

From far away to the left, where the lava flow sloped from the old crater lip, came a little pop, an innocent little sound like a champagne cork. But it was a sound that King had heard under many thousands of conditions. Galvanically he jerked round to look.

On the slope of the crater, five hundred yards away, naked black figures moved. Among them—King's heart skipped and pounded—were two white ones.

The leader at last. Whatever had delayed Van Vliet's cunningly planned flanking party, here he was finally; and in time to be deadly dangerous.

"The passage!" came King's agonized shout. "Barounggo is hit. To the passage, Yakoub."

But Barounggo's voice came up reassuringly:

"It is naught, bwana. A hole through my arm and shield. A little hole. I have had many such holes."

KING BECAME suddenly very cool. A leader five hundred yards away was a long distance from his men. But King knew exactly how dangerous that leader could be even at five hundred yards. He threw himself flat behind a lava block and pushed his rifle over the top. He waited till his breath came unhurriedly and then pressed his trigger.

One of the white figures on the far hillside flung up his hands and fell forward. King could not distinguish which one it was. The other one immediately disappeared. Faint yells of astonishment came from the black ones.

"Watch that passage," King snapped at Yakoub without taking his eyes from the far hill. "Make that fool Barounggo take cover. Shove his bunch into the passage and hold it. Stuff it with men, but hold it. And watch your wall."

He crawled forward to another sheltering block and waited.

Crash! Black splinters flew from it in front of his face, and another pop came from the hill. Then King knew the white figure that had dropped was the wrong one. Very cautiously he surveyed the terrain before him, gaging the lines of sight and cover. Then he moved forward again at an angle.

Those reenforcements from the hill must be stopped at all costs. They would stop only when the leader was stopped. King was not sure just where that leader lay hidden. There was no smoke from these high velocity cartridges to betray a position.

King watched like a hawk for a lizard. And as fast as a lizard a far figure scuttled from one rock to another. Too fast. King held his fire.

The thing became a duel at long range between two men, each of whom knew to the full the other's skill.

King called over his shoulder:

"How goes the passage? Don't show yourself."

Yakoub's voice came:

"We're holding them. They are not so anxious."

"Good," said King. "Let the natives hold the wall. Van won't waste any shots on them."

At the same instant he fired. He had caught a far glimpse of what might have been a head. Van Vliet's body lurched up into the air and flopped down behind the same rock. The natives on the wall yelled excitement.

King moved never an inch from his shelter. He grinned sourly.

"Too damned suspiciously lucky, falling that way right back behind cover. I can afford to wait," he muttered.

He judged it advisable to change his position, and he did so, relaxing not a bit of his caution. And again he changed, gaining several yards this time.

Crash! Splinters spouted a fountain all round him. He grinned, very pleased with himself.

Long minutes passed. The shouts and yelps that had marked the fighting stilled. Within the passage was a deadlock. Along the wall both sides watched the duel between the two white men; and both knew that whichever white man won, his side would also win.

Crash! King's lava block jerked convulsively and opened in an irregular line down its middle like a split apple. A nervous man might have lost his head and jumped frantically for better cover, and so exposed himself. King lay still and grunted.

"He's in a hurry." And then, "Perfect. I'll chance it."

He knew that the chances were many millions to one against another bullet finding that same slit; he knew, too, that at that distance no man could distinguish such an opening and deliberately aim for it. And he could see through the gap. It was in fact a much better view than any quick ducking and withdrawal of one eye round the edge of a rock.

Critically King studied Van Vliet's position. Not so extra good. That boulder flattened down to the right. If he could work the tiniest bit more broadside… King studied his own ground. Tumbled blocks formed a tortuous, shallow trench. By rolling into it he would lose his own view; but the other man would not know that.

Flat on his belly, King wriggled along, fearful of showing even an inch of moving surface. Sharp edges tore his shirt and breeches. Protruding points scored his ribs. He gained fifty yards.

Crash! Far behind him this time. King grinned thinly.

Forty more yards. There was a narrow V between two boulders. A splendid vantage point, if the other man did not know. King reached it and, inch by slow inch, raised his eyes above the slot. He thought he could distinguish what might be a boot and a patch of brown breeches leg behind a grass tuft and some small rubble.

A desperately small mark to hit—but even splinters and flying gravel would hurt enough to make a man jump.

King whistled through his teeth and filled his magazine. With infinite caution again he inched his rifle through the opening. No bullet came smashing to him.

It was his luck—or his skill. All set. He held his breath and fired quickly twice. He saw gravel fly. Van Vliet jerked into view. Like lightning King fired a third time. Van Vliet jerked again and flopped down. But this time a whole arm and shoulder remained visible.

King stayed motionless. But there was no need to fear a clever trick. The distant spearmen showed that. With shrill ululations naked black figures appeared from behind rocks, scrub, out of holes and streamed away over the rise.

Behind King the situation broke up just as swiftly. That shot had hit not only a cold blooded and utterly ruthless scoundrel. It had touched the magic spring of panic.

A high pitched cry of dismay broke out among the Nabu men, and they turned and ran for the ravine gap. The packed mass in the passageway fought each other to get out of the trap. The Masai's roar boomed out of the tunnel and the fiercely exultant "*sghee!*" told that his spear was at work.

The farther opening belched scrambling, screaming men. In a naked black stampede they trailed out as the faster runners got ahead. Behind them bounded the Masai and three remaining *askaris;* and behind them again a white cloud of flowing cotton garments, shouting, stabbing, stumbling.

"Stop him," yelled King. "Stop the crazy fool!"

It was one of those situations so common in any battle. The spearmen could have turned and, catching their pursuers in the open, cut them to pieces. But the leaders who had persuaded them to this war were gone. There was nobody to rally them.

One tall, heavily built fellow could not run as fast as most of the others. He lagged. Barounggo, running and roaring like a lion, overhauled him. In desperation the man turned to give battle. Barounggo yelled supreme joy.

"Oho, we meet! The herald, no less. This is my full day. What did I promise thee, naked one? Behold, this day's sun is not yet gone."

He threw away his shield and advanced upon the man, stepping high on his toes. Those behind him pulled up to watch, eyes rolling white, teeth showing, breath coming fast.

"Spear to spear, baboon," shouted Barounggo. "An Elmoran of the Masai takes no advantage over an ape."

Furiously the big man lunged at him. Barounggo, never moving his feet, swayed only his body. The spearhead swished past his side. His own spear held like a bayonet, the Masai took one swift stride in and heaved up his shoulders. The great blade ripped the naked man from groin to chest. Clutching his awful wound, he sank to the ground, dead.

"*Whau!*" shouted the Masai. "Such is the word of an Elmoran. A clean stroke, a swift stroke. So strikes the lion in his rage."

King came running.

"Shut up," he told the triumphant Masai. "There will be a time for bragging."

He had changed his mind about the disadvantage of pursuit.

"After them now; chase them well down. Roll rocks on them—give them hell, so they will have a lesson and will never come back. Go, before the sun is lost."

THAT SUN went down and the next one too. An awful mess had been cleaned up. Cuts and gashes innumerable had been stitched and plastered. Worse wounds were healing. Dead men had been buried. The valley smiled, as fair and peaceful as before the white men had brought war into it.

Yakoub conferred with King, timidly. He did not know just what to say or how to put his views and hopes before this man with whom he had gone through so much so closely and whom he had thought he understood.

"Kingi, old friend," he attempted, "we have been partners in this venture; we have agreed to share our findings. But, Kingi—you know, your own principle of the square deal; a noble principle, as I have come to learn. And what the wizard said about the right thing for the Hidden People—"

King cut him off bruskly. He knew just what the other was trying to say.

"Yes, yes, I know, I know. And a partnership is to share half the profits and half the worries. That's your principle, you told me. But I renege on that. They're your people. You found them. You can have the worry of them. And that's going to be plenty. I know what you want to do. They'll need leading by the hand; they'll need teaching and developing, slowly, carefully; they'll have to be protected from exploitation. Go ahead and develop them. Do the right thing by them, like the wizard said you would. I'll admit they're a good crowd; the best we've found in Africa. But don't drag me in on the chore."

Yakoub laid a sensitive hand on King's sleeve. His bird-like eyes were not so bright as they usually were. He wiped a ragged shirt sleeve across them to clear them.

"But—but, Kingi, the profits of our partnership that I have so boldly promised to you. This amulet—it is their secret. Nobody knows it now but ourselves. If it is developed it will—"

"Aw, shucks," King cut him short impatiently again. "It's your secret. It was my promise to you. Go ahead and use it. Dig it out in little slivers and send it out and buy plows and looms and books and whatnot. But don't sick that worry on to me. I'm no missionary to develop deserving peoples. I'm just a wandering adventurer."

Yakoub's voice was tremulous.

"But, Kingi, you are in need of money."

King's voice was hard.

"I need just about one hundred and twenty-five ounces gouged out of that block, and then I'll be quits."

Yakoub peered a question through dim eyes. King was muttering figures to himself.

"The way exchange is running, I figure a hundred and twenty-five ounces will make around five hundred pounds sterling. That's Ham Smythe's money, and then I'm clear."

The dimness of Yakoub's eyes passed to his voice.

"Kingi, old friend, Kingi Bwana M'kubwa, that is the squarest deal—"

"Shush, shush." King would not let him finish. "What would I do with that big lump of loot? I can't take it away with me. And the old wizard was all wrong. It doesn't break my heart worth a hoot. They're all wrong. Africa is chock full of secrets for me to go and find out. And I'll tell you one right now. No white man has ever been over those mountaintop trails into Abyssinia. Me, I'm going to go look-see tomorrow. There's no telling what I may turn up. Why—" his eyes narrowed and the eager, faraway look came into them—"Yakoub, I'll bet you there's gold in them thar hills. Why not quit all this and come along?"

THE IVORY KILLERS

JAN RUYS was as bad a citizen as any at large in all of East Central Africa. He was not the worst, because there were also Mink McCarthy and Tino Corra.

But when men spoke of the nefarious three, they always mentioned Ruys first because of his bulk and belligerence, though these were deceptive. It was McCarthy who was the wicked one—small, sleek, sun tanned, neutral haired, khaki clothed—a creature of low visibility at all times. In effect, a mink; and equally hard, fast and ruthless. He had brains to offset Jan Ruys's overwhelming brawn.

Tino Corra had nothing especial to recommend him above such personalities as the other two. A small, dark, Latin type, he had his own reasons for keeping out of Portuguese Mozambique. But he was a good, hard working, tough egg, and he fitted in well with the combine—three as unsavory subjects as had ever come into the Uganda Protectorate to poach ivory.

It was this trio that the chief commissioner was discussing, as he sat in his office in Entebbe. He drummed his fingers on his desk and faced a tall, wide shouldered man who paced the room with silent restlessness. The tall one looked at him with hostility.

"And why are you telling me about your hard luck?" he asked defensively. "Tell some of your policemen, game wardens— somebody. That's why you collect a white hunter's license from me."

The commissioner continued evenly:

"The three would spot my men in a minute and would lay low, as good as white mice. Or they'd just lay up by some handy *donga* and neatly bushwhack them. Down in Rhodesia some witnesses just disappeared; but the police could never get anything on those three. They're poison. And now I have them on my hands."

"Sound like nice boys," said the tall man. "I guess you'd better do something about them."

"I *am* doing something," said the commissioner. "I am negotiating with a man who knows the bush inside out, who's got the nerve of a devil and no nerves."

"Plenty of men like that on your force," said the tall man. "They've been after me for some damned silly regulation or other plenty o' times."

"I must have a man," said the commissioner, "who isn't tied down by what you call silly regulations, and who has the effrontery, if need be, to play a high handed game all on his own."

The tall man looked coldly at him.

"And I must have, essentially, a sportsman."

"Huh? I'll fall for that one," said the tall man. "Why must you have a sportsman?"

"Because," said the commissioner, "these men are using submachine guns and water hole poison. They poach ivory as a business."

"Hell!" The tall man growled. "That's swinish—beastly! Gosh, I'd like to—" He paused, then shook his head. "Well, I hope you get your man. I've got to be running along."

The commissioner smiled.

"Oh, I'll get him all right. I'll be seeing you tomorrow, my difficult Kingi Bwana."

"The hell you will!" said the tall man.

But the commissioner continued to smile and absently drummed a broken rhythm on the desk.

BUT DESPITE popular indignation and the efforts of the police, the three swaggered from Entebbe a week later with a safari of lusty porters, empty handed. That is to say, most of them were without head loads. The hard bitten trio knew their Africa. They were no tenderfeet who needed luxuries. They traveled with the minimum of impedimenta. Mobility—the ability to cover country faster than anybody else—was more precious to them than comfort. Those strong, empty handed porters were designed to carry loads that would be collected later in the dense elephant jungles of Bugoma and Semliki forests.

And until they had such contraband loads, no authority could interfere with the safari. They came, therefore, unhindered into the Semliki country; and it was there that a native approached the camp one morning and talked with the safari headman. The headman came and reported—

"That fellow he say one white man not so far."

The trio sat up and began to take notice. A white man in that corner of the wilds might interfere with stealthy plans.

"He say he sit without safari; plenty load in *boma,* no porter mans, only two servant boy mans."

Mink McCarthy swore sibilantly. With quick fingers he softly opened the breech of his gun to assure himself of what he knew to be so; then he jerked his head at Tino Corra.

"Better go quietly and look him over. If it's any blasted official—" His pause was more ominous than words. Through taut lips he added, "This is new country—hardly shot over. And it's rich. Nothing's goin' to stop us here."

In the next moment he changed his mind with characteristic high-strung abruptness.

"Wait a minute. Let's all go."

They found the white man just as the native had described him. A tall, rangy, big shouldered man, dressed in shining, new and eminently correct big game hunter's clothing, sitting marooned in a *boma* piled full of all the camping gadgets that outfitters sell to fools. As soon as he opened his mouth they knew him for one of those rich American sports.

"Howdy, strangers. Say, but I'm right glad you happened along. You see me 'way up a tall tree."

The tenderfoot's story brought grins of wearied amusement to the faces of the experienced three. He had come out from Nairobi with the usual unwieldy safari under the guidance of a licensed white hunter. A week ago the hunter had contracted something virulently African and had died. The tenderfoot, confident in his ignorance, characteristically impatient over the delay, had picked up some sort of native guide and had forged ahead.

"—hustled the outfit along. Fired some pep into those hookworm coons and kept on going."

But the simple African, it transpired, objected to being pepped up.

"—kicked like steers at a paltry twenty-five miles a day."

And when the tenderfoot—who had made his pile in railroad contracting and had run some pretty durned lazy construction gangs in his day—proceeded to inject some efficient driving methods, the untutored African safari had quite simply vanished into the bush overnight, leaving the gang driver marooned with all his expensive gear, his burly gunboy and scrawny little cook, who had remained faithful to their quite exorbitant pay.

The trio grinned sourly at the idea of anybody trying to drive safari porters at twenty-five miles a day. And what was this rich sport proposing to do now?

"Well, gee, now—" the sport was dubious—"I've got my license right here to shoot four elephant and two rhino and a raft of other stuff, and I'm not licked bad enough yet to figure on going back empty.

"And, say now—" looking the others over with calculation— "you gentlemen look like you know your way around. How about if you could see your way to signing up with me and seeing me out of the hole? The check of Cyrus P. Carmody is good in Nairobi for anything reasonable you'd like to say."

The eyelids of Mink McCarthy flickered and he spoke quickly before the others could get in a word.

"Well, now, Mr. Carmody, we don't like to see any white man bushed this way; but, you see, we're really a prospecting outfit and your idea would break up our plans to smithereens. Let me and my mates here step aside and talk it over awhile."

The three walked off together. Immediately Jan Ruys, the hasty, blurted:

"Ah, what 'cher need to talk it over? Le's leave 'im sit. He's stuck safe. Carn't foiler us—no porters nor nothin'; else we'd mebbe have to put 'im away quiet. Him an' 'is blarsted checks; just 's if we was workers for lousy wages."

Tino Corra saw the scorn growing in McCarthy's eyes and hastened to put himself on what he knew would be the winning side.

"But you are fooleesh, *amigo*," he purred in his soft Latin voice. "Pairhaps he have monnaie cash, who is so reech. Wan license for wan elephant cost heem hundred pound. So then four license—ees eet not so? And he have gun, raifle, cartridge, everytheeng of best."

Mink's impatience with stupidity was savage. His lip quivered over his small, pointed eye-teeth.

"If either of you blighted fools had a half human head, I wouldn't have to worry about any game commissioner in all Africa. You look no further'n any other monkey can see with his silly eyes. Now, listen while I say it slow."

Slowly and impressively he proceeded to lay out the quick thought that had come to him.

"License for four elephant. Let that soak in awhile. Four tuskers to be shot all due and proper under the law. Does that mean anything to you? No, of course it don't. So I'll tell you. We sign on as guides. We take this silly blighter where *we* want to go. Four licenses—" the predatory teeth clicked in anticipation—"four little bits o' stamped paper can be stretched to cover up a hell of a lot of shooting if any trouble comes sneakin' along in a uniform. And we ditch him when we come to the Belgian border with a full load. Why, the thing's a Christmas present."

Tino Corra's flashing smile came first, and the heavier one of Jan Ruys followed it more slowly.

"Meenk, he's got the haid," Tino conceded.

And Ruys, though the full possibilities of the gift would have to be assimilated later, grunted agreement.

They went back to the rich sport, all smiles. They were poor men, and prospecting was a precarious game. They would throw over their plans and would sign on with the gentleman as regular white hunters. And to show their worth they would even contrive to find porters for the gentleman's baggage—or at all events for the valuable portion of it. And then the place for elephants, of course, was the great Semliki forest, not four days' trek distant.

TO THE three who had found Rhodesia too hot for comfort this was new country. But their safari headman was a Zanzibar Arab halfbreed whose father had been a doughty Rift

Lakes slave raider in the good old days, and who himself, now that the profitable "black ivory" business was gone, had become a small scale poacher of the white. He knew his Budonga and his Semliki.

It was not long before the parched, flat, thorn scrub country began to give place to rolling grassland. Game was everywhere and foolishly tame. A splendid pair of rare roan antelopes, the hunter's prize, stood and looked at them from a little knoll, their magnificent horns curving back to their flanks. But the hurrying travelers were not interested in any such commercially valueless thing as sportsmen's prizes; and this rich sport did not even know the antelopes were rare.

He clamored buck-feverishly about all the minor items on his licenses. But Mink told him glibly:

"They'll be here when we come back. Elephants'll be movin' up into the mountain valleys before the rains come. We'd never see a one. Now's the time for tusks."

The grass country began to give place to low hills covered with clumps of timber and patches of bamboo thicket—elephant country. The safari porters, instead of stringing out in front with all their noise and confusion, were ordered to the rear. The white men took the lead with the cunning old Zanzibar headman.

Extraordinary luck was with them. On the third day the American, ranging restlessly afar, fell into a hole that looked as if a small tub had been sunk there by some mysterious jungle gardener and as mysteriously removed. It seemed as if the gardener had been a lunatic and had sunk a whole row of tubs, removing them afterward.

Without a word among the three, Ruys gave Tino Corra a hoist up a not too leafy tree. Corra was down again in two minutes, nostrils twitching and eyes shining. He reported, whispering as if already within distance of great sensitive ears:

"Wan nice ravine that side look ver likelee. Wan sweet vallee, all euphorbia, an' bamboo, leetle bit left, look best place evair I see."

Mink was tersely efficient.

"All right, we'll take the ravine first. If they're not bottled there, we'll split and jockey 'em up and down the valley. Come ahead."

The three hired white hunters gave no thought to the disposition of their greenhorn employer who had spent his thousands to shoot an elephant. Though Mink, as an afterthought, told him curtly—almost ordered him:

"You stick with the safari and see no fool comes blunderin' an' crashin' behind us." And he threw over his shoulder as they departed, "We're just goin' scoutin' to see how they stand."

They disappeared up the ravine, the Zanzibari with them, treading like cats. The greenhorn smiled thinly after them, nodding to himself. The smile went through the changing gradations from whimsicality to cold satisfaction. To his gunboy the greenhorn said in perfect Swahili—

"The safari stays here."

The gunboy replied simply: "It is an order, bwana. They stay."

He threw his blanket from his enormous shoulders and soberly, unhurriedly, went to one of the packs from which he produced an immense spear blade—a long sword of a thing that fitted snugly to the end of the strong, beautifully polished stick that he carried. And with the putting together of that weapon, as if it were a symbol of domination, he was suddenly transformed into a formidable fighting man.

To the scrawny camp cook the greenhorn said—

"How do you read the signs, little wise one?"

The little man balanced on one leg and surveyed jungle and sky with the wisdom of a wizened ape.

"The wind blows from the valley over my left shoulder," he translated from the book of the jungle. "The vultures circle high against it. The toucans and the mik-mikki fly with it. What moves will be therefore in the valley."

"Good," said the greenhorn. "Come."

The two disappeared up the valley, treading like very wary cats.

ALMOST IMMEDIATELY they were in giant bamboo jungle, each knotted stem as thick as a man's leg, grouped in close clumps of twenty or thirty. Between the clumps lay open ground carpeted with the debris of long narrow leaves that had no crackle to them.

Good jungle, that. So softly could they proceed on that velvet pile that guinea fowl scratched contentedly all around them, and once two water-buck were surprised on the far side of a score of towering stiff stems. Safe jungle, because one could see anything that came; and a charging elephant, for instance, could easily be dodged among the palisaded stems.

That jungle gave place to junipers, witch-hazels, and giant yews of the Ruwenzori foothills, all interlaced with tangled scrub and vines—bad jungle, for any quick movement, or fast getaway from danger, was impossible. The greenhorn ducked and twisted through the tangle like a ghost, and the little black man followed like his shadow.

The rain forest again gave place to a wide amphitheater of bamboo grass. Not in giant clumps here; more like a close sown field of exaggerated corn, twenty feet high, stiff, sword edged— impossible jungle. Only a steam roller, or an elephant, could penetrate this barrier. And one of the two was in it. Soft cracklings, muffled snappings, moist crunchings issued from within. A giant, trampled tunnel bored into it.

A foolhardy hunter or an ignorant novice might have plunged on into this close walled tunnel. The greenhorn climbed up into the high flung roots of a huge fallen yew that the slowly spreading bamboo grass had killed. The little black man leaped up after him like a monkey.

From the lofty perch just on a level with the grass tops the jungle amphitheater looked like an undulating green, lake; and, like a lake, the surface heaved and billowed with a heavy groundswell of monstrous motion beneath the surface.

Half an hour passed. The little black man touched his master's foot and pointed silently. Down the valley sides a cautious crackling was coming. Slowly it worked down to one edge of the amphitheater and stopped. It divided, and the careful crackling took different directions. One worked softly round in the direction of the fallen yew.

"Hmph! They know their business all right," the greenhorn muttered. "Ringing them round."

The nearest crackling came to a halt at the tunnel. A grunt of satisfaction followed. Faint shufflings indicated a man composing himself to wait.

Silence enveloped the jungle amphitheater. Even the ponderous sounds from within stilled. Suspicious, tense, the whole jungle waited. Breathless, the still air was heavy with enormous happenings.

The faintest cautious click of a breaking twig sounded from the farther side. From within the matted cane came a quick scuffle and a great, windy *woosh* of expelled air.

The little black man raised his hands to the sides of his head, fingers fanned out, and then pointed an arm snakily from his nose. It was a silent picture of great ears flapping forward and a trunk breathing questingly for the least draft of wind.

There was no wind or sound. There was nothing—only wire edged waiting.

Into the tenseness a rifle spat viciously, thin and tenuous in the vast expectancy. Thunderous echoes rolled back from the wooded hills. And on that signal, as if it had been the first primal upheaval of worlds in the making, chaos exploded into the still jungle amphitheater—siren screamings, throaty trumpetings, more fast rifle shots, shouts, vast roarings, confusion, earthquake.

On the undulating sea of grass tops the watching greenhorn saw a tidal wave rise and go hurtling across the glade to the side farthest from the rifle fire, leaving a swath of destruction behind it. Merciless rifle shots met its approach, and then a hell of machine gun fire.

The greenhorn's face grew grim with disgust; but he said nothing. The little black man spat into the air before him.

The tidal wave broke into a wild tossing of grassy billows. Enormous lurchings heaved under the surface. Terror trumpeted. Human voices screamed hysterically. Bamboo stems crackled like fireworks. Ponderous impacts thudded together. The air quivered with immense forces in confusion.

The tumbled jungle surface began to disintegrate, to melt away beneath huge trampling feet. A twisted trunk licked up into the air. A great gray back heaved itself out of the destruction. Milling, struggling forms bulked huge in the confusion. Bursts of machine gun fire crackled above the uproar.

The greenhorn on his perch sat white and silent. The little black man made a single comment which expressed more than abuse.

"Females and young with the herd."

Then, with the queer unanimity of wild things in terror, the herd hurled itself into the tossing greenery again. The tidal wave formed and went whirling and crashing off in another direction.

"Poor silly brutes. They follow their own tunnels," the greenhorn muttered. "And—" his teeth gritted—"those swine know it." A moment later, "And, by heaven, it's this tunnel."

It was true. The whole stampede came thundering down this familiar passageway, splitting it apart, smashing ruin upon devastation. The ground trembled under its rushing weight. The tidal wave resolved itself into an avalanche of hurtling flesh and elemental sound.

THE MAN hidden beneath the greenery at the tunnel's mouth coolly held his ground. He knew his own power. His rifle roared into the tunnel. Giant throats screamed. Vast momentums impacted and recoiled. The avalanche piled up on itself. Pressure from behind split its front. Huge shapes staggered aside into the thick grass wall. Shouts from the man. Again his rifle roared.

An immense head in which little eyes gleamed bloodshot appeared out of the grass fringe and crashed into the dead yew tree. The whole great stem lurched over. The watcher and the little black man were catapulted from its root. The watcher, dazed, had the wit to roll under the lee of the fallen bole. Again a shouted curse and the rifle's roar. Muddy things moved close to the fallen greenhorn's face. They were the tunnel man's boots. The greenhorn raised himself and stood behind the other. It was big Jan Ruys.

Ruys gave only a startled look and then aimed into the wrecked tunnel again. A huge bulk filled it like a rushing projectile. The heavy rifle roared. The bulk staggered but hurtled on, enormous, screaming rage. Only a shot placed in a spot as big as the palm of a hand could stop it—the most difficult shot in all elephant hunting. It was a charging, head-on shot, requiring lightning quick allowance for height and angle of head and thickness of trunk, with time for only one shot.

Ruys tore his rifle bolt out and back and aimed with a steady hand. The firing pin clicked upon emptiness. Ruys shouted a curse and stood. There was nothing else to do. His time, as it comes to most elephant hunters, had come to him.

The greenhorn snapped up his rifle and fired. The charging bulk became an avalanche slide, pushing great furrows of earth before its immense feet. The slide stopped within reaching distance of the muddy boots. The huge bulk rolled slowly and crushed a crackling hollow into the cane wall.

Ruys breathed noisily.

"Phe-ew! Gaw strike me if that ain't the damnedest tusker ever I seen. Knocked 'im endways harf a dozen times, an' he gets up an' keeps comin'."

He was admirably self-possessed in the face of his near obliteration. Suddenly he looked queerly at the greenhorn who had made that clean, cool shot. Then he shouted and crammed fresh cartridges into his gun to fire at a gray shape that milled in the tangled confusion.

The confusion broke up at last. Silence settled over the trampled tangle of what had been fresh, softly billowing jungle less than ten minutes before—ten tremendous minutes.

Then came shouts from the farther side. Shouts answered from the left. Ruys bellowed hoarsely. On the right remained silence. Ruys advanced slowly. He had to climb over the great carcass that blocked the tunnel. The greenhorn followed, wondering what lay beyond.

In a great niche in the tunnel wall formed by a falling mass lay an elephant. Beyond, in a flattened area of destruction lay another—a rounded heap that might have been a rock rising above the debris of greenery. Tusks gleamed white from a pile of twisted stems. Something bulked darkly beyond.

Ruys began to laugh, uncertainly at first, then in loud jubilation. His guffaw was a shout.

"Gawblime, but it's six ov 'em! An' I says to meself, 'Strike me if this ain't the toughest bull as ever I shot at.' Him keepin' a-comin' after I knocks 'im. Ee-yow! I'm a perisher if that ain't prize shootin'."

Joyous discovery shouts came from the other side of the slaughter pen. Ruys bellowed simian glee and tramped to meet them.

The greenhorn stood with tight pressed lips. He felt sick. Disgust swept over him in a hot wave. This was not shooting—it was a shambles. The little black man climbed upon a great rounded flank and squatted there upon his heels. Cynically he picked a snuff horn from his ear lobe and sniffed a pinch.

"It is a pity, bwana," he said, "that you did not hold your shot until after the charging elephant had taken that great ox. There would then have been only two to reckon with."

His master became aware of his presence and his eyes traveled then to where that human scream had been before the remainder of the herd had broken away. The little man clicked his tongue and his grimace was that of a pleased ape.

"That one was the Zanzibari," he said. "So screams a man when the elephant's foot is upon his belly."

The white man shivered. But his eyes were on the bodies of slaughtered elephants, not in the direction of the late Zanzibari ivory poacher.

"Pah!" He spat. "Let's get out of here."

THE GREENHORN sat in his tent alone. The others had broached a bottle from the rich sport's luxurious supplies and were celebrating their successful morning.

"Best show we ever had," said Mink McCarthy. "The perfect spot to catch 'em in. Never been another like it. Sixteen all told, and nine of 'em tuskers. And if that blighted Zanzibari hadn't been a fool we'd ha' got more. But I reckon it's close on eight hundred pounds of ivory at that, an' that's pretty good these days."

There was cause for rejoicing. But Jan Ruys had a disquieting note to inject. As sometimes happens to a stupid man, a keen idea had come into his mind earlier that morning; and it had taken root and grown alarmingly.

"This 'ere American bloke—" he lowered his great bull voice and looked cautiously out of his little eyes—"he ain't no tenderfoot sport. I seen 'im shoot. Clean an' cool as you an' me. I been thinkin' on that; an' d'yer know what?"

The others looked at him, ready for any suspicion, as in their business they had to be.

"Yer wanter know what I think?" He whispered the ill thought. "I'll bet yer he's no one else but that blarsted King feller."

The others started. Tino Corra pulled at his little mustache and considered the possibility. Mink McCarthy's keen wits raced over the pros and cons, while a tight frown contracted his brows under which his eyes glittered redly.

"Look at 'im," Ruys enlarged his accusation. "Tall an' big in the shoulder an' hard as nails. An' look at his niggers. The big feller—he's a Masai or I'm a bloody fool. An' the little un— he's the Hottentot. You've 'eard of Kingi Bwana an' his two men. We've all 'eard all about 'em. An' now I arsks yer: What's he doin' pretendin' he's a rich sport lost on a heap o' safari goods right in our road?"

Mink's narrow jaws set as if he were sinking sharp teeth into each item in turn and chewing upon it. And, as he digested each one, his face became harder and more deadly. Abstractedly, as he revolved the possibilities again, he reached for his rifle and began counting cartridges into the magazine. The vicious push of his thumb marked his decision on each separate point.

There was no more than suspicion that this man was the Kingi Bwana of camp-fire legend. But that did not matter. To those three in their ruthless game, it was sufficient that the man was not what he pretended to be.

Ruys swallowed a furious oath. He picked up his rifle with sudden resolve and made to stride for the stranger's tent. This thing would have to be finished then and there. Mink hissed throatily after him, his face bleak with rage. Quick as a small rodent, he rose and caught at Ruys's belt.

"You blasted fool!" he grated. "You'll be getting all of us lagged some day with your thick wit. Can't you see we'll have to take 'em all together—him and his niggers? If they're who you think, they're smart as monkeys. Let one of 'em escape as a witness, an' we'd be in the soup up to our necks."

Ruys stood, clumsily irresolute and half rebellious, till the blood-chilling common sense of his comrade soaked into his dull brain. Then he allowed himself to be dragged back. In a flat tone, conceding only a postponement, he said—

"When the big nigger comes to fix 'is tent an' the little devil is cookin'."

The three looked at one another, the eyes of all of them showing agreement. Slowly they nodded.

No fuss about this thing, no dramatics, without the necessity of speech. Only a glance between men who understood one another.

The stranger kept to his tent. He could not bring himself to fraternize with those three under a pretense of amity. And the three—cold, unhurried, determined—watched for the appearance of the big tent boy.

Evening came. Unsuspiciously the stranger came out of his tent. Like a blanket-wrapped baboon the little Hottentot crouched over his cook pots. But the figure of the huge Masai was nowhere in sight.

Moodily the stranger sat down to eat. A gasoline pressure lantern flooded him and his Hottentot in clear white light. Each one of the waiting three was an expert rifle shot. But, inexplicably, no Masai came.

Night fell. The man who might be the redoubtable Kingi Bwana retired to his tent. The three cursed in furious whispers and took turns to watch. Sooner or later the third witness would return to the camp—and then!

Dawn came. Mink, whose watch it was, kicked the others to snarling wakefulness.

It was just the tall stranger's luck and his inherent caution that had sent the big Masai with a message to Fort Portal, a long day's run distant.

THE THREE took council. If this were indeed the Kingi Bwana of camp-fire legend, they were up against wits as keen as all their own. Mink spat poisonous curses and fetched out a map. He pressed a pointed thumbnail upon it. His red eyes burned into the paper.

"We're too damned close to that blasted Fort Portal place. It's marked as a police outpost, curse it." The claw-like thumbnail cut a groove across the map. "There's the Semliki River. A day's fast trek beyond is the Belgian Congo border. If we can get to the river—"

Mink's fist slammed on to the map.

"By all hell, if we can get across I'll drop this fly cove at long range, I don't care who's with him or who isn't. Belgian Congo 'll be safe country, all right."

Ruys gazed at the map, judging distances. He breathed heavily. He was satisfied it could be done.

"Why not burn the two of'em now an' make a run for it? We kin get there, ivory an' all, before anybody'd ketch up."

Mink looked at him with hate. He sneered, coldly venomous.

"Don't you ever think? D'you even know what month it is? How about if the rains are breaking on the Ruwenzori, an' the river's flooded forty foot deep an' a mile wide? Then where'd we go?"

Tino Corra showed his even teeth.

"Yess, shure. Bettaire we see first the rivaire."

Ruys was forced to curb his bloodthirsty impatience once more. But he fretted. If only that Masai would show up. During the midday halt he approached the busy little Hottentot, and with immense unconcern inquired about the other man.

He might as well have hoped to pit his wits against a wise old chimpanzee. The little black man chattered as volubly as an ape and dissembled as smoothly. Oh, the big Kaffir boy? He was careful not to name him a Masai. The clumsy great oaf had stepped upon a black scorpion and his leg had swelled up like an elephant's. So he had gone to the nearest witch doctor to have the poison magic performed. He would catch up with the safari when he was well. And maliciously the wizened imp added—

"Surely will that great black one catch up; for he is a great runner and can travel distance as the antelope travels."

Later the wise little one, suspicious as a monkey, related the episode to his master over the solitary lunch at the folding canvas table; and he quoted a proverb of his own people.

"When the ox seeks for information, then must it indeed be a matter of great importance."

King cogitated over this news, his eyes very narrow, squinting out under the corners to empty distance. He fired a short question or two at the Hottentot. He whistled a tuneless air through his teeth. Then he shrugged. His bleached brows met in a straight line over his eyes. He shrugged again. With his hands deep in his breeches pockets he sauntered over to where the three squatted, heads together.

Smiling a little grimly, King teetered on widespread legs and looked down on them.

"Well," he challenged, "it seems we know each other. Now what?"

Three sets of ferocious eyes glowered at him. The three were ready for fight on the drop of a hat. But King's thumbs were hooked into his belt; and a belt holster hung at the very heel of his hand. Like the grating hiss of a ferret came Mink's words:

"Get to hell outa here before we send you sudden, you blasted police spy! Yes, sure we know you. We've heard plenty about you, but nothing that low."

King's smile was like a knife blade. He shook his head.

"Not spy. But something nobody's ever heard about me yet— deputy warden."

His voice hardened to match the smile.

"I don't give a hoot what you crooks may have done down Rhodesia way—whom you've bumped off or why. That belongs to the police. It's none of my *shauri*. But this filthy thing that you've just done is right up my street. It's the personal affair of every decent white man in Africa."

Mink smiled grimly at King.

"All right. D'you think you're going to arrest the three of us, Mr. Holy Man Game Warden Deputy?"

King knew very well he could not. While he had the drop on them just now, he had far too much respect for their collective wit to think that he could divert his attention from the group and concentrate it upon the disarming of any one man. They were all three fast and expert shots.

Mink kept his grin.

"I'd advise you to get to hell away," he spat forth again. "And you're damned lucky the breaks came the way they did. Get away—before the breaks maybe take a turn."

Again King shook his head. The smile had gone from his face; only the steely hardness was left.

"Oh, no. We don't exactly part just yet. Of course, I don't like you civet cats well enough to safari along with you. But you're not fools enough to think I won't stick right on your trail; and I'm sure you're not fools enough to try and bushwhack me as long as one of my boys remains at large. So we understand one another. I'm going to take you boys in, if I can. And you're going to do me in, if you dare."

He stood awhile longer, surveying their rage with sardonic grimness. Then he turned and left them.

Mink's grin became the throaty growl of an animal nuzzling its meat. But at no time did he lose his alertness. With a quick look he satisfied himself that Jan Ruys was making no rash move. Then very meaningly, for his friends to hear:

"We daren't bushwhack you? You think you're going to take us in. You hope? You're damn right, you hellion Yankee! We dare do nothing, until we're sure we can cross the Semliki River."

King had no fear of turning his back upon the three. He understood fully the insurance of one of his men remaining alive as a witness. To the Hottentot he said:

"We move camp swiftly. And from now on we must be as wary as the gray jackal and as sleepless as the rock snake."

The Hottentot grimaced. White man's squeamishness was a permanent sore point with him.

"Did I not say, bwana, that it would have been better to have let the elephant take that one? So there would be now only two. Even as we—" he whispered hissingly through his teeth—"even as we are two."

King was inwardly pleased at the little man's loyal hint at cooperation. But he said gruffly:

"The Masai will be returning at the hour of dusk. He surely

must be met and warned. For this is our insurance: that at no time shall the three of us be seen in one place at the same time."

Without requiring to be told, the astute little man understood the significance of that thought; and on the instant he had a thought to add.

"It is well. It is, therefore, in my head that this night bwana shall watch in the *boma* alone, as sleepless as the rock snake; and like the gray jackal, the Masai and I, we shall creep in and stab those three as they sleep."

"Out!" ordered King. "Out, little murderer! And make speed to move from these evil associations that corrupt the morals of an ape."

A N D S O that strangely divided safari trekked on its way—closely bound together, hating and helpless, hard bound by diametrically opposing restrictions. Either party was willing to do the other deadly hurt; yet each found its hands quite securely tied. Kingi Bwana could make no foolish play against those three experienced gunmen unless he could separate them. They dared not attack him unless they could get his trio all together. And somewhere in the bush, hurrying along to add the hazard of win or lose to the game, came the police from Fort Portal.

At last they reached the river. When the long line of wild fig trees that marked its course showed on the horizon, even the coldly calculating Mink was impelled to hurry. The game depended upon the river's condition. When they came near enough to look over the brim of its gully, Ruys capered uncouthly and shouted.

Down at the bottom of the great swath gouged by the monsoon into the plain a wide gray ribbon zigzagged—a good two hundred yards wide, but width mattered nothing. The water was at the bottom, not racing level with the top as it might have been.

"Here's where we settle that interferin'blighter's hash," Ruys rejoiced vindictively.

Mink McCarthy's expression was split in a lipless grin.

"Plenty of time yet," he purred. "Plenty time. We'll send the ivory over first. That son of a long legged snoop will come sticking his nose into the game sooner or later; an' then, when we're safe over—" He chuckled croakingly.

Presently a long line of black figures was stringing across the wide gray ribbon. Long white arcs gleamed on their shoulders, submerged in places. Neck deep it was and cold from the Ruwenzori heights, but easily fordable.

And presently, as prognosticated, King arrived to stick his nose into the game. Only he and the Hottentot were in sight.

Warily watching the men, his hand on his pistol butt, he surveyed the scene. It promised to be a very successful escape, unless the police should suddenly arrive like a cinema miracle. But the river seemed to offer an obstacle.

King spoke banteringly, but with a hard edge to his tone.

"Kinda like the riddle about the missionaries and the cannibals, no?"

"Meanin'?" Mink was quickly hostile.

King grinned amiably.

"Meaning the little matter of getting across. It's going to be difficult shooting for you gentlemen out in the deep spots."

Mink was suddenly affable.

"Don't you worry about that, you blasted Yank. We're not silly."

He drew his grinning friends away. Even the surly Ruys was good humored.

"Now listen," he told them. "I go first. You cover this smart Yank till I'm across. I'll hold a bead on him while Tino comes. And then the two of us covers you. And when we're all across—" he cackled harshly—"I'll lay you fifty pounds of tusk I drop him first." Suddenly he was savage. "Follow us, will he, the blasted swine! Only thing I'm sorry about is we don't get the big nigger too."

The plan was perfect. Mink waded in. He had to hold his rifle above his head out in the middle of the stream, but he had no difficulty in making it. On the far side he scrambled up the steep bank and settled himself with his back to the bush fringe, his elbows on his knees, his rifle held comfortably and steadily. He looked frail and insignificant nearly three hundred yards away; but nobody, least of all King, had any impression that the man was not deadly.

Tino Corra showed white teeth to King.

"Goodbai, senhor," he told him fondly. "Pairhaps I don' see you no more. Pairhaps nobody see you nevair no more."

He chuckled sweetly, scrambled down the bank and waded in.

King stood looking across the water. Big Jan Ruys, his back to the river, stood warily watching King, a heavy grin on his face about an impending joke that King did not know.

King scarcely looked at Ruys. His attention was all on the farther side of the river where Mink sat venomously waiting, blending with his protective coloring into the bush fringe behind him.

Hawk-like, King watched that distant figure, himself waiting for something to happen. The little Hottentot standing behind him balanced on one foot and writhed in excitement over imminent happenings. King's eyes, puckered hard and narrow in the sun, dropped for a moment to Tino Corra laboring in midstream. From him they flashed to Jan Ruys.

Ruys stiffened to alertness. He had a wholesome respect for King's wit. Had he stood alone, nervousness might have impelled him to draw a gun and precipitate a showdown. But there was comforting assurance in the steady rifle of the cold blooded Mink a scant three hundred yards across the river—an assurance of deadly precision that King fully shared. So King only stood and waited.

Jan Ruys was reassured that King knew enough not to try any foolhardy tricks against the double hazard. He felt that he could indulge in a little heavy humor before his turn to cross over.

"Yer been pretty smart, Yank, ain't yer? Well, Mink over there—" he jerked his head backward—"he's pretty smart too. Me, I'll be across there in a couple minutes." He guffawed at the thought of the long range sport that was due to commence as soon as he should be safely across. "Then you'll see how smart Mink is. He's been a damn sight too smart for a whole lot o' damned copper spies. An' he's been too smart for you."

King, tensely watching, found it in himself to grin back at the confident Ruys. Ruys instantly confronted him again with pig-eyed suspicion. So it was that he hid not see the swift events that began to take place on the other side.

And Mink, too, all his concentration fixed upon this direction from the far side, did not see what was shaping behind him. Only Tino Corra, up to his neck in water, facing Mink, saw.

T W O S T A L W A R T black arms emerged from the bush fringe behind Mink McCarthy. Mink, intent upon the sights of his rifle lined up on King's broad chest, heard not a thing, never daring to relax his attention or look about him. He knew much better than did Ruys how suddenly capable King might be of outwitting the big dullard.

Tino Corra, watching catastrophe shape itself, shrieked warning. Gray water swirled about his neck. His eyes bulged; his mouth gaped to shout. One arm holding his rifle clear waved frantically. The other arm emerged and joined it.

"Behind! Guard you behind!" Tino gurgled in his sick frenzy.

King whooped his sudden satisfaction. The little Hottentot shrieked like a steam whistle and flung his arms aloft in a demoniac leap.

Mink trained his eyes over his front sight to see what all this fuss was about. He could make nothing of the bobbing head and splashing arms out in the river. They pointed behind him; but arms pointing out of nothing are indefinite as to direction. Some damned stupidity on the fool's part, Mink was savagely deciding. Then the strong black arms descended upon him from behind.

Tino Corra shrieked his final despair. Jan Ruys snatched a look behind, and at that instant King rushed him.

Jan's quick glance over his shoulder only half took in what was happening. He turned heavily to meet King's catlike onslaught. There was not time to get his gun into play. King was at hand grips with him; and Ruys, burly, great brute that he was, felt a stab of apprehension at the expertness and power of those long, steel sinewed arms.

But Ruys was a tough barroom fighter. Though taken aback, he had the ingrained instinct to swing his hips away and to drive his knee hard for his opponent's groin.

King wilted with the numbing shock of it. He had been appraising this great bull of a man and all his instinct of competitive combat had been anticipating the inevitable tussle for the showdown. But here was no time for pretty fighting. With set teeth he clung to the cursing, shouting ox, and managed to get his pistol free. Grunting, he swung it upward. Its barrel collided with a sharp snap against the protruding bone behind the other's ear. Ruys went down without a struggle or a sound.

Tino Corra was floundering in shallower water, trying to get his rifle into play. King dropped behind Ruys's bulk. The Hottentot flung his rifle to him. King lay panting, the rifle thrust out over Ruys's side, like a cavalryman behind his fallen horse.

"Drop that!" he shouted. "Drop it! Right into the river!"

Corra had heard as much about King's marksmanship as King had heard about Mink McCarthy's. Only for a glaring moment he hesitated. He could see King's head. His own head and chest were clear of the water, but the current whirled about his legs. Slowly he let his gun drop.

"So!" King shouted, and his tenseness relaxed. "Now come ashore. This side. And don't try anything with the pistol in your belt."

On the farther bank Mink McCarthy and the strong black

arms had disappeared, swallowed up into the bush fringe that remained as peacefully blank as when Mink had disposed himself against it. But King had no apprehensions on that score.

Painfully he flexed his body while the Hottentot tied both men up with as many twists and knots as a monkey would use.

"Good," said King, and he smiled with pinched lips. "Sit on them while I go and help the Masai bring that other one across. Then the two of you can round up those ivory porters. The men from Fort Portal ought to be along any time now."

A blend of indignation and grim satisfaction chased the pain from his face, as he growled to himself—

"Go murdering elephants wholesale, will they?"